ᴋ AZUO ISHIGURO
ᴡ HEN WE WERE ORPHANS

Kazuo Ishiguro was born in Nagasaki, Japan, in 1954 and moved to Britain at the age of five. He is the author of four novels, including *The Remains of the Day,* an international bestseller that won the Booker Prize and was adapted into an award-winning film. Ishiguro's work has been translated into twenty-eight languages. In 1995, he received an Order of the British Empire for service to literature, and in 1998, the French Decoration of Chevalier dans l'Ordre des Arts et Lettres. He lives in London with his wife and daughter.

INTERNATIONAL

WHEN WE WERE ORPHANS

KAZUO ISHIGURO

WHEN WE WERE ORPHANS

VINTAGE INTERNATIONAL

VINTAGE BOOKS

A DIVISION OF RANDOM HOUSE, INC.

NEW YORK

FIRST VINTAGE OPEN MARKET EDITION, AUGUST 2000

The Library of Congress has cataloged the Knopf edition as follows:
Ishiguro, Kazuo.
When we were orphans / Kazuo Ishiguro.
1. Private investigators—China—Shanghai—Fiction.   2. British—China—Shanghai—Fiction.   3. Parents—Death—Fiction.   4. Missing persons—Fiction.   5. Shanghai (China)—Fiction.
PR6059.S5   W47   2000
823'.914—dc21
00-26120
CIP

VINTAGE OPEN-MARKET ISBN: 0-375-72610-1

www.vintagebooks.com

Printed in Canada
10 9 8 7 6 5 4 3

TO LORNA AND NAOMI.

PART ONE

*L*ONDON, 24TH JULY 1930

𝓘T WAS THE SUMMER of 1923, the summer I came down from Cambridge, when despite my aunt's wishes that I return to Shropshire, I decided my future lay in the capital and took up a small flat at Number 14b Bedford Gardens in Kensington. I remember it now as the most wonderful of summers. After years of being surrounded by fellows, both at school and at Cambridge, I took great pleasure in my own company. I enjoyed the London parks, the quiet of the Reading Room at the British Museum; I indulged entire afternoons strolling the streets of Kensington, outlining to myself plans for my future, pausing once in a while to admire how here in England, even in the midst of such a great city, creepers and ivy are to be found clinging to the fronts of fine houses.

It was on one such leisurely walk that I encountered quite by chance an old schoolfriend, James Osbourne, and discovering him to be a neighbour, suggested he call on me when he was next passing. Although at that point I had yet to receive a single visitor in my rooms, I issued my invitation with confidence, having chosen the premises with some care. The rent was not high, but my landlady had furnished the place in a tasteful manner that evoked an unhurried Victorian past; the drawing room, which received plenty of sun throughout the first half of the day, contained an ageing sofa as well as two snug armchairs, an antique sideboard and an oak bookcase filled with crumbling encyclopaedias—all of which I was convinced would win the approval of any visitor. Moreover, almost immediately upon taking the rooms, I had walked over to Knightsbridge and acquired there a Queen Anne tea service, several packets of fine teas, and a large tin of biscuits. So when Osbourne did happen along one morning a few days later, I was able to serve out the refreshments with an assurance that never once permitted him to suppose he was my first guest.

For the first fifteen minutes or so, Osbourne moved restlessly around my drawing room, complimenting me on the premises, examining this and that, looking regularly out of the windows to exclaim at whatever was going on below. Eventually he flopped down into the sofa, and we were able to exchange news—our own and that of old schoolfriends. I remember we spent a little time discussing the activities of the workers' unions, before embarking on a long and enjoyable debate on German philosophy, which enabled us to display to one another the intellectual prowess we each had gained at our respective universities. Then Osbourne rose and began his pacing again, pronouncing as he did so upon his various plans for the future.

"I've a mind to go into publishing, you know. Newspapers, magazines, that sort of thing. In fact, I fancy writing a column myself. About politics, social issues. That is, as I say, if I decide not to go into politics myself. I say, Banks, do you *really* have no idea what you want to do? Look, it's all out there for us"—he indicated the window—"Surely you have *some* plans."

"I suppose so," I said, smiling. "I have one or two things in mind. I'll let you know in good time."

"What have you got up your sleeve? Come on, out with it! I'll get it out of you yet!"

But I revealed nothing to him, and before long got him arguing again about philosophy or poetry or some such thing. Then around noon, Osbourne suddenly remembered a lunch appointment in Piccadilly and began to gather up his belongings. It was as he was leaving, he turned at the door, saying:

"Look, old chap, I meant to say to you. I'm going along tonight to a bash. It's in honour of Leonard Evershott. The tycoon, you know. An uncle of mine's giving it. Rather short notice, but I wondered if you'd care to come along. I'm quite serious. I'd been meaning to pop over to you long ago, just never got round to it. It'll be at the Charingworth."

When I did not reply immediately, he took a step towards me and said:

"I thought of you because I was remembering. I was remembering how you always used to quiz me about my being 'well connected.' Oh, come on! Don't pretend you've forgotten! You used to interrogate me mercilessly. 'Well connected? Just what does that mean, well connected?' Well, I thought, here's a chance for old Banks to see 'well connected' for himself." Then he shook his head, as though at a memory, saying: "My goodness, you were such an odd bird at school."

I believe it was at this point I finally assented to his suggestion for the evening—an evening which, as I shall explain, was to prove far more significant than I could then have imagined—and showed him out without betraying in any part the resentment I was feeling at these last words of his.

My annoyance only grew once I had sat down again. I had, as it happened, guessed immediately what Osbourne had been referring to. The fact was, throughout school, I had heard it said repeatedly of Osbourne that he was "well connected." It was a phrase that came up unfailingly when people talked of him, and I believe I too used it about him whenever it seemed called for. It was indeed a concept that fascinated me, this notion that he was in some mysterious way connected to various of the higher walks of life, even though he looked and behaved no differently from the rest of us. However, I cannot imagine I "mercilessly interrogated" him as he had claimed. It is true the subject was something I thought about a lot when I was fourteen or fifteen, but Osbourne and I had not been especially close at school and, as far as I remember, I only once brought it up with him personally.

It was on a foggy autumn morning, and the two of us had been sitting on a low wall outside a country inn. My guess is that we would have been in the Fifth by then. We had been appointed as markers for a cross-country run, and were waiting for the runners to emerge from the fog across a nearby field so that we could point them in the correct direction down a muddy lane. We were not expecting the runners for some time yet, and so had been idly chatting. It was on this occasion, I am sure, that I asked Osbourne about his "well connectedness." Osbourne, who for all his exuberance, had a modest nature, tried to change the subject. But I persisted until he said eventually:

"Oh, do knock it off, Banks. It's all just nonsense, there's nothing to analyse. One simply knows people. One has parents, uncles, family friends. I don't know what there is to be so puzzled about." Then quickly realising what he had said, he had turned and touched my arm. "Dreadfully sorry, old fellow. That was awfully tactless of me."

This *faux pas* seemed to cause Osbourne much more anguish than it had me. Indeed, it is not impossible it had remained on his conscience for all those years, so that in asking me to accompany him to the Charingworth Club that evening, he was in some way trying to make amends. In any case, as I say, I had not been at all upset that foggy morning by his admittedly careless remark. In fact, it had become a matter of some irritation to me that my schoolfriends, for all their readiness to fall into banter concerning virtually any other of one's misfortunes, would observe a great solemnness at the first mention of my parents' absence. Actually, odd as it may sound, my lack of parents—indeed, of any close kin in England except my aunt in Shropshire—had by then long ceased to be of any great inconvenience to me. As I would often point out to my companions, at a boarding school like ours, we had *all* learned to get on without parents, and my position was not as unique as all that. Nevertheless, now I look back on it, it seems probable that at least some of my fascination with Osbourne's "well connectedness" had to do with what I then perceived to be my complete lack of connection with the world beyond St. Dunstan's. That I would, when the time came, forge such connections for myself and make my way, I had no doubts. But it is possible I believed I would learn from Osbourne something crucial, something of the way such things worked.

But when I said before that Osbourne's words as he left my flat had somewhat offended me, I was not referring to his raising the matter of my "interrogating" him all those years before. Rather, what I had taken exception to was his casual judgement that I had been "such an odd bird at school."

In fact, it has always been a puzzle to me that Osbourne should have said such a thing of me that morning, since my own memory is that I blended perfectly into English school life. During even my earliest weeks at St. Dunstan's, I do not believe I did anything to cause myself embarrassment. On my very first day, for instance, I recall observing a mannerism many of the boys adopted when standing and talking—of tucking the right hand into a waistcoat pocket and moving the left shoulder up and down in a kind of shrug to underline certain of their remarks. I distinctly remember reproducing this mannerism on that same first day with sufficient expertise that not a single of my fellows noticed anything odd or thought to make fun.

In much the same bold spirit, I rapidly absorbed the other gestures, turns of phrase and exclamations popular among my peers, as well as grasping the deeper mores and etiquettes prevailing in my new surroundings. I certainly realised quickly enough that it would not do for me to indulge openly—as I had been doing routinely in Shanghai—my ideas on crime and its detection. So much so that even when during my third year there was a series of thefts, and the entire school was enjoying playing at detectives, I carefully refrained from joining in in all but a nominal way. And it was, no doubt, some remnant of this same policy that caused me to reveal so little of my "plans" to Osbourne that morning he called on me.

However, for all my caution, I can bring to mind at least two instances from school that suggest I must, at least occasionally, have lowered my guard sufficiently to give some idea of my ambitions. I was unable even at the time to account for these incidents, and am no closer to doing so today.

The earlier of these occurred on the occasion of my fourteenth birthday. My two good friends of that time, Robert Thornton-Browne and Russell Stanton, had taken me to a tea-shop in the village and we had been enjoying ourselves over scones and cream cakes. It was a rainy Saturday afternoon and all the other tables were occupied. This meant that every few minutes more rain-soaked villagers would come in, look around, and throw disapproving looks in our direction as though we should immediately vacate our table for them. But Mrs. Jordan, the proprietress, had always been welcoming towards us, and on that afternoon of my birthday, we felt we had every right to be occupying the choice table beside the bay window with its view of the village square. I do not recall much of what we talked about that day; but once we had eaten our fill, my two companions exchanged looks, then Thornton-Browne reached down into his satchel and presented to me a gift-wrapped package.

As I set about opening it, I quickly realised the package had been wrapped in numerous sheets, and my friends would laugh noisily each time I removed one layer, only to be confronted by another. All the signs, then, were that I would find some joke item at the end of it all. What I did eventually uncover was a weathered leather case, and when I undid the tiny catch and raised the lid, a magnifying glass.

I have it here now before me. Its appearance has changed little over the years; it was on that afternoon already well travelled. I remember noting this, along with the fact that it was very powerful, surprisingly weighty, and that the ivory handle was chipped all down one side. I did not notice until later—one needs a second magnifying glass to read the engraving—that it was manufactured in Zurich in 1887.

My first reaction to this gift was one of huge excitement. I snatched it up, brushing aside the bundles of wrapping covering the table surface—I suspect in my enthusiasm I caused a few sheets to flutter to the floor—and began immediately to test it on some specks of butter smeared on the tablecloth. I became so absorbed that I was only vaguely aware of my friends laughing in that exaggerated way that signifies a joke at one's expense. By the time I looked up, finally self-conscious, they had both fallen into an uncertain silence. It was then that Thornton-Browne gave a half-hearted snigger, saying:

"We thought since you're going to be a detective, you'd be needing one of these."

At this point, I quickly recovered my wits and made a show of pretending the whole thing had been an amusing jest. But by then, I fancy, my two friends were themselves confused about their intentions, and for the remainder of our time at the tea-shop, we never quite regained our former comfortable mood.

As I say, I have the magnifying glass here now in front of me. I used it when investigating the Mannering case; I used it again, most recently, during the Trevor Richardson affair. A magnifying glass may not be quite the crucial piece of equipment of popular myth, but it remains a useful tool for the gathering of certain sorts of evidence, and I fancy I will, for some time yet, carry about with me my birthday gift from Robert Thornton-Browne and Russell Stanton. Gazing at it now, this thought occurs to me: if my companions' intention was indeed to tease me, well then, the joke is now very much on them. But sadly, I have no way now of ascertaining what they had in mind, nor indeed how, for all my precautions, they had ever gleaned my secret ambition. Stanton, who had lied about his age in order to volunteer, was killed in the third battle of Ypres. Thornton-Browne, I heard, died of tuberculosis two years ago. In any case, both boys left St. Dunstan's in the fifth year and I had long since lost touch with them by the time I heard of their deaths. I still remember, though, how disappointed I was when Thornton-Browne left the school; he had been the one real friend I had made since arriving in England, and I missed him much throughout the latter part of my career at St. Dunstan's.

The second of these two instances that comes to mind occurred a few years later—in the Lower Sixth—but my recollection of it is not as detailed. In fact, I cannot remember at all what came before and after this particular moment. What I have is a memory of walking into a classroom—Room 15 in the Old Priory—where the sun was pouring through the narrow cloister windows in shafts, revealing the dust hanging in the air. The master had yet to arrive, but I must have come in slightly late, for I remember finding my classmates already sitting about in clusters on the desk-tops, benches and window ledges. I was about to join one such group of five or six boys, when their faces all turned to me and I saw immediately that they had been discussing me. Then, before I could say anything, one of the group, Roger Brenthurst, pointed towards me and remarked:

"But surely he's rather too short to be a Sherlock."

A few of them laughed, not particularly unkindly, and that, as far as I recall, was all there was to it. I never heard any further talk concerning my aspirations to be a "Sherlock," but for some time afterwards I had a niggling concern that my secret had got out and become a topic for discussion behind my back.

Incidentally, the need to exercise caution around this whole topic of my ambitions had been impressed upon me before I ever arrived at St. Dunstan's. For I had spent much of my first few weeks in England wandering about the common near my aunt's cottage in Shropshire, performing amidst the damp ferns the various detective scenarios Akira and I had evolved together in Shanghai. Of course, now that I was alone, I was obliged to take on all his roles as well; moreover, aware as I was that I could be seen from the cottage, I had had the sense to enact these dramas with restrained movements, muttering our lines under my breath—in marked contrast to the uninhibited manner in which Akira and I had been accustomed to carry on.

Such precautions, however, had proved inadequate. For one morning I had overheard from the little attic room I had been given, my aunt talking with some friends down in the drawing room. It was the sudden lowering of their voices that had first aroused my curiosity, and I soon found myself creeping out on to the landing and leaning over the rail.

"He's gone for hours," I could hear her saying. "It's hardly healthy, a boy his age, sunk in his own world like that. He has to start looking ahead."

"But it's only to be expected, surely," someone said. "After everything that's happened to him."

"He has nothing at all to gain by brooding," my aunt said. "He's been well provided for, and in that sense he's been lucky. It's time he looked forward. I mean to put a stop to all this introspection."

From that day on I ceased to go to the common, and in general, took steps to avoid any further displays of "introspection." But I was then still very young, and at nights, lying in that attic room, listening to the creak of the boards as my aunt moved about the cottage winding her clocks and seeing to her cats, I would often enact again, in my imagination, all our old detective dramas in just the way Akira and I had always done.

But let me return to that summer's day Osbourne called at my

Kensington flat. I do not wish to imply that this remark of his, about my being "an odd bird," preoccupied me for more than a few moments. In fact, I went out myself, not long after Osbourne, in rather good spirits, and was soon to be found in St. James's Park, strolling about the flower beds, growing ever more eager for the evening ahead.

Thinking again of that afternoon, it strikes me I had every right to feel a little nervous, and it is entirely typical of the foolish arrogance that carried me through those early London days that I did not. I was aware, of course, that this particular evening would be on a different level from anything I had ever attended at university; that I might well, moreover, encounter points of custom as yet unfamiliar to me. But I felt sure I would, with my usual vigilance, negotiate any such difficulties, and in general acquit myself well. My concerns as I drifted around the park were of a quite different order. When Osbourne had talked of "well-connected" guests, I had immediately assumed these to include at least a few of the leading detectives of the day. I fancy, then, that I spent a lot of my time that afternoon working out just what I would say should I be introduced to Matlock Stevenson, or perhaps even to Professor Charleville. I rehearsed over and over how I would—modestly, but with a certain dignity—outline my ambitions; and I pictured to myself one or the other of them taking a fatherly interest in me, offering all kinds of advice and insisting I come to him for guidance in the future.

Of course, the evening turned out to be a major disappointment—even if, as you will presently see, it was to prove particularly significant for quite other reasons. What I did not know at this point was that in this country, detectives tend not to participate in society gatherings. This is not through any lack of invitations; my own recent experience will testify to the fact that fashionable circles are forever trying to recruit the celebrated detectives of the day. It is just that these same persons tend to be earnest, often reclusive individuals who are dedicated to their work and have little inclination to mingle with one another, let alone with "society" at large.

As I say, this was not something I appreciated as I arrived at the Charingworth Club that evening and followed Osbourne's example of cheerily greeting the grandly uniformed doorman. But I was quickly disabused within minutes of our entering the crowded room on the first floor. I do not know how exactly this occurred— for I had not had the time to ascertain the identities of anyone present—but a kind of intuitive revelation swept over me which made me feel utterly foolish about my earlier excitement. Suddenly it seemed unbelievable that I had ever expected to find Matlock Stevenson or Professor Charleville hob-nobbing with the financiers and government ministers I knew were around me. Indeed, I was so thrown by this discrepancy between the event I had arrived at and the one I had been thinking about throughout the afternoon, that all my poise, at least temporarily, deserted me, and for half an hour or so, much to my annoyance, I could not bring myself to leave Osbourne's side.

I am sure this same agitated frame of mind accounts for the fact that when I now think back to that evening, so many aspects seem somewhat exaggerated or unnatural. For instance, when I now try to picture the room, it is uncommonly dark; this despite the wall lamps, the candles on the tables, the chandeliers above us—none of which seem to make any impression on the pervading darkness. The carpet is very thick, so that to move about the room, one is obliged to drag one's feet, and all around, greying men in black jackets are doing just this, some even pressing forward their shoulders as if walking into a gale. The waiters, too, with their silver trays, lean into conversations at peculiar angles. There are hardly any ladies present, and those one can see seem oddly self-effacing, almost immediately melting from one's view behind the forest of black evening suits.

As I say, I am sure these impressions are not accurate, but that is how the evening remains in my mind. I remember standing about frozen with awkwardness, repeatedly sipping from my glass, as Osbourne chatted amiably with one guest after another, most of them a good thirty years older than us. I did once or twice try to join in, but my voice sounded conspicuously child-like, and in any case, most conversations centred on people or issues about which I knew nothing.

After a while, I grew angry—at myself, at Osbourne, at the whole proceedings. I felt I had every right to despise the people around me; that they were for the most part greedy and self-seeking, lacking any idealism or sense of public duty. Fuelled by this anger, I was at last able to tear myself away from Osbourne and move off through the darkness into another part of the room.

I came to an area illuminated by a dull pool of light cast by a small wall lantern. The crowd was thinner here, and I noticed a silver-haired man of perhaps seventy smoking with his back to the room. It took a moment for me to realise he was gazing into a mirror, and by then he had noticed me looking at him. I was about to hurry on, when he said without turning:

"Enjoying yourself?"

"Oh yes," I said with a light laugh. "Thank you. Yes, a splendid occasion."

"But a little lost, eh?"

I hesitated, then gave another laugh. "Perhaps a little. Yes, sir."

The silver-haired man turned and studied me carefully. He then said: "If you wish, I'll tell you who some of these people are. Then if there's anyone you want especially to talk to, I'll take you over and introduce you. What do you say to that?"

"That would be most kind. Most kind indeed."

"Good."

He came a step closer and surveyed what was visible to us of the room. Then leaning towards me, he proceeded to point out this personage and that. Even when the name was an illustrious one, he would remember to add for my benefit "the financier," "the composer," or whatever. With the less well known, he would summarise in some detail the person's career and the reason for his importance. I believe he was in the midst of telling me about a clergyman standing quite near us, when he broke off suddenly and said:

"Ah. I see the attention has drifted."

"I'm terribly sorry . . ."

"Quite all right. Perfectly natural, after all. Young fellow like you."

"I assure you, sir . . ."

"No apology required." He gave a laugh and nudged my arm. "Find her pretty, eh?"

I did not know quite how to respond. I could hardly deny I had been diverted by the young woman several yards to our left, at that moment in conversation with two middle-aged men. But as it happened, that first time I saw her, I did not think her at all pretty. It is even possible I somehow sensed, there and then, at my first sight of her, those qualities which I have since discovered to be so significantly a part of her. What I saw was a small, rather elf-like young woman with dark, shoulder-length hair. Even though at that moment she was clearly wishing to charm the men she was talking to, I could see something about her smile that might in an instant turn it into a sneer. A slight crouch around her shoulders, like that of a bird of prey, gave her posture a suggestion of scheming. Above all, I noticed a certain quality around her eyes—a kind of severity, something ungenerously exacting—which I see now, in retrospect, was what more than anything else caused me to stare at her with such fascination that evening.

Then, as we were both still gazing at her, she looked our way, and recognising my companion, sent him a quick, cold smile. The silver-haired man gave a salute and a respectful bow of the head.

"A charming young lady," he murmured, as he began leading me away. "But no sense in a chap like you wasting time pursuing her. I don't mean to be offensive, you look a jolly decent type. But you see, that's Miss Hemmings. Miss *Sarah* Hemmings."

The name meant nothing to me. But whereas my guide had earlier been so conscientious in supplying me with the backgrounds of those he had pointed out, he uttered the name of this woman clearly expecting me to be familiar with it. So it was that I nodded and said:

"Oh yes. So that's Miss Hemmings."

The gentleman paused again and surveyed the room from our new vantage point.

"Now let me see. I take it you're looking for someone to give you a leg up in life. Correct? Don't worry. Played much the same game myself when I was young. Now let me see. Who do we have here?" Then he turned back to me suddenly to ask: "Now what was it again you said you wanted to do with your life?"

Of course, I had not at that point told him anything. But now, after a slight hesitation, I answered simply:

"Detective, sir."

"Detective? Hmm." He continued to gaze around the room. "You mean . . . a policeman?"

"More a private consultant."

He nodded. "Naturally, naturally." He continued to draw on his cigar, deep in thought. Then he said: "Not interested in museums, by any chance? Chap over there, known him for years. Museums. Skulls, relics, that kind of thing. Not interested? Didn't think so." He went on gazing around the room, sometimes craning his neck to see someone. "Of course," he said eventually, "a lot of young men dream of becoming detectives. I dare say I did once, in my more fanciful moments. One feels so idealistic at your age. Longs to be the great detective of the day. To root out single-handedly all the evil in the world. Commendable. But really, my boy, it's just as well to have, let us say, a few other strings to your bow. Because a year or two from now—I don't mean to be offensive—but pretty soon you'll feel quite differently about things. Are you interested in furniture? I ask because over there stands none other than Hamish Robertson himself."

"With all respect, sir. The ambition which I just confided to you is hardly the whim of a moment. It's a calling I've felt my whole life."

"Your whole life? But what are you? Twenty-one? Twenty-two? Well, I suppose I shouldn't discourage you. After all, if our young men won't entertain idealistic notions of this sort, who is there to do so? And no doubt, my boy, you believe today's world to be a far more evil place than the one of thirty years ago, is that it? That civilisation's on the brink and all that?"

"As a matter of fact, sir," I said curtly, "I do believe that to be the case."

"I remember when I thought so too." Suddenly his sarcasm had been replaced by a more kindly tone, and I even thought I saw tears fill his eyes. "Why is it, do you suppose, my boy? Is the world really getting more evil? Is *Homo sapiens* degenerating as a species?"

"I don't know about that, sir," I replied, this time more gently. "All I can say is that to the objective observer, the modern criminal is growing increasingly clever. He has grown more ambitious, more daring, and science has placed a whole new array of sophisticated tools at his disposal."

"I see. And without gifted chaps like you on our side, the future's bleak, is that it?" He shook his head sadly. "You might have something there. Too easy for an old chap to scoff. Perhaps you're right, my boy. Perhaps we've allowed things to slide for too long. Ah."

The silver-haired man bowed his head again as Sarah Hemmings came drifting past us. She was moving through the crowd with a haughty grace, her gaze moving from left to right in search—so it seemed to me—of someone she deemed worthy of her presence. Noting my companion, she gave him the same quick smile as before, but did not break her stride. For just a second, her gaze fell on me, but almost instantly—before I could so much as smile—she had dismissed me from her mind and was making her way towards someone she had spotted on the other side of the room.

Later that night, as Osbourne and I sat together in a taxicab speeding us back towards Kensington, I tried to find out something more concerning Sarah Hemmings. Osbourne, for all his pretending that he had found the evening a bore, was well pleased with himself, and eager to recount to me in detail the many conversations he had had with influential persons. It was not easy then to get him on to the subject of Miss Hemmings without my appearing unduly curious. Eventually, however, I did get him to say:

"Miss Hemmings? Oh yes, her. Used to be engaged to Herriot-Lewis. You know, the conductor fellow. Then he went and gave that Schubert concert at the Albert Hall last autumn. Remember that debacle?"

When I confessed my ignorance of it, Osbourne went on:

"They didn't quite throw chairs about, but I dare say they would have done if the things hadn't been fixed to the floor. The fellow from _The Times_ described the performance as a 'complete travesty.' Or did he say, 'a violation?' Anyway, he didn't much care for it."

"And Miss Hemmings . . ."

"Dropped him like a hot potato. Threw the engagement ring back at him, apparently. And she's kept a huge distance from the chap ever since."

"All because of this concert?"

"Well, it _was_ pretty ghastly, by all accounts. Caused quite a stir. Her breaking off the engagement, I mean. But what a lot of bores they were tonight, Banks. Do you suppose when we're that age, we'll be carrying on like that?"

DURING THAT FIRST YEAR after Cambridge, largely through my friendship with Osbourne, I found myself attending other smart social events on a fairly regular basis. Thinking back to that period of my life, it now strikes me as a singularly frivolous one. There were supper parties, luncheons, cocktail parties held usually in apartments around Bloomsbury and Holborn. I was determined to put behind me the awkwardness I had displayed that evening at the Charingworth, and my manner at these events grew steadily more assured. Indeed, for a time, it is reasonable to say I came to occupy a place within one of the fashionable London "sets."

Miss Hemmings was not part of my particular set, but I found that whenever I mentioned her to friends, they would know of her. Moreover, I would glimpse her from time to time at functions, or else, often, in the tea-rooms of the grander hotels. In any case, in one way or another, I ended up accumulating a fair amount of information concerning her career in London society.

How curious to recall a time when such vague second-hand impressions were all I knew of her! It did not take long to establish that there were many who did not regard her with approval. Even before the business of the broken engagement to Anthony Herriot-Lewis, it seemed she had made enemies on account of what many referred to as her "forthrightness." Friends of Herriot-Lewis—whose objectivity, to be fair, could hardly be counted on by this point—described how ruthlessly she had pursued the conductor. Others accused her of manipulating Herriot-Lewis's friends in order to get close to him. Her subsequent dropping of the conductor, after all her determined efforts, was viewed by some as puzzling, by others simply as conclusive evidence of her cynical motives. On the other hand, I came across plenty who spoke rather well of Miss Hemmings. She was frequently described as "clever," "fascinating," "complicated." Women in particular defended her right to break off an engagement, whatever her reasons. Even her defenders, however, agreed that she was a "terrible snob of a new sort"; that she did not consider a person worthy of respect unless he or she possessed a celebrated name. And I must say, observing her from afar as I did that year, I came across little to counter such claims. Indeed, I sometimes got the impression she was unable properly to breathe anything other than the air surrounding the most distinguished persons. For a time she became linked with Henry Quinn, the barrister, only to distance herself again after his failure in the Charles Browning case. Then there came rumours of her growing friendship with James Beacon, who at that time was a rising young government minister. In any case, by this point, it had become abundantly clear to me what the silver-haired man had meant when he had declared there was little point in a "chap like me" pursuing Miss Hemmings. Of course, I had not really understood his words at the time. Now that I did so, I found myself following Miss Hemmings's activities with a peculiar interest that year. For all that, I did not actually speak to her until one afternoon almost two years after I first saw her at the Charingworth Club.

I HAD BEEN TAKING TEA at the Waldorf Hotel with an acquaintance when some business had suddenly called him away. I was thus sitting there by myself on the floor of the Palm Court, indulging in the scones and jam, when I noticed Miss Hemmings, also sitting alone, up at one of the balcony tables. As I have said, this was by no means the first time I had glimpsed her at such places, but that afternoon things were different. For this was barely a month after the conclusion of the Mannering case, and I was still on something of a cloud. Certainly, that period after my first public triumph was a heady one: many new doors suddenly opened to me; invitations poured in from entirely new sources; those who previously had been no more than pleasant to me exclaimed with great enthusiasm when I entered a room. It is no wonder I lost my bearings a little.

In any case, on that afternoon at the Waldorf, I found myself rising and making my way up to the balcony. I am not sure what I expected. It is again typical of my smugness of those days that I did not stop to consider if Miss Hemmings would really be so delighted to make my acquaintance. Perhaps a flicker of doubt did cross my mind as I strolled past the pianist and approached the table where she sat reading her book. But I remember feeling rather pleased with the way my voice came out, urbane and jocular, as I said:

"Excuse me, but I thought it time I introduced myself to you. We have so many mutual friends. I'm Christopher Banks."

I managed to pronounce my name with a flourish, but already by this point, my assurance had started to fade. For Miss Hemmings was looking up at me with a cold, searching gaze. And in the silence that followed, she gave a quick glance back to her book, as though it had let out a groan of complaint. Finally she said, in a voice filled with bafflement:

"Oh yes? How do you do?"

"The Mannering case," I said, foolishly. "You might have read about it."

"Yes. You investigated it."

It was this utterance, made so matter-of-factly, which quite threw me off my balance. For she had spoken with no note whatsoever of realisation; it was simply a flat statement implying that she had been quite aware of my identity all along, and that she was still far from being enlightened as to why I was standing beside her table. Suddenly I felt the giddy elation of the past weeks evaporating. And I believe it was then, as I let out a nervous laugh, it occurred to me that the Mannering case, for all the self-evident brilliance of my investigation, for all the praise of my friends, somehow did not carry as much importance in the wider world as I had assumed.

It is quite possible we had a perfectly civil exchange before I began my retreat back down to my own table. And it seems to me today that Miss Hemmings was more than entitled to respond as she did; how absurd to have imagined something like the Mannering case would be sufficient to impress her! But I remember, once I had sat down again, feeling both angry and dejected. The thought came to me that I had not only just made an ass of myself with Miss Hemmings, but that I had perhaps been doing so continuously throughout the previous month; that my friends, for all their congratulations, had been laughing at me.

By the following day, I had come to accept that I fully deserved the jolt I had received. But this episode at the Waldorf probably did arouse in me feelings of resentment towards Miss Hemmings which I never fully shook off—and which undoubtedly contributed to yesterday evening's unfortunate events. At the time though, I tried to see the whole incident as providential. It had, after all, brought home to me how easy it was to become distracted from one's most cherished goals. My intention was to combat evil—in particular, evil of the insidious, furtive kind—and as such had little to do with courting popularity within society circles.

I began thereafter to socialise far less and became more deeply immersed in my work. I studied notable cases from the past, and absorbed new areas of knowledge that might one day prove useful. Around this time, too, I began scrutinising the careers of various detectives who had established their names, and found I could discern a line between those reputations that rested on solid achievement, and those that derived essentially from a position within some influential set; there was, I came to see, a true and a false way for a detective to gain renown. In short, much as I had been excited by the offers of friendship extended to me following the Mannering affair, I did, after that encounter at the Waldorf, remember again the example set by my parents, and I resolved not to allow frivolous preoccupations to deflect me.

$\mathscr{S}$INCE I AM NOW RECALLING that period in my life following the Mannering case, it is perhaps worth mentioning here
my unexpected reunion with Colonel Chamberlain after all those
years. It is perhaps surprising, given the role he played at such a
pivotal juncture in my childhood, that we had not kept in closer
contact. But for whatever reason, we had failed to do so, and when
I did meet him again—a month or two after that encounter with
Miss Hemmings at the Waldorf—it was quite by chance.

I was standing in a bookshop on the Charing Cross Road one
rainy afternoon, examining an illustrated edition of *Ivanhoe*. I had
been aware for some time of someone hovering close behind me,
and assuming he was wishing access to that part of the shelf, had
moved aside. But then when the person continued to loiter around
me, I finally turned.

I recognised the colonel immediately, for his physical features
had hardly changed. However, through adult eyes, he appeared to
me meeker and shabbier than the figure from my boyhood. He was
standing there in a mackintosh, regarding me shyly, and only when
I exclaimed: "Ah, Colonel!" did he smile and hold out his hand.

"How are you, my boy? I was sure it was you. My goodness!
How are you, my boy?"

Although tears had appeared in his eyes, his manner remained awkward, as though he were afraid I might be annoyed at this reminder of the past. I did my best to convey delight at seeing him again, and as a downpour commenced outside, we stood there exchanging conversation in the cramped bookshop. I discovered that he was still living in Worcestershire, that he had come to London to attend a funeral and had decided "to make a few days of it." When I asked where he was staying, he answered vaguely, leading me to suspect he had taken modest lodgings. Before parting, I invited him to dine with me the following evening, a suggestion he took up with enthusiasm, though he seemed taken aback when I mentioned the Dorchester. But I continued to insist—"It's the least I can do after all your past kindness," I had pleaded—until finally he gave in.

LOOKING BACK NOW, my choice of the Dorchester strikes me as the height of inconsideration. I had, after all, already surmised that the colonel was short of funds; I should have seen too how wounding it would be for him not to pay at least his half of the bill. But in those days such things never occurred to me; I was much too concerned, I suspect, about impressing the old man with the full extent of my transformation since he had last seen me.

In this latter aim, I was probably rather successful. For as it happened, I had just around that point been taken to the Dorchester on two occasions, so that on the evening I met Colonel Chamberlain there, the *sommelier* greeted me with a "nice to see you again, sir." Then, after he had witnessed me exchanging witticisms with the *maître d'* as we started on our soup, the colonel broke into sudden laughter.

"And to think," he said, "this is the same little squirt I had snivelling at my side on that boat!"

He gave a few more laughs, then broke off abruptly, perhaps fearing he should never have alluded to the subject. But I smiled calmly and said:

"I must have been a trial to you on that trip, Colonel."

The old man's face clouded for a moment. Then he said solemnly: "Considering the circumstances, I thought you were extremely brave, my boy. Extremely brave."

At this stage, I recall, there was a slightly awkward silence, which was broken when we both commented on the fine flavour of our soup. At the next table, a large lady with much jewellery was laughing gaily, and the colonel glanced rather indiscreetly towards her. Then he appeared to come to a decision.

"You know, it's funny," he said. "I was thinking about it, before I came out tonight. That time you and I first met. I wonder if you remember, my boy. I don't suppose you do. After all, you had so much else on your mind then."

"On the contrary," I said, "I have the most vivid memory of the occasion."

This was no lie. Even now, if I were for a moment to close my eyes, I could with ease transport myself back to that bright morning in Shanghai and the office of Mr. Harold Anderson, my father's superior in the great trading company of Morganbrook and Byatt. I was sitting in a chair that smelt of polished leather and oak, the sort of chair normally found behind some impressive desk, but which, on this occasion, had been pulled out into the centre of the room. I could sense it was a chair reserved for only the most important of personages, but on this occasion, owing to the gravity of the circumstances, or perhaps as a sort of consolation, it had been given to me. I can remember that, no matter how I tried, I could not find a dignified way to sit in it; in particular, I could discover no posture which would enable me to keep both elbows at once upon its finely carved arms. Moreover, I had on that morning a brand new jacket made from some coarse grey material—where it had come from, I do not know—and I was most self-conscious about the ugly way I had been made to button it almost to my chin.

The room itself had tall grand ceilings, a large map on one wall, and behind Mr. Anderson's desk, great windows through which the sun was beating and a breeze blowing. I should think there were ceiling fans moving above me, though I do not actually remember this. What I do remember is that I was sitting in that chair in the middle of the room, the centre of solemn concern and discussion. All around me, adults were conferring, most of them on their feet; sometimes a few would drift over to the windows, their voices lowering as they argued a point. I remember too being surprised by the way Mr. Anderson himself, a tall greying man with a large moustache, behaved towards me as though we were old friends—so much so that for a while I assumed we had known each other when I was younger and that I had forgotten him. Only much later did I ascertain that we could not possibly have met until that morning. In any case, he had assumed for himself the role of uncle, continually smiling at me, patting my shoulder, nudging me and winking. Once he offered me a cup of tea, saying: "Now, Christopher, this will cheer you up," and had bent right down to peer at me as I had taken it. After that came more murmuring and conferring around the room. Then Mr. Anderson appeared in front of me again and said:

"So then, Christopher. It's all decided. This is Colonel Chamberlain. He's most kindly agreed to see you safe to England."

I remember at this point a hush descending over the room. In fact, my impression was that all the adults shrank back until they were lining the walls like spectators. Mr. Anderson too withdrew with a final encouraging smile. It was then that I first laid eyes on Colonel Chamberlain. He came up to me slowly, bent down to look into my face, then held out his hand. I had a feeling I should stand up to shake it, but he had thrust it out so quickly, and I had felt so fixed to that chair, that I had grasped his hand still sitting. Then I remember him saying:

"My poor lad. First your father. Now your mother. Must feel like the whole world's collapsed around your ears. But we'll go to England tomorrow, the two of us. Your aunt's waiting for you there. So be brave. You'll soon pick up the pieces again."

For a moment I was quite unable to find my voice. When I finally did so, I said: "It's awfully kind of you, sir. I'm very grateful for your offer, and I hope you don't think me very rude. But if you don't mind, sir, I think I oughtn't to go to England just now." Then, when the colonel did not respond immediately, I went on:

"Because you see, sir, the detectives are working extremely hard to find my mother and father. And they're the very best detectives in Shanghai. I think they're bound to find them very soon."

The colonel was nodding. "I'm sure the authorities are doing everything possible."

"So you see, sir, though I very much appreciate your kindness, I think my going to England, it won't be necessary after all."

I remember a murmur passing around the room at this point. The colonel went on nodding, as though weighing things up carefully.

"You may well be right, my boy," he said eventually. "I sincerely hope you are. But just in case, why don't you come with me anyway? Then once your parents are found, they can send for you. Or who knows? Perhaps they'll decide to come to England too. So what do you say? Let's you and me go to England tomorrow. Then we can wait and see what happens."

"But you see, sir, excuse me. But you see, the detectives looking for my parents. They're the *very best* detectives."

I am not sure what exactly the colonel said to this. Perhaps he just went on nodding. In any case, the next moment, he leaned in even closer to me and placed a hand on my shoulder.

"Look here. I realise how it must feel. Entire world's collapsed about your ears. But you've got to be brave. Besides, your aunt in England. She's expecting you, don't you see? Can't very well let the lady down at this stage, can we?"

When, sitting over our soup that evening, I related to him my memory of these last words of his, I rather expected him to laugh. Instead, he said solemnly:

"I felt so sorry for you, my boy. So terribly sorry." Then perhaps sensing he had misjudged my mood, he gave a short laugh and said more lightly: "I remember waiting at the harbour with you. I kept saying: 'Look here, we're going to have a lot of fun on that ship, aren't we? We're going to have a jolly good time.' And you just kept saying: 'Yes, sir. Yes, sir. Yes, sir.' "

I allowed him, for the next several minutes, to drift through reminiscences concerning various of his old acquaintances who had been present in Mr. Anderson's office that morning. Without exception, their names meant nothing to me. Then the colonel paused and a frown crossed his face.

"As for that Anderson himself," he said eventually, "that chap always gave me an uneasy feeling. Something fishy about him. There was something fishy about the whole damn business, if you ask me."

No sooner had he said this than he looked up at me with a start. Then before I could respond, he began to talk again rapidly, moving us on to what he no doubt considered the safer territory of our voyage to England. Before long, he was chuckling to himself as he recounted memories of our fellow passengers, the ship's officers, amusing little incidents I had long forgotten or had not registered in the first place. He was enjoying himself and I encouraged him to do so, often pretending to remember something just to please him. However, as he continued with these reminiscences, I found myself becoming somewhat irritated. For gradually, from behind his cheerful anecdotes, there was emerging a picture of myself on that voyage to which I took exception. His repeated insinuation was that I had gone about the ship withdrawn and moody, liable to burst into tears at the slightest thing. No doubt the colonel had an investment in giving himself the role of an heroic guardian, and after all this time, I saw it was as pointless as it was unkind to contradict him. But as I say, I began to grow steadily more irritated. For according to my own, quite clear memory, I adapted very ably to the changed realities of my circumstances. I remember very well that, far from being miserable on that voyage, I was positively excited about life aboard the ship, as well as by the prospect of the future that lay before me. Of course, I did miss my parents at times, but I can remember telling myself there would always be other adults I would come to love and trust. In fact, there were a number of ladies on the voyage who had heard what had happened to me and who, for a time, came fussing around me with pitying expressions, and I can recall feeling much the same irritation with them as I did towards the colonel that evening at the Dorchester. The fact was, I was not nearly as distressed as the adults around me seemed to suppose. As far as I can recall, there was only a single instance during the whole of that long voyage when I might conceivably have merited that title of "snivelling little squirt," and even that occurred on the very first day of our journey.

The sky that morning was overcast, the waters around us very muddy. I was standing on the deck of the steamer gazing back towards the harbour, towards the messy shoreline of boats, gangplanks, mud huts, dark wood jetties, behind them the large buildings of the Shanghai Bund, all now fading together into a single blur.

"Well, lad?" the colonel's voice had said near me. "Think you'll be back again one day?"

"Yes, sir. I expect I'll come back."

"We'll see. Once you're settled in England, I dare say you'll forget all this quickly enough. Shanghai's not a bad place. But eight years is about as much as I can take of it, and I expect *you*'ve had about as much as you need. Much more, you'll be turning into a Chinaman."

"Yes, sir."

"Look here, old fellow. You really ought to cheer up. After all, you're going to England. You're going home."

It was this last remark, this notion that I was "going home," which caused my emotions to get the better of me for—I am certain of this—the first and last time on that voyage. Even then, my tears were more of anger than sorrow. For I had deeply resented the colonel's words. As I saw it, I was bound for a strange land where I did not know a soul, while the city steadily receding before me contained all I knew. Above all, my parents were still there, somewhere beyond that harbour, beyond that imposing skyline of the Bund, and wiping my eyes, I had cast my gaze towards the shore one last time, wondering if even now I might catch sight of my mother—or even my father—running on to the quay, waving and shouting for me to return. But I was conscious even then that such a hope was no more than a childish indulgence. And as I watched the city that had been my home grow less and less distinct, I remember turning to the colonel with a cheerful look and saying: "We should be reaching the sea fairly soon, don't you think so, sir?"

BUT I BELIEVE I managed to betray none of my irritation with the colonel that evening. Certainly, by the time he boarded a taxicab in South Audley Street, and we said our farewells, he was in a splendid mood. It was only when I heard of his death just over a year later that I felt somewhat guilty I had not been warmer towards him that evening at the Dorchester. He had, after all, once done me a good turn, and from all I had observed, had been a very decent man. But I suppose the role he had played in my life—the fact of his being so overwhelmingly associated with what happened at that point—will ensure he remains for ever an ambivalent figure in my memory.

FOR AT LEAST THREE or four years after that Waldorf episode, Sarah Hemmings and I had little to do with one another. I remember seeing her once during this period at a cocktail party in a flat in Mayfair. The event was very crowded, but I did not know many of those there and had decided to leave early. I was making my way towards the door, when I spotted Sarah Hemmings talking with someone, standing directly in my path. My first instinct was to turn and go another way. But this was around the time of my success with the Roger Parker case, and it did occur to me to wonder if Miss Hemmings would still dare to be quite so high-handed as she had been at the Waldorf a few years earlier. I thus continued to squeeze my way past the guests and made sure to pass right in front of her. As I did so, I saw her gaze move to check over my features. A look of bemusement crossed her face as she struggled to remember who I was. Then I saw recognition dawn, and without a smile, without a nod, she turned her gaze back to the person to whom she was talking.

But I hardly gave such an incident any thought. For it came during a period when I was deeply engrossed in many challenging cases. And although this was still a good year before my name acquired anything of the standing it has today, I was already beginning to appreciate for the first time the scale of responsibility that befalls a detective with any sort of renown. I had always understood, of course, that the task of rooting out evil in its most devious forms, often just when it is about to go unchecked, is a crucial and solemn undertaking. But it was not until my experience of such cases as the Roger Parker murder that it came home to me just how much it means to people—and not only those directly concerned, but the public at large—to be cleansed of such encroaching wickedness. As a result, I became more determined than ever not to be diverted by the more superficial priorities of London life. And I began to understand, perhaps, something of what had made it possible for my parents to take the stand they had. In any case, the likes of Sarah Hemmings did not much impinge on my thoughts during that time, and it is even possible I would have forgotten of her existence altogether had I not run into Joseph Turner that day in Kensington Gardens.

I was at that time investigating a case in Norfolk and had returned to London for a few days with the intention of studying the extensive notes I had made. It was while I was strolling around Kensington Gardens one grey morning, pondering the many curious details surrounding the victim's disappearance, that I was hailed from afar by a figure I quickly recognised to be Turner, a man I had come to know vaguely from my social rounds. He came hurrying up to me, and after asking why I was so rarely "seen about the place these days," invited me to a dinner he and a friend were giving in a restaurant that evening. When I politely declined on the grounds that my present case was demanding all my time and attention, he said:

"Shame. Sarah Hemmings is coming along, and she's so wanting to have a good chat with you."

"Miss Hemmings?"

"Remember her, don't you? She certainly remembers you. Said you got to know each other a bit a few years ago. She's always complaining how you're no longer to be found."

Resisting the urge to make some comment, I said simply: "Well, please do give her my good wishes."

I left Turner fairly promptly after that, but on returning to my desk I confess I found myself somewhat distracted by this report of Miss Hemmings's wishing to see me. In the end, I told myself that in all likelihood Turner had made some mistake; or at the least, was exaggerating his point in an effort to entice me to his dinner. But then over the following months a number of similar reports reached my ears. Sarah Hemmings had been heard expressing annoyance at how, despite our once having been friends, I had now become impossible for her to find. I heard from several sources, moreover, how she was threatening to "ferret me out." Then finally, last week, while I was staying in the village of Shackton, in Oxfordshire, to investigate the Studley Grange business, Miss Hemmings turned up in person, presumably with the intention of doing just that.

I HAD FOUND the walled garden—containing the pond where Charles Emery's body had been discovered—in the lower grounds of the house. Four stone steps had brought me down into a rectangular space so perversely sheltered from the sun that even on that bright morning everything around me was in shadow. The walls themselves were covered with ivy, but somehow one could not avoid the impression of having stepped into a roofless prison cell.

The pond dominated this enclosure. Though several people had told me it contained goldfish, I could see no sign of life; in fact, it was hard to imagine how anything could thrive in such dank water—a fitting place indeed to discover a corpse. Surrounding the pond was a circle of square mossy slabs embedded into the mud. I would suppose I had been examining this area for about twenty minutes—I was on my front, scrutinising with my magnifying glass one of the slabs that projected over the water—when I became conscious of someone observing me. At first I assumed this to be some family member wishing yet again to pester me with questions. Since earlier I had insisted on uninterrupted time, I decided, at the cost of appearing rude, to pretend not to have noticed anything.

Then eventually I heard the sound of a shoe scraping on stone somewhere near the entrance to the garden. By then it was starting to seem unnatural that I should remain on my belly for such a long time, and in any case, I had exhausted the investigations I could usefully carry out in such a posture. Moreover, I had not entirely forgotten I was lying at almost the exact spot where a murder had been committed, and that the murderer was still at large. A chilly sensation passed through me as I clambered to my feet, and dusting my clothes, turned to face the intruder.

The sight of Sarah Hemmings did of course rather surprise me, but I am sure nothing unusual showed on my face. I had set my features to convey annoyance, and I would suppose that is what she saw, for her opening words to me were:

"Oh! Didn't mean to spy on you. But it seemed too good an opportunity. To watch the great man at his work, I mean."

I searched her face carefully, but could detect no sarcasm. Nevertheless, I kept my voice cold as I said: "Miss Hemmings. This is most unexpected."

"I heard you were here. I'm spending a few days with my friend in Pemleigh. It's only just up the road."

She paused, no doubt expecting me to respond. When I remained silent, she showed no sign of being perturbed, but instead came walking towards me.

"I'm quite a good friend of the Emerys, did you know?" she continued. "Awful business, this murder."

"Yes, awful."

"Ah. So you too believe it to be murder. Well, I suppose that sort of clinches it. Do you have a theory, Mr. Banks?"

I gave a shrug. "I've formed a few ideas, yes."

"It's too bad for the Emerys they didn't think to ask you for help when it all first happened last April. I mean to say, bringing Celwyn Henderson on to a case like this! What did they expect? That man should have been put out to pasture long ago. Just shows you how out of touch people get living out here. Anyone in London could have told them all about you, of course."

This last remark did, I have to confess, intrigue me somewhat, so that after a moment's hesitation, I found myself asking her: "Excuse me, but told them what, exactly?"

"Why, that you're the most brilliant investigative mind in England, of course. We could all have told them that last spring, but the Emerys—it's taken them this long to cotton on. Better late than never, perhaps, but I suppose the trail's gone rather cold for you by now."

"As it happens, there are some advantages in coming to a case after some time has elapsed."

"Really? How fascinating. I always thought it was essential to get there quick, to pick up the scent, you know."

"On the contrary, it's never too late to, as you put it, pick up the scent."

"But isn't it so depressing, how this crime's eaten away at people's spirits here? And not just the household. It's the whole of Shackton that's started to rot. This used to be a happy and thriving market town. Now look at them, they barely meet each other's eyes. This whole business has dragged them down into a mire of suspicion. I tell you, Mr. Banks, if you can solve this thing, they'll remember you here for ever."

"Do you really think so? That would be curious."

"No doubt about it. They'd be so grateful. Yes, they'll be talking about you here for *generations*."

I let out a short laugh. "You seem to know the village well, Miss Hemmings. And I thought you spent all your time in London."

"Oh, I can only take so much of London, then I've just got to come away. I'm not a city girl at heart, you know."

"You surprise me. I always thought you were much drawn to city life."

"You're quite right, Mr. Banks." A note of resentment had come into her voice, as though I had tricked her into a corner. "Something does draw me to the city. It does have its . . . its attractions for me." For the first time, she turned away from me and glanced around the walled garden. "Which reminds me," she said. "Well, to be honest, it doesn't remind me at all. Why should I pretend? I've been thinking of it all the time we've been talking. I wanted to ask a favour of you."

"And what's that, Miss Hemmings?"

"Reliable sources tell me you've been invited to this year's Meredith Foundation dinner. Is that right?"

I paused slightly before replying: "Yes. That's correct."

"Quite a thing, to be invited at your age. I've heard this year it's in honour of Sir Cecil Medhurst."

"Yes, I believe so."

"I've heard too that Charles Wolfe is expected to attend."

"The violinist?"

She laughed brightly. "Does he do something else? And Thomas Byron too, apparently."

She had become visibly excited, but now she once again turned away and gazed at our surroundings with a slight shudder.

"Did you say," I asked eventually, "you wished me to grant you a favour?"

"Oh yes, yes. I wanted you to . . . I wished you to ask me to accompany you. To the Meredith Foundation dinner."

She was now holding me with an intense look. It took me a moment to find a response, but when I did so, I spoke quite calmly.

"I'd like to oblige you, Miss Hemmings. But unfortunately I've already replied to the organisers some days ago. I fear it'll be rather late to inform them of my wish to bring a guest . . ."

"Nonsense!" she broke in angrily. "Yours is the name on everyone's lips just now. If you wish to bring a companion, they'd be only too pleased. Mr. Banks, you aren't about to let me down, are you? That would be quite unworthy of you. After all, we've been good friends for some time now."

It was this last remark—reminding me as it did of the actual history of our "friendship"—that brought me back to myself.

"Miss Hemmings," I said with finality, "this is hardly a favour within my power to grant."

But there was now a determined look in Sarah Hemmings's eyes.

"I know all the details, Mr. Banks. At Claridge's Hotel. Next Wednesday evening. I mean to be there. I shall look forward to the evening, and I shall be waiting for you in the lobby."

"The lobby of Claridge's is, as far as I'm aware, open to respectable members of the public. If you choose to stand there next Wednesday evening, there is nothing I can do to prevent you, Miss Hemmings."

She looked at me very carefully, now uncertain about my intentions. Finally she said: "Then you shall most certainly see me there next Wednesday, Mr. Banks."

"As I've said, that is your affair, Miss Hemmings. Now, if you'll excuse me."

CHAPTER 3

*I*T TOOK NO MORE than a few days to unravel the mystery of Charles Emery's death. The matter did not attract publicity on the scale of some of my other investigations, but the deep gratitude of the Emery family—indeed, of the whole community of Shackton—made the case as satisfying as any thus far in my career. I returned to London in a glow of well-being and consequently failed to give much thought to my encounter with Sarah Hemmings in the walled garden on that first day of the investigation. I would not say I forgot entirely her declared intentions regarding the Meredith Foundation dinner, but as I say, I was in a triumphant frame of mind and I suppose I chose not to dwell on such things. Perhaps deep down I believed her "threat" to have been no more than a ploy of the moment.

In any case, when I stepped out of my taxicab outside Claridge's yesterday evening, my thoughts were elsewhere. I was, for one thing, reminding myself that my recent triumphs had more than entitled me to my invitation; that far from questioning my presence at such a gathering, other guests were likely to press me eagerly for inside information regarding my cases. I was reminding myself too of my resolution not to leave the proceedings prematurely, even if it meant putting up with the odd period of standing about alone. As I entered that grand lobby, then, I was quite unprepared for the sight of Sarah Hemmings waiting there with a smile.

She was dressed rather impressively in a dark silk dress and discreet but elegant jewellery. Her manner as she came towards me was utterly assured, so much so that she even found time to smile a greeting to a couple walking past us.

"Ah, Miss Hemmings," I said, while in my mind I tried hurriedly to retrieve all that had passed between us that day at Studley Grange. At that moment, I must confess, it seemed to me perfectly possible she had every right to expect me to offer my arm and lead her inside. No doubt, she sensed my uncertainty and appeared to grow even more confident.

"Dear Christopher," she said, "you're looking quite dashing. I'm overcome! Oh, and I haven't had a chance to congratulate you. That was so marvellous, what you did for the Emerys. It was ever so clever of you."

"Thank you. It was hardly such a complicated matter."

She had now taken my arm and had she at that instant moved towards the footman directing dinner guests towards the staircase, I am sure I would have been powerless to do anything other than her bidding. But here, I see now, she made an error. Perhaps she wished to savour the moment; perhaps her audacity had for a second given out. In any case, she made no move to proceed upstairs, but instead, gazing at the other guests filing into the lobby, said to me:

"Sir Cecil hasn't arrived yet. I do hope I shall get a chance to speak to him. So fitting he's the one being honoured this year, don't you think?"

"Indeed."

"You know, Christopher, I don't suppose it will be so many years until we'll all be here to honour *you*."

I laughed. "I hardly think . . ."

"No, no. I feel sure of it. All right, we might have to give it a few more years. But the day will come, you'll see."

"It's kind of you to say so, Miss Hemmings."

She continued to hold my arm as we stood there talking. Not infrequently, someone passing would smile or utter a greeting to one or the other of us. And I have to say, I found I was rather enjoying the notion of all these people—many of them very distinguished—seeing me arm in arm with Sarah Hemmings. I fancied I saw in their eyes, even as they greeted us, the idea: "Oh, she's caught *him* now, has she? Well, that's natural enough." Far from making me feel foolish or in any way humiliated, this notion rather filled me with pride. But then suddenly—and I am not sure what caused this—quite without warning I began to feel a great fury towards her. I am sure there was no detectable change in my manner at that moment and for a few minutes more we went on chatting amiably, nodding the occasional greeting to a passing guest. But when I unlinked her arm from mine and turned to her, I did so with a steely resolve.

"Well, Miss Hemmings, it was very good to see you again. But now I must leave you and go up to this function."

I gave a slight bow and began to move away. This clearly took her by surprise, and if she had ready some strategy for my failing to co-operate, she was for the moment unable to act on it. Only when I had gone several paces from her, and had in fact fallen in step with an elderly couple who had greeted me, did she suddenly come rushing up.

"Christopher!" she said in a frantic whisper. "You wouldn't dare! You promised me!"

"You know I did nothing of the sort."

"You wouldn't dare! Christopher, you wouldn't!"

"I wish you a pleasant evening, Miss Hemmings."

Turning away from her—and also, incidentally, from my elderly companions, who were doing their best to hear nothing—I began to make my way rapidly up the great staircase.

• • •

ON REACHING THE UPPER LEVEL, I was ushered into a brightly lit anteroom. There I duly joined a line of guests filing past a desk, behind which sat a uniformed man with a frosty face, checking people's names against a register. When it came to my turn, I was gratified to see a flicker of excitement cross the frosty man's face as he ticked off my name. I signed the guest book, then moved on towards a doorway leading into a large room, within which, I could see, there was already a sizeable crowd of guests. As I crossed the threshold and the hubbub engulfed me, a tall man with a thick dark beard greeted me and shook my hand. I supposed he was one of the evening's hosts, but I failed to register much of what he said to me because, to be frank, I was at that moment finding it hard to think about anything other than what had just occurred downstairs. I was experiencing a curiously hollow sensation, and I had to remind myself that I had not in any way ensnared Miss Hemmings; that any humiliation that had befallen her was entirely of her own making.

But as I parted from the bearded man and drifted further into the room, Sarah Hemmings continued to dominate my thoughts. I was vaguely aware of a waiter approaching me with a tray of aperitifs; of various people turning to greet me. At some point I fell into conversation with a group of three or four men—all of whom turned out to be scientists, and who seemed to know who I was. Then, when I had been in the room for perhaps fifteen minutes, I sensed a slight change in the atmosphere, and looking about me, perceived from the glances and murmurs all around that some sort of commotion was occurring near the doorway through which we had entered.

No sooner had I noted this than a sense of grave foreboding came over me and my first impulse was to escape deeper into the room. But it was as though some mysterious force were pulling me back to the doorway, and I soon found myself once more beside the bearded man—who at that moment was standing with his back to the reception, watching with a pained expression the drama unfolding in the anteroom.

Peering past him, I ascertained that Miss Hemmings was indeed at the heart of the disturbance. She had brought to a halt the procession of guests signing in their names at the desk. She was not shouting exactly, but seemed quite beyond caring who heard her. I watched her shake off an elderly hotel employee trying to restrain her; then, leaning right over the desk so as to glare all the more intently at the frosty-faced man still sitting there as before, she said in a voice close to a sob:

"But you simply have no idea! I simply *must* go in, don't you see? I have so many friends in there, I *belong* in there, I really do! Oh, do be reasonable!"

"I really am sorry, Miss . . ." the frosty-faced man began. But Sarah Hemmings, whose hair had tumbled over one side of her face, did not let him finish.

"It's all the most silly mix-up anyway, don't you see? That's all it is, the most silly old mix-up! And just because of that, you're being beastly, I can't believe it! I just can't believe it . . ."

All of us witnessing this scene seemed for a moment united in frozen embarrassment. Then the bearded man regained his wits and strode into the anteroom with authority.

"What has occurred?" he said soothingly. "My dear young lady, has there been some error? There, there, we'll sort it out, I'm sure. I'm at your disposal." Then he gave a start and exclaimed: "Why, it's Miss Hemmings, isn't it?"

"Of course it is! It's me! Don't you see? This man's being so beastly to me . . ."

"But Miss Hemmings, my dear young lady, there's no need to upset yourself like this. Come, let's go over here a moment . . ."

"No! No! You won't turn me away! I won't have it! I tell you I must, I absolutely *must* go in! I've dreamt of it for so long . . ."

"Surely, something can be done for the young lady," a man's voice said from among the bystanders. "Why be so petty? If she's taken the trouble to come here, why can't she be allowed in?"

This produced a general murmur of assent, though I noticed too some faces set in disapproval. The bearded man hesitated, then appeared to decide that his priority was to bring the scene to an end.

"Well perhaps, in this particular case . . ." Then turning to the frosty-faced man behind the desk, he went on: "I'm sure we can find a way to accommodate Miss Hemmings, don't you think, Mr. Edwards?"

I would have lingered further, but throughout this exchange I had been seized by the fear that, at any stage, Miss Hemmings might notice me and draw me into this unseemly spectacle with an accusation. In fact, just as I began to retreat, she did for one second gaze straight at me. But she did nothing, and the next moment her anguished eyes were back on the bearded man. I took the opportunity to hurry away.

For the next twenty minutes or so, I confined myself to those areas of the ballroom furthest from the doorway. A surprising number of those present appeared needlessly overawed by the occasion, so much so that most of the conversations—those I could hear around me as well as those I took part in—consisted almost entirely of mutual compliments. Once the compliments had been exhausted, people would resort to eulogising the guest of honour. At one stage, after one such speech listing exhaustively Sir Cecil Medhurst's achievements, I said to the elderly man who had just made it:

"I wonder if Sir Cecil has arrived yet?"

My companion indicated with his glass, and I saw a little way across the room the tall figure of the great statesman stooped in conversation with two middle-aged ladies. Then, just as I was looking over at him, I saw Sarah Hemmings emerge through the crowd, making straight for him.

There was now no trace left of the pitiful creature from the ante-room. She looked positively radiant. As I watched, she strode up to Sir Cecil with not a hint of hesitation and laid a hand on his arm.

The elderly man began to introduce me to someone, so that I was obliged for the moment to turn away. When I next looked towards Sir Cecil, I saw that the two middle-aged ladies were standing to one side, looking on with awkward smiles, and that Miss Hemmings had succeeded in engaging his complete attention. Even as I watched, Sir Cecil leant back his head to laugh loudly at something she was saying.

In time we were ushered into the banqueting hall and seated around a vast, long table under bright chandeliers. I was relieved to find that Miss Hemmings had been seated some way away from me, and for a while, I did rather enjoy the occasion. I chatted in turn to the ladies sitting on either side of me—both of whom, in their different ways, were quite charming—and the food was pleas-antly sumptuous. But as the meal went on, I found myself leaning forward time and again to catch sight of Miss Hemmings further down the table, and I began yet again to rehearse in my head all the reasons why I had been entitled to behave as I had.

It is perhaps owing to such preoccupations that I cannot now remember much more concerning the dinner itself. Somewhere towards the end there were speeches; various personages stood up to heap praise on Sir Cecil for his contribution to world affairs, and in particular, for his role in building the League of Nations. Then finally, Sir Cecil himself rose to his feet.

His speech, as I recall it, was self-deprecating and optimistic. In his view, mankind had learnt from its mistakes, the structures were now firmly in place to ensure we would never again see on this globe a calamity on the scale of the Great War. The war, ghastly as it was, represented no more than "an awkward window in Man's evo-lution" when for a few years our technical progress had run ahead of our organisational capacities. We had all surprised ourselves with the rapid development of our engineering might, and the consequent ability to wage war with modern weaponry, but now we had made good the gap. Having been reminded of the horrors that could be let loose among us, the forces of civilisation had prevailed and legislated. His speech was along some such lines, and we all applauded it heartily.

After dinner, the ladies did not leave us, but instead we were all asked to proceed through into the ballroom. There we found a string quartet playing, and waiters moving about with trays of liqueurs, cigars, and coffee. The guests began immediately to circulate, and the atmosphere was far more relaxed than before dinner. At one point, I happened to catch Miss Hemmings's eye across the room, and was surprised to see her smile at me. My initial thought was that this was the smile of an enemy plotting some awful revenge; but then I continued to observe her as the evening went on, and decided I was wrong about this. I realised that Sarah Hemmings was utterly happy. After months, perhaps years of planning, she had succeeded in being at this place at this time, and having achieved her goal, she had—much like, so we are told, a woman who has just given birth—consigned to oblivion all memories of the pain she had endured along the way. I watched her drifting from group to group, chatting amiably. It occurred to me I should go over and make my peace with her while her mood lasted, but then the possibility of her suddenly turning and creating another scene kept me a good distance from her.

It was perhaps half an hour into this portion of the evening when I was finally introduced to Sir Cecil Medhurst. I had been making no special efforts to meet him, but I suppose I might have been a little disappointed had I left the occasion without having exchanged any words at all with the illustrious statesman. As it was, it was he who was led up to me—by Lady Adams, whom I had met several months ago during an investigation. Sir Cecil grasped my hand warmly, saying: "Ah, my young friend! So here you are!"

For a few minutes, we were left alone together in the middle of the room. All around us, by this time, there was a very lively hub-bub, and when we exchanged the usual pleasantries, we were obliged to lean towards one another and raise our voices. At one point, he nudged me and said:

"All of that I was saying earlier at dinner. About this world being made a safer, more civilised place. I do believe it, you know. At least"—here he grasped my hand and gave me a droll look—"at least, I'd *like* to believe it. Oh yes, I'd dearly love to believe it. But I don't know, my young friend. I don't know if in the end we'll be able to hold the line. We'll do what we can. Organise, confer. Get the greatest men from the greatest nations to put their heads together and talk. But there'll always be evil lurking around the corner for us. Oh yes! They're busy, even now, even as we speak, busy conspiring to put civilisation to the torch. And they're clever, oh, devilishly clever. Good men and women can do what they can, devote their lives to keeping them at bay, but I fear it won't be enough, my friend. I fear it won't be enough. The evil ones are much too cunning for your ordinary decent citizen. They'll run rings around him, corrupt him, turn him against his fellows. I see it, I see it all the time now and it will grow worse. That's why we'll need to rely more than ever on the likes of you, my young friend. The few on our side every bit as clever as they are. Who'll spot their game quickly, destroy the fungus before it takes hold and spreads."

Possibly he was more than a little drunk; possibly the occasion had overwhelmed him. In any case, he went on in this vein for some time, clasping my arm emotionally as he spoke. And perhaps simply because this distinguished man was being so effusive—or perhaps it was that I had had it in my mind all evening to ask him some such thing—when at last he came to a halt, I said to him:

"Sir Cecil, I believe you've spent time recently in Shanghai."

"Shanghai? Certainly, my friend. Been back and forth. What

happens in China is crucial. We can no longer look just at Europe, you see. If we wish to contain chaos in Europe, we now have to look further afield."

"I ask, sir, because I was born in Shanghai."

"Is that so? Well, well."

"I did just wonder, sir, if you came across an old friend of mine there. Of course, there's no real reason why you would have done. But his name is Yamashita. Akira Yamashita."

"Yamashita? Hmm. Japanese, I take it. A lot of Japanese in Shanghai, of course. They have more influence there by the day. Yamashita, you say."

"Akira Yamashita."

"Can't say I came across him. Diplomatist or something?"

"Actually, sir, I wouldn't know. He was a childhood friend."

"Oh, I see. In that case, do you know for sure he's still in Shanghai? Perhaps your man's left and gone back to Japan."

"Oh no, I'm sure he's still there. Akira was very fond of Shanghai. Besides, he was determined never to return to Japan. No, I'm sure he'll still be there."

"Well, I didn't come across him. Saw quite a lot of that chap Saito. And a few of the military fellows. But no one by that name."

"Well . . ." I gave a laugh to cover my disappointment. "It was always unlikely. But I did just wonder."

Just at this moment, somewhat to my alarm, I realised that Sarah Hemmings was standing beside me.

"So you've finally cornered the great detective, Sir Cecil," she said cheerily.

"Indeed, my dear," the old gentleman replied, beaming at her. "I was just telling him how we'll all have to depend on him in the years to come."

Sarah Hemmings smiled at me. "I have to say, Sir Cecil, I haven't always found Mr. Banks to be *utterly* dependable. But perhaps he's the best we can do."

I decided at this juncture that I should leave as quickly as possible, and pretending to notice someone across the room, I made my apologies and moved away.

I DID NOT SET EYES on Miss Hemmings again until some time later. By then, many of the guests had started to leave and the ballroom was less stuffy. Moreover, the waiters had opened a number of doors on to the balconies, so that a refreshing night breeze was blowing across the room. For all that, the evening had remained warm, and wishing for a little air, I drifted over to one of the balconies. I had all but stepped out on to it before I realised that Sarah Hemmings was already standing there, her back to the room, a cigarette in her holder, gazing out at the night sky. I started back, but then something told me, despite her not having stirred, that she had become aware of my presence. I thus made my way on to the balcony and said:

"So, Miss Hemmings. You've had your evening after all."

"It's been the most marvellous evening," she said without turning. She gave a contented sigh, drew on her cigarette, then gave me one quick smile over her shoulder before turning her gaze back to the night sky. "It's exactly as I imagined it would be. All these marvellous people. Everywhere you care to glance. Marvellous people. And Sir Cecil, he's such a darling, don't you think? I had the most wonderful talk with Eric Mitchell about his exhibition. He's going to invite me to the private view next month."

I said nothing to this, and for a few moments we continued simply to stand there side by side against the balcony rail. Curiously—perhaps it was to do with the string quartet, whose gentle waltz was drifting out to us—the silence was not as uncomfortable as one might have expected. Eventually she said:

"I suppose you're surprised at me."

"Surprised?"

"At how determined I was. To get in here tonight."

"I was surprised, yes." Then I said: "Why do you suppose it is, Miss Hemmings? That you should find it so imperative to seek out company such as this, tonight."

"Imperative? You believe I find it imperative?"

"I would say so. And what I witnessed at the door earlier on might tend to support that view."

Rather to my surprise, she responded with a light laugh, then gave me a smile. "But why shouldn't I, Christopher? Why shouldn't I wish to be in company like this. Isn't it simply . . . heaven?"

When I remained silent, her smile faded.

"I suppose you rather disapprove of me," she said, in a quite different voice.

"I merely remarked . . ."

"It's all right. You've every right. You find all of that, earlier on, you find it embarrassing, and you disapprove. But what else am I to do? I don't wish to look back at my life when I'm old and see something empty. I want to see something I can be proud of. You see, Christopher, I'm *ambitious*."

"I'm not sure I quite understand you. You're under the impression you'll lead a more worthwhile life if you consort with famous people?"

"Is that really how you see me?"

She turned away, perhaps genuinely hurt, and drew again on her cigarette. I watched her staring down at the deserted street below, and at the white stucco-fronted buildings opposite. Then she said quietly:

"I can see it might look that way. At least to someone observing me with a cynical eye."

"I hope I don't observe you in that way. It would upset me to think I did so."

"Then you should try to be more understanding." She turned to me with an intent expression, before looking away again. "If my parents were alive today," she said, "they'd be telling me it's high time I was married. And perhaps it is. But I won't do what I've seen so many girls do. I won't waste all my love, all my energy, all my intellect—modest as that is—on some useless man who devotes himself to golf or to selling bonds in the City. When I marry, it will be to someone who'll really *contribute*. I mean to humanity, to a better world. Is that such an awful ambition? I don't come to places like this in search of famous men, Christopher. I come in search of distinguished ones. What do I care about a little embarrassment here and there?"—she waved towards the room—"But I won't accept it's my fate to waste my life on some pleasant, polite, morally worthless man."

"When you put it like that," I said, "I can see how you might see yourself as, well, almost a zealot."

"In a way, Christopher, I do. Oh, what's that piece they're playing now? It's something I know. Is it Mozart?"

"I believe it's Haydn."

"Oh yes, you're right. Yes, Haydn." For several seconds, she looked at the sky and appeared to be listening.

"Miss Hemmings," I said, eventually, "I'm not proud of the way I behaved towards you earlier. In fact, I now very much regret it. I'm sorry. I hope you'll forgive me."

She went on looking out into the night, stroking her cheek lightly with her cigarette holder. "That's very decent of you, Christopher," she said quietly. "But I should be the one to apologise. I was just trying to use you, after all. Of course I was. I'm sure I made myself look dreadful earlier on, but I don't care about that. I do care, though, I treated you badly. You perhaps won't believe me, but it's true."

I laughed. "Well, then, let's both try and forgive each other."

"Yes, let's." She turned to me and her face suddenly broke into a smile that was almost childlike in its glee. Then a weariness fell over it once more and she turned back to the night. "I often treat people badly," she said. "I suppose that comes with being ambitious. And not having so much time left."

"Did you lose your parents long ago?" I asked.

"It seems like for ever. But in another way, they're always with me."

"Well, I'm glad you enjoyed the evening, after all. I can only say again I'm sorry for my own part in it."

"Oh look, everyone's leaving. What a pity! And I wanted to talk to you about all kinds of things. About your friend, for instance."

"My friend?"

"The one you were asking Sir Cecil about. The one in Shanghai."

"Akira? He was just a childhood friend."

"But I could tell he was someone very important to you."

I straightened and looked behind us. "You're right. Everyone *is* leaving."

"Then I suppose I should leave too," she said. "Otherwise my departure will be as much noticed as my entrance."

But she made no move to go and in the end it was I who excused myself and went back into the room. At one point, when I glanced back, I thought she cut a lonely figure there on the balcony, smoking her cigarette into the night air, the room behind her fast emptying. It even ran through my mind I should go back and offer to escort her out of the proceedings. But then her mentioning Akira had slightly alarmed me, and I decided I had done sufficient for one evening towards improving relations between myself and Sarah Hemmings.

PART TWO

LONDON, 15TH MAY 1931

CHAPTER 4

*A*T THE REAR of our garden in Shanghai, there was a grass mound with a single maple tree rising out of its summit. From the time Akira and I were around six years old, we enjoyed playing on and around that mound, and whenever I now think of my boyhood companion, I tend to remember the two of us running up and down its slopes, sometimes jumping right off where the sides were at their steepest.

From time to time, when we had worn ourselves out, we would sit panting at the top of the mound with our backs against the trunk of the maple tree. From this vantage point, we had a clear view over my garden and of the big white house standing at the end of it. If I close my eyes a moment, I am able to bring back that picture very vividly: the carefully tended "English" lawn, the afternoon shadows cast by the row of elms separating my garden and Akira's; and the house itself, a huge white edifice with numerous wings and trellised balconies. I suspect this memory of the house is very much a child's vision, and that in reality, it was nothing so grand. Certainly, even at the time, I was conscious that it hardly matched the splendour of the residences round the corner in Bubbling Well Road. But the house was certainly more than adequate for a household comprising simply my parents, myself, Mei Li, and our servants.

It was the property of Morganbrook and Byatt, which meant there were many ornaments and pictures around the place I was forbidden to touch. It meant also that from time to time, we would have boarding with us a "house guest"—some employee newly arrived in Shanghai who had yet to "find his feet." I do not know if my parents objected to this arrangement. I did not mind at all, since usually a house guest would be some young man who brought with him the air of the English lanes and meadows I knew from *The Wind in the Willows,* or else the foggy streets of the Conan Doyle mysteries. These young Englishmen, no doubt eager to create a good impression, were inclined to indulge my lengthy questions and sometimes unreasonable requests. Most of them, it occurs to me, were probably younger then than I am today, and were probably all at sea so far from their home. But to me at the time, they were all of them figures to study closely and emulate.

But to return to Akira: there is a particular instance that now comes to mind from one such afternoon, after the two of us had been running frantically up and down that mound to enact one of our extended dramas. We were for a moment sitting down against the maple tree to recover our breath, and I was gazing across the lawn towards the house, waiting for my chest to stop heaving, when Akira said behind me:

"Be careful, old chip. Centipede. By your foot."

I had clearly heard him say "old chip," but did not at this point think anything of it. But having once used the phrase, Akira seemed rather pleased with it, and over the following several minutes, once we resumed our game, proceeded to address me so over and over: "This way, old chip!" "More fast, old chip!"

"Anyway, it's not old chip," I told him in the end, during one of our disputes over how our game should proceed. "It's old *chap.*"

Akira, as I knew he would, protested vigorously. "Not at all. Not at all. Mrs. Brown. She make me say again and again. Old chip. Old chip. Correct pronunciation, everything. She say old chip. She *teacher!*"

It was pointless to try to convince him; since starting his English lessons, he was immensely proud of his position within his family as the expert English speaker. All the same, I was unwilling to concede the point, and in the end the quarrel grew to such proportions, Akira simply stalked off in a fury, our game abandoned, through our "secret door"—a gap in the hedge separating the two gardens.

On the next few occasions we played together, he did not call me "old chip," or make any reference to this altercation on the mound. I had all but forgotten the matter when one morning a few weeks later, it came up again suddenly as we were walking back together along Bubbling Well Road past the grand houses and beautiful lawns. I cannot remember quite what I had just said to him. In any case, he responded by saying:

"Very kind of you, old chap."

I remember resisting the temptation to point out that he had come round to my view. For by then I knew Akira well enough to realise he was not saying "old chap" by way of a subtle admission that he had previously been wrong; rather, in some odd way we both understood, he was implying that *he* had always been the one to claim it was "old chap"; that he was now merely reasserting his argument, and my lack of protest simply confirmed his conclusive victory. Indeed, for the rest of the afternoon, he continued to "old chap" me with an ever more smug expression, as though to say: "So you're no longer determined to be ridiculous. I'm glad you're seeing more sense."

This kind of behaviour was not at all untypical of Akira, and though I always found it infuriating, for some reason I rarely made the effort to protest. In fact—and today I find this hard to explain—I felt a certain need to preserve such fantasies on Akira's behalf, and had, say, an adult tried to arbitrate in the "old chip" dispute, I would just as likely have taken Akira's side.

I do not wish to imply by this that Akira dominated me, or that ours was in any sense an unbalanced friendship. I took as much initiative in our games, and if anything, made more of the crucial decisions. The fact was, I believed myself his intellectual superior, and at some level, Akira probably accepted this. On the other hand, there were various things that gave my Japanese friend great authority in my eyes. There were, for instance, his arm-locks—which he would often administer if I made statements that displeased him, or if during one of our dramas, I became resistant to adopting a particular plot-turn he was keen on. More generally, even though he was actually only a month my senior, I did have a sense that he was the more worldly. He did seem to know about many things I did not. There was, above all, his claim to having ventured on several occasions beyond the boundaries of the Settlement.

It is slightly surprising to me, looking back today, to think how as young boys we were allowed to come and go unsupervised to the extent that we were. But this was, of course, all within the relative safety of the International Settlement. I for one was absolutely forbidden to enter the Chinese areas of the city, and as far as I know, Akira's parents were no less strict on the matter. Out there, we were told, lay all manner of ghastly diseases, filth and evil men. The closest I had ever come to going out of the Settlement was once when a carriage carrying my mother and me took an unexpected route along that part of the Soochow creek bordering the Chapei district; I could see the huddled low rooftops across the canal, and had held my breath for as long as I could for fear the pestilence would come airborne across the narrow strip of water. No wonder then that my friend's claim to have undertaken a number of secret forays into such areas made an impression on me.

I remember quizzing Akira repeatedly about these exploits. The truth concerning the Chinese districts, he told me, was far worse even than the rumours. There were no proper buildings, just shack upon shack built in great proximity to one another. It all looked, he claimed, much like the marketplace in Boone Road, except that whole families were to be found living in each "stall." There were, moreover, dead bodies piled up everywhere, flies buzzing all over them, and no one there thought anything of it. On one occasion, Akira had been strolling down a crowded alley and had seen a man—some powerful warlord, he supposed—being transported on a sedan chair, accompanied by a giant carrying a sword. The warlord was pointing to whomever he pleased and the giant would then proceed to lop his or her head off. Naturally, people were trying to hide themselves the best they could. Akira, though, had simply stood there, staring defiantly back at the warlord. The latter had spent a moment considering whether to have Akira beheaded, but then obviously struck by my friend's courage, had finally laughed and, reaching down, patted him on the head. Then the warlord's party had continued on its way, leaving many more severed heads in its wake.

I cannot remember ever attempting to challenge Akira on any of these claims. Once I mentioned casually to my mother something about my friend's adventures beyond the Settlement, and I remember her smiling and saying something to cast doubt on the matter. I was furious at her, and thereafter I believe I carefully avoided revealing to her anything at all intimate concerning Akira.

My mother, incidentally, was one person Akira regarded with a peculiar awe. If, say, despite his having got me in an arm-lock, I was still loath to concede a point to him, I could always resort to declaring that he would have my mother to answer to. Of course, this was not something I liked to do readily; it rather hurt my pride to have to invoke my mother's authority at such an age. But on those occasions I was obliged to do so, I was always amazed by the transformation brought about—how the merciless fiend with the vice-like grip could turn in a second into a panic-stricken child. I was never sure why my mother should have such an effect on Akira; for although he was always exceedingly polite, he was on the whole unintimidated by adults. I could not, moreover, recall my mother ever having spoken to him in anything but a gentle and friendly way. I can remember pondering this question at the time, and various possibilities occurring to me.

I did, for a while, consider the notion that Akira regarded my mother as he did because she was "beautiful." That my mother was "beautiful" was something I accepted, quite dispassionately, as fact throughout my growing up. It was always being said of her, and I believe I regarded this "beautiful" as simply a label that attached itself to my mother, no more significant than "tall" or "small" or "young." At the same time, I was not unaware of the effect her "beauty" had on others. Of course, at that age, I had no real sense of the deeper implications of feminine allure. But accompanying her from place to place as I did, I came to take for granted, for instance, the admiring glances of strangers as we strolled through the Public Gardens, or the preferential treatment from the waiters at the Italian Café in Nanking Road where we would go for cakes on Saturday mornings. Whenever I look now at my photographs of her—I have seven in all, in the album that accompanied me here from Shanghai—she strikes me as a beauty in an older, Victorian tradition. Today, she might perhaps be regarded as "handsome"; certainly, she is not "pretty." I cannot imagine her, for instance, ever having had the repertoire of coquettish little shrugs and tosses of the head that we expect of our young women today. In the photographs—all of them taken before my birth, four in Shanghai, two in Hong Kong, one in Switzerland—she is certainly elegant, stiff-backed, perhaps even haughty, but not without the gentleness around her eyes I remember well. In any case, the point I am making is that it was quite natural for me to suspect, initially at least, that Akira's odd attitude towards my mother derived, like so many other things, from her beauty. But when I thought the thing over more carefully, I recall settling on a more likely explanation: namely, that Akira had been unusually impressed by what he had witnessed the morning the company's health inspector visited our house.

IT WAS AN ACCEPTED FEATURE of our lives to be visited from time to time by an official from Morganbrook and Byatt, some man who would spend an hour or so wandering about the house, noting things in his notebook, mumbling the occasional question. I remember my mother once telling me that when I was very young, I liked to play at "being" a Byatt's health inspector, and that she often had to dissuade me from spending prolonged periods studying our lavatory arrangements with a pencil in my hand. This may well have been so, but as far as I can recall, these visits were mostly entirely eventless, and for years I did not think anything of them. I can see now, though, that these inspections, checking as they did not only on hygiene matters, but also for signs of disease or parasites among household members, were potentially very embarrassing, and no doubt the individuals selected by the company to conduct them tended to be those with a gift for tact and delicacy. Certainly, I remember a series of meek, shuffling men—usually English, though occasionally French—who were always carefully deferential not just to my mother, but also to Mei Li—a point which always went down well with me. But the inspector who turned up on that morning—I must then have been eight—was not at all typical.

Today, I can remember in particular two things about him: that he had a drooping moustache, and that there was a brown mark—perhaps a tea stain—at the back of his hat disappearing into its band. I was playing alone at the front of the house, on the round island of lawn encircled by our carriage track. I remember it being overcast that day. I had been absorbed in my game when the man appeared at the gate and came walking towards the house. As he passed me, he muttered: "Hello, young man. Mother in?" then carried on without waiting for my reply. It was as I was staring at his back view that I noticed the stain on his hat.

What I remember next must have occurred around an hour later. By that time Akira had arrived and we were busy up in my playroom. It was the sound of their voices—not raised exactly, but filled with a growing tension—that caused us both to look up from our game, then eventually, to move stealthily out on to the landing and crouch beside the heavy oak cabinet outside the playroom door.

Our house had a rather grand staircase, and from our vantage point beside the oak cabinet, we could see the gleaming banister rail following the curve of the stairs down to the spacious entrance hall. There, my mother and the inspector were standing facing each other, both very stiff and straight, near the centre of the floor, so that they looked rather like two opposing chess pieces left on the board. The inspector, I noticed, was clutching to his chest his hat with the stain. For her part, my mother had her hands clasped just below her bosom, the way she did before she burst into song on those evenings Mrs. Lewis, the American curate's wife, came to play the piano.

The altercation that followed, though of no apparent significance in itself, I believe came to mean something special to my mother, representing perhaps a key moment of moral triumph. I remember she would refer to it regularly as I grew older, as though it were something she wished me to take to my heart; and I remember often listening to her recount the whole story to visitors, usually concluding with a little laugh and the observation that the inspector had been removed from his post shortly after the encounter. Consequently, I cannot be sure today how much of my memory of that morning derives from what I actually witnessed from the landing, and to what extent it has merged over time with my mother's accounts of the episode. In any case, my impression is that as Akira and I peered round the edge of the oak cabinet, the inspector was saying something like:

"I have every respect for your sentiments, Mrs. Banks. Nevertheless, out here, one can't be too careful. And the company does have a responsibility for all employees' welfare, even the more seasoned, such as yourself and Mr. Banks."

"I am sorry, Mr. Wright," my mother responded, "but your objections have yet to make themselves clear to me. These servants you talk of have given excellent service over the years. I can vouch utterly for their standards of hygiene. And you have yourself admitted they show no signs of any contagious illness."

"Nevertheless, madam, they are from Shantung. And the company is obliged to counsel all our employees against taking natives of that province into their houses. A stricture, may I say, derived from bitter experience."

"Can you be serious? You wish me to drive out these friends of ours—yes, we've long considered them *friends!*—for no other reason than that they hail from Shantung?"

At this, the inspector's manner grew rather pompous. He proceeded to explain to my mother that the company's objections to servants from Shantung were based on doubts about not just their hygiene and health, but also their honesty. And with so many items of value in the house belonging to the company—the inspector gestured around him—he was obliged to reiterate most strongly his recommendation. When my mother broke in again to ask on what basis such astonishing generalisations had been made, the inspector gave a weary sigh, then said:

"In a word, madam, opium. Opium addiction in Shantung has now advanced to such deplorable levels that entire villages are to be found enslaved to the pipe. Hence, Mrs. Banks, the low standards of hygiene, the high incidence of contagion. And inevitably, those who come from Shantung to work in Shanghai, even if essentially of an honest disposition, tend sooner or later to resort to thieving, for the sake of their parents, brothers, cousins, uncles, what have you, all of whose cravings must somehow be pacified . . . Good gracious, madam! I'm simply trying to make my point . . ."

Not only was it the inspector who recoiled at this point; beside me, Akira gave a sharp intake of breath, and when I glanced at him he was staring down at my mother open-mouthed. It is this picture of him at that moment which led me later to believe his subsequent awestruck view of my mother originated from that morning.

But if the inspector and Akira both started at something my mother did at that point, I did not myself see anything out of the ordinary. To me, she appeared to do no more than brace herself a little in preparation for what she was about to assert. But then, I suppose I was well used to her ways; possibly to those less familiar with them, certain of my mother's customary looks and postures in such situations might indeed have come over as somewhat alarming.

This is not to say that I was not fully alert to the explosion that was to follow. In fact, from the instant the inspector had uttered the word "opium," I had known that the unfortunate man was done for.

He had come to an abrupt halt, no doubt expecting to be cut off. But I recall my mother letting hang a trembling silence— throughout which her glare never moved off the inspector—before finally asking in a quiet voice that nevertheless threatened to brim over with fury:

"You presume, sir, to talk to *me*, on behalf of *this* of all firms, about *opium*?"

There followed a tirade of controlled ferocity in which she put to the inspector the case with which I was by then already familiar and which I was to hear outlined again many more times: that the British in general, and the company of Morganbrook and Byatt especially, by importing Indian opium into China in such massive quantities had brought untold misery and degradation to a whole nation. As she spoke, my mother's voice often grew taut, but never quite lost its measured quality. Finally, still fixing her foe with her glare, she asked him:

"Are you not ashamed, sir? As a Christian, as an Englishman, as a man with scruples? Are you not ashamed to be in the service of such a company? Tell me, how is your conscience able to rest while you owe your existence to such ungodly wealth?"

Had he had the temerity to do so, the inspector might have pointed out the inappropriateness of my mother's admonishing him in such terms, of such words issuing from the wife of a fellow company employee, residing in a company house. But by this point he had realised he was out beyond his depth, and muttering a few stock phrases to preserve his dignity, retreated from the house.

In those days, it was still a surprise to me when any adult displayed—as had the inspector—ignorance of my mother's campaigns against opium. Throughout much of my growing up, I held the belief that my mother was known and admired far and wide as the principal enemy of the Great Opium Dragon of China. The opium phenomenon, I should say, was not something adults in Shanghai made much effort to hide from children, but of course, when I was very young, I understood little concerning the matter. I was accustomed to seeing each day, from the carriage that took me to school, the Chinese men in doorways along Nanking Road, sprawled in the morning sun, and for some time, whenever I heard of my mother's campaigns, I imagined her to be assisting this specific group of men. Later though, as I grew older, I had more opportunities to glimpse something of the complexity surrounding the issue. I was, for instance, required to present myself at my mother's luncheons.

These would take place at our house, usually during the week when my father was at the office. Typically, four or five ladies would arrive and be led into the conservatory, where a table would have been laid amidst the creepers and palms. I would assist by passing around cups, saucers and plates, and wait for the moment I knew would come: that is, when my mother asked her guests how, when they "searched their hearts and consciences," they viewed their companies' policies. At this point the pleasant chatter would cease and the ladies would listen silently as my mother went on to express her own deep unhappiness with "our company's actions," which she regarded as "un-Christian and un-British." As I remember it, these luncheons always became quiet and awkward from this stage on, until the moment, not so long afterwards, when the ladies would utter their frosty farewells and drift out to the waiting carriages and motor cars. But I knew from what my mother told me that she did "win through" to a number of these company wives, and the converts were then invited to her meetings.

These latter were much more serious affairs and I was not permitted to attend them. They would take place in the dining room behind closed doors, and if by chance I was still in the house while a meeting was in progress, I would be required to tip-toe around silently. Occasionally I would be introduced to a personage my mother held in special esteem—a clergyman, say, or a diplomatist—but by and large Mei Li was instructed to have me well out of the way before the first guests arrived. Of course, Uncle Philip was one of those always present, and I often endeavoured to be visible as the participants departed so as to catch his eye. If he spotted me, then invariably he would come over with a smile and we would have a little talk. Sometimes, if he had no pressing engagement, I would take him aside to show him the drawings I had done that week, or else we might go and sit together for a while out on the back terrace.

Once everyone had left, the atmosphere in the house would undergo a complete change. My mother's mood would invariably lighten, as though the meeting had swept away every one of her cares. I would hear her singing to herself as she went around the house putting things back in order, and as soon as I did so, I would hurry out into the garden to wait. For I knew that once she had finished tidying, she would come out to find me, and whatever time was left before lunch she would devote entirely to me.

Once I was older, it was during these periods, just after a meeting, that my mother and I went for our walks in Jessfield Park. But when I was six or seven, we tended to stay at home and play a board game, or sometimes even with my toy soldiers. I can still remember a certain routine we developed around this time. In those days, there had been a swing on our lawn not far from the terrace. My mother would emerge from the house, still singing, step on to the grass and sit on the swing. I would be waiting up on my mound at the back of the garden, and come running up to her, pretending to be furious.

"Get off, Mother! You'll break it!" I would jump up and down before the swing, waving my arms about. "You're much too big! You'll break it!"

And my mother, pretending she could neither see nor hear me, would swing herself higher and higher, all the time continuing to sing at the top of her voice some song like: "Daisy, Daisy, Give Me Your Answer Do." When all my pleading had failed, I would—the logic of this now eludes me—attempt a succession of headstands on the grass in front of her. Her singing would then become punctuated by gales of laughter, until eventually she would come down from the swing, and we would go off to play with whatever I had prepared for us. Even today, I cannot think about my mother's meetings without remembering those eagerly anticipated moments that would always follow.

A few years ago, I did spend some days in the Reading Room of the British Museum researching into the arguments that raged over the opium trade in China during those times. As I sifted through many newspaper articles, letters and documents of the day, a number of issues that had mystified me as a child became much clearer. However—and I might as well admit this—my main motive in undertaking such research was the hope that I would come across reports of my mother. After all, as I have said, I had been given to believe as a child that she was a key figure in the anti-opium campaigns. It was something of a disappointment then that I did not once find her name. There were others repeatedly quoted, praised, denigrated, but in all that material I collated, I did not once find my mother. I did though stumble upon several mentions of Uncle Philip. Once, in a letter to the *North China Daily News*, a Swedish missionary, in the process of condemning a number of European companies, referred to Uncle Philip as "that admirable beacon of rectitude." The absence of my mother's name was disappointment enough, but this was a cruel twist indeed, and I abandoned my researches thereafter.

BUT I HAVE NO WISH to recall Uncle Philip here just now. There was a time, earlier this evening, when I was convinced I had mentioned his name to Sarah Hemmings during our bus ride this afternoon—even told her one or two basic things about him. But going over yet again all that took place, I am now reasonably sure Uncle Philip did not come up at all—and I must say I am relieved. It may be a foolish way to think, but it has always been my feeling that Uncle Philip will remain a less tangible entity while he exists only in my memory.

I did though tell her a little about Akira this afternoon, and now that I have had a chance to think it over, I do not really regret having done so. I did not, in any case, tell her very much, and she did appear genuinely interested. I have no idea what it was that caused me suddenly to start talking to her of such matters; I certainly had no such intention when I first boarded that bus with her in the Haymarket.

I had been invited by David Corbett, a man I have come vaguely to know, to lunch with him and "a few friends" at a restaurant in Lower Regent Street. It is a fashionable lunch spot, and Corbett had booked a long table at the rear of the room for a dozen of us. I was pleased to see Sarah among the party—and a little surprised, since I had not been aware she was a friend of Corbett's—but arriving rather late, I was not able to sit within speaking range of her.

It had clouded over by that time, and the waiter had lit for us a brace of candles on our table. One of our party, a fellow called Hegley, thought it a good joke to blow the candles out, and then to summon the waiter back to relight them. He did this at least three times in the space of twenty minutes—whenever he judged the boisterous atmosphere to be sagging—and the others did seem to find this very amusing. From what I could see, Sarah was at this stage enjoying herself, laughing with the rest of them. We had been there for perhaps an hour—a couple of the men had excused themselves to return to their offices—when attention turned to Emma Cameron, a rather intense girl, sitting at Sarah's end of the table. For all I knew, she had already been talking for some time to those nearest her about her problems; but it was at this stage that a lull falling over the rest of the table suddenly made her the focus of the whole party. There followed a half-serious, half-ironic discussion of Emma Cameron's troubled relationship with her mother—which was evidently reaching a new crisis on account of Emma's recent engagement to a Frenchman. All kinds of advice were offered to her. The man called Hegley, for instance, proposed that all mothers—"and aunts too, naturally"—be kept in a large zoo-like institution to be constructed beside the Serpentine. Others made more helpful comments based on their own experiences, and Emma Cameron, relishing all the attention, kept the topic well stoked with ever more theatrical anecdotes to illustrate the thoroughly exasperating nature of this particular parent. The discussion had been going on for perhaps fifteen minutes when I saw Sarah rise and, mumbling a word into the host's ear, leave the room. The ladies' powder room was located in the lobby area of the restaurant, and the others—those who noticed her exit at all—no doubt assumed that was where she was bound. But I had caught something in her face as she had left, and after a few minutes, I too rose and went out after her.

I found her standing at the entrance of the restaurant, looking out of the windows into Lower Regent Street. She did not notice me come up to her until I touched her arm and asked:

"Is everything all right?"

She gave a start, and I noticed little traces of tears in her eyes, which she quickly tried to mask with a smile.

"Oh yes, I'm fine. I felt a little stuffy, that's all. I'm fine now." She gave a little laugh and gazed out searchingly into the street. "I'm sorry, it must have looked awfully rude. I really should go back in."

"I see no reason why you should if you don't want to."

She studied me carefully, then asked: "Are they still talking about what they were talking about?"

"They were when I left." Then I added: "I suppose neither of us is able to contribute much to a symposium on troublesome mothers."

She suddenly laughed and wiped away the tears, now no longer trying to hide them from me. "No," she said, "I suppose we're disqualified." Then she smiled again and said: "It's so silly of me. After all, they're just having a nice lunch."

"Are you expecting a car?" I asked, for she was still looking out earnestly at the traffic.

"What? Oh no, no. I was just looking." Then she said: "I was wondering if a bus would come. You see, look, over the street. There's a stop. My mother and I, we used to spend a lot of time on buses. Just for the pleasure of it. I'm talking about when I was small. If we couldn't get the front seat on the top deck, then we'd just come straight down and wait for another one. And we'd spend hours sometimes, going around London, looking at everything, and talking, and pointing things out to each other. I so used to enjoy it. Don't you ever go on buses, Christopher? You should. You can see so much from the top."

"I must confess I tend to walk or get a cab. I'm rather afraid of London buses. I'm convinced if I get on one, it'll take me some-where I don't want to go, and I'll spend the rest of the day trying to find my way back."

"Shall I tell you something, Christopher?" Her voice had become very quiet. "It's very silly, but I only realised it recently. It had never occurred to me before. But Mother must already have been in a lot of pain. She wasn't strong enough to do other things with me. That's why we spent so much time on buses. It was something we could still do together."

"Would you care to ride on a bus now?" I asked.

She looked out again into the street. "But aren't you very busy?"

"It would be a pleasure. As I say, I'm rather frightened to go on buses alone. Since you're something of a veteran, then this is my opportunity."

"Very well." She suddenly beamed. "I'll show you how you ride on a London bus."

We eventually boarded not in Lower Regent Street—we did not wish the lunch party to emerge and see us waiting—but in nearby Haymarket. When we climbed to the upper deck, she showed a childish delight in finding her front seat vacant, and we sat there swaying together as the vehicle lumbered its way towards Trafalgar Square.

London looked very grey today, and down on the pavements, the crowds were well prepared with their mackintoshes and umbrel-las. I would suppose we spent a half-hour on that bus, perhaps longer. We took in the Strand, Chancery Lane, Clerkenwell. Some-times we sat looking at the view below us in silence; at other times, we talked, usually of innocuous things. Her mood had lightened considerably since the lunch, and she did not mention her mother again. I am not sure how we got on to the subject, but it was just after a lot of passengers had got off at High Holborn, and we were moving down Gray's Inn Road, that I found myself talking about

Akira. I believe at first I did no more than mention him in passing, describing him as a "childhood friend." But she must have probed me, for I remember not long afterwards saying to her with a laugh:

"I always think about the time we stole something together."

"Oh!" she exclaimed. "So that's it! The great detective has a secret criminal past! I knew this Japanese boy was significant. Do tell me about your robbery."

"Hardly a robbery. We were ten years old."

"But it torments your conscience, even still?"

"Not at all. It was just a small thing. We stole something from a servant's room."

"But how fascinating. And this was in Shanghai?"

I suppose I must then have told her a few further things from the past. I did not reveal anything of any real significance, but after parting with her this afternoon—we eventually got off in New Oxford Street—I was surprised and slightly alarmed that I had told her anything at all. After all, I have not spoken to anyone about the past in all the time I have been in this country, and as I say, I had certainly never intended to start doing so today.

But perhaps something of this sort has been on the cards for some time. For the truth is, over this past year, I have become increasingly preoccupied with my memories, a preoccupation encouraged by the discovery that these memories—of my childhood, of my parents—have lately begun to blur. A number of times recently I have found myself struggling to recall something that only two or three years ago I believed was ingrained in my mind for ever. I have been obliged to accept, in other words, that with each passing year, my life in Shanghai will grow less distinct, until one day all that will remain will be a few muddled images. Even tonight, when I sat down here and tried to gather in some sort of order these things I still remember, I have been struck anew by how hazy so much has grown. To take, for instance, this episode I have just recounted concerning my mother and the health inspector:

while I am fairly sure I have remembered its essence accurately enough, turning it over in my mind again, I find myself less certain about some of the details. For one thing, I am no longer sure she actually put to the inspector the actual words: "How is your conscience able to rest while you owe your existence to such ungodly wealth?" It now seems to me that even in her impassioned state, she would have been aware of the awkwardness of these words, of the fact that they left her quite open to ridicule. I do not believe my mother would ever have lost control of the situation to such a degree. On the other hand, it is possible I attributed these words to her precisely because such a question was one she must have put to herself constantly during our life in Shanghai. The fact that we "owed our existence" to a company whose activities she had identified as an evil to be scourged must have been a source of true torment for her.

In fact, it is even possible I have remembered incorrectly the context in which she uttered those words; that it was not to the health inspector she put this question, but to my father, on another morning altogether, during that argument in the dining room.

CHAPTER 5

$\mathcal{I}$ DO NOT REMEMBER NOW if the dining-room episode occurred before or after the health inspector's visit. What I recall is that it was raining hard that afternoon, making it gloomy throughout the house, and that I had been sitting in the library, watched over by Mei Li as I went through my arithmetic books.

We called it the "library," but I suppose it was really just an anteroom whose walls happened to be lined with books. There was just enough space in the middle of the floor for a mahogany table, and it was there I always did my schoolwork, my back to the double doors leading into the dining room. Mei Li, my *amah*, saw my education as a matter of solemn importance, and even when I had been working for an hour, it never occurred to her, as she stood sternly over me, to lean her weight on the shelf behind her, or else to sit down in the upright chair opposite mine. The servants had long since learnt not to blunder in during these moments of study, and even my parents had accepted they should not disturb us unless absolutely necessary.

It was, then, something of a surprise when my father came striding through the library that afternoon, oblivious of our presence, and went into the dining room, closing the doors firmly behind him. This intrusion was followed within minutes by another from my mother, who also strode past briskly and disappeared into the dining room. During the minutes that followed I could catch, even through the heavy doors, the occasional word or phrase that told me my parents were locked in argument. But frustratingly, whenever I tried to hear a little more, whenever my pencil hovered too long over my sums, there would come Mei Li's inevitable reprimand.

But then—I do not remember quite how this came about—Mei Li was called away, and I was suddenly left alone at the library table. At first I just continued to work, too fearful of what would happen if Mei Li returned and found me out of my chair. But the longer she was gone, the greater grew my urge to hear more clearly the muffled exchanges in the next room. I did finally rise and go to the doors, but even then, I would hurry back to the table every few seconds, convinced I could hear my *amah's* footsteps. In the end, I managed to remain at the door only by keeping a ruler in my hand, so that if surprised by Mei Li, I could claim to be in the process of measuring the dimensions of the room.

Even so, I managed to hear whole phrases only when my parents forgot themselves and raised their voices. I could make out in my mother's angry voice the same righteous tone she had used that morning to the health inspector. I heard her repeat: "A disgrace!" a number of times, and she referred often to what she called "the sinful trade." At one point she said: "You're making us all party to it! All of us! It's a disgrace!" My father too sounded angry, though in a defensive, despairing sort of way. He kept saying things like: "It's not so simple. It's not nearly so simple." And at one point he shouted:

"It's too bad! I'm *not* Philip. I'm not made that way. It's too bad, it's just too bad!"

There was something in his voice as he shouted this, a kind of terrible resignation, and I suddenly became furious at Mei Li for having abandoned me in such a situation. And it was perhaps then, as I was standing by those doors, my ruler in my hand, caught between the urge to continue listening and the desire to flee to the sanctuary of my playroom and my toy soldiers, that I heard my mother utter those words:

"Are you not ashamed to be in the service of such a company? How can your conscience rest while you owe your existence to such ungodly wealth?"

I DO NOT REMEMBER what occurred after that: whether Mei Li came back; if I was still there in the library when my parents emerged. I do recall, though, that the episode heralded one of the longer periods of silence between my parents—that is to say, one that was maintained for weeks, rather than days. I do not mean, of course, that my parents did not communicate at all during this time, just that all exchanges were kept to the strictly functional.

I was well used to such periods and never concerned myself unduly with them. In any case, it was only in the smallest ways that they ever impinged upon my life. For instance, my father might appear at breakfast with a cheerful: "Good morning, everyone!" and slap his hands together, only to be met by my mother's frosty glare. On such occasions, my father might try to cover his embarrassment by turning to me and, still in the same cheery tone, asking:

"And what about you, Puffin? Any interesting dreams last night?"

To which I knew from experience I should respond by giving a vague sound and continuing to eat. Otherwise, as I say, I was able to go about my business more or less as usual. But I suppose I must, at least sometimes, have given thought to these matters, for I do have a memory of a particular conversation I had with Akira once when we were playing in his house.

MY MEMORY of Akira's house is that, from an architectural stand-point, it was very similar to ours; in fact, I remember my father telling me both houses had been built by the same British firm some twenty years earlier. But the inside of my friend's house was a quite different affair, and the source of some fascination for me. It was not so much the preponderance of Oriental pictures and ornaments—in Shanghai, at that stage in my life, I would have seen nothing unusual in this—but rather his family's eccentric notions regarding the usage of many items of Western furniture. Rugs I would have expected to see on floors were hung on walls; chairs would be at odd heights to tables; lamps would totter under overly large shades. Most remarkable were the pair of "replica" Japanese rooms Akira's parents had created at the top of the house. These were small but uncluttered rooms with Japanese tatami mats fitted over the floors, and paper panels fixed to the walls, so that once inside—at least according to Akira—one could not tell one was not in an authentic Japanese house made of wood and paper. I can remember the doors to these rooms being especially curious; on the outer, "Western" side, they were oak-panelled with shining brass knobs; on the inner, "Japanese" side, delicate paper with lac-quer inlays.

In any case, one sweltering day, Akira and I had been playing in one of these Japanese rooms. He had been trying to teach me a game involving piles of cards with Japanese characters on them. I had managed to pick up the rudiments and we had been playing for several minutes when I suddenly asked him:

"Does your mother sometimes stop talking to your father?"

He looked at me blankly, probably because he had failed to understand me; his English often let him down if I spoke out of context like this. Then, when I repeated my question, he shrugged and said:

"Mother not talk to Father when he at office. Mother not talk to Father when he in toilet!"

With that, he roared with theatrical laughter, rolled on to his back and began kicking his feet in the air. I was thus obliged for the moment to drop the matter. But having raised it, I was determined to get his view, and a few minutes later, brought it up again.

This time he seemed to sense my earnestness, and leaving aside the card game, asked me a number of questions until I had more or less told him the nature of my worries. He then rolled on to his back again, but this time gazed thoughtfully up at the ceiling fan rotating above us. After a few moments he said:

"I know why they stop. I know why." Then turning to me, he said: "Christopher. You not enough Englishman."

When I asked him to explain this, he once more looked at the ceiling and went quiet. I too rolled on to my back and followed his example of staring at the fan. He was lying a little way across the room from me, and when he spoke again, I remember his voice sounded oddly disembodied.

"It same for me," he said. "Mother and Father, they stop talk. Because I not enough Japanese."

As I may have said already, I tended to regard Akira as a worldly authority on many aspects of life, and so I listened to him that day with great care. My parents stopped talking to one another, he told me, whenever they became deeply unhappy with my behaviour— and in my case, this was on account of my not behaving sufficiently like an Englishman. If I thought about it, he said, I would be able to link each of my parents' silences to some instance of my failing in this way. For his part, he always knew when he had let down his Japanese blood, and it never came as a surprise to him to discover that his parents had ceased talking to one another. When I asked him why they did not scold us in the usual manner when we misbehaved in this way, Akira explained to me that it was not like that; he was talking of offences quite different from the usual misdemeanours for which we might be punished. He was referring to moments that disappointed our parents so deeply they were unable even to scold us.

"Mother and Father so very very disappoint," he said quietly. "So they stop talk."

Then he sat up and pointed to one of the slatted sun-blinds at that moment hanging partially down over a window. We children, he said, were like the twine that kept the slats held together. A Japanese monk had once told him this. We often failed to realise it, but it was we children who bound not only a family, but the whole world together. If we did not do our part, the slats would fall and scatter over the floor.

I do not remember anything more of our conversation that day, and besides, as I say, I did not spend much time dwelling on such matters. All the same, I remember more than once being tempted to ask my mother about what my friend had said. In the end, I never did so, though I did broach the subject once with Uncle Philip.

UNCLE PHILIP WAS NOT a real uncle. He had stayed with my parents as a "house guest" upon his arrival in Shanghai sometime before my birth, in the days when he was still in the employ of Morganbrook and Byatt. Then, while I was still very young, he had resigned from the company owing to what my mother always described as "a profound disagreement with his employers over how China should mature." By the time I was old enough to be aware of him, he was running a philanthropic organisation called The Sacred Tree dedicated to improving conditions in the Chinese areas of the city. He had always been a family friend, but as I have said, became a particularly frequent visitor during the years of my mother's anti-opium campaigns.

I can remember often going with my mother to Philip's office. This was located within the grounds of one of the churches in the city centre—my guess now is that it was the Union Church in Soochow Road. Our carriage would drive right into the grounds and stop beside a large lawn shaded by fruit trees. Here, despite the noises from the city around us, the atmosphere was tranquil, and my mother, stepping out of the carriage, would pause, raise her head and remark: "The air. It's so much purer here." Her mood would lighten visibly, and sometimes—if we were a little early—my mother and I would while away some minutes playing games on the grass. If we played tag, chasing one another all around the fruit trees, my mother would often laugh and squeal as excitedly as I did. I remember once, in the middle of one such game, she stopped suddenly on seeing a clergyman emerge from the church. We had then stood quietly on the edge of the lawn and exchanged greetings with him as he had passed. But no sooner had he gone out of our sight than my mother had turned, and stooping right down to me, given a conspiratorial giggle. It is even possible this kind of thing occurred more than once. In any case, I remember being fascinated by the notion of my mother participating in something for which, just like me, she could be "told off." And it was perhaps this dimension to these moments of careless play around the churchyard that made them seem always a little special for me.

My memory of Uncle Philip's office is that it was very ramshackle. There were everywhere boxes of all sizes, heaps of papers, even loose drawers, still with their contents, stacked precariously one on another. I would have expected my mother to disapprove of such untidiness, but she only ever talked of Uncle Philip's office being "cosy" or "busy."

He never failed to make a fuss of me on these visits, shaking my hand heartily, sitting me down then engaging me in conversation for several minutes while my mother looked on smiling. Often he would give me a gift, something he would pretend he had had ready and waiting—though I soon came to realise he was presenting me with whatever caught his eye at the time. "Guess what I've got for you, Puffin!" he would declare, while his gaze travelled the room in search of something suitable. In this way I acquired an extensive collection of office items, which I kept in an old chest in my playroom: an ashtray, an ivory pen stand, a lead weight. There was one occasion when, after announcing he had a present for me, his eye failed to alight on anything at all. There followed an awkward pause, before he sprang up and began wandering about his office, muttering: "And where did I put it? What on earth have I done with it?"—until finally, perhaps in desperation, he went over to the wall, pulled down a map of the Yangtze region, tearing a corner as he did so, rolled it up and presented it to me.

That time I confided in him, Uncle Philip and I were sitting together in his office, waiting for my mother to come back from somewhere. He had persuaded me to take his own chair behind his desk, while he himself roamed aimlessly around the place. He was making his usual amusing small-talk, and normally he would have had me laughing in no time, but on that occasion—only days after my discussion with Akira—I was not in that sort of mood. Uncle Philip soon saw this and said:

"So, Puffin. We're rather glum today."

I saw my chance and said: "Uncle Philip, I was just wondering. How do you suppose one might become more English?"

"More English?" He stopped whatever it was he was doing and looked at me. Then, with a thoughtful expression, he came nearer, pulled a chair up to the desk and sat down.

"Now why would you want to be more English than you are, Puffin?"

"I just thought . . . well, I just thought I might."

"Who says you're not sufficiently English already?"

"No one really." Then after a second I added: "But I think perhaps my parents think so."

"And what do *you* think, Puffin? Do you think you ought to be more English?"

"I can't tell really, sir."

"No, I suppose you can't. Well, it's true, out here, you're growing up with a lot of different sorts around you. Chinese, French, Germans, Americans, what have you. It'd be no wonder if you grew up a bit of a mongrel." He gave a short laugh. Then he went on: "But that's no bad thing. You know what I think, Puffin? I think it would be no bad thing if boys like you *all* grew up with a bit of everything. We might all treat each other a good deal better then. Be less of these wars for one thing. Oh yes. Perhaps one day, all these conflicts will end, and it won't be because of great statesmen or churches or organisations like this one. It'll be because people have changed. They'll be like you, Puffin. More a mixture. So why not become a mongrel? It's healthy."

"But if I did, everything might . . ." I stopped.

"Everything might what, Puffin?"

"Like that blind there"—I pointed—"if the twine broke. Everything might scatter."

Uncle Philip stared at the blind I had indicated. Then he rose, went to the window and touched it gently.

"Everything might scatter. You might be right. I suppose it's something we can't easily get away from. People need to feel they belong. To a nation, to a race. Otherwise, who knows what might happen? This civilisation of ours, perhaps it'll just collapse. And everything scatter, as you put it." He sighed, as though I had just defeated him in an argument. "So you want to be more English. Well, well, Puffin. So what are we to do about it?"

"I wondered, if it's all right, sir, if you didn't awfully mind. I wondered if I might copy you sometimes."

"Copy me?"

"Yes, sir. Just sometimes. Just so that I learn to do things the English way."

"That's very flattering, old fellow. But don't you think your father's the one to have this great privilege? About as English as they come, I'd say."

I looked away, and Uncle Philip must immediately have sensed he had said the wrong thing. He came back to his chair and sat down again in front of me.

"Look," he said quietly. "I'll tell you what we'll do. If you're ever worried how you should go about things, anything, if you're worried about the proper way to go about it, then just you come to me and we'll have a good talk about it. We'll talk it all through until you know exactly what's what. Now. Feel better?"

"Yes, sir. I think I do." I managed a smile. "Thank you, sir."

"Look here, Puffin. You're a right little horror. You know that, of course. But as little horrors go, you're a pretty decent specimen. I'm sure your mother and father are very, very proud of you."

"Do you really think so, sir?"

"I do. I really do. So, you feel better?"

With that, he sprang to his feet to resume his wanderings around his office. Reverting to his light-hearted tone, he began some nonsensical story about the lady in the office next door, which soon had me in stitches.

How fond I was of Uncle Philip! And is there any real reason to suppose he was not genuinely fond of me? It is perfectly possible that at that stage, he wished nothing but good for me, that he had no more inkling than I did of the course things would take.

$\mathcal{I}$T WAS AROUND that same time—that same summer—when certain aspects of Akira's behaviour began seriously to irk me. In particular, there was his endless harping on the achievements of the Japanese. He had always tended to do this, but that summer things seemed to reach obsessive levels. Time and again my friend would bring to a stop some game we were playing just to lecture me on the latest Japanese building being erected in the business district, or the imminent arrival of another Japanese gunboat in the harbour. He would then oblige me to listen to the most minute details and, every few minutes, his claim that Japan had become a "great, great country just like England." Most irritating of all were those occasions on which he would try to start arguments about who cried the easiest, the Japanese or the English. If I spoke up at all on behalf of the English, my friend would immediately demand we put things to the test, which meant in practice his putting me in one of his dreadful arm-locks until I either capitulated or gave in to tears.

At the time, I put Akira's obsession with the prowess of his race down to the fact that he was due to start school in Japan that coming autumn. His parents had arranged for him to stay with relatives in Nagasaki, and although he would return to Shanghai during school holidays, we realised we would see a lot less of each other and initially the news had made us both despondent. But as the summer drew on, Akira appeared to convince himself about the superiority of every aspect of life in Japan and became increasingly excited about the prospect of his new school. I in turn grew so weary of his persistent boasting about all things Japanese that by the late summer I was actually looking forward to being rid of him. Indeed, when the day eventually came, and I stood outside his house waving off the motor car taking him to the harbour, I believe I was not at all sorrowful.

VERY SOON. HOWEVER, I began to miss him. It was not that I did not have other friends. There were for instance the two English brothers living nearby with whom I played regularly, and of whom I saw much more after Akira's departure. I got on well with them, especially when it was just the three of us. But sometimes we would be joined by their schoolfriends—other boys from Shanghai Public School—and then their behaviour towards me would change, and I would sometimes become the target of certain pranks. I did not mind this at all, of course, since I could see they were all essentially decent sorts intending no real malice. Even at the time, I could see that if within a group of five or six boys, all but one attended the same school, the outsider was bound now and then to become the butt of some harmless banter. What I mean is that I did not think badly of my English friends; but then, all the same, such things did prevent me developing with them the same level of intimacy I had had with Akira, and as the months went on, I suppose I began to miss his company more and more.

But that autumn of Akira's absence was not a particularly unhappy one by any means. I remember it rather as a period when I was often at a loose end, of empty afternoons following one

another, much of which has now faded from my mind. Nevertheless, a few small events did occur during that period which I have
subsequently come to regard as being of particular significance.

THERE WAS, FOR EXAMPLE, the incident surrounding our trip
to the racecourse with Uncle Philip, which I am reasonably sure
occurred after one of my mother's Saturday morning meetings. As I
may have said already, for all my mother's encouraging me to mingle with her fellow campaigners in the drawing room where they
first gathered, I was not permitted into the dining room for the
meetings themselves. I remember once asking her if I could attend
a meeting, and to my surprise she had given it long consideration.
Finally she had said:

"I'm sorry, Puffin. Neither Lady Andrews nor Mrs. Callow appre-
ciates the company of children. It's a pity. You might well have
learnt some important things."

My father, of course, was not barred from the meetings, but
there seemed to exist an understanding that he too should refrain
from attending them. It is hard for me now to say which, if either of
them, was responsible for this state of affairs; but certainly, there
was always an odd atmosphere at breakfast on those Saturdays a
meeting was to take place. My mother would not actually mention
the meeting itself to my father, but would regard him throughout
the meal with an air almost of disgust. For his part, my father
would become infected by a forced joviality which would grow
throughout the morning right up until when my mother's guests
began to arrive. Uncle Philip was always among the first, and he
and my father would chat for a few minutes in the drawing room,
laughing a lot. Then as more guests arrived, my mother would
come and take Uncle Philip away into a corner, where they would
confer solemnly about the coming meeting. It was always at around
this point that my father would absent himself, usually by going up
to his study.

On that day I am recalling, I remember I heard the visitors starting to leave at the end of the meeting, and went out into the garden to await my mother—who I assumed would, as usual, emerge before long to commandeer my swing, singing all the while in her wonderfully carrying tones. When after a time there was no sign of her, I went into the house to investigate, and coming into the library saw that the doors of the dining room were now ajar; that the meeting had indeed broken up, but that Uncle Philip and my mother were still there, deep in discussion at the table, papers strewn before them. And then my father appeared behind me, no doubt also believing the morning's business to be over. On hearing the voices from the dining room, he stopped and said to me:

"Oh, they're still here."

"Just Uncle Philip."

My father smiled, then drifted past me into the dining room. Through the doors I could see Uncle Philip rising to his feet, and then I could hear the two men laughing loudly together. A moment later my mother emerged looking somewhat annoyed, her documents gathered in her arms.

By then it was past noon. Uncle Philip stayed for lunch and there was more good-humoured laughter. Then, as we were finishing our meal, Uncle Philip made his suggestion: why did we not all go down to the racecourse for the afternoon? My mother thought about this and declared it an excellent idea. My father too said he thought it a fine idea, but he would have to be excused on account of the work awaiting him in his study.

"But by all means, darling," he said, turning to my mother, "why don't you go along with Philip? It's turning into the most splendid afternoon."

"Well, you know, I rather think I might," my mother said. "A little excitement might do us all some good. Christopher too."

And at that moment they all looked at me. Although I was then only nine years old, I believe I read the situation with some accuracy. I knew of course that I was being offered a choice: to go out to the racecourse or to stay at home with my father. But I believe I grasped also the deeper implications: if I chose to stay in, then my mother would decline to go to the racecourse solely in Uncle Philip's company. In other words, the outing depended on my going with them. Moreover I knew—and I did so with a calm certainty—that at that moment my father was desperately wishing us not to go, that for us to do so would cause him huge pain. It was not anything in his manner that suggested this to me, but rather what I had—perhaps unwillingly—absorbed over the preceding weeks and months. Of course, there were many things I did not understand at all in those days, but this much I saw with great clarity: at that instant, my father was entirely depending on me to save the situation.

But perhaps I did not understand enough. For when my mother said: "Come on, Puffin. Hurry and get your shoes on," I did so with conspicuous enthusiasm, an enthusiasm I manufactured for show. And I can remember to this day my father seeing us to the front door, shaking hands with Philip, laughing and waving us off as the carriage took my mother, Uncle Philip and me away on our afternoon's outing.

THE ONLY OTHER MEMORIES to have remained distinct from that autumn also concern my father: namely, those curious instances of his "boasting." My father was always modest in his manners and found boastfulness in others embarrassing. This is why it struck me at the time as so odd to hear him talk in the way he did on a number of separate occasions around that time. These were all small instances which caused me only mild surprise, but they have none the less remained in my memory over the years.

There was the moment, for example, when at the dinner table he said quite suddenly to my mother:

"Did I tell you, darling? That fellow came back to see me, that representative from the dock workers. Wanted to thank me for all I'd done for them. Spoke jolly good English too. Of course these Chinese always speak very effusively, these speeches of theirs have all to be taken with a pinch of salt. But you know, dear, I had the distinct impression he meant it. Said I was their 'honoured hero.' How do you like that? Honoured hero!"

My father laughed, then watched my mother carefully. She went on eating for a moment, then said:

"Yes, darling. You've told me already."

My father looked a little deflated, but then the next second he smiled cheerfully again and said with another laugh: "So I have!" Then turning to me, he said: "But Puffin here hasn't heard it yet. Have you, Puffin? Honoured hero. That's what they're calling your father."

I cannot remember what any of this was about, and I probably did not much care even at the time. I have remembered the episode only because, as I have said, it was so uncharacteristic of my father to talk of himself in this way.

Another incident of this sort occurred one afternoon my parents and I were going to the Public Gardens to listen to the brass band. We had just stepped out of our carriage at the upper end of the Bund, and my mother and I were gazing across the wide boulevard towards the gateway into the gardens. It was a Sunday afternoon and I remember the pavements on both sides being filled with finely dressed promenaders enjoying the breeze from the harbour. The Bund itself was busy with carriages, motor cars and rickshaws, and my mother and I were preparing to cross it, when my father, having paid our driver, came up behind us and said suddenly and quite loudly:

"You see, darling, they know now at the firm. They know now I'm not one to back down. Bentley knows it, for one. Oh yes, he jolly well knows it now!"

As on that occasion at the dinner table, my mother initially gave no sign of having heard. She took my hand and we made our way across the traffic towards the gardens. "Does he really?" was all she murmured under her breath as we reached the other side.

But that was not quite the end of the matter. We went into the Public Gardens and for a while, like every other family who went to the gardens on a Sunday afternoon, we strolled around the lawns and flower beds greeting friends and acquaintances, stopping occasionally for a short chat. I would sometimes see boys I knew—from school or from my piano lessons at Mrs. Lewis's—but they were, like me, walking beside their parents on their best behaviour, and we would acknowledge one another only shyly, if at all. The brass band would start to play at half past five on the dot, and although everyone knew this, most people would wait until the horns came drifting across the grounds before making a move towards the bandstand.

We were always late to set off, so that the seats would all be taken by the time we arrived. I did not mind this so much, since it was around the bandstand that we children were allowed a looser leash, and I too would sometimes mingle and play there with the other boys. On that particular afternoon—it must have been well into the autumn for I remember the sun already low over the water behind the bandstand—my mother had moved a few paces away to talk with some friends standing nearby, and after several minutes of attending to the music, I asked my father's permission to go over to some American boys I knew playing on the outer fringe of the crowd. He went on gazing at the band and did not answer, so I was about to ask him again, when he said quietly:

"All these people here, Puffin. All these people. Ask them and they'll all profess to have standards. But you'll see as you get older, very few of them really do. Your mother, though, she's different. She never lets herself down. And you know, Puffin, that's why she's finally succeeded. She's made your father a better man. A much better man. Very well, she may be strict, I don't need to tell *you* that, ha ha! Well, she's been every bit as strict with me as she has with you. And the result is, by golly, I'm a better human being for it. Took a long time, but she managed it. I want you to know this, Puffin, your father is no longer today the same person you saw that time, you know, that time you and Mother burst in on me. You remember that, of course you do. That time I was in my study. I'm sorry you ever had to see your own father like that. Well anyway, that was then. Today, thanks to your mother, I'm someone much much stronger. Someone, I dare say, Puffin, you'll one day be proud of."

I understood little of what he was saying, and besides, I had the feeling that if my mother—who was only a little way away—caught any of these words, she would be angry. So I did not really respond to my father. I have a feeling I simply asked him again, after a few moments, if I could go over to join my American friends, and that was the end of the matter.

But over the days that followed, I did find myself thinking about this curious speech from my father, and in particular his reference to some occasion when my mother and I had "burst in" upon him in his study. For a long time, I had no clear idea what he might have been referring to, and I tried in vain to match one recollection or another to his words. Eventually I did settle on one memory from very early in my life, from when I could have been no older than four or five—a memory which even then, when I was nine years old, had already grown hazy in my mind.

MY FATHER'S STUDY WAS on the uppermost floor of the house with a commanding view over the rear grounds. I was not usually permitted to enter it, and in general was discouraged from playing anywhere near it. There was, however, a narrow corridor leading from the landing to the study door, along which a row of pictures hung in heavy gilt frames. These were each precise, draughtsman-like paintings of Shanghai harbour seen from the viewpoint of someone standing on the shore at Pootung; that is to say, all the numerous vessels in the harbour were shown with the great buildings of the Bund in the background. The pictures probably dated back at least to the 1880s and my guess is that like many of the ornaments and pictures in the house, they belonged to the company. Now I do not actually remember this myself, but my mother often told me how, when I was very young, she and I would stand in front of these pictures and entertain ourselves giving amusing names to the various vessels in the water. According to my mother, I would quickly be in fits of laughter and would sometimes refuse to abandon the game until we had named every visible vessel. If this were so—if we were really in the habit of laughing boisterously throughout this game of ours—then almost certainly we would not have come up to amuse ourselves in this way while my father was working in his study. But when I thought further about my father's words at the bandstand that day, I began to remember an occasion my mother and I had indeed been standing together up on that attic floor, for all I know playing this game of ours, when she suddenly stopped and became very still.

My first thought was that I was about to be scolded, perhaps for something I had just said which had displeased her. It was not even unheard of for my mother to switch moods abruptly in the midst of a harmonious exchange and scold me for some suddenly remembered misdemeanour committed earlier in the day. But as I fell silent in readiness for just such an explosion, I realised she was listening. Then the next instant she had turned and pushed open with great suddenness the door to my father's study.

I caught a glimpse past my mother's frame of the inside of the room. My abiding image is of my father slumped forward over his bureau, his face covered in perspiration and contorted with frustration. It is possible he was sobbing and it was this sound that had caught my mother's attention. In front of him, all over his desk, there were papers, ledgers, notebooks. I noticed—I believe I followed my mother's gaze—more papers and notebooks on the floor, as though he had hurled them there in a temper fit. He was looking up at us, startled, and then the next moment he said in a voice that rather shocked me:

"We can't do it! We'll never get back! We can't do it! You're asking too much, Diana. It's too much!"

My mother said something to him under her breath, no doubt some reprimand to make him pull himself together. My father did collect himself a little at this point and, glancing past my mother, looked at me for the first time. But almost instantly his face creased again with despair and, turning to my mother, he said again, shaking his head helplessly:

"We can't do it, Diana. It'll be the ruin of us. I've looked at everything. We'll never get back to England. We can't raise enough. Without the firm, we're simply stranded."

Then he seemed to lose control again, and as my mother began to say something else—something in her quiet, angry voice—my father began to shout, not so much at her as at the walls of his study:

"I won't do it, Diana! My God, who do you take me for? It's beyond me, you hear? Beyond me! I can't do it!"

Possibly at this point my mother closed the door on him and led me away. I have no further memory of the episode. And of course, I cannot be sure of the exact sentiments, let alone the exact words, my father was uttering that day. But this is how, admittedly with some hindsight, I have come to shape that memory.

At the time, it was simply a bewildering experience for me, and although I probably found it interesting that my father should, like me, have moments of crying and shouting, I did not much ask myself what it had all been about. Besides, when I next saw my father he was his normal self again, and for her part my mother never alluded to the incident. If my father had not, years later, made that curious speech beside the bandstand, I would probably never have dredged up this memory at all.

But as I say, apart from these curious little episodes, there is little that seems worth remembering from that autumn and the dull winter that followed it. I was listless for much of that period and was delighted when one afternoon Mei Li quite casually gave me the news that Akira had returned from Japan, that at that very moment, in the drive next door, his luggage was being unloaded off the motor car.

CHAPTER 7

*A*KIRA. I WAS DELIGHTED to learn, had returned to Shanghai not just for a visit, but for the foreseeable future, with plans to resume at his old school in the North Szechwan Road at the start of the summer term. I cannot remember if the two of us celebrated his return in any special way. I have the impression we simply picked up our friendship where we had left off the previous autumn with minimum fuss. I was quite curious to hear about Akira's experiences in Japan, but he persuaded me it would be childish—somehow beneath us—to discuss such matters, and so we made a show of continuing with our old routines as if nothing had ever interrupted them. I guessed of course that all had not gone well for him in Japan, but did not begin to suspect the half of it until that warm spring day he tore the sleeve of his kimono.

When we played outside, Akira usually dressed much as I did— in shirt, shorts and, on the hotter days, sun hat. But on that particular morning we were playing on the mound at the back of our garden, he was wearing a kimono—not anything special, just one of the garments he often wore around his house. We had been running up and down the mound enacting some drama when he suddenly stopped near the summit and sat down with a frown. I thought he had injured himself but, when I came up to him, saw he was examining a tear on the sleeve of the kimono. He was doing so with the utmost concern, and I believe I said to him something like:

"What's wrong? Your maid or someone will sew that in no time."

He did not respond—he seemed for the moment to have forgotten my presence entirely—and I realised he was sinking into a deep gloom before my eyes. He went on examining the tear for a few more seconds, then letting down his arm, stared blankly at the earth in front of him as though a great tragedy had just occurred.

"This is third time," he muttered quietly. "Third time same week I do bad thing."

Then as I continued to gaze at him somewhat baffled, he said: "Third bad thing. Now mother and father, they make me go back Japan."

I could not, of course, see how a small tear in an old kimono could bring such consequences, but I was for the moment sufficiently alarmed by this prospect to crouch down beside him and urgently demand an explanation for his words. But I could get little more out of my friend that morning—he grew increasingly sulky and closed—and I seem to remember our parting not on the best of terms. Over the following weeks, however, I gradually discovered what had lain behind his odd behaviour.

From his very first day in Japan, Akira had been thoroughly miserable. Although he never admitted this explicitly, I surmised that he had been mercilessly ostracised for his "foreignness"; his manners, his attitudes, his speech, a hundred other things had marked him out as different, and he had been taunted not just by his fellow pupils, but by his teachers and even—he hinted at this more than once—by the relatives in whose house he was staying. In the end, so profound was his unhappiness, his parents had been obliged to bring him home in the middle of a school term.

The thought that he might have to return again to Japan was one that haunted my friend. The fact was his parents missed Japan badly and often talked of the family returning there. With his older sister, Etsuko, not at all averse to living in Japan, Akira realised he was alone in wishing the family to remain in Shanghai; that it was only his strong opposition to the idea that prevented his parents packing their things and sailing for Nagasaki, and he was not at all sure how much longer his preferences could expect to take precedence over those of his sister and parents. Things were very much in the balance, and any displeasure he incurred—any misdemeanour, any falling off of his schoolwork—could tip the scales against him. Hence his supposition that a small tear in a kimono sleeve might easily produce the gravest of consequences.

As it turned out, the torn kimono did not incur his parents' wrath nearly to the extent feared, and certainly nothing momentous came of the matter. But throughout those months following his return, there would come along one little mishap after another to plunge my friend back into his pit of worry and despondency. The most significant of these, I suppose, was the affair concerning Ling Tien and our "robbery"—the "crime from my past" which so aroused Sarah's curiosity during our bus ride this afternoon.

LING TIEN HAD BEEN with Akira's family for as long as they had been in Shanghai. Among my earliest memories of going next door to play are those of the old servant shuffling about the place with his broom. He looked very old, always wore a heavy dark gown even in the summer, a cap and a pigtail. Unlike the other Chinese servants in the neighbourhood, he rarely smiled at children, but then nor did he scowl or shout at us, and had it not been for Akira's attitude to him, it is unlikely I would ever have regarded him as an object of fear. Indeed, I remember I was initially more puzzled than anything by the alarm that would seize Akira whenever the servant came within our vicinity. If for instance Ling Tien was passing in the corridor, my friend would break off whatever we were doing to stand rigidly in a part of the room not visible to the old man and not move again until the danger had passed. In those early days of our friendship, I had yet to become infected by Akira's sense of dread, assuming that it derived from something specific that had occurred between him and Ling Tien. As I say, I was more puzzled than anything, but whenever I asked Akira to explain his behaviour, he simply ignored me. In time I came to appreciate how deeply embarrassed he was by his inability to control his dread of Ling Tien and learnt to say nothing whenever our games were disrupted in this manner.

But then as we grew older, I imagine Akira began to feel the need to justify his fear. By the time we were seven or eight, the sight of Ling Tien would no longer cause my friend to freeze; instead, he would break off whatever he was doing and look at me with a strange grin. Then putting his mouth close to my ear, he would recite in a curious monotone—not unlike that of the monks we sometimes heard chanting at the Boone Road market—the most terrifying revelations concerning the old servant.

I thus learnt of Ling Tien's fearful passion for hands. Akira had once happened to glance down the servants' corridor towards Ling Tien's room on a rare occasion when the old man had left his door ajar, and had seen heaped upon the floor the severed hands of men, women, children, apes. Another time, late at night, Akira had spotted the servant carrying a basket into the house piled with the dismembered little arms of monkeys. We had always to be on our guard, Akira warned me. If we gave him the slightest opportunity, Ling Tien would not hesitate to cut off our hands.

When after a number of such briefings, I enquired as to why Ling Tien was so keen on hands, Akira looked at me carefully, then asked if I could be entrusted with his family's darkest secret. When I assured him I could, he thought a little longer before saying finally:

"Then I tell you, old chap! Terrible reason! Why Ling cut off hands. I tell you!"

Ling Tien, evidently, had discovered a method by which he could turn severed hands into spiders. In his room were many bowls filled with various fluids in which he soaked for several months at a time the many hands he had collected. Slowly the fingers would start to move by themselves—just little twitches at first, then coiling motions; finally dark hairs would grow and Ling Tien would then take them out of the fluids and set them loose, as spiders, all around the neighbourhood. Akira had often heard the old servant creeping out in the dead of night to do just this. My friend had once even seen in the garden, moving through the undergrowth, a mutant Ling had taken prematurely from its solution which did not yet fully resemble a spider and could easily be identified as a severed hand.

Although even at that age I did not entirely believe these stories, they certainly upset me and for some time the mere sight of Ling Tien was enough to set off terrors within me. Indeed, as we grew older, we neither of us quite shook off our horror of Ling Tien. This was something that always nagged at Akira's pride, and around the time we were eight, he seemed to develop a need constantly to challenge these old fears. I often remember him dragging me off to some point in his house where we could spy on Ling Tien sweeping the path or whatever. I did not mind these spying sessions so much, but what I came to dread were those occasions Akira would persistently dare me to go near Ling Tien's room.

Until this point we had kept well clear of that room, especially since Akira had always maintained the fumes from Ling Tien's fluids were liable to hypnotise us and draw us in through the door. But now the notion of going near the room became for my friend something of an obsession. We might be having a conversation about something quite different, and then suddenly that strange grin would appear on his face and he would start to whisper: "Are you frighten? Christopher, are you frighten?"

He would then oblige me to follow him through his house, through those oddly furnished rooms, to the heavy-beamed arch that marked the start of the servants' quarters. Going under the arch, we would find ourselves standing in a gloomy corridor of bare polished boards, at the far end of which, facing us, was the door of Ling Tien's room.

First, I would only be required to stand at the arch and watch as Akira pushed himself step by step along the corridor until he had covered perhaps half the distance to that awful room. I can still see my friend, his tubby figure stiff with tension, his face, whenever he glanced back at me, shining with perspiration, willing himself a few steps further before turning and running back with his triumphant grin. Then would come all his goading and bullying until I eventually found the nerve to match his feat. For quite a time, as I say, these tests of courage concerning Ling Tien's room came rather to obsess Akira, and took much out of the pleasure of going to play at his house.

For some time yet, though, it was to remain beyond either of us to walk right up to the door, let alone to go through it. By the time we finally entered Ling Tien's room, we were both ten, and it was— although of course I did not know it then—my last year in Shanghai. That was when Akira and I committed our little theft—an impulsive act whose wider repercussions, in our excitement, we failed entirely to anticipate.

WE HAD ALWAYS KNOWN Ling Tien would be going away for six days in early August to visit his home village near Hangchow, and we had talked often about how we would then take the opportunity finally to enter that room. And sure enough, on the first afternoon after Ling Tien's departure, I turned up at Akira's house to find my friend entirely preoccupied with the matter. By this time, I should say, I was in general a much more confident person than even a year earlier, and if I still felt a little of that old dread of Ling Tien, I would certainly not have shown it. In fact, I believe I was much the calmer about the prospect of entering the room—

something I am sure my friend noticed and saw as an extra dimension to the challenge.

But as it turned out, throughout that afternoon, Akira's mother was making a dress, which for some reason required her constantly to move from room to room, and Akira declared it too risky even to contemplate our venture. I was certainly not displeased, but I am sure Akira was the one more grateful for the excuse.

The following day, however, was a Saturday and when I arrived at Akira's house towards mid-morning, both his parents had gone out. Akira did not have an *amah*, as I did, and when we were younger we had often argued over which of us was the more fortunate. He had always taken the position that Japanese children did not need an *amah* because they were "braver" than Western children. I had once asked him during one such argument who would see to his needs if his mother was out and he wanted, say, some iced water, or if he cut himself. I remember his telling me Japanese mothers *never* went out unless the child specifically permitted them to do so—a claim I found hard to believe, since I knew for a fact Japanese ladies met in their circles, much as the European ladies did, at Astor House or Marcell's Tea Room in Szechwan Road. But when he pointed out that in his mother's absence there was the maid to see to his every need, while at the same time he was free to do whatever he pleased with no restrictions at all, I did begin to believe I was the one hard done by. Oddly, I continued to hold this view even though in practice, on those occasions we played at his house when his mother was out, one or another servant was always delegated to watch over our every move. Indeed, especially when we were younger, this would mean some unsmiling figure, no doubt fearing dire consequences should any misfortune befall us, standing within inhibiting proximity while we did our best to play.

Naturally, though, by that summer, we were allowed to move much more freely without supervision. On that morning we entered Ling Tien's room, we had been playing in one of Akira's sparse

tatami-floored rooms up on the third floor while an elderly maid—
the only other person in the house—occupied herself with some
sewing in the room directly below. I remember at one point Akira
breaking off from what we were doing, tip-toeing to the balcony
and leaning right over the rail, so far I feared he might topple over.
Then when he came hurrying back, I noticed the strange grin had
appeared on his face. The maid, he reported in a whisper, had as
expected fallen asleep.

"Now we must go in! Are you frighten, Christopher? Are you
frighten?"

Akira had suddenly become so tense that for a moment all my
old fears concerning Ling Tien came flooding back. But by this
point a retreat for either of us was out of the question, and we made
our way as quietly as possible down to the servants' quarters until
we were once more standing together in that gloomy corridor with
its bare polished boards.

What I recall is that we strode down the corridor with little
hesitation until we were all but four or five yards from Ling Tien's
door. Then something made us pause, and for a second neither of
us appeared capable of continuing; if at that moment Akira had
turned and run, I am sure I would have done the same. But then
my friend seemed to find some extra resolve, and holding out his
arm to me, said: "Come on, old chap! We go together!"

We linked arms and took the final few steps like that. Then
Akira pulled back the door and we both peered in.

We saw a small, sparse, tidy room with a well-swept boarded
floor. The window was covered by a sun-blind, but the light was
leaking in brightly at the edges. There was a faint smell of incense
in the air, a shrine in the far corner, a low narrow bed, and a surprisingly grand chest of drawers, beautifully lacquered, with ornate
handles hanging on each little drawer.

We stepped inside, and for a few seconds remained still, barely
breathing. Then Akira let out a sigh and turned to me with a

huge smile, clearly delighted finally to have conquered his old fear. But the next moment his sense of triumph seemed quickly to be replaced by a concern that the room's lack of any obviously sinister features would make him look ridiculous. Before I could say anything, he pointed quickly to the chest of drawers and whispered urgently:

"There! In there! Careful, careful, old chap! The spiders, they inside there!"

He was hardly convincing and he must have realised it. Nevertheless, for a second or two, an image went through my head of those small drawers opening before our eyes as creatures—at various stages between hand and spider—put out tentative limbs. But now Akira was indicating excitedly a small bottle standing on a low table beside Ling Tien's bed.

"Lotion!" he whispered. "The magic lotion he uses! There it is!"

I was tempted to pour ridicule over this desperate attempt to preserve a fantasy we had in truth long outgrown, but at that moment I had another sudden vision of the drawers opening, and a residue of my old fear kept me from saying anything. Moreover, I was beginning to grow anxious about a much more likely eventuality: namely, that we would be discovered in that room by the maid or some other unexpected adult. I could not begin to imagine the disgrace that would then follow, the punishments, the long discussions between my parents and Akira's. I could not even think how we might start to explain our behaviour.

Just then Akira quickly stepped forward, grabbed the bottle and clasped it to his chest.

"Go! Go!" he hissed, and suddenly we were both gripped by panic. Giggling under our breaths, we rushed out of the room and down the corridor.

Back in the safety of the upstairs room—the maid had remained asleep below—Akira reasserted his claim that the drawers had been filled with severed hands. I could see now he was seriously worried about my ridiculing our long-standing fantasy and somehow I too felt the need to preserve it. I thus said nothing to undermine his claim, nor gave any suggestion that Ling Tien's room had been a let-down or that our courage had been summoned on false pretences. We placed the bottle on a plate in the middle of the floor, then sat down to examine it.

Akira carefully removed the stopper. There was inside a pale liquid with a vague smell of aniseed. To this day I have no idea for what the old servant used this lotion; my guess is that it was some patent medicine he had purchased to combat some chronic condition. In any case, its nondescript appearance served our purpose well. Very carefully we dipped twigs into the bottle and let them drip on to some paper. Akira warned that we should not let even a drop touch our hands lest we wake up the next day with spiders at the end of our arms. Neither of us really believed this, but again, it seemed important for Akira's feelings that we pretend to do so, and thus we went about our task with exaggerated caution.

Finally, Akira replaced the stopper and put away the bottle in the box he kept for his special things, saying that he wished to conduct a few more experiments with the lotion before returning it. All in all, when we parted that morning, we were both well pleased with ourselves.

But when Akira came to my house the following afternoon, I saw immediately some difficulty had arisen; he was very preoccupied and unable to concentrate on anything. Dreading to hear that his parents had somehow found out about our previous day's deeds, I for some time avoided asking what was troubling him. In the end, though, I could bear it no longer and demanded he tell me the worst. Akira, however, denied that his parents suspected anything, then sank once more into his gloom. Only after much more pressure did he finally give in and tell me what had happened.

Finding it impossible to contain his sense of triumph, Akira had revealed to his sister Etsuko what we had done. To his surprise,

Etsuko had reacted with horror. I say surprise because Etsuko—who was four years older than us—had never gone along with our view of Ling Tien's sinister nature. But now, on hearing Akira's story, she had glared at him as though she expected him to curl over and die before her eyes. Then she had told Akira we had had the luckiest of escapes; that she personally had known of servants previously employed in the house who had dared do what we had done, and who as a consequence had vanished—their remains discovered weeks later in some alley beyond the Settlement boundaries. Akira had told his sister she was simply trying to frighten him, that he did not for a moment believe her. But clearly he had been shaken, and I too felt a chill pass through me on hearing this "confirmation"—and from no less an authority than Etsuko—of all our old fears concerning Ling Tien.

It was then I appreciated what was so troubling Akira: someone had to put back the bottle in Ling Tien's room before the old servant's return in three days' time. Yet it was plain to see our bravado of the previous day had all but evaporated, and the prospect of going into that room again now seemed beyond us.

Unable to settle to any of our usual games, we decided to walk to our special spot beside the canal. All the way there, we talked over our problem from every angle. What would happen if we did not return the bottle? Perhaps the lotion was very precious and the police would be called in to investigate. Or perhaps Ling Tien would tell no one of its disappearance, but decide personally to wreak some terrible vengeance on us. I remember we became quite confused about how much we wished to maintain our fantasy about Ling Tien, and to what extent we wanted to consider logically how best to avoid getting into serious trouble. I remember, for instance, our considering at one point the possibility the lotion was a medicine Ling Tien had bought after months of saving his money, and that without it he would become horribly ill; but then in the next breath, without abandoning this last notion, we considered other hypotheses which assumed the lotion to be what we had always said it was.

Our spot by the canal, some fifteen minutes' walk from our homes, was behind some storehouses belonging to the Jardine Matheson Company. We were never sure if we were actually trespassing; to reach it we would go through a gate that was always left open, and cross a concrete yard past some Chinese workers, who would watch us suspiciously, but never impede us. We would then go round the side of a rickety boathouse and along a length of jetty, before stepping down on to our patch of dark hard earth right on the bank of the canal. It was a space only large enough for the two of us to sit side by side facing the water, but even on the hottest days the storehouses behind us ensured we were in the shade, and each time a boat or junk went past, the waters would lap soothingly at our feet. On the opposite bank were more storehouses, but there was, I remember, almost directly across from us, a gap between two buildings through which we could see a road lined with trees. Akira and I often came to the spot, though we were careful never to tell our parents of it for fear they would not trust us to play so near the water's edge.

On that afternoon, once we had sat down, we tried for a while to forget our worries. I remember Akira starting to ask me, as he often did when we came to our spot, if in an emergency I would manage to swim to this or that vessel visible further up the water. But he could not keep it up, and suddenly, to my astonishment, he began to cry.

I had hardly ever seen my friend cry. In fact, today, this is the only recollection I have of him crying. Even when a large piece of mortar fell on to his leg when we were playing behind the American Mission, for all his turning a ghastly white, he did not cry. But that afternoon by the canal, Akira had clearly reached his wits' end.

I remember he had in his hands some piece of damp flaking wood from which, as he sobbed, he broke off bits to hurl into the water. I wanted very much to comfort him, but being at a loss for anything to say, I recall getting up to find more such pieces of wood to break off into pieces and hand to him, as though this were some urgent remedy. Then there was no more wood left for him to throw, and Akira brought his tears under control.

"When parents find out," he said eventually, "they be so angry. Then they not let me stay here. Then we all go to Japan."

I still did not know what to say. Then, staring at a boat going by, he murmured: "I don't ever want to live in Japan."

And because this was what I always said when he made this statement, I echoed: "And I don't ever want to go to England."

With that, we both fell silent for a few more moments. But as we continued to stare at the water, the one obvious course of action to prevent all these awful repercussions loomed ever larger in my mind, and in the end I simply put it to him that all we had to do was to replace the bottle in time, then all would be well.

Akira did not appear to hear me, so I repeated the point. He continued to ignore me, and it was then I realised how very real his fear of Ling Tien had grown since our adventure the previous day; indeed, I could see it was as great now as it had ever been in our younger days, except of course that Akira was now unable to admit to it. I could see his difficulty and tried hard to think of a way out. In the end, I said quietly:

"Akira-chan. We'll do it again together. Just like last time. We'll join arms again, go in, put the bottle where we found it. If we do it together like that, then we'll be safe, nothing bad can happen to us. Nothing at all. Then no one will ever find out anything about what we did."

Akira thought about this. Then he turned and looked at me and I could see deep and solemn gratitude in his face.

"Tomorrow, in afternoon, three o'clock," he said. "Mother will go out to park. If maid fall asleep again, then we have chance."

I assured him the maid was bound to fall asleep again, and

repeated that if we went into the room together, there was nothing at all to fear.

"We do together, old chap!" he said with a sudden smile and got to his feet.

On the walk back, we finalised our plans. I promised to come to Akira's house the next day well before his mother's departure, and as soon as she left, we would go upstairs and wait together, Ling Tien's bottle ready, for the maid to fall asleep. Akira's mood lightened considerably, but I remember, as we parted that afternoon, my friend turning to me with an unconvincing nonchalance and warning me not to be late the next day.

THE FOLLOWING DAY was again hot and humid. I have down the years gone over many times everything I can remember of that day, trying to put the various details in some coherent order. I cannot remember a great deal about the first part of the morning. I have a picture of how I said goodbye to my father as he went off to work. I was already outside, loitering around the carriage track waiting for him to emerge. He eventually did so, in a white suit and hat, holding a briefcase and a stick. He squinted and glanced out towards our gateway. Then, as I waited for him to come further towards me, my mother appeared on the doorstep behind him and said something. My father walked back a few steps, exchanged some words with her, smiled, kissed her lightly on the cheek, then came striding out to where I was waiting. That is all I remember of how he left that day. I do not remember now if we shook hands, if he patted my shoulder, if he turned back at the gate for a last wave. My overall recollection is that there was nothing in the manner of his parting that morning to set it apart from the way he had left for work on every other day.

All I remember of the rest of the morning is that I played with my toy soldiers on the rug in my bedroom, my mind forever drifting to the daunting task awaiting us later in the day. I remember my mother going out at some point and that I ate lunch with Mei Li in the kitchen. After lunch, needing to kill time until three o'clock, I walked the short distance along our road to the spot where two large oak trees stood, set back from the road, yet well in front of the nearest garden wall.

Perhaps it was because I was already stoking up my courage, but I succeeded that day in climbing one of the oaks to a new height. Perched triumphantly in its branches, I found I had a view across the hedges and grounds of all the neighbouring houses. I remember I sat up there for some time, the wind on my face, growing ever more anxious about the task ahead. It occurred to me that, apprehensive as I was, Akira's fear of Ling Tien's room was now much the greater, and I would this time have to be the "leader." I saw the responsibility this entailed, and resolved to appear as confident as possible when I presented myself at his house. But as I continued to sit there in the tree, there kept occurring to me any number of eventualities that could thwart us: the maid would fail to fall asleep; she might even choose this of all days to clean the corridor outside Ling Tien's room; or else Akira's mother would change her mind and not go out as expected. And then of course, there were the older, less rational fears which, try as I might, I could not quite dispel from my mind.

Eventually I climbed down the oak, wishing to go home for a glass of water and to check the time. As I came in through our gate, I saw two motor cars in the drive. I was mildly curious about these, but by this stage was far too preoccupied to give them much attention. Then as I was crossing the hallway I glanced through the open doors of the drawing room and saw the three men, standing with their hats in their hands, talking with my mother. There was nothing so untoward about this—it was perfectly possible they had come to discuss my mother's campaign—but something in the atmosphere made me pause a moment there in the hall. As I did so, the voices broke off and I saw their faces turn to me. I recognised one of the men to be Mr. Simpson, my father's colleague at Byatt's; the other two were strangers. Then my mother came into view as she too leant forward and looked at me. I suppose I might have sensed then that something out of the ordinary was unfolding. In any case, the next moment, I was hurrying off in the direction of the kitchen.

No sooner had I reached the kitchen than I heard footsteps, and my mother came in. I have often tried to recall her face—the exact expression she was wearing—at that moment, but with no success. Perhaps some instinct told me not to look at it. What I do remember is her presence, which seemed looming and large, as though suddenly I were very young again, and the texture of the pale summer frock she was wearing. She said to me in a lowered, but perfectly composed voice:

"Christopher, the gentlemen with Mr. Simpson are from the police. I must finish talking with them. Then I want to talk to you straight afterwards. Will you wait for me in the library?"

I was about to protest, but my mother fixed me with a stare that silenced me.

"In the library then," she said, turning away. "I'll come as soon as I've finished with the gentlemen."

"Has something happened to Father?" I asked.

My mother turned back to me. "Your father never arrived at the office this morning. But I'm sure there's a perfectly simple explanation. Wait for me in the library. I won't be long."

I followed her out of the kitchen and made my way to the library. There I sat down at my homework table and waited, thinking not about my father, but of Akira and how I was already going to be late for him. I wondered if he would have the courage to return the bottle on his own; even if he did, he would still be very angry with me. I felt at that moment such an urgency about Akira's situation, I actually contemplated disobeying my mother and simply going off. Meanwhile the discussion in the drawing room seemed to go on interminably. There was a clock on the library wall and I stared at its hands. At one point, I went out into the hall, hoping to catch my mother's attention and ask her permission to leave, but I found the doors to the drawing room had now been closed. Then, as I was hovering there in the hall, once more thinking about sneaking off, Mei Li appeared and pointed sternly towards the library. Once I had gone back in, she closed the door on me and I could hear her pacing about outside. I seated myself again and went on watching the clock. As the hands passed half past three, I fell into a gloom, full of anger at both my mother and Mei Li.

Then at last I heard the men being shown out. I heard one of them say:

"We'll do everything we can, Mrs. Banks. We must hope for the best and trust in God."

I could not hear my mother's reply.

As soon as the men had gone, I rushed out and asked for permission to go to Akira's. But my mother, to my fury, completely ignored my request, saying: "Let's go back into the library."

Frustrated though I was, I did as bidden, and it was there in the library that she sat me down, crouched before me and told me, very calmly, that my father had been missing since the morning. The police, alerted by his office, were carrying out a search, so far to no avail.

"But he may well turn up by supper time," she said with a smile.

"Of course he will," I said in a voice I hoped would convey my annoyance at this great fuss. Then I got off the chair and asked again for permission to leave. But this time I did so with less fervour, for I could see from the clock there was no longer any point in going to Akira's. His mother would have returned; his evening meal would be served before long. I felt a huge resentment that my mother should have kept me in simply to tell me something I had more or less gleaned in the kitchen an hour and a half earlier. When at last she told me I could go, I simply went up to my room, laid my soldiers out on my rug and did my best not to think about Akira or his feelings towards me at that moment. But I kept remembering all that had been said beside the canal, and the look of gratitude he had given me. Moreover, I did not wish Akira to return to Japan any more than he did.

My sullenness stayed with me well into the night, but of course this was interpreted as my reaction to the situation regarding my father. Throughout the evening my mother would say to me things like: "Let's not get gloomy. There's sure to be a very simple explanation." And Mei Li was uncharacteristically gentle with me when helping with my bath. But I remember too, as the evening went on, my mother having a number of those "distant" moments I was to come to know well over the weeks that followed. In fact I believe it was that same night, as I lay in my bed still preoccupied about what to say to Akira when I next saw him, that my mother murmured, looking blankly across the room:

"Whatever happens, you can be proud of him, Puffin. You can always be proud of what he's done."

CHAPTER 8

𝒥 DO NOT REMEMBER MUCH about the days immediately following my father's disappearance, other than that I was often so concerned about Akira—in particular, what I would say when I next saw him—that I could not settle to anything. Nevertheless I found myself continually putting off a visit next door, even contemplating for a while the notion that I might never need face him at all—that his parents, so angered by our misdemeanour, were even at that moment packing their bags for Japan. During these days any sort of loud noise outside would send me rushing upstairs to the front windows, from where I could scrutinise the next-door courtyard for signs of piling luggage.

Then after three or four days had passed, on an overcast morning, I was playing by myself out on the circle of lawn in front of our house when I became conscious of the sounds coming from Akira's side of the fence. I quickly realised that Akira was moving about on his sister's bicycle around his carriage track; I had often enough watched him trying to ride this bicycle, which was far too large for him, and recognised the scraping noises the wheels made as he struggled for balance. At one stage I heard a crash and a yell as he fell off altogether. The possibility occurred to me that Akira had spotted me out playing from his upstairs window and had come out with the bicycle expressly to attract my attention. After several further moments of hesitation—during which Akira continued to crash about on his side—I finally strode out of our gateway, turned and stared into his front garden.

Akira was indeed astride Etsuko's bicycle, absorbed in attempts to execute some circus-like manoeuvre that required taking his hands from the handlebar just as he turned a tight circle. He appeared too absorbed to notice me, and even when I walked up to him, gave no sign of having seen me. Finally I said simply:

"I'm sorry I couldn't come the other day."

Akira gave me a sulky glance, then went back to his manoeuvres. I was about to give him my explanation for having let him down, but for some reason, found I could say nothing more. I stood there watching him for a little longer. Then taking a further step towards him, I said, lowering my voice to a whisper:

"What happened? Did you put it back?"

My friend gave me a glare that rejected the intimacy implied by my tone, then spun his bicycle round. I felt tears coming, but remembering in time our long-standing feud about whether the English or Japanese cried easiest, I managed to stifle them. I thought again of telling him about my father's disappearance, and suddenly it seemed a hugely substantial reason not only for my having let him down, but for great self-pity on my part. I pictured the shock and shame that would transform Akira's face once I uttered the words: "I couldn't come the other day because . . . because my father's been *kidnapped!*"—but somehow I could not say it. Instead, I believe I simply turned and ran back to my house.

I DID NOT SEE AKIRA for the next few days. Then one after-noon he came to our back door, asking Mei Li for me as usual. I was in the middle of something, but dropped it all and went out to my friend. He greeted me smilingly, and as he led me away to his garden, patted me affectionately on the back. I was of course anxious to discover just what had transpired over the Ling Tien matter, but being even more keen not to re-open wounds, resisted the urge to ask anything about it.

We went to the back of his garden—to the thick shrubs we called our "jungle"—and soon became immersed in one of our dramatic narratives. I have a feeling we acted out scenes from *Ivanhoe*, which I was reading at that time—or perhaps it was one of Akira's Japanese samurai adventures. In any case, after an hour or so, my friend suddenly stopped and looked oddly at me. Then he said:

"If you like, we play new game."

"A new game?"

"New game. About Christopher father. If you like."

I was taken aback and I do not recall what I said next. He came a few steps closer in the long grass and I saw he was looking at me almost tenderly.

"Yes," he said. "If you like, we play detective. We search for father. We rescue father."

I then realised that it was hearing the news about my father—which no doubt had started to do the rounds of the neighbourhood—that had brought Akira back to my door. I understood too that this present proposal was his way of showing his concern and wish to help, and I felt my affection for him welling up. But in the end, I said quite nonchalantly:

"All right. If you want to play that, we can."

And that was how it began, what today in my memory feels like an entire era—though in truth it could only have been a period of two months or less—when day after day we invented and played out endless variations on the theme of my father's rescue.

Meanwhile the real investigations into my father's disappearance were continuing. I knew this from the visits we received from the men who held their hats in their hands and talked solemnly to my mother; from the hushed exchanges between my mother and Mei

Li when my mother came in, tight-lipped, at the end of an afternoon; and in particular, there was that conversation I had with her at the foot of the staircase.

I have no real memory of what either of us had been doing prior to that moment. I had started to run up the stairs, eager to fetch something from the playroom, when I realised my mother had appeared at the top and was making her way down. She must have been about to go out, for she had on her special beige dress, the one that gave off a peculiar smell like mouldering leaves. I suppose I must have sensed something in her manner, for I stopped where I was on the third or fourth step and waited for her. As she came towards me, she smiled and reached out a hand. She did this while still a number of steps above me, so that I thought for a moment she was wishing me to assist her down the rest of the stairs, the way my father sometimes did when he waited for her at the foot of the staircase. But as it turned out, she simply put her arm around my shoulder and we descended the last steps together. Then she let go of me and walked over towards the hat-stand on the other side of the hall. It was as she did so that she said:

"Puffin, I know how difficult these last few days have been for you. It must seem as though the whole world's caving in. Well, it's been difficult for me too. But you must do as I have. You must keep praying to God and remain hopeful. I hope you are remembering your prayers, aren't you, Puffin?"

"Yes, I am," I replied, rather off-handedly.

"It's a sad fact," she went on, "that in a city like this, from time to time, people do get kidnapped. In fact it happens rather often, and a lot of the time, I'd go so far as to say *most* of the time, the people come back perfectly safely. So we have to be patient. Puffin, are you listening to me?"

"Of course I'm listening." I had by this time turned my back to her and was dangling by my arms from the banister post.

"What we have to appreciate," my mother said after a pause, "is that the city's very best detectives have been assigned to the case. I've spoken with them, and they're very optimistic a solution will be found soon."

"But how long will that be?" I asked sullenly.

"We have to be hopeful. We have to trust the detectives. And it may take a little time, but we must be patient. Then in the end things may well come right, and everything will be just as it was before. We must continue to pray to God and always keep hopeful. Puffin, what are you doing? Did you hear me?"

I did not respond immediately, because I was trying to see how many steps my feet could climb while I continued to cling to the banister post. Then I asked:

"But what if the detectives are too busy? With all the other things they have to solve? Murders and robberies. They can't do everything."

I could hear my mother coming back a few steps towards me, and when she next spoke, a careful, deliberate tone had entered her voice.

"Puffin, there is no question whatsoever of the detectives being 'too busy.' *Everyone* in Shanghai, the most important people in this community are extremely anxious about Father, and very concerned to have the matter cleared up. I mean gentlemen like Mr. Forester. And Mr. Carmichael. Even the consul-general himself. I know they've made it their personal concern to see Father return safely as soon as possible. So you see, Puffin, there is no chance at all of the detectives giving anything but their utmost. And that's what they're doing, now, at this very moment. Do you realise, Puffin, Inspector Kung himself has been put in charge of this investigation? Yes, that's right: Inspector Kung. So you see, we've every reason to be hopeful."

This exchange undoubtedly made some impact, for I remember I did not worry nearly so much during the following several days. Even at nights, when my anxieties tended to return, I would often go to sleep thinking of Shanghai's detectives moving all around the city, closing in ever more tightly on the kidnappers. Sometimes, lying in the dark, I found myself weaving quite elaborate dramas before dropping off to sleep, many of which would then serve as material for Akira and me the next day.

I do not mean to imply, incidentally, that during this period Akira and I did not play games quite unconnected with my father; sometimes we could lose ourselves for hours in one of our more traditional fantasies. But whenever my friend sensed I was preoccupied, or that my heart was not in what we were doing, he would say: "Old chap. We play father rescue game."

Our narratives concerning my father had, as I say, endless variations, but fairly quickly we established a basic recurring story-line. My father was held captive in a house somewhere beyond the Settlement boundaries. His captors were a gang intent on extorting a huge ransom. Many smaller details evolved quite rapidly until they too became fixtures. It was always the case, for instance, that despite being surrounded by the horrors of the Chinese district, the house in which my father was held was comfortable and clean. In fact, I can still remember how this particular convention came to be established. It was perhaps our second or third time of trying the game, and Akira and I had been taking it in turns to play the role of the legendary Inspector Kung—whose handsome features and dandily worn hat we both knew well from newspaper photographs. We had been quite absorbed in the excitements of our fantasy, when suddenly, at the point when my father first appeared in our story, Akira gestured to me—indicating that I should play him—and said: "You tied up in chair."

We had been in full flow but now I stopped.

"No," I said. "My father isn't tied up. How can he be tied up all the time?"

Akira, who never liked to be contradicted when unfolding a narrative, repeated impatiently that my father was tied up in a chair and that I should mimic this at the foot of a tree without further delay. I shouted back: "No!" and stalked off. I did not, however, leave Akira's garden. I remember standing at the spot where his lawn started—where our "jungle" ended—and staring blankly at a lizard climbing the trunk of an elm. After a moment I heard Akira's footsteps behind me and braced myself for a full-blown argument. But to my surprise, when I turned to him, I saw my friend gazing at me with a conciliatory look. He came closer and said gently:

"You right. Father not tied up. He very comfortable. Kidnappers' house comfortable. Very comfortable."

After this it was always Akira who took great care to ensure my father's comfort and dignity in all our dramas. The kidnappers always addressed him as though they were his servants, bringing him food, drink and newspapers as soon as he requested them. Accordingly the characters of the kidnappers softened; it turned out they were not evil after all, simply men with starving families. They truly regretted having to take such drastic action, they would explain to my father, but they could not bear to see their children starve to death. What they were doing was wrong, they knew it, but what else were they to do? They had chosen Mr. Banks precisely because his kind views towards the plight of the poorer Chinese were well known, and he was likely to understand the inconvenience to which they were putting him. To this, my father—whom I always represented—would sigh sympathetically, but then go on to say that whatever the hardships of life, crime could not be condoned. Besides, inevitably, Inspector Kung would sooner or later come with his men to arrest them, then they would be thrown into prison, perhaps executed. Where would that leave their families? The kidnappers—represented by Akira—would respond by saying that once the police discovered their hideout, they would give themselves up quietly, and wish Mr. Banks well as he rejoined his family. But until then, they were obliged to do their utmost to make their scheme work. They would then ask my father what he required for his dinner, and I would order on his behalf a vast meal of his favourite dishes—roast sirloin, buttered parsnips and poached haddock always among them. As I say, it was Akira rather than myself who tended to be the more insistent on these luxurious aspects, and it was he who added many of the other small but important details: my father's room would have a fine view over the rooftops to the river; the bed would be one his captors had stolen for him from the Palace Hotel, and thus the ultimate in comfort. In time, Akira and I would become the detectives—though sometimes we played ourselves—until in the end, after the chases, fist-fights, and gun-battles around the warren-like alleys of the Chinese districts, whatever our variations and elaborations, our narratives would always conclude with a magnificent ceremony held in Jessfield Park, a ceremony that would see us, one after the other, step out on to a specially erected stage—my mother, my father, Akira, Inspector Kung, and I—to greet the vast cheering crowds. This was, as I say, our basic story-line, and I suppose, incidentally, it was more or less the one I enacted over and over during those first drizzly days in England, when I filled my empty hours wandering about the ferns near my aunt's cottage, muttering Akira's lines for him under my breath.

IT WAS NOT UNTIL perhaps a month after my father's disappearance that I finally found the nerve to ask Akira what had happened about Ling Tien's bottle. We had been taking a moment's break from our playing, sitting together in the shade of the maple at the top of our mound, drinking the iced water Mei Li had brought out to us in two tea-bowls. To my relief Akira no longer showed any sign of bitterness.

"Etsuko take back bottle," he said.

His sister had initially been most obliging. But now, whenever she wanted to force Akira to do something, she would threaten to reveal his secret to their parents. Akira though was not unduly troubled by this ploy.

"She go to room too. So she just as bad as me. She not tell."

"So there wasn't any trouble," I said.

"No trouble, old chap."

"So you won't have to go and live in Japan."

"No Japan." He turned to me and smiled. "I stay Shanghai for ever." Then he looked at me solemnly and asked: "If father not found. You must go England?"

This startling notion for some reason had never before occurred to me. I thought it over, then said:

"No. Even if Father isn't found, we'll live here for ever. Mother will never want to go back to England. Besides, Mei Li wouldn't want to go. She's a Chinese."

For a moment, Akira went on thinking, staring at the ice-cubes floating in his bowl. Then he looked up at me and beamed broadly.

"Old chap!" he said. "We live here together, always!"

"That's right," I said. "We'll live in Shanghai for ever."

"Old chap! Always!"

THERE WAS ONE other small incident from those weeks following my father's disappearance which I have now come to believe highly significant. I did not always regard it so; in fact, I had more or less forgotten it altogether when a few years ago, quite by chance, something happened which caused me not only to recall it again, but to appreciate for the first time the deeper implications of what I had witnessed that day.

It was during the period shortly after the Mannering case, when I was undertaking some research into the background of those years I spent in Shanghai. I believe I have mentioned this research before, much of which I conducted in the British Museum. I suppose it was, at least in part, my attempt as an adult to grasp the nature of those forces which as a child I could not have had the chance of comprehending. It was also my intention to prepare my ground for the day I began in earnest my investigations into the whole affair concerning my parents—which despite the continuing efforts of the Shanghai police has remained unresolved to this day. It remains, incidentally, my intention to embark on such an investigation in the not-too-distant future. In fact, I am sure I would have done so already had the demands on my time not been so relentless.

In any case, as I say, I spent a good many hours in the British Museum a few years ago gathering material on the history of the opium trade in China, on the affairs of Morganbrook and Byatt, on the complex political situation in Shanghai at that time. I did also, at various points, write off letters to China seeking information unavailable to me in London. So it was that I received one day a yellowed cutting taken from the *North China Daily News* dated some three years after my departure from Shanghai. My correspondent had sent me an article about changes to trading regulations in the concession ports—which no doubt I had requested—but it was the photograph which happened to be on the reverse side that immediately captured my attention.

I have kept that old newspaper photograph in the drawer of my desk, inside a tin cigar box, and from time to time I take it out and stare at it. It shows three men in a leafy avenue, standing in front of a grand motor car. All three are Chinese. The two on the outside are wearing Western suits with stiff collars, and hold bowler hats and canes. The plump man in the centre is in traditional Chinese dress: a dark gown, cap and pigtail. As with most newspaper photographs of the time, there is a stagy, posed feeling to it, and my correspondent's scissors have cut off perhaps an entire quarter of it to the left. Nevertheless, from the moment my glance first fell on it, the picture—more precisely, the central figure in the dark gown—has been a source of exceptional interest to me.

Alongside this photograph, in my tin cigar box in the drawer, I keep the letter I received from the same correspondent a month or so afterwards in reply to further enquiries. In it, he informs me that the plump man in the gown and cap is Wang Ku, a warlord who at the time of the photograph wielded much power in the Hunan province, employing a motley army of almost three hundred men. Like most of his sort, he lost much of his power after the ascendancy of Chiang Kai-shek, but was rumoured to be still alive and well, languishing in reasonable comfort somewhere in Nanking. Regarding my specific query, my correspondent states that he has been unable to ascertain whether or not Wang Ku ever had any known connections with Morganbrook and Byatt. In his own opinion, however, there is "no reason to suppose he would not at some point have had dealings with the aforesaid company." In those days, my correspondent points out, any shipments of opium—or of any other desirable goods—travelling along the Yangtze through Hunan would have been vulnerable to raids from the bandits and pirates who terrorised the region. Only the warlords through whose territories the shipments travelled could offer any sort of effective protection, and a company like Byatt's almost certainly would have gone some way to securing the friendship of such men. At the time of my childhood in Shanghai, Wang Ku, with the power he then commanded, would have been regarded as a particularly desirable ally. My correspondent's letter closes with his apologies for being unable to provide more concrete details.

As I have said, I did not solicit this information from my correspondent until some five or six weeks after discovering the newspaper picture. The reason for my delay was that annoyingly, though I was certain I had seen the plump man somewhere in my past, I could not for a long time remember anything about the context in which I had done so. The man was associated for me with some scene of embarrassment or unpleasantness, but beyond that my memory would yield nothing. Then one morning, quite unexpectedly, as I was strolling along Kensington High Street in search of a taxicab, it all suddenly came back to me.

I HAD NOT PAID much attention to the plump man when he had first arrived at our house. It was after all only two or three weeks after my father's disappearance and any number of strangers had been coming and going: policemen, men from the British consulate, men from Byatt's, ladies who on entering the house and catching sight of my mother would hold out their arms with a cry of anguish. To these latter, I recall, my mother always responded with a self-possessed smile, and walking up to the lady, would pointedly avoid the embrace, saying instead in her most assured tones something like: "Agnes, how delightful." She would then take her guest's hands—perhaps still proffered awkwardly in the air—and lead the way into the drawing room.

In any case, as I say, the arrival of the plump Chinese man that day did not much excite my interest. I remember glancing down from my playroom window and seeing him getting out of his motor car. His appearance on that occasion was, I believe, much as it is in my newspaper picture: dark gown, cap, pigtail. I noticed the car was a vast gleaming affair, and that he had two men to assist him as well as his chauffeur, but even this was not so remarkable; in those days following my father's disappearance, a number of very grand visitors had already turned up at the house. I was, though, vaguely struck by the way Uncle Philip, who had been in the house for the past hour or so, marched out to greet the plump man. They exchanged the most effusive greetings—as though they were the dearest friends—then Uncle Philip led the visitor into our house.

I do not remember what I got up to for the next little while. I did remain in the house—though not on account of the plump man, who, as I say, had not much interested me. In fact when I first heard the commotion downstairs, I remember being surprised the visitor was still with us. Rushing back to my playroom window I saw the motor car still on the carriage track, and the three servants who had stayed in the car—who too had heard the disturbance—hastening out of the vehicle with looks of alarm. Then I saw below me the plump man walking quite calmly towards the car, signalling to his men not to worry. The chauffeur held open the door for the plump man and as he was climbing in, my mother came into view. In fact, it had been her voice that had first sent me rushing to the window. I had been trying to convince myself it was just the same voice she used when angry with me or our servants, but by the time my mother's figure appeared below me, her every word now clearly audible, the effort became pointless. There was something about her that had lost control, something I had never seen before, and yet which I at once registered as something I would have to accept in the wake of my father's disappearance.

She was yelling at the plump man, having actually to be restrained by Uncle Philip. My mother was telling the plump man he was a traitor to his own race, that he was an agent of the devil, that she did not want help of his sort, that if he ever returned to our house, she would "spit on him like the dirty animal he was."

The plump man took all this very calmly. He signalled to his men to get in the car, and then, as his chauffeur wound the crank, he smiled from his window almost approvingly towards my mother, as though she were uttering the most gracious of farewells. Then the car was gone and Uncle Philip was persuading my mother to come inside.

By the time they came into the hall, my mother had gone silent. I could hear Uncle Philip saying: "But we have to pursue every possible avenue, don't you see?" His footsteps followed my mother's into the drawing room, the door closed and I heard no more.

Of course, to see my mother behaving in such a way was most disturbing to me. But if she had found shouting at her visitor a liberation after weeks of keeping her feelings on a tight rein, then I too experienced something similar. It was witnessing her outburst that allowed me, after at least two or three weeks, finally to acknowledge the momentous nature of what had happened to us, and this brought with it a tremendous sense of relief.

I will have to admit, incidentally, that I cannot say with complete certainty that the plump Chinese man I saw that day was one and the same as the man in the newspaper photograph—the man now identified as the warlord Wang Ku. All I can say is that from the moment I first set eyes on the photograph, that face—and it was the face, not the gown, cap and pigtail, which of course could have been those of any Chinese gentleman—struck me unmistakably as one I had seen during the days immediately after my father's disappearance. And the more I have turned that particular incident over in my mind, the more convinced I have become that the man in the photograph was the one who visited our house that day. This discovery I believe to be most significant—one that may well help shed light on my parents' present whereabouts, and prove central to those investigations upon which, as I have said, I intend before long to embark.

$\mathcal{T}$HERE IS A FURTHER ASPECT to this incident I have just described which I hesitate to mention here, uncertain as I am that there is any substance to it. It has to do with Uncle Philip's manner that day as he tried to restrain my mother in front of our house; and again, something in his voice when he said as they came in: "But we have to pursue every possible avenue, don't you see?" There was nothing at all concrete I could put my finger on, but then a child is sometimes very receptive to these less tangible things. Anyway, my feeling was that there was something definitely odd about Uncle Philip that day. I do not know why, but I got the distinct impression that on this occasion, Uncle Philip was not on "our side"; that the intimacy he shared with the plump Chinese man was greater than the one he shared with us; even—and quite possibly this *was* merely my fancy—that he and the plump man exchanged looks as the car drove off. As I say, I cannot point to anything solid to support these impressions, and it is more than possible I am projecting back certain perceptions in the light of what ultimately occurred with Uncle Philip.

Even today, I find it brings me some pain to remember the way my relationship with Uncle Philip concluded. As I have probably made clear, he had become over the years a figure to idolise, so much so that in the first days after my father's disappearance, I remember contemplating the notion that I need not mind so much since Uncle Philip could always take my father's place. Admittedly, this was an idea I found in the end curiously unconvincing, but my point is that Uncle Philip was a special person for me, and it is no wonder at all I should have lowered my guard that day and followed him.

I say "lowered my guard" because for some time before that final day, I had been keeping watch over my mother with increasing anxiety. Even when she demanded to be left alone, I continued to keep a careful eye over the room she had gone into, and over the doors and windows through which kidnappers might enter. At nights I lay awake listening to her movements around the house, and always kept close to hand my weapon—a stick with a sharpened end Akira had given me.

However, when I think further about this, I have a feeling that deep down, I still did not at that stage truly believe my fears could be realised. Even the fact that I considered a pointed stick an adequate deterrent to kidnappers—that I often fell asleep fantasising I was locked in combat with dozens of intruders coming up our staircase, whom I would fell one by one with my stick—testifies perhaps to the oddly unreal level at which my fears still operated at that time.

For all that, there is no doubting the anxiety I felt for my mother's safety, and my bewilderment that the other adults had taken no steps at all to protect her. I did not like to let my mother out of my sight during this period, and as I say, I would never have lowered my guard on that day had it been anyone other than Uncle Philip.

IT WAS A SUNNY, windy morning. I remember watching from the playroom windows the leaves blowing in the front yard over the carriage track. Uncle Philip had been downstairs with my mother since shortly after breakfast, and I had been able to relax for a while, believing as I did that nothing could happen to her while he was with her.

Then midway through the morning I heard Uncle Philip calling me. I went out on to the landing and, looking down over the balcony rail, saw my mother and Philip standing in the hall, gazing up at me. For the first time in weeks I sensed something cheerful about them, as though they had just been enjoying a joke. The front door was ajar and a long streak of sunlight was falling across the hall. Uncle Philip said:

"Look here, Puffin. You're always saying you want a piano accordion. Well, I intend to buy you one. I spotted an excellent French model in a window in Hankow Road yesterday. Shopkeeper obviously has no idea what it's worth. I propose the two of us go and look it over. If it takes your fancy, then it's yours. Good plan?"

This brought me down the staircase at great speed. I jumped the last four steps and circled round the adults, flapping my arms in impersonation of a bird of prey. As I did so, to my delight, I heard my mother laughing—laughing in a way I had not heard her laugh for a while. In fact it is possible it was this very atmosphere—this feeling that things were perhaps starting to return to what they had been—which played a significant part in causing me to "lower my guard." I asked Uncle Philip when we could go, to which he shrugged and said:

"Why not now? If we leave it, someone else might spot it. Perhaps someone's buying it at this moment, even as we speak!"

I rushed to the doorway and again my mother laughed. Then she told me I would have to put on proper shoes and a jacket. I remember thinking of protesting about the jacket, but then deciding not to in case the adults changed their minds, not only about the accordion, but also about this whole light-hearted mood we were enjoying.

I waved casually to my mother as Uncle Philip and I set off across the front courtyard. Then several steps on, as I was hurrying towards the waiting carriage, Uncle Philip grasped me by the shoulder, saying: "Look! Wave to your mother!" despite my already having done so. But I thought nothing of it at the time, and turning as bidden, waved once more to my mother's figure, elegantly upright in the doorway.

For much of the way, the carriage followed the route my mother and I usually took to the city centre. Uncle Philip was quiet on the journey, which surprised me a little, but I had never before been alone with him in a carriage and assumed this was perhaps his normal custom. Whenever I pointed out to him anything we were passing, he would reply cheerfully enough; but the next moment he would be staring silently once more out at the view. The leafy boulevards gave way to the narrow crowded streets, and our driver began to shout at the rickshaws and pedestrians in our path. We passed the little curio shops in Nanking Road, and I remember craning to see the window of the toy shop on the corner of Kwangse Road. I had just begun to anticipate the smell of rotting produce as we approached the vegetable market, when Uncle Philip suddenly rapped his cane to make the carriage stop.

"From here, we'll go on foot," he said to me. "I know a good short cut. It'll be much quicker."

This made perfectly good sense. I knew from experience how the little streets off Nanking Road could become so clogged with people that a carriage or motor car would often not move for five, even ten minutes at a time. I thus allowed him to help me down from the carriage with no argument. But it was then, I recall, that I had my first presentiment that something was wrong. Perhaps it was something in Uncle Philip's touch as he handed me down; perhaps there was something else in his manner. But then he smiled and made some remark I did not catch in the noise around us. He pointed towards a nearby alley and I stayed close behind him as we pushed our way through the good-humoured throng. We moved from bright sun to shade, and then he stopped and turned to me, right there in the midst of the jostling crowd. Placing a hand on my shoulder, he asked:

"Christopher, do you know where we are now? Can you guess?"

I looked around me. Then pointing towards a stone arch under which crowds were pressing around the vegetable stalls, I replied: "Yes. That's Kiukiang Road through there."

"Ah. So you know exactly where we are." He gave an odd laugh. "You know your way around here very well."

I nodded and waited, the feeling rising from the pit of my stomach that something of great horror was about to unfold. Perhaps Uncle Philip was about to say something else—perhaps he had planned the whole thing quite differently—but at that moment, as we stood there jostled on all sides, I believe he saw in my face that the game was up. A terrible confusion passed across his features, then he said, barely audibly in the din:

"Good boy."

He grasped my shoulder again and let his gaze wander about him. Then he appeared to come to a decision I had already anticipated.

"Good boy!" he said, this time more loudly, his voice trembling with emotion. Then he added: "I didn't want you hurt. You understand that? I didn't want you hurt."

With that he spun round and vanished into the crowd. I made a half-hearted effort to follow, and after a moment caught sight of his white jacket hurrying through the people. Then he had passed under the arch and out of my view.

For the next few moments I remained standing there in the crowd, trying not to pursue the logic of what had just occurred. Then suddenly I began to move, back in the direction we had just come, to the street in which we had left the carriage. Abandoning all sense of decorum, I forced my way through the crowds, sometimes pushing violently, sometimes squeezing myself through gaps, so that people laughed or called angrily after me. I reached the street to discover of course that the carriage had long since gone on its way. For a few confused seconds I stood in the middle of the street, trying to form in my head a map of my route back home. I then began to run as fast as I could.

I ran down Kiukiang Road, across the hard uneven stones of Yunnan Road, pushed through more crowds along Nanking Road. When at last I reached Bubbling Well Road, my breath was already coming in gasps, but I was encouraged that I now had left only this one long straight road, relatively free of people.

Perhaps it was because I was conscious of the highly private nature of my fears—or perhaps some profound shift in attitude was already taking place within me—but it did not once occur to me to solicit help from any of the adults I passed, or to try and hail a passing carriage or motor car. I set off at a run down that long road, and even though I soon began to pant pathetically, even though I knew my gait must look appalling to an onlooker, even though the heat and exhaustion reduced me at times to little more than walking pace, I believe I did not stop at all. Then at last I was going past the American consul's residence, and then the Robertsons' house. I turned off Bubbling Well Road into our road and a second wind took me the remaining distance to our gate.

I knew as soon as I turned through our gateway—though there was nothing obvious to tell me so—that I was too late, that the thing had finished long ago. I found the front door bolted. I ran to the back door, which opened for me, and ran through the house shouting for some reason not for my mother, but for Mei Li—perhaps even at that stage, I did not wish to acknowledge the implications of shouting for my mother.

The house appeared to be empty. Then as I was standing bewildered in the entrance hall, I heard a giggling sound. It had come from the library, and as I turned and went towards it, I saw through the half-open door Mei Li sitting at my work table. She was sitting very upright and as I appeared in the doorway, she looked at me and made another giggling sound, as if she were enjoying a private joke and trying to suppress her laughter. It dawned on me then that Mei Li was weeping, and I knew, as I had known throughout that punishing run home, that my mother was gone. And a cold fury rose within me towards Mei Li, who for all the fear and respect she had commanded from me over the years, I now realised was an impostor: someone not in the least capable of controlling this bewildering world that was unfolding all around me; a pathetic little woman who had built herself up in my eyes entirely on false pretences, who counted for nothing when the great forces clashed and battled. I stood in the doorway and stared at her with the utmost contempt.

IT IS NOW LATE—a good hour has passed since I set down that last sentence—and yet here I am, still at my desk. I suppose I have been turning over these recollections, some of which I had not brought to the fore of my mind for many years. But I have also been looking ahead, to the day when I eventually return to Shanghai; to all the things Akira and I will do there together. Of course, the city will have undergone many changes. But then I know Akira would like nothing more than to take me around, showing off all his great knowledge of the city's more intimate reaches. He will know just the right places to eat, to drink, to take a walk; the best establishments where we might go after a hard day, to sit and talk late into the night, swapping stories about all that has happened to us since our last meeting.

But I must now get some sleep. There is much work to be done in the morning, and I must catch up on the time lost this afternoon going about London with Sarah on the upper deck of that bus.

PART THREE

LONDON, 12TH APRIL 1937

ESTERDAY, BY THE TIME young Jennifer returned from her shopping trip with Miss Givens, the light in my study was already murky. This tall narrow house, bought with my inheritance following my aunt's death, overlooks a square which, while moderately prestigious, catches less sun than any of its neighbours. I watched her from the study window, down in the square, going back and forth from the taxicab, lining up shopping bags against the railings, while Miss Givens searched in her purse for the fare. When eventually they came in, I could hear them quarrelling, and though I shouted a greeting from the landing, decided not to go down. Their quarrel seemed trivial—something about what they had and had not bought—but at that moment I was still excited by the morning's letter—and the conclusions to which it had led me— and I did not want my triumphant mood broken.

By the time I came downstairs, they had long ceased their argument, and I found Jennifer roaming around the drawing room with a blindfold over her eyes, hands outstretched before her.

"Hello, Jenny," I said, as though spotting nothing unusual about her. "Did you get all you needed for the new term?"

She was drifting dangerously towards the display cabinet, but I resisted the temptation to call out. She stopped just in time, felt with her hands and giggled.

"Oh, Uncle Christopher! Why didn't you warn me?"

"Warn you? About what?"

"I've gone blind! Can't you tell? I'm blind! Look!"

"Ah yes. So you are."

I left her groping around the furniture and went through to the kitchen, where Miss Givens was unpacking a bag on to the table. She greeted me politely, but made sure I noticed her glance towards the remains of my lunch abandoned at the far end of the table. Since the departure last week of Polly, our maid, Miss Givens has despised any implication that she should even temporarily undertake such duties.

"Miss Givens," I said to her, "there's something I must discuss with you." Then looking over my shoulder, I lowered my voice: "It's something that has an important bearing on Jennifer."

"Of course, Mr. Banks."

"In fact, Miss Givens, I wonder if we might step into the conservatory. As I say, it's a matter of some significance."

But just at this moment a crashing noise came from the drawing room. Miss Givens, brushing past me, shouted from the doorway:

"Jennifer, stop that! I told you this would happen!"

"But I'm blind," came the reply. "I can't help it."

Miss Givens, remembering I had been addressing her, seemed caught in two minds. In the end, she came back and said quietly: "Excuse me, Mr. Banks. You were saying?"

"Actually, Miss Givens, I think we'll be able to speak more freely this evening after Jennifer has gone to bed."

"Very well. I shall come and see you then."

If Miss Givens had any forebodings about what I wished to discuss, she did not at that stage show it. She gave me one of her unrevealing smiles, before going through to her charge in the drawing room.

• • •

IT IS NOW almost three years ago that I first heard of Jennifer. I had been invited to a supper party by my old schoolfriend, Osbourne, whom I had not seen for a little while. He was still living in those days on the Gloucester Road, and I met for the first time that night the young woman who has since become his wife. Among his other guests that evening was Lady Beaton, the widow of the well-known philanthropist. Perhaps because the guests were all strangers to me—they spent much of the evening telling jokes about people I knew nothing about—I found myself talking rather a lot to Lady Beaton, so much so that I feared at times I was becoming a burden to her. In any case, it was just after the soup had been served that she began to tell me about a sad case she had recently come across in her capacity as treasurer of a charity concerned with the welfare of orphans. A couple had been drowned in a boating accident in Cornwall two years earlier, and their only child, a girl now of ten, was at present living out in Canada with her grandmother. This old lady was evidently in poor health, rarely went out or received callers.

"When I was over in Toronto last month," Lady Beaton told me, "I decided to call on them myself. The poor little thing was miserable, she so misses England. And as for the old lady, she can barely look after herself, never mind a young girl."

"Will your organisation be able to help her?"

"I'll do my best for her. But we have so many cases, you see. And strictly speaking, she isn't a priority. After all, she does have a roof over her head and her parents have left her reasonably well provided for. The big thing about this sort of work is not to get too personal about it. But having met the poor girl, one can't help but get involved. She has such a spirit about her, quite unusual, even though she was clearly so unhappy."

It is possible she told me a few further things about Jennifer as we continued with the meal. I remember listening politely, but saying little. It was only much later, out in the hall, as the guests were leaving, and Osbourne was appealing to us all to stay a little longer, that I took Lady Beaton to one side.

"I hope you don't think this inappropriate," I said. "But this girl you were telling me of earlier. This Jennifer. I'd like to do something to help. In fact, Lady Beaton, I'd be quite prepared to take her in."

Perhaps I should not hold it against her that her first reaction was to recoil with a look of suspicion. At least, that is how it appeared to me. Eventually she said:

"That's very good of you, Mr. Banks. I will, if I may, get in touch with you about the matter."

"I'm quite serious, Lady Beaton. I recently came into an inheritance, so I'll be quite able to provide for her."

"I'm sure that's so, Mr. Banks. Well, let us speak further about it." With that, she turned to some other guests to exchange boisterous farewells.

But Lady Beaton did indeed get in touch with me less than a week later. Possibly she had been making enquiries about my character; perhaps it was simply that she had had time to think things over; in any case, her attitude had quite changed. Over lunch at the Café Royal, and during our subsequent meetings, she could not have been warmer towards me, and Jennifer duly arrived at my new house just four months after the dinner at Osbourne's apartment.

She was accompanied by a Canadian nurse named Miss Hunter, who departed again a week later, cheerfully kissing the girl on the cheek and reminding her to write to her grandmother. Jennifer considered carefully the choice of three bedrooms I offered her, and decided on the smallest, because, she said, the little wooden ledge running along one wall would be perfect for her "collection." This, I soon discovered, comprised some carefully selected sea-shells, nuts, dried leaves, pebbles and a few other such items she had gathered over the years. She positioned the objects carefully along the ledge and called me in one day to inspect.

"I've given each a name," she explained. "I realise that's a silly sort of thing to do, but I do so love them. One day, Uncle Christopher, when I'm not so busy, I'll tell you all about each of them. Please will you tell Polly to be extra careful when she cleans along here."

Lady Beaton came to assist me in conducting the interviews for a nanny, but it was Jennifer herself, eavesdropping on proceedings from the next room, who proved the most decisive influence. She would emerge after each candidate had left to deliver a damning verdict. "A complete horror," she pronounced of one woman. "That's obvious nonsense about her last charge dying of pneumonia. She poisoned her." Of another, she said: "We can't possibly have her. Far too nervous."

Miss Givens struck me during her interview as dull and rather cold, but for some reason it was she who immediately won Jennifer's approval, and it must be said, in the two and a half years since then she has amply justified Jennifer's belief in her.

Almost everyone to whom I introduced Jennifer remarked on how self-possessed she appeared for one who had experienced such tragedy. Indeed, she did have a remarkably assured manner, and in particular a capacity to make light of setbacks which might have brought other girls her age to tears. A good example of this was her reaction concerning her trunk.

She had for some weeks after her arrival made repeated references to her trunk that would arrive by sea from Canada. I remember, for instance, her describing to me once in some detail a wooden merry-go-round someone had made for her that was coming in the trunk. On another occasion, when I had complimented her on a particular costume she and Miss Givens had brought back from Selfridge's, she had looked at me solemnly and said: "And I have a hair-band to match it *perfectly*. It's coming in my trunk."

However, I received one day a letter from the shipping company apologising for the loss of the trunk at sea and offering compensation. When I told Jennifer of this, she first simply stared. Then she gave a light laugh and said:

"Well in that case, Miss Givens and I will just have to go on an *enormous* spending spree."

When after two or three days she had still shown no sign of distress over her loss, I felt inclined to have a talk with her, and one morning after breakfast, spotting her wandering about in the garden, went out to join her.

It was a crisp, sunny morning. My garden is not large, even by city standards—a green rectangle overlooked by any number of our neighbours—but it is well laid out and has, despite everything, a pleasing sense of sanctuary. When I stepped down on to the lawn, Jennifer was drifting about the garden with a toy horse in her hand, dreamily walking it along the tops of the hedges and bushes. I remember being rather concerned the toy might be harmed by the dew and was on the verge of pointing this out to her. But in the end, as I came up, I said simply:

"That was rotten luck about your things. You've taken it awfully well, but it must have been a terrible shock."

"Oh . . ." She went on moving her horse carelessly. "It *was* a bit of a bore. But I can always get more things with the compensation money. Miss Givens said we could go shopping on Tuesday."

"All the same. Look, I think you're awfully brave. But there's no need, you know, to put up a show, if you see what I mean. If you want to let your guard down a bit, you should do so. I'm not going to let on to anyone, and neither, I'm sure, is Miss Givens."

"It's all right. I'm not upset. After all, they were just *things*. When you've lost your mother and your father, you can't care so much about *things*, can you?" With that, she gave her little laugh.

This is one of the few instances I can now recall of her mentioning her parents. I laughed too, and saying: "I suppose not," started to walk back to the house. But then I turned to her again and said:

"You know, Jenny, I'm not sure that's true. You might say a thing like that to a lot of people and they'd believe you. But you see, I know it's not true. When I came from Shanghai, the things that came in *my* trunk, those things, they were important to me. They remain so."

"Will you show them to me?"

"Show them to you? Well, most of it wouldn't mean anything to you."

"But I love Chinese things. I'd like to see them."

"Most of it isn't Chinese as such," I said. "Well, what I'm trying to say is that for me, my trunk was special. If it had got lost, I'd have been upset."

She shrugged and put her horse up to her cheek. "I was upset. But I'm not any more. You have to look forward in life."

"Yes. Whoever told you that is quite right in a way. All right, as you will. Forget your trunk for now. But remember . . ." I trailed off, not knowing what I had intended to say.

"What?"

"Oh nothing. Just remember, if there's anything you want to tell me, or anything that's troubling you, I'm always here."

"All right," she said brightly.

As I stepped back up to the house, I glanced behind me and saw she was roaming about the garden once more, moving her horse in dreamy arcs through the air.

I DID NOT MAKE such promises to Jennifer lightly. At that time, it was my intention entirely to fulfil them, and my fondness for Jennifer only grew in the days that followed. And yet here I am today, planning to desert her; for how long, I do not even know. It is, of course, possible I am exaggerating her dependence on me. If all goes well, moreover, I may well be back in London before the next school holidays and she will hardly notice my absence. And yet, I am obliged to admit, as I was to Miss Givens when she asked me flatly last night, that I may be gone a lot longer. It is this very indefiniteness that betrays my priorities, and I have no doubt Jennifer will not be slow to draw her own conclusions. Whatever brave face she puts on it, I know she will see my decision as a betrayal.

It is not easy to explain how things have come to this. What I can say is that it began some years ago—from well before Jennifer's arrival—as a vague feeling I would get from time to time; a feeling that someone or other disapproved of me, and was only just managing to conceal it. Curiously, these moments tended to occur in the company of the very people whom I might have expected to be most appreciative of my achievements. When talking to some statesman at a dinner, say, or to a police officer, or even a client, I would be suddenly surprised by the coldness of a handshake, a curt remark inserted amidst pleasantries, a polite aloofness just where I might have expected gushing gratitude. Initially, whenever such incidents occurred, I would search my memory for some offence I might inadvertently have caused the particular individual; but eventually I was obliged to conclude that such reactions had to do with something more general in people's perceptions of me.

Because what I am talking of here is so nebulous, it is not easy to recall instances to serve as clear illustrations. But I suppose one example is the odd exchange I had last autumn with the police inspector from Exeter in that gloomy lane outside the village of Coring, in Somerset.

It was one of the most dispiriting crimes I have ever investigated. I did not arrive in the village until four days after the bodies of the children had been discovered in the lane, and the constant rainfall had turned the ditch where they had been found into a muddy stream—making the gathering of relevant evidence no simple affair. None the less, by the time I heard the inspector's footsteps approaching, I had formed a fairly clear view of what had occurred.

"A most disturbing business," I said to him as he came up to me.

"It's sickened me, Mr. Banks," the inspector said. "Truly sickened me."

I had been crouching down examining the hedge, but now rose to my feet, and we stood facing one another in the steady drizzle. Then he said:

"You know, sir, just at this moment, I dearly wish I'd become a carpenter. That's what my father wished of me. I really do, sir. Today, after this, I really do."

"It's awful, I agree. But one mustn't turn away. We have to see to it justice prevails."

He shook his head forlornly. Then he said: "I came out here to ask you, sir, if you'd formed a view of this case. Because you see . . ." He looked up at the dripping trees above him, then went on with an effort: "You see, my own investigations do lead me towards a certain conclusion. A conclusion I'm somewhat loath to reach."

I looked at him gravely and nodded. "I fear your conclusion is correct," I said solemnly. "Four days ago, this looked to be as horrific a crime as one could imagine. But now, it seems the truth is even more ghastly."

"How can it be, sir?" The inspector had gone very pale. "How can such a thing be possible? Even after all these years I can't comprehend such . . ." He fell silent and turned away from me.

"Unfortunately, I see no other possibility," I said quietly. "It is indeed shocking. It's as if we're looking right into the depths of the darkness."

"Some madman who was passing, something of that order I could have accepted. But this . . . I am still loath to believe it."

"I fear you must," I said. "We must accept it. Because it's what happened."

"You're sure of it, sir?"

"I'm sure of it."

He was gazing across the neighbouring fields to the row of cottages in the distance.

"At times like these," I said, "I can well understand, one gets very discouraged. But if I may say so, it's well you didn't follow your father's advice. Because men of your calibre, inspector, are rare. And those of us whose duty it is to combat evil, we are . . . how might I put it? We're like the twine that holds together the slats of a wooden blind. Should we fail to hold strong, then everything will scatter. It's very important, Inspector, that you carry on."

He remained silent for another moment. Then when he spoke again, I was rather taken aback by the hardness in his voice.

"I'm just a small person, sir. So I'll stay here and do what I can. I'll stay here and do my best to fight the serpent. But it's a beast with many heads. You cut one head off, three more will grow in its place. That's how it seems to me, sir. It's getting worse. It's getting worse every day. What's happened here, these poor little children . . ." He turned around and I could now see fury in his face. "I'm just a small man. If I was a greater man"—and here, without a doubt, he looked accusingly straight into my eyes—"if I was a greater man, then I tell you, sir, I'd hesitate no longer. I'd go to its heart."

"Its heart?"

"The heart of the serpent. I'd go to it. Why waste precious time wrestling with its many heads? I'd go this day to where the heart of the serpent lies and slay the thing once and for all before . . . before . . ."

He appeared to run out of words and simply stood there glaring at me. I do not remember quite what I said in response. Possibly I muttered something like:

"Well, that would be most commendable of you," and turned away.

THEN THERE WAS ALSO that incident from last summer, on the occasion I visited the Royal Geographical Society to hear H. L. Mortimer deliver his lecture. It was a very warm evening. The audience of around a hundred was made up of specially invited figures from all walks of life; I recognised, among others, a Liberal peer and a famous Oxford historian. Professor Mortimer spoke for just over an hour, while the lecture hall grew steadily more stuffy. His paper, entitled: "Does Nazism pose a threat to Christianity?," was in fact a polemic to argue that universal suffrage had severely weakened Britain's hand in international affairs. When questions were invited at the end, a fairly vigorous argument started up around the room, not about Professor Mortimer's ideas, but concerning the German army's move into the Rhineland. There were passionate voices both condoning and condemning the German action, but I was exhausted that night after weeks of intense work, and made no real effort to follow.

Eventually we were ushered out of the hall into a neighbouring room, where refreshments were being served. The room was not nearly large enough, so that by the time I entered—and I was by no means among the last—people were already squeezed uncomfortably up against one another. A picture I have of that evening is of large, aproned women elbowing their way ferociously through the crowd with their trays of sherry, and of greying, bird-like professors talking in pairs, their heads tilted right back to maintain a civilised speaking distance. I felt it was impossible to remain in such an environment, and was pushing my way towards the exit when I felt a touch on my shoulder. I turned to find smiling at me Canon Moorly, a cleric who had been of invaluable service to me on a recent case, and saw nothing for it but to stop and greet him.

"What a most fascinating evening it's been," he said. "It's given me so much to think about."

"Yes, most interesting."

"But I must say, Mr. Banks, when I saw you there across the room, I did rather hope you'd say something."

"I'm afraid I was feeling rather tired this evening. Besides, virtually everyone else in the room seemed to know so much more about the topic."

"Oh, nonsense, nonsense." He laughed and tapped me on the chest. Then he leant in closer—perhaps someone behind him had pushed him—so that his face was only inches from mine, and said: "To be quite truthful, I was a little surprised you didn't feel compelled to make an intervention. All this talk of a crisis in Europe. You say you were tired; perhaps you were being polite. All the same, I'm surprised you let it go."

"Let it go?"

"What I mean to say, forgive me, is that it's quite natural for some of these gentlemen here tonight to regard Europe as the centre of the present maelstrom. But you, Mr. Banks. Of course, *you* know the truth. You know that the real heart of our present crisis lies further afield."

I looked at him carefully, then said: "I'm sorry, sir. But I'm not quite sure what you're getting at."

"Oh come, come." He was smiling knowingly. "You of all people."

"Really, sir, I've no idea why you think I should have any special knowledge concerning such things. It's true, I've investigated many crimes over the years, and perhaps I've built up a general picture of how certain forms of evil manifest themselves. But on the question of how the balance of power might be maintained, how we can contain the violent conflict of aspirations in Europe, on such things I'm afraid I have no large theory as such."

"No theory? Perhaps not." Canon Moorly went on smiling at me. "But you do have, shall we say, a special relationship to what is, in truth, the source of all our current anxieties. Oh come, my dear fellow! You know perfectly well to what I'm referring! You know better than anyone the eye of the storm is to be found not in Europe at all, but in the Far East. In Shanghai, to be exact."

"Shanghai," I said lamely. "Yes, I suppose . . . I suppose there are some problems in that city."

"Problems indeed. And what was once just a local problem has been allowed to fester and grow. To spread its poison over the years ever further across the world, right through our civilisation. But I hardly need remind *you* of this."

"I think you'll find, sir," I said, no longer trying to hide my irritation, "that I've worked hard over the years to check the spread of crime and evil wherever it has manifested itself. But of course I've been able to do so only within my own limited sphere. As for what occurs in faraway places, surely, sir, you can hardly expect me to . . ."

"Oh come! Really!"

I might well have lost my patience, but just at this point another clergyman came squeezing through the crowd to greet him. Canon Moorly introduced us, but I quickly took the opportunity to slip away.

There were a number of other such incidents which, if they were not quite so overt, nevertheless built up over a period of time to push me steadily in a certain direction. And then of course, there was the encounter with Sarah Hemmings at the Draycoats' wedding.

CHAPTER 11

*I*T IS NOW ALREADY over a year ago. I had been sitting near the back of the church—the bride was not expected for several more minutes—when I saw Sarah come in with Sir Cecil Medhurst on the other side of the nave. Certainly, Sir Cecil did not look appreciably older than when I had last seen him on the evening of the Meredith Foundation banquet in his honour; but the many reports that he had been hugely rejuvenated by his marriage to Sarah appeared to be something of an exaggeration. He looked happy enough, none the less, as he gave jovial waves to people he recognised.

I did not speak to Sarah until after the service. I was strolling around the churchyard amidst the chattering guests, and had paused to admire a flower bed, when suddenly she appeared at my side.

"Now, Christopher," she said. "You're virtually the only one here not to have congratulated me on my hat. Celia Matheson made it for me."

"It's splendid. Really very impressive. And how are you?"

It was the first time we had spoken for some time and I believe we chatted politely for a while as we moved slowly around the fringes of the crowd. Then when we paused again, I asked:

"And Sir Cecil is well? He's certainly looking very fit."

"Oh, he's on splendid form. Christopher, you can tell me. Were people utterly horrified I married him?"

"Horrified? Oh no, no. Why should they be?"

"I mean, about his being so much older. Of course, no one will say so to *us*. But you tell me. People were horrified, weren't they?"

"As far as I was aware, everyone was delighted. Of course, people were surprised. It was all so sudden. But no, I believe everyone was delighted."

"Well then, that only proves what I feared. They must have seen me as an old maid. That's why they weren't horrified. A few years ago, I'm sure they would have been."

"Really . . ."

Sarah laughed at my discomfort and touched my arm. "Christopher, you're so sweet. Don't worry. Don't worry about it at all." Then she added: "You know, you must come and visit. Cecil remembers meeting you, at that banquet. He'd love to see you again."

"I'd be delighted."

"Oh, but it's probably too late now. We're going away, you see. Sailing for the Far East in eight days' time."

"Really. Will you be gone for long?"

"Might be months. Perhaps even years. Still, you must come and see us when we get back."

I suspect I was a little lost for words at this news. But just at that moment, the bride and groom came into view across the grass, and Sarah said:

"Don't they look so handsome together? And they're so suited." For a moment she gazed at them dreamily. Then she said: "I was asking them just now what they wished of the future. And Alison said they just want a little cottage in Dorset, from which neither of them need emerge for years and years. Not until there are children, and they're getting grey hairs and wrinkles. Don't you think that's so wonderful? I do so wish it for them. And it's so wonderful, the way they happened to meet just by chance like that."

She went on gazing at them as though hypnotised. Eventually she came out of her trance, and I believe we spent a few minutes exchanging news of mutual friends. Then others came to join us, and after a while I drifted away.

I was to encounter Sarah once more, later in the day, at the country house hotel overlooking the South Downs where the reception was held. It was towards the end of that afternoon, and the sun was low in the sky. An unusual amount of drink had been consumed by then, and I remember walking through the hotel past groups of dishevelled guests, scattered across sofas and propped uncertainly in alcoves, until coming out on to the windy terrace I spotted Sarah, leaning against the balustrade, looking out over the grounds. I was walking towards her, when I heard a voice behind me, and saw a stout, red-faced man hurrying across the terrace after me. He grasped my arm, then stood there recovering his breath, looking into my face with a serious expression. Then he said:

"Look, I've been watching. I saw what happened, and I saw them earlier too. It's a disgrace, and as the brother of the groom, I want to extend my apologies to you. Those drunken oafs, I don't know who they are. I'm sorry, old chap, it must have been awfully upsetting."

"Oh, please don't worry," I said with a laugh. "I'm not in the least offended. They've had a little to drink and they were just amusing themselves."

"It's barbaric behaviour. You're a guest, just as they are, and if they can't be civil, they'll have to go."

"Well really, I think you've got the wrong end of the stick. They didn't mean anything. In any case, I certainly took no offence. A fellow's got to be able to take a little joke sometimes."

"But they've been at it all afternoon. I saw them earlier, even at the church. This is my brother's wedding. I won't have behaviour of this sort. In fact, I'm going to sort the whole thing out here and now. Come with me, old fellow. We'll see if they still find you so amusing."

"No, look, you don't understand. If anything, I was enjoying the joke just as much as they were."

"But I won't have it! Far too much of this kind of thing goes on these days. They get away with it more and more, but not today. Not at my brother's wedding. Come on, you come with me."

He was tugging at my arm and I saw beads of sweat all over his face. I am not sure what I would have done next, but just then, Sarah came strolling up to us, a cocktail in one hand, and said to the red-faced man:

"Oh, Roderick, you *have* got the wrong end of the stick. Those are *friends* of Christopher's. Besides, Christopher's the last person you need to protect."

The red-faced man looked from one to the other of us. Finally he asked Sarah: "Are you sure? Because I've seen it go on the whole day. Every time this chap goes anywhere near them . . ."

"You worry too much, Roderick. Those are friends of Christopher's. If he were in the least bit cross with them, you'd soon know all about it. Christopher's *quite* capable of dressing them down himself. In fact, Christopher here could have them cowering, or else eating out of his hand, whatever he pleases, in the wink of an eye. So off you go, Roderick. Go off and enjoy yourself."

The red-faced man regarded me with a new respect, then in his confusion held out his hand. "I'm Jamie's brother," he said, as I took it. "Pleased to meet you. If I can do anything, well, you come and find me. I'm sorry if there was some misunderstanding. Well, enjoy yourself."

We watched him lurch back towards the house. Then Sarah said:

"Come on, Christopher. Why don't you come and talk to me for a while."

She took a sip from her glass and strolled off. I followed her across the terrace until we were at the balustrade, looking out over the grounds.

"Thank you for that," I said eventually.

"Oh, it's all part of the service. Christopher, what have you been up to all afternoon?"

"Oh, nothing much. In fact, I was just thinking. About that night a few years ago, that banquet for Sir Cecil. I was wondering if when you met him that night you had any idea you'd one day . . ."

"Oh, Christopher"—she cut across my words and I realised she was fairly drunk—"I'll tell you, I can tell you. When I met Cecil that night, I found him very charming. But really, I thought nothing more of him. It was only much later, oh, a year later, even more. Oh yes, I'll tell you, you're such a dear friend. I was at this supper and people were talking about Mussolini, and some of the men were saying it wasn't a joke any more, there could well be another war, even worse than the last one. That's when someone brought up Cecil's name. Said we needed people like him more than ever at a time like this, and he really shouldn't have retired, surely he had plenty of steam left yet. Then someone said, he's the man to undertake the great mission, and someone else said, no, it's not fair on him, he's too old, he's got no close colleagues left, he doesn't even have a wife now. And that's when it came to me. I thought, well, even a great man like that, with all his achievements, he needs someone, someone who'll make the difference. Someone to help him, at the end of his career, to summon up what's needed for one last great push."

She fell quiet for a moment, so I said: "And it would appear Sir Cecil came to see it that way too."

"I can be persuasive when I wish to be, Christopher. Besides, he says he fell in love with me right from that time he first saw me, at that banquet."

"How splendid."

Below us, down on the grass, some way in the distance, several guests were larking about by the pond. I could see one man, his collar sticking out behind his neck, charging at some ducks. Eventually, I said:

"This business of Sir Cecil making a final push. His crowning achievement. What exactly was it you had in mind for him? Is this why you're going away for months?"

Sarah took a deep breath and her gaze became serious and steady. "Christopher. You must know the answer."

"If I knew the answer . . ."

"Oh, for goodness' sake. We're going to Shanghai, of course."

It is hard to describe just what I felt when I heard her say this. Perhaps there was still some element of surprise. But more than anything else, I recall a kind of relief; an odd feeling that from the time I had first laid eyes on her all those years ago at the Charingworth Club, a part of me had been waiting for this moment; that in some sense, my whole friendship with Sarah had always been moving towards this one point, and now at last it had arrived. The few words we then went on to exchange had about them a strangely familiar ring, as though we had rehearsed them somewhere many times already.

"Cecil knows the place well," she was saying. "He feels he might be able to help sort things out over there and he felt he should go. So go we shall. Next week. Our bags are virtually packed."

"Well, then, I wish Sir Cecil, I wish you *both*, the very best in accomplishing your mission in Shanghai. Are you looking forward to it? I get the impression you are."

"Of course I am. Of course I'm looking forward to it. I've waited a long time for something like this. I'm so tired of London and . . . and all of this"—she waved back towards the hotel. "I wasn't getting any younger, and sometimes I thought my chance would never come. But here we are, we're going to Shanghai. Now, Christopher, what's the matter?"

"I suppose this might sound rather feeble to you," I said. "But I'll say it anyway. You see, it's always been my intention to return to Shanghai myself. I mean, to . . . to solve the problems there. That's always been my intention."

For a moment, she went on gazing out at the sunset. Then she turned and smiled at me, and I thought her smile was full of sadness, and tinged with rebuke. She reached out a hand and touched me gently on the cheek, then turned back to the view again.

"Perhaps Cecil will solve things quickly in Shanghai," she said. "Perhaps he won't. In any case, we might be there a long time. So if what you just said is true, Christopher, then it's quite possible we shall see you out there. Isn't it?"

"Yes," I said. "Indeed."

I WAS NOT to see Sarah Hemmings again before she set sail. If she had every right to rebuke me for my procrastination over the years, then how much more deserving of her disappointment would I be should I now fail to act? For it is self-evident, whatever progress Sir Cecil has made out in Shanghai during the intervening months, a solution is still nowhere in sight. Tensions continue to mount the world over; knowledgeable people liken our civilisation to a haystack at which lighted matches are being hurled. Meanwhile, here I am, still languishing in London. But with the advent of yesterday's letter, it might be said that the last pieces of the jigsaw have come together. Surely the time has finally arrived for me to go out there myself, to Shanghai, to go there and—after all these years—"slay the serpent," as that decent West Country inspector put it.

But it will be at some cost. Earlier this morning, as yesterday, Jennifer went out shopping—for a few last items she claims are imperative for the new school term. When she left, she appeared excited and happy; she knows nothing yet of my plans, or of the things Miss Givens and I discussed last night.

I asked Miss Givens into the drawing room and had to invite her to sit down three times before she did so. Perhaps she had an inkling of what I wished to say, and felt that to sit with me would amount to some form of collusion. I laid the situation out to her as best I could; tried to make her understand the vast importance of the case; that it was, moreover, one I had been involved with for many, many years. She listened impassively, and then when I paused, asked her simple question: how long would I be gone? I believe then I talked for some time, trying to explain to her why it was impossible to place a clear time frame on a case of this sort. I have a feeling it was she who interrupted me eventually to raise some query, and after that we spent several minutes on the various practical implications of my going away. It was only after we had discussed these matters fairly exhaustively, and she had risen to leave, that I said to her:

"Miss Givens, I'm fully aware that in the short term, even with your best efforts, my absence will bring difficulties for Jennifer. But I wonder if you've considered that in the longer term, it's almost certainly in our best interests, Jenny's and mine, that I pursue the course I've just outlined to you. After all, how will Jennifer ever be able to love and respect a guardian who she knew had turned away from his most solemn duty when the call finally came? Whatever she may wish for now, she'll come to have only contempt for me when she's older. And what good would that do either of us?"

Miss Givens gazed at me steadily, then said: "You have a point, Mr. Banks." Then she added: "But she will miss you, Mr. Banks, none the less."

"Yes. Yes, I dare say so. But Miss Givens, don't you see?" I might have raised my voice at this point. "Don't you see how very urgent things have got? The growing turmoil all over the world? I have to go!"

"Of course, Mr. Banks."

"I'm sorry. I do apologise. I'm somewhat overwrought tonight. All in all, it's been quite a day."

"Would you like me to tell her?" Miss Givens asked.

I thought about this, then shook my head. "No, I'll speak to her. I'll speak to her in good time. I'd appreciate it if you said nothing to her until I've seen her."

I had intended last night to talk to Jennifer some time today. But on further thought, I feel to do so might be premature; it might, moreover, quite unnecessarily sully her current very positive mood concerning her forthcoming school term. It will be better, all in all, to leave the matter for now, and I will be able to go and see her at her school once I have finalised my arrangements. Jennifer is a child of remarkable spirit, and there is no reason to suppose she would be so devastated just on account of my departure.

I cannot help, though, recalling now that winter's day two years ago when I first visited her at St. Margaret's. I had been conducting an investigation not far away, and this still being early in her career at the school, I had decided to call to check that all was well.

The school comprises a large manor house surrounded by several acres of grounds. Behind the house, the lawn slopes down to a lake. Perhaps on account of this latter, on each of the four occasions I have visited the school, I have found mist enveloping the place. Geese wander freely, while sullen gardeners tend to the marshy grounds. It is, by and large, a rather austere atmosphere, though the mistresses, in so far as I have seen them, present a warmer face. On that particular day, I remember a certain Miss Nutting, a kindly woman in her fifties, leading me through the chilly corridors. At one point, she paused by an alcove and, lowering her voice, said to me:

"All things considered, Mr. Banks, she's settling in as well as can be expected. After all, there are bound to be a few difficulties for her at the start, while the other girls still see her as a newcomer. And one or two of them *can* be a little cruel sometimes. But by next term, that will all be behind her, I'm sure."

Jennifer was waiting for me in a large, oak-panelled room where a log was smouldering in the fireplace. The mistress left us, and

Jennifer smiled rather shyly from where she was standing in front of the mantelpiece.

"They don't keep things very warm here," I said, rubbing my hands and moving towards the fire.

"Oh, you should feel how cold it is in our dorm. Icicles on your sheets!" She giggled.

I sat down in a chair close to the fire, but she remained standing. I had feared she might feel awkward seeing me in this different context, but she soon began to chat quite freely, about her badminton, the girls she liked, the food, which she said was "stew, stew, stew."

"It's sometimes difficult," I put in at one point, "when you're new. They're not . . . ganging up on you or anything?"

"Oh no," she said. "Well, there's a bit of teasing sometimes, but they mean nothing by it. They're all nice girls here."

We had been talking for twenty minutes or so when I rose to my feet and handed her the cardboard box I had brought in my briefcase.

"Oh, what's this?" she exclaimed excitedly.

"Jenny, it's not . . . it's not a present as such."

She caught the warning in my voice, and looked at the box in her hands with a sudden wariness. "Then what is it?" she asked.

"Open it. See for yourself."

I watched her remove the lid of the box—roughly the size of a shoe box—and stare inside. Her expression, already cautious, did not change at all. Then she reached in a hand and touched something.

"I'm afraid," I said gently, "that's all I could recover. Your trunk, I discovered, wasn't lost at sea at all, but stolen along with four others from a London depot. I did what I could, but I fear the thieves simply destroyed what they couldn't sell easily. I could find no trace of the clothes and such. Just these little things."

She had brought out a bracelet, and was examining it carefully as though checking for blemishes. She put it back, then took out a pair of tiny silver bells and examined them in the same way. Then she put the lid back on the box and looked at me.

"It was very kind of you, Uncle Christopher," she said quietly. "And you must be so busy."

"It wasn't any trouble. I'm just sorry I couldn't recover any more."

"It was very kind of you."

"Well, I'd better let you get back to your geography lesson. I didn't come at a very convenient time."

She did not move, but continued to stand there quietly, gazing at the box in her hands. Then she said:

"When you're at school, sometimes, you forget. Just sometimes. You count the days until the holidays like the other girls do, and then you think you'll see Mother and Papa again."

Even in these circumstances, it still came as a surprise to hear her mention her parents. I waited for her to say more but she did not; she simply gazed up at me as though she had just put to me a question. In the end, I said:

"It's very difficult sometimes, I know. It's as though your whole world's collapsed around you. But I'll say this for you, Jenny. You're making a marvellous job of putting the pieces together again. You really are. I know it can never be quite the same, but I know you have it in you to go on now and build a happy future for yourself. And I'll always be here to help you, I want you to know that."

"Thank you," she said. "And thank you for these."

As far as I recall, that is how our meeting ended that day. We moved beyond the relative warmth of the fire, across the draughty room and out into the corridor, where I watched her walk away back to her class.

That winter's afternoon two years ago, I had no idea that my words to her were anything other than well founded. When I next visit St. Margaret's, to say goodbye, we may well meet again in that same draughty room, by that same fire. If so, things will be all the harder for me, for there is little chance Jennifer will fail to remember very clearly our last encounter there. But she is an intelligent girl, and whatever her immediate emotions, she may well understand all that I will say to her. She may even grasp, more quickly than did her nanny last night, that when she is older—when this case has become a triumphant memory—she will be truly glad I rose to the challenge of my responsibilities.

PART FOUR

*C*ATHAY HOTEL, SHANGHAI,
20TH SEPTEMBER 1937

TRAVELLERS IN THE ARAB COUNTRIES have often remarked on the way a native will position his face disconcertingly close during conversation. This, of course, is simply a local custom that happens to differ from our own, and any open-minded visitor will before long come to think nothing of it. It has occurred to me that I should try and view in a similar spirit something which, over these three weeks I have been here in Shanghai, has come to be a perennial source of irritation: namely, the way people here seem determined at every opportunity to block one's view. No sooner has one entered a room or stepped out from a car than someone or other will have smilingly placed himself right within one's line of vision, preventing the most basic perusal of one's surroundings. Often as not, the offending person is one's very host or guide of that moment; but should there be any lapse in this quarter, there is never a shortage of bystanders eager to make good the shortcoming. As far as I can ascertain, all the national groups that make up the community here—English, Chinese, French, American, Japanese, Russian—subscribe to this practice with equal zeal, and the inescapable conclusion is that this custom is one that has grown up uniquely here within Shanghai's International Settlement, cutting across all barriers of race and class.

It took me a good few days to put my finger on this local eccentricity, and to appreciate that it was what lay at the root of the disorientation which threatened to overwhelm me for a time upon first arriving here. Now, although I still find myself occasionally annoyed by it, it is not a thing of undue concern. Besides, I have discovered a second, complementary Shanghai practice to make life a little easier: it appears to be quite permissible here to employ surprisingly rough shoves to get people out of one's way. Though I have not yet found the nerve to take advantage of this licence myself, I have already witnessed on a number of occasions refined ladies at society gatherings giving the most peremptory pushes without provoking as much as a murmur.

When on my second night here I entered the ballroom on the penthouse floor of the Palace Hotel, I had yet to identify either of these curious practices, and consequently found much of that evening undermined by my frustration with what I then took to be the inordinately crowded nature of the International Settlement. Stepping out of the lift, I had barely glimpsed the plush carpet leading into the ballroom—a row of Chinese doormen lined all along it—when one of my hosts for the evening, Mr. MacDonald from the British consulate, put his broad frame before me. As we strode on towards the doorway, I noticed the rather charming way each doorman, as we passed, would bow and bring his white-gloved hands up together. But we were hardly past the third man—there were probably six or seven in all—when even this view was obstructed by my other host, a certain Mr. Grayson, representing the Shanghai Municipal Council, who stepped up beside me to continue whatever he had been saying during our ascent in the lift. And I had no sooner entered the room in which, according to my two hosts, we were to witness "the city's smartest cabaret and a gathering of Shanghai's elite" than I found myself in the midst of a drifting crowd. The tall ceilings above me, with their elaborate chandeliers, led me to suppose the dimensions of the room were pretty vast, though for some time I had no way to corroborate this. As I followed my hosts through the throng, I saw large windows all along one side of the room through which, at that moment, the sunset was streaming in. I glimpsed too a stage at the far end, upon which several musicians in white tuxedos were wandering about talking. They, like everyone else, appeared to be waiting for something—perhaps simply for night to fall. In general there was a restlessness, with people pushing and circling one another to no clear purpose.

I almost lost sight of my hosts, but then saw MacDonald beckoning to me, and I eventually found myself sitting down at a small table with a starchy white cover to which my companions had pushed their way. From this lower vantage point I could see that in fact a large expanse of floor had been left vacant—presumably for the cabaret—and that almost all present had squeezed themselves into a relatively narrow strip along the glazed side of the room. The table we were sitting at was part of a long row, though when I tried to see how far the row extended, I was once again thwarted. No one was sitting at the tables immediately neighbouring ours, probably because the jostling crowd made it impractical to do so. Indeed, before long, our table came to feel like a tiny boat assailed on all sides by the tides of Shanghai high society. My arrival, moreover, had not gone unnoticed; I could hear murmurs spreading around me conveying the news, and more and more gazes turned our way.

In spite of all this, until things grew quite impossible, I recall trying to continue the conversation I had started with my hosts in the car bringing us to the Palace Hotel. At one point I remember I was saying to MacDonald:

"I very much appreciate your suggestion, sir. But in truth, I'm happy to pursue my lines of enquiry alone. It's how I'm accustomed to working."

"As you will, old fellow," MacDonald said. "Just thought I'd mention it. Some of these fellows I'm talking of, they certainly know their way about this city. And the best of them are as good as anything you'll find at Scotland Yard. Just thought they might save you, all of us, some valuable time."

"But you'll recall my telling you, Mr. MacDonald. I left England only once I'd formed a clear view of this case. In other words, my arrival here isn't a starting point, but the culmination of many years' work."

"In other words," Grayson suddenly put in, "you've come here to us in order to tie up the case once and for all. How marvellous! It's wonderful news!"

MacDonald gave the Municipal Council man a disdainful glance, then continued as though the latter had not spoken.

"I don't mean to cast any doubt upon your abilities, old fellow. Your record speaks for itself, after all. I was only suggesting a little back-up in the way of personnel. Strictly under your command, naturally. Just, you know, to quicken things up. Having only just got here, it mightn't be so clear how urgent our situation's become now. It all looks pretty relaxed here, I know. But I rather fear we don't have a great deal of time left."

"I fully appreciate the urgency, Mr. MacDonald. But I can only say again, I've every reason to believe things will be brought to a satisfactory conclusion in a relatively short time. Provided, that is, I'm allowed to go about my enquiries unhindered."

"That's splendid news!" Grayson exclaimed, earning another cold look from MacDonald.

For much of the time I had been in his company that day, I had been growing increasingly impatient with MacDonald's pretence at being nothing more than a consulate official charged with protocol matters. It was not just his inordinate curiosity concerning my plans—or his eagerness to foist "assistants" on me—that gave him away; it was the air of refined duplicity he carried along with his languid, well-bred manners that marked him out so readily as a senior intelligence man. By that point in the evening, I must have grown weary of humouring him in his charade, for I put my request to him as though the truth had been acknowledged between us long before.

"Since we're on the question of assistance, Mr. MacDonald," I said to him, "there is in fact something you might be able to do for me that would be of immense help."

"Try me, old fellow."

"As I mentioned before, I have a particular interest in what I believe the police forces here are calling the Yellow Snake killings."

"Oh yes?" I could see a guardedness falling over MacDonald's face. Grayson, on the other hand, seemed not to know to what I was referring, and looked from one to the other of us.

"In fact"—I went on, looking carefully at MacDonald—"it was when I'd gathered sufficient evidence on these so-called Yellow Snake killings that I made the decision finally to come here."

"I see. So you're interested in the Yellow Snake business." MacDonald glanced about the room nonchalantly. "Nasty affair. But not all that significant, I wouldn't have thought, in terms of the larger picture."

"On the contrary. I believe it to be highly relevant."

"I'm so sorry," Grayson managed finally to put in. "But just what are these Yellow Snake killings? I've never heard of them."

"It's what people are calling these communist reprisals," Mac-Donald told him. "Reds murdering relatives of one of their number who's turned informer on them." Then he said to me: "We get this happening from time to time. The Reds are savages in such matters. But it's a matter between the Chinese. Chiang Kai-shek's well on top of the Reds and plans to stay that way, Japanese or no Japanese. We try to keep above it, you know. Surprised you're so interested in all that, old fellow."

"But this particular set of reprisals," I said, "these Yellow Snake killings. They've been continuing for a long time. Off and on for the last four years. During which time thirteen people have to date been murdered."

"You'll know the details better than me, old fellow. But from what I've heard, the reason the reprisals are protracted is that the Reds don't know who their traitor is. They began by slaughtering the wrong people. A little approximate, you see, this Bolshevik vision of justice. Every time they change their ideas about who this Yellow Snake chap might be, they go out and slaughter another family."

"It would help things greatly, Mr. MacDonald, if I were able to speak to this informer. The man referred to as the Yellow Snake."

MacDonald shrugged. "That's all between the Chinese, old fellow. None of us even know who this Yellow Snake is. In my view, the Chinese government would do well to announce his identity before more innocent people get mistaken for his relatives. But honestly, old fellow. It's all between the Chinese. Best leave it that way."

"It's important I get to speak to the informer."

"Well, since you feel so strongly about it, I'll have a word with a few people. But I can't promise much. This chap seems pretty useful to the government. Chiang's men keep him pretty well under wraps, I'd imagine."

I had become aware by this point of ever more people pressing in on all sides, eager not just to glimpse me in the flesh, but to overhear something of our conversation. In such circumstances, I could hardly expect MacDonald to talk frankly, and I decided I should abandon the matter for the time being. In fact, I was overcome at that moment by a strong urge to rise and get a little air, but before I could move, Grayson had leant forward with a cheerful smile, saying:

"Mr. Banks, I appreciate this might not be the best time. But I wanted just to have a quick word. You see, sir, I've been charged with the happy task of organising the ceremony. That's to say, the welcoming ceremony."

"Mr. Grayson, I don't wish to seem ungrateful, but as Mr. MacDonald here just put it, time is rather pressing. And I feel I've been welcomed already with so much lavish hospitality . . ."

"No, no, sir"—Grayson laughed nervously—"I was referring to *the* welcoming ceremony. I mean, the one welcoming back your parents after their years of captivity."

This, I admit, rather took me by surprise and perhaps for a second I just stared at him. He let out another nervous laugh and said:

"Of course, it's somewhat jumping ahead, I realise. You've first to do your work. And of course, I don't wish to tempt fate. All the same, you see, we *are* obliged to prepare. As soon as you announce the solving of the case, everyone will look to us, the Municipal Council, to provide an occasion worthy of such a moment. They'll want a pretty special event, and they'll want it promptly. But you see, sir, to organise something on the scale we're talking of, it's no simple matter. So you see, I wondered if I could put a few very basic options before you. My first question, sir, before anything else, is if you're happy with the choice of Jessfield Park for the ceremony? We will, you see, require substantial space . . ."

While Grayson had been speaking, I had become steadily aware of the sound—from somewhere behind the hubbub of the crowd—of distant gunfire. But now Grayson's words were suddenly cut off by a loud boom which shook the room. I looked up in alarm, only to see all around me people smiling, even laughing, their cocktail glasses still in their hands. After a moment, I could discern a movement in the crowd towards the windows, rather as though a cricket match had resumed outside. I decided to seize the opportunity to leave the table, and rising, joined the drift. There were too many people in front of me to see anything, and I was trying to edge my way forward when I became aware that a grey-haired lady by my shoulder was talking to me.

"Mr. Banks," she was saying, "do you have any idea at all how relieved we all feel now that you're finally with us? Of course, we didn't like to show it, but we were getting extremely concerned about, well"—she gestured towards the sound of gunfire—"my husband, he insists the Japanese will never dare attack the International Settlement. But then you know, he says it at least twenty times a day, and that's hardly reassuring. I tell you, Mr. Banks, when news of your impending arrival reached us, that was the first good news we'd had here in months. My husband even stopped repeating that little mantra of his about the Japanese, stopped for at least a few days. Good heavens!"

Another thunderous explosion had rocked the room, provoking a few ironic cheers. I then noticed that a little way in front of me, some French windows had been opened, and people had pushed out on to a balcony.

"Don't worry, Mr. Banks," a young man said, grasping my elbow. "There's no chance of any of that coming over here. Both sides are *extremely* careful now after Bloody Monday."

"But where's it coming from?" I asked him.

"Oh, it's the Jap warship in the harbour. The shells actually arc over us and land over there across the creek. After dark, it's quite a sight. Rather like watching shooting stars."

"And what if a shell falls short?"

Not only the young man I was talking to, but several others around me laughed at this idea—I thought rather too loudly. Then another voice said:

"We'll have to trust the Japs to get it right. After all, if they get sloppy, they're just as likely to drop one behind their own lines."

"Mr. Banks, would you care for these?"

Someone was holding out a pair of opera glasses. When I took hold of them, it was as if I had given a signal. The crowd parted before me, and I found myself virtually conveyed towards the open French windows.

I stepped out on to a small balcony. I could feel a warm breeze and the sky was a deep pink. I was looking down from a considerable height, and the canal was visible past the next row of buildings. Beyond the water was a mass of shacks and rubble out of which a column of grey smoke was rising into the evening sky.

I put the glasses to my eyes, but the focus was entirely wrong for me and I could see nothing. When I fiddled with the wheel, I found myself gazing on to the canal, where I was faintly surprised to see various boats still going about their normal business right next to the fighting. I picked out one particular boat—a barge-like vessel with a lone oarsman—that was so piled up with crates and bundles it seemed impossible for it to pass under the low canal bridge just beneath me. As I watched, the vessel approached the bridge rapidly, and I was sure I would see at least a crate or two fall from the top of the pile into the water. For the next few seconds, I went on staring through the glasses at the boat, having quite forgotten the fighting. I noted with interest the boatman, who like me was utterly absorbed by the fate of his cargo and oblivious of the war not sixty yards to his right. Then the boat had vanished under the bridge, and when I saw it glide gracefully out the other side, the precarious bundles still intact, I lowered the glasses with a sigh.

I realised a large crowd had been gathering at my back while I had been looking on to the canal. I handed the glasses to someone nearby and said to no one in particular: "So that's the war. Most interesting. Are there many casualties, do you suppose?"

This set off a lot of talking. A voice said: "Plenty of death over there in Chapei. But the Japs will have it in a few more days and it'll go quiet again."

"Wouldn't be so sure," someone else said. "The Kuomintang's surprised everyone so far, and my bet is they'll keep doing so. I'd bet on them holding out a good while yet."

Then everyone around me seemed to start arguing at once. A few days, a few weeks, what difference did it make? The Chinese would have to surrender sooner or later, so why did they not do so now? To which several voices objected that the conclusion was not nearly so cut and dried. Things were changing by the day, and there were many factors each impinging on the others.

"And besides," someone asked loudly, "hasn't Mr. Banks turned up?"

This question, obviously intended to be rhetorical, nevertheless hung oddly in the air, causing a hush to fall and all eyes to turn to me once more. In fact, I got the idea that it was not only the immediate group around the balcony, but the entire ballroom that had fallen into silence and was awaiting my response. It struck me that this was as good a time as any to make an announcement—one that perhaps had been called for from the moment I had entered the room—and clearing my throat, I declared loudly:

"Ladies and gentlemen. I can well see the situation here has grown rather trying. And I have no wish to raise false expectations at such a time. But let me say that I would not be here now if I were not optimistic about my chances of bringing this case, in the very near future, to a happy conclusion. In fact, ladies and gentlemen, I would say I am *more* than optimistic. I beg then for your patience over this coming week or so. After that, well, let us see what we have achieved."

As I uttered these last words, the jazz orchestra suddenly started up within the ballroom. I have no idea if this was simply a coincidence, but in any case the effect was to round off my statement rather nicely. I felt the focus of the room shifting away from me, and saw people starting to return inside. I too made my way back into the room, and as I tried to find our table again—I had for a moment lost my bearings somewhat—I noticed that a troupe of dancing girls had taken the floor.

There were perhaps as many as twenty dancers, many of them "Eurasians," dressed skimpily in matching outfits with a bird motif. As the dancers proceeded with their floor show, the room seemed to lose all interest in the battle across the water, though the noises were still clearly audible behind the cheery music. It was as though for these people, one entertainment had finished and another had begun. I felt, not for the first time since arriving in Shanghai, a wave of revulsion towards them. It was not simply the fact of their having failed so dismally over the years to rise to the challenge of the case, of their having allowed matters to slip to the present appalling level with all its huge ramifications. What has quietly shocked me, from the moment of my arrival, is the refusal of everyone here to acknowledge their drastic culpability. During this fortnight I have been here, throughout all my dealings with these citizens, high or low, I have not witnessed—not once—anything that could pass for honest shame. Here, in other words, at the heart of the maelstrom threatening to suck in the whole of the civilised world, is a pathetic conspiracy of denial; a denial of responsibility which has turned in on itself and gone sour, manifesting itself in the sort of pompous defensiveness I have encountered so often. And here they now were, the so-called elite of Shanghai, treating with such contempt the suffering of their Chinese neighbours across the canal.

I was moving along the line of backs that had formed to watch the cabaret, trying to contain my sense of disgust, when I realised someone was tugging on my arm and turned to find Sarah.

"Christopher," she said, "I've been trying to get over to you all evening. Have you no time to say hello to your old friends from home? Look, Cecil's over there, he's waving to you."

It took me a little while to get a view of Sir Cecil through the crowd; he was seated alone at a table in a far corner of the room, and indeed was waving to me. I waved back, then looked at Sarah.

It was our first encounter since my arrival. The impression I received of her that evening was that she seemed very well; the Shanghai sun had removed her customary pallor to some advantage. Moreover, as we exchanged a few friendly words, her manner remained light-hearted and assured. It is only now, after the events of last night, that I find myself thinking over again that first encounter, in an attempt to discover how I could have been so deceived. Perhaps it is only hindsight that makes me recall something overly deliberate in her smile, particularly whenever she mentioned Sir Cecil. And although we exchanged little more than pleasantries, after last night, one phrase she uttered that evening—which even at the time rather puzzled me—has continued to return to me all day.

I had been enquiring how she and Sir Cecil had enjoyed the year they had spent here. She had been assuring me that although Sir Cecil had not achieved the breakthrough he had hoped for, he had none the less done much to earn the gratitude of the community. It was then that I had asked, with nothing much in mind:

"So then you've no immediate plans to leave Shanghai?"

At which Sarah had laughed, cast another gaze towards Sir Cecil's corner, and said: "No, we're quite settled for now. The Metropole's very comfortable. I don't expect we'll be going anywhere in a hurry. Not unless someone comes to the rescue, that is."

She had said all this—including this last remark about being rescued—as though telling a joke, and although I did not know exactly what she meant, I had responded with a small laugh to go with hers. We had then, as far as I recall, talked about mutual friends in England until Grayson's arrival effectively put an end to a seemingly uncomplicated conversation.

It is only now, as I say, after last night, that I find myself searching back through my various encounters with Sarah over these three weeks, and it is this one phrase, added as a kind of afterthought to her breezy reply, to which I continue to return.

CHAPTER 13

I SPENT MOST of the afternoon yesterday inside the dark, creaking boathouse where the three bodies had been discovered. The police respected my wish to carry out my investigations undisturbed to the extent that I lost all track of time and hardly noticed the sun setting outside. By the time I crossed the Bund and strolled down Nanking Road, the bright lights had come on and the pavements were filled with the evening crowds. After the long, dispiriting day, I felt the need to unwind a little and made my way to the corner of Nanking and Kiangse Road, to a small club I had been taken to in the days soon after my arrival. There is nothing so special about the place; it is just a quiet basement where most nights a lone French pianist will give melancholy renditions of Bizet or Gershwin. But it meets my needs well enough and I have returned there several times over these weeks. Last night, I spent perhaps an hour at a corner table, eating a little French food and making notes on what I had discovered in the boathouse, while the taxi-dancers swayed with their clients to the music.

I had climbed the staircase back up to the street intending to return to the hotel, when I happened to fall into conversation with the Russian doorman. He is some sort of count, and speaks excellent English learnt, he tells me, from his governess before the Revolution. I have got into the habit of passing a few words with him whenever I visit the club, and was doing so again last night when—I no longer remember what we were discussing—he happened to mention that Sir Cecil and Lady Medhurst had passed by earlier in the evening.

"I suppose," I remarked, "they were off home for the night."

At this, the count thought for a moment, then said: "Lucky Chance House. Yes, I believe Sir Cecil mentioned they were on their way there."

It was not an establishment I knew, but the count proceeded without prompting to give me directions, and since it was not far, I set off towards it.

His instructions were clear enough, but I am still uncertain of my way around the side-streets off Nanking Road, and managed to get a little lost. This was not something I minded so much. The atmosphere in that part of the city is not intimidating, even after dark, and although I was accosted by the odd beggar, and at one point a drunken sailor collided with me, I found myself drifting with the night-time crowd in a mood not far from tranquillity. After the depressing work in the boathouse, it was a relief to be amidst these pleasure-seekers of every race and class; to have the smells of food and incense come wafting towards me as I passed each brightly lit doorway.

Last night, too, as I have come increasingly to do of late, I believe I looked about me, scanning the faces in the passing crowd, hoping to spot Akira. For the fact is, I had almost certainly seen my old friend shortly after my arrival in Shanghai—on my second or third night here. It was the night Mr. Keswick of Jardine Matheson and some other prominent citizens had decided I should "taste the night-life." I was still at that stage in something of a disorientated condition, and was finding the tour of dance-bars and clubs tiresome. We were in the entertainment area of the French Concession—I can see now my hosts were rather enjoying shocking me with some of the more lurid establishments—and we were just emerging from a club when I had seen his face go by in the crowd.

He was one of a group of Japanese men dressed in sharp suits, evidently out on the town. Of course, glimpsed so fleetingly—the figures had been virtually silhouettes against a row of lanterns hanging in a doorway—I could not be completely sure it was Akira. Perhaps for this reason, perhaps for some other, I did nothing to attract the attention of my old friend. This might be hard to understand, but I can only say it was so. I suppose I was assuming then there would be many more such opportunities; perhaps I felt that to meet in such a way, by chance, when we each had other companions, was inappropriate—unworthy, even, of the reunion I had anticipated for so long. In any case, I had let the moment pass, and had simply followed Mr. Keswick and the others to the awaiting limousine.

Over these past weeks, however, I have had much cause to regret my inaction that evening. For although, even at the busiest times, I have persisted in searching the crowd, in streets or in hotel lobbies, as I have gone about my business, I have yet to spot him again. I am aware I could take active steps to try and locate him; but really, the case must for now take priority. And Shanghai is not such a vast place; we are sure to happen upon one another sooner or later.

But to return to the events of last night. The doorman's directions eventually brought me to a kind of square where a number of little streets intersected and the crowd was thicker than ever. There were people trying to sell things, others trying to beg, while yet others were just standing about talking and watching. A lone rickshaw that had ventured into the throng had become stuck in its midst, and as I passed, the rickshawman was arguing furiously with a bystander. I could see Lucky Chance House on the far corner, and before long was being conducted up a narrow stairway covered in scarlet plush.

I first entered a room the size of an average hotel room, where a dozen Chinese were crowded around a gaming table. When I enquired if Sir Cecil was in the building, two of the staff conferred quickly, then one of them signalled for me to follow.

I was led up another flight of stairs, along a dim corridor, then into a room filled with smoke in which a group of Frenchmen were playing cards. When I shook my head, the man shrugged and beckoned me again. In this way I soon established that the building was a gambling emporium of some size, comprising many smallish rooms, each with some game or other in progress. But I grew exasperated at the way my guide would nod knowingly each time I repeated Sarah or Sir Cecil's name, just to lead me into yet another smoky room where only the wary eyes of strangers would look up at me. In any case, the more I saw of the establishment, the more unlikely it seemed Sir Cecil would bring Sarah into such a place, and I was on the point of giving up when I stepped through a door to find Sir Cecil sitting at a table, staring at a roulette wheel.

There were as many as twenty people present, mostly men. The room was not so smoky as some others, but felt hotter. Sir Cecil was utterly absorbed and gave me only the most cursory of waves before fixing his eyes back on the wheel.

Placed around the periphery of the room were some worn armchairs covered in a reddish material. In one of these, an old Chinese man—in a Western suit and drenched in sweat—was snoring away. The only other chair occupied was in the shadowy corner furthest from the gaming table, where Sarah was resting her head on the heel of a hand, her eyes half-closed.

She gave a start when I sat down beside her. "Oh, Christopher. What are you doing here?"

"I was just passing by. I'm sorry. I didn't mean to startle you."

"Just passing by? This place? I don't believe it. You've been pursuing us."

We were speaking in lowered tones so as not to distract the players at the table. From somewhere in the building, I could hear faintly someone practising a trumpet.

"I have to confess," I said, "I did happen to hear you'd come here. And since I was walking past . . ."

"Oh, Christopher, you were lonely."

"Hardly. But I've had rather a gloomy day, and I felt like unwinding a little, that's all. Though I must admit, I'd have hesitated if I'd known you were in a place like this."

"Don't be cruel. Cecil and I, we enjoy being low-life. It's fun. It's all part of what Shanghai's about. Now tell me about your gloomy day. You're looking despondent. No breakthrough yet on your case, I suppose."

"No breakthrough, but I'm not despondent. Things are starting to take shape."

When I then began to describe to her how I had spent over two hours on my hands and knees in a rotting boat in which three decaying corpses had been found, she pulled a face and stopped me.

"It's all so ghastly. Someone was saying at the tennis club today, the bodies all had their arms and legs cut off. Is that true?"

"I'm afraid so."

She pulled another face. "It's too ghastly for words. But these were Chinese factory workers, weren't they? Surely, they can't have much to do with . . . with your parents."

"Actually, I believe this crime has a very significant bearing on my parents' case."

"Really? They were saying at the tennis club these murders are all part of this Yellow Rat business. They're saying the victims were the Yellow Rat's nearest and dearest."

"Yellow Snake."

"Pardon?"

"The communist informer. Yellow *Snake.*"

"Oh yes. Well anyway, it's so ghastly. What are the Chinese

doing, tearing at each other's throats at a time like this? You'd think the Reds and the government might put up a united front against the Japanese just for a little while at least."

"I suppose hatred between communists and nationalists runs pretty deep."

"That's what Cecil says. Oh, look at him, how can he play like that?"

I followed her gaze and saw that Sir Cecil—who had his back to us—had slumped over to one side, so that most of his weight was on the table. There seemed every possibility of his sliding off the chair altogether.

Sarah looked at me a little awkwardly. Then rising, she went over to him, placed a hand on each of his shoulders, and spoke gently into his ear. Sir Cecil came awake and glanced about him. It is possible that at this point I took my gaze off them for a second, for I am not at all certain about what exactly happened next. I saw Sarah reel back, as though she had been struck, and for a second she seemed about to lose her balance, but then recovered. Sir Cecil, when I scrutinised his back, was sitting upright again, concentrating on the game, and I could not say it was he who had caused Sarah to stumble.

She saw me staring at her, and smiling, came back and sat down beside me again.

"He's tired," she said. "He has so much energy. But at his age, he really needs to rest more."

"Do the two of you often come to this place?"

She nodded. "And a few others very similar. Cecil doesn't much like those big glittering places. He doesn't think it's possible to come out a winner in those places."

"Do you always accompany him on these expeditions?"

"Someone has to look after him. He's not a young man, you see. Oh, I don't mind it. It's rather exciting. It's what this city's all about really."

A collective sigh went around the gaming table and the players broke into conversation. I saw Sir Cecil attempt to rise, and only then did I realise how inebriated he was. He slumped back down in the chair, but on a second attempt, managed to rise and come unsteadily towards us. I stood up, expecting to shake hands, but he rested his hand on my shoulder, as much for balance as anything else, saying:

"My dear boy, my dear boy. Delighted to see you."

"Did you have any luck just now, sir?"

"Luck? Oh no, no. Tonight's been a foul night. Whole wretched week, it's been bad, bad, bad. But you never know. I'll rise up again, ha ha! Rise from the ashes."

Sarah too was on her feet and put out a hand to support him, but he brushed her off without looking at her. Then he said to me:

"I say. Care for a cocktail? There's a bar downstairs."

"That's very kind, sir. But I really should be getting back to my hotel. Another hard day tomorrow."

"Good to see you're working hard. Of course, I came out here to this city wanting to sort things a little myself. But you see"—he bent his face right down to me until it was only an inch or two away—"too deep for me, my boy. Too deep by far."

"Cecil, darling, let's go home now."

"Home? You call that rat-hole of a hotel home? You have an advantage on me, my dear, being the vagabond that you are. That's why you don't mind it."

"Let's go now, darling. I'm tired."

"You're tired. My little vagabond's tired. Banks, do you have a car outside?"

"I'm afraid not. But if you like I'll try and find a taxi."

"Taxi? Think you're in Piccadilly? Suppose you can hail a cab out there? Just as soon cut your throat, these Chinamen."

"Cecil, darling, please sit down here while Christopher finds Boris." Then she said to me: "Our driver should be somewhere not far. Would you mind terribly? Poor Cecil's a little the worse for wear tonight."

Doing my best to look good-humoured, I made my way out of the building, making a mental note of how to return to the room. The square outside was as dense as ever with people, but a little further on I could see a street in which rickshaws and motor cars were waiting in rows. I made my way over, and after a while of going from car to car uttering Sir Cecil's name at chauffeurs of varying nationalities, I eventually got a response.

When I returned to the gambling house, Sarah and Sir Cecil were already outside. She was supporting him with both her hands, but his tall, bent form looked likely to overwhelm her at any second. As I came hurrying up, I could hear him saying:

"It's you they don't like in there, my dear. When I used to frequent this place by myself, they always treated me like royalty. Oh yes, like royalty. Don't like women of your sort. They only want real ladies or else whores. And you're neither. So you see, they don't like you one bit. Never had any trouble here until you insisted on tagging along."

"Come along, darling. Here's Christopher. Well done, Christopher. Look, darling, he's found Boris for us."

It was not a great distance to the Metropole, but the car could often move at no more than a crawl through the pedestrians and rickshaws. Throughout the journey, Sarah continued to hold Sir Cecil by the arm and shoulder while he drifted in and out of sleep. Whenever he came round, he would try to shake Sarah off, but she would laugh and continue to hold him steady in the lurching vehicle.

It was my turn to assist him as we negotiated the revolving doors of the Metropole, and then the lift, while Sarah exchanged cheerful greetings with the lobby staff. Then we were finally up in the Medhursts' suite and I was able to lower Sir Cecil into an armchair.

I thought he would doze off, but instead he grew suddenly alert again and began asking me some meaningless questions of which I could make neither head nor tail. Then when Sarah emerged from the bathroom with a flannel and began to mop his forehead, he said to me:

"Banks, my boy, you can speak frankly. This wench here. As you see, she's a good few years younger than me. No spring chicken herself, mind you, ha ha! But still, a good few years my junior. Tell me frankly, my boy, do you suppose, in a place like tonight's, where you found us tonight, a place like that, do you suppose a stranger looking at the two of us together . . . Well, let's speak frankly! What I'm asking you is, do you suppose people take my wife for a harlot?"

Sarah's expression, as far as I could see it, did not change, though a slight urgency entered her ministrations, as though she hoped the treatment would bring a change of mood. Sir Cecil waved his head in irritation as though avoiding a fly, then said:

"Come on, my boy. Do speak frankly now."

"Now, now, darling," Sarah said quietly. "You're being unpleasant."

"I'll tell you a secret, my boy. I'll tell you a secret.. I rather enjoy it. I like people to mistake my wife for a harlot. That's why I like to frequent places like that one tonight. Get off me! Leave me alone!" He pushed Sarah aside, then continued: "Other reason I go, of course, no doubt you guessed it, I owe a little money. Run up bit of a debt, you know. Nothing I won't win back, of course."

"Darling, Christopher's been very kind. You mustn't bore him."

"What's the harlot saying? Hear what she said, my boy? Well, don't. Don't listen to her. Don't listen to trollops, that's what I say. They'll lead you astray. Particularly in times of war and conflict. Never listen to a trollop in times of war."

He climbed to his feet unaided, and for a moment stood swaying before us in the middle of the room, his unfastened collar sticking out from his neck. Then he moved off into the bedroom, closing the door behind him.

Sarah gave me a smile, then went in after him. Had it not been for that smile—or rather, something like an appeal I detected behind it—I would certainly have withdrawn at that point. As it was, I remained in the room, examining absent-mindedly a Chinese bowl on a stand near the entrance. For a time, I could hear Sir Cecil shouting something; then there was silence.

Sarah emerged after perhaps five minutes and looked surprised to find me still there.

"Is he all right?" I asked.

"He's asleep now. He'll be fine. I'm sorry you were inconvenienced, Christopher. Hardly what you were seeking when you came looking for us this evening. We'll arrange something to make up. We'll take you out to dinner somewhere. Astor House has good food still."

She was guiding me out of the room, but I turned at the door and said:

"This sort of thing. Does it happen a lot?"

She gave a sigh. "Often enough. But you mustn't think I mind. It's just that I do worry sometimes. About his heart, you know. That's why I always go with him now."

"You look after him well."

"You mustn't get the wrong impression. Cecil's a dear man. We must take you out to dinner very soon. When you're not busy. But I suppose you're always busy."

"Is this how Sir Cecil tends to pass all his evenings?"

"Most of them. Some of his days too."

"Is there anything at all I can do?"

"Anything you can do?" She gave a light laugh. "Look, Christopher, I'm fine. Really, you mustn't get the wrong impression about Cecil. He's a dear. I . . . I do love him so."

"Well, then, I'll say goodnight."

She took another step towards me and raised a hand vaguely. I found myself grasping it, but not quite knowing what to do next, kissed the back of it. Then, mumbling another goodnight, I stepped into the corridor.

"You're not to worry about me, Christopher," she whispered from the door. "I'm perfectly all right."

Those were her words to me last night. But today, it is those earlier words of hers, uttered three weeks ago when I first saw her at the ballroom of the Palace Hotel, that return to me with particular pertinence. "I don't expect we'll be going anywhere in a hurry," she had said. "Unless someone comes to the rescue." What could she have intended by making such a remark to me that evening? As I say, even at the time it puzzled me, and I may well have quizzed her further about it had not Grayson, just at that moment, emerged out of the crowd, looking for me.

PART FIVE

*C*ATHAY HOTEL, SHANGHAI,

29TH SEPTEMBER 1937

I MISHANDLED my meeting this morning with MacDonald at the British consulate, and recalling it tonight only fills me with frustration. The fact is, he had prepared himself well and I had not. Time and again, I allowed him to lead me down false avenues, to waste my energy arguing over things he had decided to concede to me from the start. If anything, I was further forward with him four weeks ago, that evening at the ballroom of the Palace Hotel, when I first put to him this notion of an interview with the Yellow Snake. I had caught MacDonald unawares then, and had at least got him to admit, in so many words, his true role here in Shanghai. This morning, however, I had not obliged him even to relinquish his charade of being simply an official charged with protocol matters.

I suppose I underestimated him. I had thought it simply a matter of going in and reprimanding him for his slow progress in arranging what I had requested. Only now do I see how he laid his traps, realising that once I became annoyed, he would easily get the better of me. It was foolish to show my irritation in the way I did; but these continuous days of intense work have left me tired. And of course, there was the unexpected encounter with Grayson, the

Municipal Council man, as I was going up to MacDonald's office. In fact, I would say it was this more than anything else which threw me off balance this morning, to the extent that for much of my subsequent discussion with MacDonald, my mind was actually elsewhere.

I had been kept waiting for several minutes in the little lounge on the second floor of the consulate building. The secretary finally came to inform me MacDonald was ready, and I had crossed the marbled landing and was standing before the lift doors when Grayson came hurrying down the staircase, calling to me.

"Good morning, Mr. Banks! I'm so sorry, perhaps this isn't the best time."

"Good morning, Mr. Grayson. As a matter of fact, it isn't ideal. I was just on my way up to see our friend Mr. MacDonald."

"Oh well then, I won't keep you. It's just that here I was in the building and I heard you were here too." His cheerful laugh echoed around the walls.

"It's splendid to see you again, Mr. Grayson. But just now . . ."

"I won't keep you a second, sir. But if I may, you see, you've been a little difficult to track down recently."

"Well, Mr. Grayson, if it can be dealt with very briefly."

"Oh very briefly. You see, sir, I realise this may seem like jumping ahead, but a certain amount of forward planning is required in these matters. If things aren't up to scratch at such an important event, if things look even a little shoddy or amateurish . . ."

"Mr. Grayson . . ."

"I'm so sorry. I just wished to have your thoughts on a few details concerning the welcome reception. We've now settled on Jessfield Park as the venue. We shall erect a marquee with a stage and public address system . . . I'm so sorry, I'll come to the point. Mr. Banks, I really wished to discuss with you your own role in the proceedings. Our feeling is that the ceremony should be kept simple. What I had in mind was that perhaps you would say a few words concerning how you went about solving the case. Which vital clues finally led you to your parents, that sort of thing. Just a few words, the crowd would be so delighted. And then at the end of your speech, I thought they might care to come out on to the stage."

"They, Mr. Grayson?"

"Your parents, sir. My idea was that they might come on to the platform, wave, acknowledge the cheers, then withdraw. But of course, this is no more than an idea. I'm sure you'll have some other excellent suggestions . . ."

"No, no, Mr. Grayson"—I suddenly felt a great weariness coming over me—"it all sounds splendid, splendid. Now, if that's all. I really must . . ."

"Just one other thing, sir. A small matter, but one that might lend a most effective touch if pulled off just so. My idea was that at the moment your parents come out on to the platform, the brass band should strike up. Perhaps something like 'Land of Hope and Glory.' Some of my colleagues are less keen on this idea, but to my mind . . ."

"Mr. Grayson, your idea sounds a marvellous one. What's more, I'm exceedingly flattered by your utter confidence in my ability to solve this case. But now, please, I'm keeping Mr. MacDonald waiting."

"Of course. Well, thank you so much for taking the time to talk to me."

I pressed the button for the lift, and while I stood waiting, Grayson continued to hover. I had actually turned away from him to face the doors, when I heard him say:

"The only other thing I wondered about, Mr. Banks. Have you any idea where your parents will be staying on the day of the ceremony? You see, we shall need to ensure they're conveyed to and from the park with minimum bother from the crowds."

I cannot remember what I said to him in reply. Perhaps the lift doors opened at that moment, and I was able to take my leave of him with nothing more than a cursory response. But it was this last question which hung in my mind throughout my meeting with MacDonald, and which, as I say, probably did more than anything else to prevent me thinking clearly about the matter in hand. And tonight, again, now that the demands of the day are behind me, I find this same question returning to my mind.

It is not that I have given no thought at all to the matter of where my parents should eventually be accommodated. It is just that it has always seemed to me premature—perhaps even "tempting fate"—to contemplate such questions while the great complexities of the case have still to be unravelled. I suppose the only occasion over these past weeks when I gave the matter any real thought was on that evening I met up with my old schoolfriend, Anthony Morgan.

IT WAS NOT LONG after my arrival here—my third or fourth night. I had known for some time that Morgan was living in Shanghai, but since we had never been especially friendly at St. Dunstan's—despite our being in the same class throughout—I had made no special arrangements to meet up with him. But then I received from him a telephone call on the morning of that third day. I could tell he was rather hurt at my failure to get in touch, and eventually found myself agreeing to a rendezvous that evening in a hotel in the French Concession.

It was well after dark when I found him waiting in the dimly lit hotel lounge. I had not laid eyes on him since school and was shocked by how worn and heavy-set he had become. But I tried to keep any such impression out of my voice as we exchanged warm greetings.

"Funny," he said, patting me on the back. "Doesn't seem so long ago. And yet in some ways, it feels like another age."

"It certainly does."

"Do you know," he went on, "I got a letter the other day from

Emeric the Dane? Remember him? Emeric the Dane! Hadn't heard from him in years! Living in Vienna now, it seems. Old Emeric. You remember him?"

"Yes, of course," I said, though I could summon only the vaguest memory of such a boy. "Good old Emeric."

For the next half-hour or so, Morgan chattered on with hardly a break. He had come out to Hong Kong straight after Oxford, then moved to Shanghai eleven years ago after securing a position at Jardine Matheson. Then at one point he broke off his story to say:

"You wouldn't believe the God-awful trouble I've been having with chauffeurs since all this trouble started. Regular one got killed the first day the Japs started shelling. Found another man, turned out to be a bandit of some sort. Kept having to rush off to perform his gang duties, could never be found when you wanted to go somewhere. Picked me up once at the American Club with blood all over his shirt. Not his own, I soon gathered. Didn't say a word in apology, typical Chinaman. That was the last straw for me. Then I had two others, couldn't drive at all. One actually hit a rickshawman, hurt the poor fellow quite badly. Driver I've got now's not much better, so let's keep fingers crossed he gets us there all right."

I had no idea what he meant by this last statement, since as far as I could recall we had not agreed to go anywhere else that night. But I did not feel like picking him up on it, and then he had quickly moved on to telling me about the shortages afflicting the hotel. The lounge we were sitting in, he confided, was not always so dimly lit: the war had stopped the supply of light bulbs from the Chapei factories; in some other parts of the hotel, guests were having to wander about through darkness. He pointed out also that at least three members of the dance-band at the far end of the room were not playing their instruments.

"That's because they're really porters. The real musicians have either fled Shanghai or been killed in the fighting. Still, they do a fair impersonation, don't you think?"

Now that he had pointed it out, I saw that their impersonations were, in fact, poor in the extreme. One man looked utterly bored and was hardly bothering to hold his violin bow near his instrument; another was standing with a clarinet virtually forgotten in his hands, staring in open-mouthed wonder at the real musicians playing around him. It was only when I congratulated Morgan on his intimate knowledge of the hotel that he told me he had in fact been living there for over a month, having judged his apartment in Hongkew "too close for comfort" to the fighting. When I muttered some words of sympathy that he had had to abandon his home, his mood suddenly changed, and for the first time I saw about him a melancholy that brought to mind the unhappy and lonely boy I had known at school.

"Wasn't much of a home anyway," he said, looking into his cocktail. "Just me, a few servants that came and went. Miserable little place really. In some ways, it was just an excuse, the fighting. Gave me a good reason to walk out. It was a miserable little place. All my furniture was Chinese. Couldn't sit comfortably anywhere. Had a songbird once, but it died. It's better for me here. Much quicker to my watering holes." Then he looked at his watch, drained his glass and said: "Well, better not keep them waiting. Car's outside."

There was something about Morgan's manner—a kind of nonchalant urgency—that made it hard to raise any objections. Besides, these were still my early days in the city, when I was in the habit of being taken from function to function by various hosts. I thus followed Morgan out of the building and before long was sitting with him in the back of his car, moving through the lively night-time streets of the French Concession.

Almost immediately, the driver only just avoided an oncoming tram, and I thought this would start Morgan off again on his chauffeur problems. But now he had fallen into an introspective mood, staring silently out of his window at the passing neon and Chinese banners. At one point, when I remarked to him, in an attempt to glean something about the event to which we were going: "Do you suppose we'll be late?" he glanced at his watch again and replied distractedly: "They've been waiting for you this long, they won't mind a few more minutes." Then he added: "This must feel so odd for you."

For a while after that we travelled on, speaking little. Once we went down a side-street on both sides of which the pavements were filled with huddled figures. I could see them in the lamplight, sitting, squatting, some curled up asleep on the ground, squeezed one upon the other, so that there was only just enough space down the middle of the street for traffic to pass. They were of every age—I could see babies asleep in mothers' arms—and their belongings were all around them; ragged bundles, bird-cages, the occasional wheelbarrow piled high with possessions. I have now grown used to such sights, but on that evening I stared out of the car in dismay. The faces were mostly Chinese, but as we came towards the end of the street, I saw clusters of European children—Russians, I supposed.

"Refugees from north of the canal," Morgan said blandly, and turned away. For all his being a refugee himself, he appeared to feel no special empathy with his poorer counterparts. Even when once I thought we had run over a sleeping form, and glanced back in alarm, my companion merely murmured: "Don't worry. Probably just some old bundle."

Then after several minutes of silence, he startled me with a laugh. "Schooldays," he said. "All comes back to you. They weren't so bad, I suppose."

I glanced at him and noticed tears welling in his eyes. Then he said:

"You know, we should have teamed up. The two miserable loners. That was the thing to do. You and me, we should have teamed up together. Don't know why we didn't. We wouldn't have felt so left out of things if we'd done that."

I turned to him in astonishment. But his face, caught in the changing light, told me he was somewhere far away.

As I have said, I could remember well enough Anthony Morgan's being something of a "miserable loner" at school. It was not that he was particularly bullied or teased by the rest of us; rather, as I recall it, it was Morgan himself who from an early stage cast himself in that role. He it was who always chose to walk by himself, lagging several yards behind the main group; who on bright summer days refused to join in the fun, and was to be found instead alone in a room, filling a notebook with doodles. All this I can remember clearly enough. In fact, as soon as I had spotted him that night in the gloomy hotel lounge, what had come instantly to mind was an image of his sulky, solitary walk behind the rest of us as we crossed the quadrangle between the art room and the cloisters. But his assertion that I had likewise been a "miserable loner," one with whom he might have made a matching pair, was such an astounding one, it took me a little while to realise it was simply a piece of self-delusion on Morgan's part—in all likelihood something he had invented years ago to make more palatable memories of an unhappy period. As I say, this did not occur to me instantly, and thinking about it now I see I may have been a little insensitive in my response. For I remember saying something like:

"You must have me mixed up with someone else, old fellow. I was always one for mucking in. I dare say you're thinking of that fellow Bigglesworth. Adrian Bigglesworth. He was certainly a bit of a loner."

"Bigglesworth?" Morgan thought about this, then shook his head. "I remember the chap. Rather heavy-set, jug ears? Old Bigglesworth. My, my. But no, I wasn't thinking of him."

"Well, it wasn't me, old man."

"Extraordinary." He shook his head again, then turned back to his window.

I too turned away, and for the next little while gazed out at the night-time streets. We were once again moving through a busy entertainment area, and I glanced through the faces in the crowds, hoping to glimpse Akira's. Then we were in a residential district full of hedges and trees, and before long the driver brought the car to a halt inside the grounds of a large house.

Morgan left the vehicle hurriedly. I too got out—the chauffeur made no effort to assist—and followed him along a gravelled path leading around the side of the house. I suppose I had been expecting a big reception of some sort, but I could now see this was not what awaited us; the house was for the most part dark, and aside from our own car, there was only one other in the courtyard.

Morgan, who was clearly familiar with the house, brought us to a side door flanked by tall shrubs. He opened it without ringing and ushered me inside.

We found ourselves in a spacious hallway lit by candles. Peering before me, I could make out musty-looking scrolls, huge porcelain vases, a lacquered chest of drawers. The smell in the air—of incense mingled with that of excrement—was oddly comforting.

No servant or host appeared. My companion continued to stand beside me, not saying a word. After a time, it occurred to me he was waiting for me to make some comment on our surroundings. So I said:

"I know little about Chinese artwork. But even to my eye, it's clear we're surrounded by some rather fine things."

Morgan stared at me in astonishment. Then he shrugged and said: "I suppose you're right. Well, let's go in."

He led the way further into the house. We were in darkness for several steps, and then I heard voices talking in Mandarin, and saw light coming from a doorway hung with beaded threads. We passed through the beads, then a further set of drapes, into a large warm room lit with candles and lanterns.

What do I remember now of the rest of that evening? It has already grown a little hazy in my mind, but let me try and piece it together as clearly as I can. My first thought on entering that room was that we had disturbed some family celebration. I glimpsed a

big table laden with food, and seated around it, eight or nine people. All were Chinese; the youngest—two men in their twenties—
were dressed in Western suits, but the rest were in traditional dress.
An old lady, seated at one end of the table, was being assisted in her
eating by a servant. An elderly gentleman—surprisingly tall and
broad for an Oriental—whom I took to be the head of the household, had immediately risen upon our arrival, and now the other
males in the company followed his example. But at this stage, my
impression of these people remained vague, for very rapidly it was
the room itself that had begun to command all my attention.

The ceiling was high and beamed. Beyond the diners, right at
the back, was a kind of minstrels' gallery, from the rail of which
hung a brace of paper lanterns. It was this section of the room that
had drawn my gaze, and I now continued to stare past the table
towards it, hardly hearing my host's words of welcome. For what
was dawning upon me was that the entire rear half of the room in
which I was now standing was in fact what used to be the entrance
hall of our old Shanghai house.

Obviously some vast restructuring had taken place over the
years. I could not, for instance, work out at all how the areas
through which Morgan and I had just entered related to our old
hall. But the minstrels' gallery at the back clearly corresponded to
the balcony at the top of our grand curving staircase.

I drifted forward, and probably remained standing there for
some time, gazing up at the gallery, tracing with my eye the route
our stairs had once taken. And as I did so, I found an old memory
coming back to me, of a period in my childhood when I had made
a habit of coming down the long curve of the stairs at huge speed
and taking off two or three steps from the bottom—usually while
flapping my arms—to land in the depths of a couch positioned just
a little way away. My father, whenever he witnessed this, would
laugh; but both my mother and Mei Li disapproved. Indeed, my
mother, who could never quite explain why this particular practice

was wrong, would always threaten to have the couch removed if I persisted with the habit. Then once, when I was around eight, I attempted this feat for the first time in months to discover the couch could no longer take the impact of my increased weight. One end of the frame completely collapsed, and I tumbled on to the floor, utterly shocked. The next instant, though, I had remembered my mother was coming down the stairs behind me, and had braced myself for the most terrible dressing down. But my mother, looming over me, had burst out laughing. "Look at your face, Puffin!" she had exclaimed. "If you could only see your face!"

I had not been hurt at all, but when my mother had continued to laugh—and perhaps because I was still afraid of a scolding—I had begun to make the most of a pain I could feel in my ankle. My mother had then stopped her laughing and had helped me up gently. I remember her then walking me slowly round and round the hall, an arm around my shoulder, saying: "There now, that's better, isn't it? We'll just walk it off. There now, it's nothing."

I never was scolded over the incident and a few days later I came in to find the couch had been mended; but although I continued often to jump from the second or third step, I never again attempted a dive into the couch.

I took a few paces around the room, trying to work out the exact spot where the couch would have been. As I did so, I found I could conjure up only the haziest picture of what it had actually looked like—though I could recall quite vividly the feel of its silky fabric.

Then eventually I became conscious of the others in the room, and the fact that they were all watching me with gentle smiles. Morgan and the elderly Chinese man had been conferring quietly. Seeing me turn, Morgan took a step forward, cleared his throat and began the introductions.

He was obviously friendly with the family and reeled off the names without hesitation. As he did so, each of them gave a little bow and smile, touching hands together. Only the old lady at the end of the table, whom Morgan introduced with extra deference, went on gazing at me impassively. The family was called Lin— beyond this, I do not now remember any names—and it was Mr. Lin himself, the elderly, bulky gentleman, who from this point took charge.

"I trust, my good sir," he said in an English only slightly accented, "that it gives a warm feeling to return here again."

"Yes, it does." I gave a little laugh. "Yes. And it's a little strange also."

"But that is natural," Mr. Lin said. "Now please make yourself comfortable. Mr. Morgan tells me you have already dined. But as you see, we have prepared food for you. We did not know if you cared for Chinese cuisine. So we borrowed the cook of our English neighbour."

"But perhaps Mr. Banks isn't hungry."

This was said by one of the young men in suits. Then turning to me the latter continued: "My grandfather is rather the old-fashioned type. He gets very offended if a guest doesn't accept every piece of hospitality." The young man smiled broadly at the old man. "Please don't let him bully you, Mr. Banks."

"My grandson believes me to be an old-fashioned Chinese," Mr. Lin said, coming closer to me, the smile never leaving his face. "But the truth is, I am born and bred in Shanghai, here in the International Settlement. My parents were obliged to flee the Empress Dowager's forces, and take sanctuary here, in the foreigner's city, and I have grown up a Shanghailander through and through. My grandson here has no idea what life is like in the real China. He considers *me* old-fashioned! Ignore him, my dear sir. There is no need to worry about protocol in this house. If you do not wish to eat, then never mind. I will certainly not bully you."

"But you're all so kind," I said, perhaps a little distractedly, for in truth I was still trying to work out how the building had been altered.

Then suddenly the old lady said something in Mandarin. The young man who had addressed me before, then said:

"My grandmother says she thought you would never come. It was such a long wait. But now she's seen you, she's very happy you are here."

Even before he had finished translating, the old lady was talking again. This time, when she finished, the young man remained silent for a moment. He looked at his grandfather as though for guidance, then appeared to come to a decision.

"You must excuse Grandmother," he said. "She is sometimes a little eccentric."

The old lady, perhaps understanding the English, gestured impatiently for a translation. Finally the young man sighed and said:

"Grandmother says that until you came in this evening, she resented you. That is to say, she was angry that you are to take our home from us."

I looked at the young man, quite baffled, but now the old lady was talking again.

"She says that for a long time," her grandson translated, "she hoped you would stay away. She believed this home belonged to our family now. But tonight, seeing you in person, seeing the emotion in your eyes, she is able to understand. She now feels in her heart that the agreement is correct."

"The agreement? But surely . . ."

I allowed the words to fade in my mouth. For puzzled as I was, while the young man had been translating his grandmother's words, I had started to locate some vague recollection concerning some such arrangement regarding the old house and my eventual return to it. But as I say, my memory of it was only a very hazy one, and I sensed that by opening a discussion on the matter I would only embarrass myself. In any case, just at that moment Mr. Lin said:

"I fear we are all being most inconsiderate to Mr. Banks. Here we are, making him chatter to us, when in fact he must be longing to look about this house once more." Then turning to me with a kindly smile, he said: "Come with me, good sir. There will be time enough to talk to everyone later. Come this way and I will show you the house."

𝒻OR THE NEXT SEVERAL MINUTES, I followed Mr. Lin all around the building. Despite his age, my host showed little sign of infirmity; he carried his bulk steadily, if slowly, hardly ever pausing for breath. I pursued his dark gown and whispering slippers up and down narrow stairs, and along back corridors lit often only by a single lantern. He led me through areas that were bare and cobwebbed, past numerous neatly stacked wooden crates of rice wine. Elsewhere the house became sumptuous; there were beautiful screens and wall hangings, clusters of porcelain displayed within alcoves. Every so often, he would open a door, then stand back to let me pass. I entered various kinds of room, but—for some time at least—saw nothing at all familiar to me.

Then finally I stepped through a door and felt something tugging at my memory. It took a few seconds more, but I then recognised with a wave of emotion our old "library." It had been greatly altered: the ceiling was much higher, a wall had been knocked through to make the space L-shaped; and where there had once been double doors through into our dining room, there was now a partition against which were stacked more crates of rice wine. But it was unmistakably the same room where as a child I had done much of my homework.

I drifted further into the room, looking all around me. After a while I became aware of Mr. Lin regarding me and gave him a self-conscious smile. At which point, he said:

"No doubt much has been changed. Please accept my apologies. But you must understand, over eighteen years, which is how long we have lived here, a few alterations have been inevitable to meet the needs of my household and of my business. And I understand the occupants before us, and those before them, carried out extensive alterations. Most unfortunate, my good sir, but I suppose few could have foreseen that one day you and your parents . . ."

He trailed off, perhaps because he thought I was not listening, perhaps because like most Chinese, he was uncomfortable with apologies. I went on gazing about me for a while longer, then asked him:

"So this house, it's no longer owned by Morganbrook and Byatt?"

He looked astonished, then laughed. "Sir, I am the owner of this house."

I saw I had insulted him, and said hurriedly: "Yes, of course. I do beg your pardon."

"Don't worry, my good sir"—his genial smile had quickly returned—"it was not an unreasonable question. After all, when you and your dear parents lived here, that was no doubt the situation. But I believe that has long ceased to be. My good sir, if you will only consider how much Shanghai has changed over the years. Everything, everything has changed and changed again. All this"—he sighed and gestured about us—"by comparison these are small changes. There are parts of this city I once knew so well, places I would walk every day, I now go there and I know not which way to turn. Change, change all the time. And now the Japanese, they wish to make *their* changes here. The most terrible changes may yet overtake us. But one must not be pessimistic."

For a moment, we both stood there in silence, continuing to look about us. Then he said quietly:

"My family, of course, will be saddened to leave this house. My father died here. Two grandchildren were born here. But when my wife spoke earlier—and you must forgive her frankness, Mr. Banks—she did speak for us all. We will consider it a great honour and privilege to return this house to you and your parents. Now, my good sir, let us continue if we may."

I believe it was not long after that we climbed a carpeted staircase—one which certainly did not exist in my time—and stepped into a luxuriously furbished bedroom. There were rich fabrics, and lanterns casting a reddish glow.

"My wife's room," Mr. Lin said.

I could see it was a sanctuary, a cosy boudoir where the old lady probably whiled away most of her day. In the warm lantern light, I could make out a card table upon which a number of different sorts of game appeared to be in progress; a writing desk with a column of tiny gold-tasselled drawers running down one side; a large four-poster bed with layers of veil-like drapes. Elsewhere my gaze caught various fine ornaments, and items of amusement whose exact natures I could not guess.

"Madame must like this room," I said eventually. "I can see her world here."

"It suits her. But you mustn't concern yourself on her behalf, my good sir. We will find her another room she will come to love equally."

He had spoken to reassure me, but something fragile had entered his voice. He now drifted further into the room, over to a dressing table, and became absorbed by some small object there— perhaps a brooch. After several moments, he said quietly:

"She was very beautiful when she was younger. The most beautiful flower, my good sir. You cannot imagine. In this respect, I am like a Westerner in my heart. I have never wanted any wife but her. One wife, quite enough. Of course, I took others. I am Chinese, after all, even if I have lived all my life here in the foreigners' city. I felt obliged to take other wives. But she is the one I truly cared for. The others have all gone now, and she is left. I miss the others, but I'm glad, in my heart I'm glad that in our old age, it is just the two of us again." For a few seconds, he seemed to forget my presence. Then he turned to me and said: "This room. I wonder how you will come to use it. Pardon me, this is very impertinent. But do you think this room will be for your own good wife? Of course, I am aware that for many foreigners, however wealthy, husband and wife will share the same room. I wonder then if this room will go to yourself and your good wife. My curiosity, I realise, is most impertinent. But this room is very special for me. It is my hope that you will put it to special use."

"Yes . . ." I looked around it again carefully. Then I said: "Perhaps not my wife. My wife, you see, to speak frankly . . ." I realised that in this talk of a wife, I had had a picture of Sarah in my mind. Covering my embarrassment, I went on quickly: "What I mean, sir, is I'm not yet married. I have no wife. But I think this room will suit my mother."

"Ah yes. After all the inconveniences she has had to suffer, this room will be ideal for her. And your father? I wonder, will he share it with her in the Western manner? Please forgive my great intrusion."

"It's no intrusion, Mr. Lin. After all, by letting me in here, it is you who have allowed me great intimacy. You have every right to ask these questions. It's just that this is all rather sudden, and I've not yet had time fully to make my plans . . ."

I drifted into silence and went on gazing at the room. Then after a moment, I said to him: "Mr. Lin, I'm afraid this may upset you. But you've been more open and generous than I could ever have expected, and I feel you deserve my honesty. You said yourself just now, how inevitable it is that a house undergoes alteration whenever its occupants change. Well, sir, dear as these rooms are to you, I'm afraid that once my family are again living here, we will carry out our own alterations. This room too, I fear, will change beyond recognition."

Mr. Lin closed his eyes, and there was a heavy silence. I wondered if he would become angry, and for a second regretted being so honest with him. But then when he opened his eyes again, he was regarding me gently.

"Of course," he said, "it is quite natural. You will wish to restore this house to just the way it was when you were a boy. That is quite natural. My good sir, I understand it perfectly."

I thought about this for a moment, then said: "Well, actually, Mr. Lin, we would probably not turn it back exactly to what it was then. For one thing, as I remember it, there were many things we were unhappy about. My mother, for instance, never had her own study. With all her campaign work, a little bureau in the bedroom was never adequate. My father too wanted a little workshop for his woodwork. What I'm saying is that there's no need to turn back the clock just for the sake of it."

"That is most wise, Mr. Banks. And although you have not yet taken a wife, perhaps soon there will come the day when you have the needs of a wife and children to consider."

"That's certainly possible. Unfortunately, just at present, this question of a wife, in my case, Western customs notwithstanding . . ." I became very confused and stopped. But the old man nodded sagely, saying:

"Of course, in matters of the heart, things are never simple." Then he asked: "You wish for children, good sir? I wonder how many you will have."

"As a matter of fact, I already have a child. A young girl. Though she isn't really my daughter as such. She was an orphan and now she's in my care. I do look on her as a daughter."

I had not thought about Jennifer for some time, and mentioning her like this so unexpectedly caused a powerful feeling to well up within me. Images of her ran through my mind; I thought of her at her school, and wondered how she was, and what she had been doing that day.

I perhaps turned away to hide my emotions. In any case, when I next looked at him, Mr. Lin was nodding again.

"We Chinese are well used to such arrangements," he said. "Blood is important. But so is household. My father took in an orphan girl and she grew up with us as though she were my sister. I regarded her as such, though I knew always of her origins. When she died, in the cholera epidemic when I was still a young man, I felt as much grief as when my blood sisters passed away."

"If I may say so, Mr. Lin, it's a great pleasure to talk to you. It's rare to find someone so immediately understanding."

He gave a small bow, bringing his fingertips together before him. "When one has lived as long as I have, and through the turmoil of these years, one knows many joys and sadnesses. I hope your adopted daughter will be happy here. I wonder which room you will give her. But of course, forgive me! As you say, you will alter."

"In fact, one of the rooms we saw earlier would be ideal for Jennifer. It had a little wooden ledge running along the wall."

"She likes such a ledge?"

"Yes. For her things. And in fact there's one further person I shall be accommodating here in this house. I suppose she was officially a sort of servant, but in our household she was always much more. Her name is Mei Li."

"She was your *amah*, good sir?"

I nodded. "She would be older now and I'm sure she'd appreciate a rest from her work. Children can be very taxing. It was always my intention that when she was old, she'd go on living with us here."

"That is most kind-hearted of you. One so often hears of foreign families who throw out the *amah* once her charges are grown. Such women are often to be seen ending their days as street beggars."

I gave a laugh. "I hardly think that could ever happen to Mei Li. In fact, the very thought is quite absurd. In any case, as I say, she'll be living here with us. As soon as my task is accomplished, I'll turn my mind to locating her. I don't imagine it will be so difficult."

"And tell me, good sir, will you give her a room in the servants' quarters or with the family?"

"With the family, certainly. My parents might take a dim view of that. But then really, I'm the head of the household now."

Mr. Lin smiled. "According to your custom, that will certainly be so. For us Chinese, fortunately for me, the old are permitted to go on ruling the house well into their foolish years."

The old man laughed to himself and turned towards the door. I was about to follow, but just at that moment—quite suddenly and very vividly—I found another memory returning to me. I have thought about it since, and I have no idea why it was that particular recollection rather than any other. It was of an occasion when I was six or seven, when my mother and I had raced each other along a stretch of lawn. I do not know where exactly this was; I would suppose now we were in one of the parks—perhaps Jessfield Park—for I can remember a trellised fence beside where we ran, covered in climbing flowers and creepers. It was a warm day, but not especially sunny. I had impulsively challenged my mother to the race, to some marker a short distance before us, as a way of showing off to her my improved running ability. I had assumed completely that I would outpace her, and that she would then express, in her usual way, her delighted surprise at this latest manifestation of my maturing prowess. But to my annoyance she had kept up with me all the way, laughing as she went, although I was running with all my strength. I do not remember which of us actually "won," but I still recall my fury at her, and my sense that I had suffered a grave injustice. It was this incident that came back to me that night as I stood in the snugly sheltered atmosphere of Madam Lin's bedroom. Or rather, a fragment of it: a memory of me pushing into the wind with all my might; my mother's laughing presence beside me; the rustling of her skirt, and my rising frustration.

"Sir," I said to my host, "I wonder if I may ask you. You say you've lived all your life here in the Settlement. I wonder then if during that time you ever met my mother."

"I never had the good fortune to meet her in person," Mr. Lin said. "But of course, I knew of her, and of her great campaign. I admired her, like all decent-minded people. I am sure she is a fine lady. And I've heard it said she is very beautiful."

"I suppose she might be. One never thinks about whether one's mother is beautiful."

"Oh, I've heard it said she is the most beautiful Englishwoman in Shanghai."

"I suppose she might be. But of course, she'll be older now."

"Certain kinds of beauty never fade. My wife"—he gestured at the room—"she is as beautiful to me now as the day I married her."

When he said this, I suddenly felt as though I were intruding, and this time it was I who made the first move to leave.

I DO NOT REMEMBER a great deal more about my visit to the house that evening. Perhaps we stayed another hour, talking and eating with the family around the table. In any case, I know I parted from the Lin family on the best of terms. It was during the journey back, however, that Morgan and I rather fell out.

It was probably my fault. I was by that stage tired and somewhat overwrought. We had been travelling through the night for a while in silence, and my mind had perhaps begun to drift back to the immense task before me. For I remember I said to Morgan, quite out of the blue:

"Look, you've been here a few years now. Tell me, have you come across a certain Inspector Kung?"

"Inspector Kung? Policeman or something?"

"When I was a child here, Inspector Kung was something of a legend. As a matter of fact, he was the officer originally in charge of my parents' case."

To my surprise, I heard Morgan beside me give a guffaw. Then he said:

"Kung? *Old Man* Kung? Yes, of course, he used to be a police inspector. Well then, it's no wonder nothing got sorted out at the time."

His tone took me aback, and I said rather coldly: "In those days, Inspector Kung was the most revered detective in Shanghai, if not the whole of China."

"Well, he still has something of a name for himself, I can tell you. Old Man Kung. Well I never."

"I'm glad at least to hear he's still in the city. Do you have any idea where I'd find him?"

"Simplest way's just to wander around Frenchtown any night after dark. Bound to come across him sooner or later. You usually see him in a heap on the pavement. Or if he's been let into some hole of a bar, he'll be snoring away in a dark corner."

"Are you implying Inspector Kung's become a drunk?"

"Drink. Opium. Usual Chinaman stuff. But he's a character. Tells stories about his glory days and people give him coins."

"I think you're thinking of the wrong man, old fellow."

"Don't think so, old chap. Old Man Kung. So he really was a policeman. I always fancied he was making all that up. Most of his stories *are* preposterous. What's the matter, old fellow?"

"The trouble with you, Morgan, is you keep muddling things. First you muddle up me and Bigglesworth. Now you get Inspector Kung muddled with some worthless ragamuffin. Being out here's got your head all soft, old man."

"Now look here, pipe down a bit. What I'm telling you, you'll hear from anyone else you care to ask. And I rather take exception to your comments. Nothing soft about my head."

We may have returned to slightly more civil terms by the time he dropped me off at the Cathay, but our parting was distinctly cold and I have not seen Morgan again since. As for Inspector Kung, it had been my intention after that evening to seek him out without delay, but for whatever reason—perhaps I feared Morgan might have been telling the truth—I have never made it a priority—at least, not until yesterday, when my search through the police archives threw up the inspector's name again in the most dramatic fashion.

This morning, incidentally, when I mentioned Inspector Kung in passing to MacDonald, his reaction was not dissimilar to Morgan's that night, and I suspect here was yet another reason for my impatience with MacDonald as we faced each other in his airless little office overlooking the consulate grounds. All the same, with a little more effort, I know I could have made a much better job of it. My central error this morning was to allow him to goad me into losing my temper. At one point, I fear, I was practically shouting at him.

"Mr. MacDonald, it simply isn't enough to leave things to what you insist on calling my 'powers!' I have no such 'powers!' I am a mere mortal, and I can only achieve my goals if I am given the sort of basic assistance that allows me to go about my work. I've not asked much of you, sir. Hardly anything at all! And what I've asked, I've put to you very clearly. I wish to speak to this communist informer. Just speak with him, a short interview will suffice. I made this request to you in the clearest terms. I fail to understand why arrangements still have not been made. Why is that, sir? Why is that? What can possibly be impeding you?"

"But look here, old fellow, this is hardly a matter for my office. If you wish, I'll get the police commissioner over to see you. Mind you, even then, you see, I'm not at all sure you'll get anywhere useful. It's not they who have the Yellow Snake . . ."

"I fully appreciate it's the Chinese government who are keeping the Yellow Snake under their protection. That is why I have come to you and not to the police. I'm aware that in a matter of this magnitude, the police are an irrelevance."

"I'll see what I can do, old chap. But you must understand, this isn't a British colony. We can't go ordering the Chinese about. But I'll talk to someone in the appropriate office. Don't bet on anything happening too quickly though. Chiang Kai-shek's had informers before, but never one with quite such extensive knowledge of the Reds' network. Chiang would lose a good few battles with the Japs before allowing anything to happen to this Yellow Snake chap. As far as Chiang is concerned, you see, the real enemy's not the Japs but the Reds."

I gave a loud sigh. "Mr. MacDonald, I do not care about Chiang Kai-shek or his priorities. Just now, I have a case to solve, and I would like you to do whatever you can to secure an interview for me with this informer. I am putting it to you personally, and if all my efforts come to nothing because this simple request is not granted, I shan't hesitate to let it be known that it was you I came to . . ."

"Now really, old fellow, please! There's no need to take this sort of line! No need at all! We're all friends here. We all wish you to succeed. Take my word for it, we really do. Look here, I've said I'll do all I can. I'll talk to a few people, you know, people in that line of work. I'll talk to them, tell them how strongly you feel. But you have to understand, there's only so much we can do with the Chinese." Then he leant forward and said confidingly: "You know, you might try the French. They have a lot of little understandings with Chiang. You know, of the off-the-record sort. The kind of thing we wouldn't touch. That's the French for you."

Perhaps there is something in MacDonald's suggestion. Perhaps I might indeed get some useful help from the French authorities. But frankly, since this morning, I have not given this option much thought. It is clear to me that MacDonald, for reasons which as yet remain unclear, is prevaricating, and that once he has recognised the overwhelming importance of granting my request, he will do whatever is necessary. Unfortunately, it is probable I handled this morning's meeting so incompetently I will have to tackle him one further time. It is not a prospect to which I particularly look forward, but at least the next time my approach will be different, and he will not find it so easy to send me away empty-handed.

PART SIX

CATHAY HOTEL, SHANGHAI,
20TH OCTOBER 1937

$\mathcal{I}$ KNEW WE WERE somewhere in the French Concession, not far from the harbour, but otherwise I had lost my bearings. The chauffeur had for some time been steering us through tiny alleys quite unsuitable for a car, sounding his horn repeatedly to get pedestrians out of our way, and I had begun to feel ridiculous, like a man who has brought a horse into a house. But eventually the car stopped, and the driver, opening my door, pointed out the entrance to the Inn of Morning Happiness.

I was led inside by a thin Chinese man with one eye. What comes back to me today is an overall impression of low ceilings, dark damp wood and the usual smell of sewage. But the establishment seemed clean enough; at one point we stepped around three old women on their knees, diligently scrubbing the floorboards. Somewhere near the rear of the building, we came to a corridor with a long row of doors. I was reminded of stables, or even a prison, but these cubicles, it turned out, contained the inn's guests. The one-eyed man knocked on one of the doors, then opened it before any reply had been given.

I stepped into a small narrow space. There was no window, but the partitions did not go right up to the ceiling—the last foot or so being wire mesh—thus allowing light and air to circulate. For all that, the cubicle was stuffy and dark, and even when the afternoon sun broke brightly outside, it resulted only in the mesh throwing odd patterns over the floor. The figure lying on the bed appeared to be asleep, but then moved his legs when I took up a position in the gap between the bed and the wall. The one-eyed man mumbled something and vanished, the door closing behind him.

Former Inspector Kung looked to be little more than bones. The skin on his face and neck was shrivelled and spotted; his mouth hung open slackly; a bare, stick-like leg was protruding from the coarse blanket, though on his top half I saw he had on a surprisingly white undershirt. He did not at first make any attempt to sit up, and appeared only vaguely to register my presence. And yet he did not seem directly under the sway of opium or alcohol, and eventually, as I continued to state who I was and my purpose in coming to see him, he became more coherent, and began to show signs of courtesy.

"I'm sorry, sir"—his English, when it came, was fluent enough— "I have no tea." He began to mumble something in Mandarin, shuffling his legs about beneath his blanket. Then he appeared to remember himself again and said: "Please forgive me. I'm not well. But soon, I will recover my good health."

"I sincerely hope so," I said. "After all, you were one of the finest detectives ever to serve in the SMP."

"Really? How kind of you to say so, sir. Yes, perhaps I was a good officer once." With a sudden effort, he raised himself, and placed his bare feet gingerly down on to the floor. Perhaps out of modesty, perhaps because he was cold, he kept his blanket gathered around his middle. "But in the end," he went on, "this city defeats you. Every man betrays his friend. You trust someone, and he turns out to be in the pay of a gangster. The government are gangsters too. How is a detective to do his duty in a place like this? I might have a cigarette for you. Would you care for a cigarette?"

"No, thank you. Sir, let me just say this. When I was a boy, I followed your exploits with great admiration."

"When you were a boy?"

"Yes, sir. The boy next door and I"—I gave a little laugh—"we used to play at being you. You were . . . you were our hero."

"Is that so?" The old man shook his head and smiled. "Is that so indeed. Well then, I am all the more sorry I cannot offer you anything. No tea. No cigarette."

"Actually, sir, you may be able to offer me something much more important. I came to you today because I believe you may be able to provide a vital clue. In the spring of 1915, there was a case you investigated, a shooting incident in a restaurant called Wu Cheng Lou in Foochow Road. Three people died and several more were injured. You arrested the two men responsible. In the police records, the matter is referred to as the Wu Cheng Lou Shooting Incident. It's many years ago now, I realise, but Inspector Kung, I wonder if you remember this case?"

Behind me, from perhaps two or three rooms away, there came the sound of frantic coughing. Inspector Kung remained deep in thought, then said: "I remember the Wu Cheng Lou case very well. It was one of my more satisfying moments. I sometimes think about that case, even these days, lying here in this bed."

"Then perhaps you'll remember that you interrogated a suspect whom you subsequently established was unconnected with the shooting. According to the records, the man's name was Chiang Wei. You interrogated him concerning the Wu Cheng Lou, but he instead made some other quite unrelated confessions."

Though his body remained a sagging sack of bones, the old detective's eyes were now full of life. "That's correct," he said. "He had nothing to do with the shooting. But he was afraid and he began to talk. He confessed everything. He confessed, I remember, to having been a member of a kidnapping gang some years earlier."

"Excellent, sir! That's just as it's recorded in the files. Now,

Inspector Kung, this is very important. This man gave you some addresses. Addresses of houses the gang had used to hold their captives."

Inspector Kung had been gazing at the flies buzzing around the wire mesh near the ceiling, but now his eyes turned slowly to where I was standing. "That is so," he said quietly. "But Mr. Banks, we had all those houses checked thoroughly. The kidnappings he talked of were years in the past. We found nothing suspicious in those houses."

"I know, Inspector Kung, you would have done everything duty required of you most thoroughly. But of course, you were investigating the shooting. It would be perfectly natural if you didn't expend your energy on such a side issue. What I'm suggesting is that if powerful people had gone to some lengths to prevent you searching one of those houses, you would perhaps not have persisted."

The old detective was deep in thought again. He said finally: "There was one house. I remember now. My men brought me reports. All the other houses, seven of them, I received reports. I remember it troubled me at the time. One last house, no report. My men were being prevented in some way. Yes, I remember wondering about it. A detective's nose. You will know what I mean, sir."

"And that remaining house. You never did see a report on it."

"Correct, sir. But as you say, it was not a great priority. You understand, the Wu Cheng Lou was a large matter. It had caused much outrage. The hunt for the killers had gone on for weeks."

"And I believe it had defeated two of your more senior colleagues."

Inspector Kung smiled. "As I have said, it was a most satisfying moment in my career. I came on to the case when others had failed. The city was talking of nothing else. I was able after a few days to apprehend the killers."

"I read the records. I was filled with admiration."

But now the old man was staring at me intently. Eventually he said slowly: "That house. The house my men failed to go to. That house. You are saying . . . ?"

"Yes. It's my belief that is where my parents are being held."

"I see." He fell silent for a time, digesting this colossal idea.

"There's no question of negligence on your part," I said. "Let me say again, I read the reports with great admiration. Your men didn't get to the house because they were obstructed by persons in the higher echelons of the police force. People we now know were in the pay of criminal organisations."

The coughing had started up again. Inspector Kung remained silent for a moment longer, then looked up at me again and said slowly: "You've come to ask me. You've come to ask if I can help you find this house."

"Unfortunately, the archives are in chaos. It's a disgrace how things have been run in this city. Papers have been misfiled, others lost altogether. In the end, I decided I'd do better if I came here to you. To ask you, unlikely though it is, if you remember. Something, anything about that house."

"That house. Let me try to remember." The old man closed his eyes in concentration, but then after a time, he shook his head. "The Wu Cheng Lou shooting. It is over twenty years ago. I am sorry. I can remember nothing about this house."

"Please try and remember something, sir. Do you recall even which district it was in? Whether for instance it was in the International Settlement?"

He thought for another moment, then shook his head again. "It is a long time ago. And my head, it doesn't work in a normal way. Sometimes I remember nothing, not even of the day before. But I shall try and remember. Perhaps tomorrow, perhaps the next day, I shall wake up and remember something. Mr. Banks, I am so sorry. But just now, no, I remember nothing."

IT WAS EVENING by the time I returned to the International Settlement. I believe I spent an hour or so in my room, going through my notes once again, trying to put behind me the disappointment of my meeting with the old inspector. I did not go down to supper until after eight, when I took my usual corner table in that splendid dining room. I remember I did not have much of an appetite that evening, and was about to abandon my main course and return to my work when the waiter brought in Sarah's note.

I have it here now. It is no more than a scribble on unlined paper, the upper edge torn off. It is doubtful whether she gave the words much thought; it simply asks me to meet her at once on the half-landing between the third and fourth floors of the hotel. Looking at it again now, its connection with that small incident at Mr. Tony Keswick's house a week previously seems all too obvious; that is to say, Sarah probably would not have written the note at all had it not been for what took place between us then. Oddly enough, though, when the waiter first presented it to me, I failed to make any such association, and I sat there for some moments, quite mystified as to why she should summon me in such a way.

I should say here that by this point I had run into her a further three times since the night at Lucky Chance House. On two of these occasions, we had seen each other only fleetingly in the presence of others, and little had passed between us. On the third occasion too—the night of the dinner at the home of Mr. Keswick, the chairman of Jardine Matheson—I suppose we were again in a public place, and exchanged barely a word; yet, with hindsight, our encounter there could well be viewed as some sort of important turning point.

I had turned up a little late that evening, and by the time I was shown into Mr. Keswick's vast conservatory, upwards of sixty guests were already taking their places at the several tables situated among the foliage and trailing vines. I spotted Sarah on the far side of the room—Sir Cecil was not present—but I could see she too was searching for her seat, and so made no attempt to approach her.

It appears to be a Shanghai custom at such events for guests, as soon as dessert has been served—even before they have had time properly to eat it—to abandon the original seating plan and mingle freely. No doubt then, it was in my mind that once this point came along, I might go over and exchange a few words with Sarah. However, when dessert finally appeared, I was unable to get away from the woman seated beside me, who wished to explain in some detail the political position in Indo-China. Then no sooner had I extricated myself from her than our host stood up to announce that the time had come for "the turns." He proceeded to introduce the first performer—a willowy lady who, emerging from a table behind me, went to the front and began to recite an amusing poem, evidently composed by herself.

She was followed by a man who sang unaccompanied a few verses of Gilbert and Sullivan, and I surmised that the majority of those around me had come ready to perform. Guests went up one after another, sometimes in twos and threes; there were madrigals, comic routines. The tone was invariably frivolous, sometimes even bawdy.

Then a large red-faced man—a director of the Hong Kong and Shanghai Bank, I learnt later—made his way to the front wearing a kind of tunic over his dinner jacket, and began to read from a scroll a monologue satirising various aspects of Shanghai life. Almost all the references—to individuals, to the bathroom arrangements at particular clubs, to incidents that had occurred on recent paper chases—were entirely lost on me, but very quickly every section of the room became filled with laughter. At this point I looked around for Sarah, and saw her sitting over in a corner amidst a group of ladies, laughing as heartily as any of them. The woman beside her, who clearly had had a fair amount to drink, was roaring with almost indecent abandon.

The red-faced man's performance had been going for perhaps five minutes—during which time the level of hilarity seemed only to rise—when he delivered a particularly effective volley of three or four lines which set the room virtually howling. It was at this point that I happened to glance over once more to Sarah. At first the scene appeared much as it had before: there was Sarah, laughing helplessly amidst her companions. If I went on watching her for several more seconds, it was simply because I was rather surprised that after barely a year, she was already so intimate with Shanghai society to the extent that these obscure jokes could reduce her to such a state. And it was then, as I was gazing at her, pondering this point, that I suddenly realised she was not laughing at all; that she was not, as I had supposed, wiping away tears of laughter, but was in fact weeping. For a moment I went on staring at her, unable quite to credit my eyes. Then, as the uproar continued, I rose quietly and moved through the crowd. After a little manoeuvring, I found myself standing behind her, and now there was no further doubt. Amidst all the gaiety, Sarah was crying uncontrollably.

I had approached from behind, so that when I offered her my handkerchief, she gave a start. Then looking up at me, she fixed me—for perhaps as long as four or five seconds—with a searching gaze in which gratitude was mixed with something like a question. I inclined my head to read better her look, but then she had taken my handkerchief and turned back towards the red-faced man. And when the next burst of laughter seized the room, Sarah, too, with an impressive show of will, let out a laugh, even as she pressed the handkerchief to her eyes.

Conscious that I might draw unwanted attention to her, I then made my way back to my seat, and indeed, did not go near her again that evening other than to exchange rather formal goodnights with her in the entrance hall alongside the many other guests taking their leave of one another.

But I suppose, for a few days afterwards, I entertained a vague expectation of hearing something from her concerning what had occurred. It is, then, a measure of how much I had become engrossed in my investigations that by the time that note was brought to me in the dining room of the Cathay Hotel, I failed to make any connection with the earlier incident, and made my way up the grand staircase, wondering why it was she wished to see me.

What Sarah described as the "half-landing" is in fact a substantial area strewn with armchairs, occasional tables and potted palms. In the morning particularly, with the great windows open and the ceiling fans whirring, I imagine it is a pleasant enough place for a guest to read a newspaper and take some coffee. At night, though, it has a rather abandoned atmosphere; perhaps owing to the shortages, there is no lighting other than that coming from the staircase, and whatever leaks in through the windows from the Bund down below. On that particular evening, the area was deserted aside from Sarah, whose figure I could see silhouetted against the huge panes, gazing out at the night sky. As I made my way towards her, I knocked into a chair, and the sound made her turn.

"I thought there'd be a moon," she said. "But there isn't. There aren't even any shells being fired tonight."

"Yes. It's been quiet the last few nights."

"Cecil says the soldiers on both sides are exhausted for now."

"I dare say."

"Christopher, come over here. It's all right, I'm not going to do anything to you. But we have to talk more quietly."

I moved closer till I was beside her. I could now see the Bund below, and the line of lights marking the waterfront promenade.

"I've arranged everything," she said quietly. "It wasn't easy, but it's all done now."

"You've done what exactly?"

"Everything. Papers, boats, everything. I can't stay here any more. I tried my best, and I'm so tired now. I'm going away."

"I see. And Cecil. Does he know of your intentions?"

"It won't come entirely as a surprise to him. But I suppose it'll be a shock, all the same. Are *you* shocked, Christopher?"

"No, not really. From what I'd observed, I could see something like this might be on the cards. But before you take such a drastic step, are you sure there aren't . . . ?"

"Oh, I've thought of everything there is to think about it. It's no good. Even if Cecil were willing to go back to England tomorrow. Besides, he's lost so much money here. He's determined not to leave until he's won it all back."

"I can see this trip out here's rather fallen short of your hopes. I'm sorry."

"It's hardly just the trip out here." She gave a laugh, then went quiet. After a moment she said: "I tried to love Cecil. I tried very hard. He's not a bad man. You probably think he is, the way you've seen him here. But that's not how he always was. And I realise a lot of it's to do with me. What he needed at this stage of his life was a good rest. But then I came along and he felt he had to do a little more. That was my fault. When we came out here, he did try at first, tried awfully hard. But it was beyond him, and I think that's what it was, that's what broke him. Perhaps once I've gone, he'll be able to pull himself together again."

"But where will you go? Will you return to England?"

"Just now, there's not enough money to return. I'm going to Macao. Then after that, I shall have to see. Anything might happen then. In fact, that's why I wanted to talk with you. Christopher, I'll confess, I'm rather frightened. I don't want to go out there all by myself. I did wonder if you'd go with me."

"Do you mean go with you to Macao? Go with you tomorrow?"

"Yes. Go with me to Macao tomorrow. We can decide after that where to go next. If you wanted to, we could just drift around the South China Sea for a while. Or we could go to South America, run away like thieves in the night. Wouldn't that be fun?"

I suppose I was surprised when I heard her utter these words; but what I remember now, overwhelming anything else, was an almost tangible sense of relief. Indeed, for a second or two I experienced the sort of giddiness one might when coming suddenly out into the light and fresh air after being trapped a long time in some dark chamber. It was as though this suggestion of hers—which for all I knew she had thrown out on an impulse—carried with it a huge authority, something that brought me a kind of dispensation I had never dared hope for.

Hardly had this feeling swept over me, however, than I suppose another part of me grew quickly alert to the possibility of this being some test she had set for me. For I remember that when I at last responded, it was to say:

"The difficulty is my work here. I'll have to finish here first. After all, the whole world's on the brink of catastrophe. What would people think of me if I abandoned them all at this stage? Come to that, what would *you* think of me?"

"Oh, Christopher, we're both as bad as each other. We've got to stop thinking like that. Otherwise there'll be nothing for either of us, just more of what we've had all these years. Just more loneliness, more days with nothing in our lives except some whatever-it-is telling us we haven't done enough yet. We have to put that all behind us now. Leave your work, Christopher. You've spent enough of your life already on all of that. Let's go away tomorrow, let's not waste a single day more, let's go before it's too late for us."

"Too late for what, exactly?"

"Too late for . . . oh, I don't know. All I know is that I've wasted all these years looking for something, a sort of trophy I'd get only if I really, really did enough to deserve it. But I don't want it any more, I want something else now, something warm and sheltering, something I can turn to, regardless of what I do, regardless of who I become. Something that will just be *there*, always, like tomorrow's sky. That's what I want now, and I think it's what you should want too. But it *will* be too late soon. We'll become too set to change. If we don't take our chance now, another may never come for either of us. Christopher, what are you doing to that poor plant?"

Indeed, I realised I had been absent-mindedly stripping leaves off a palm standing next to us and depositing them on to the carpet.

"I'm sorry"—I let out a laugh—"rather destructive." Then I said: "Even if you're right, what you were saying just now, even then, it's not so easy for me. Because, you see, there's Jennifer."

When I said this, a vivid image came back to me of the last time she and I had spoken, the time we had said our goodbyes in the pleasant little sitting room at the rear of her school, the sunshine of a gentle English spring afternoon falling across the oak-panelled walls. I suddenly remembered again her face as she first took in what I was saying, the thoughtful nod she gave as she thought it over, and then those quite unexpected words she came out with.

"You see, there's Jennifer," I said again, aware that I was in danger of drifting off into a daydream. "Even now, she'll be waiting for me."

"But I've thought of that. I've thought about it all very carefully. I just know she and I can be friends. More than friends. The three of us, we could be, well, a little family, just like any other family. I've thought about it, Christopher, it could be wonderful for us all. We could send for her, as soon as we've settled on a plan. We might even go back to Europe, to Italy, say, and she could join us there. I know I could be a mother to her, Christopher, I'm sure I could."

I went on thinking quietly for a moment, then said: "Very well."

"What do you mean, Christopher, 'very well?' "

"I mean, yes, I'll go with you. I'll go with you, we'll do as you say. Yes, you might be right. Jennifer, us, everything, it might turn out well."

As soon as I said this, I could feel a massive weight lifting off me, so much so that I may well have let out a loud sigh. Sarah, meanwhile, had come another step closer, and for a second gazed deep into my face. I even thought she would kiss me, but she seemed to check herself at the last moment, and said instead:

"Then listen. Listen carefully, we must do this correctly. Pack no more than one suitcase. And don't send on any trunks. There'll be some money waiting for us in Macao, so we can buy what we need there. I'll send someone to come and get you, a driver, tomorrow afternoon at half past three. I'll see to it he's someone to be trusted, but all the same, don't tell him anything you don't need to. He'll bring you to where I'll be waiting. Christopher, you look as if something heavy just hit you on the head. You're not going to let me down, are you?"

"No, no. I'll be ready. Half past three tomorrow. Don't worry, I'll . . . I'll follow you anywhere, wherever you want to go in the world."

Perhaps it was simply an impulse; perhaps it was the memory of how we had parted that night we had brought Sir Cecil back from the gaming house; in any case, I suddenly reached forward, grasped one of her hands in both of mine, and kissed it. After that, I believe I looked up, still clutching her hand, uncertain what to do next; it is even possible I let out an awkward giggle. In the end, she freed the hand gently and touched my cheek.

"Thank you, Christopher," she said quietly. "Thank you for agreeing. Everything suddenly feels so different. But you'd better go now, before someone sees us here. Go on, off you go."

CHAPTER 17

T WENT TO BED that night somewhat preoccupied, but awoke the next morning to find a kind of tranquillity had come over me. It was as though a heavy burden had been removed, and when, as I dressed, I thought again of my new situation, I realised I was rather excited.

Much of that morning has now become a haze to me. What I recall is that I became seized by the idea that I should complete, in the time remaining to me, as many as possible of the tasks I had planned for the next few days; that to do otherwise would be less than conscientious. The obvious illogic of this position somehow failed to trouble me, and after breakfast, I set about my work with much urgency, rushing up and down staircases, and urging my drivers on through the crowded city streets. And although today it makes little sense to me, I have to say I took considerable pride in being able to sit down to lunch a little after two o'clock having more or less fulfilled all I had set out to do.

And yet at the same time, when I look back on that day, I have the overwhelming impression I remained peculiarly detached from my activities. As I hurried around the International Settlement talking with many of the city's most prominent citizens, there was a part of me virtually laughing at the earnest way they tried to answer my questions, at the pathetic way they tried to be of help. For the truth is, the longer I had been in Shanghai, the more I had come to despise the so-called leaders of this community. Almost every day my investigations had revealed yet another piece of negligence, corruption or worse on their part down the years. And yet in all the days since my arrival, I had not come across one instance of honest shame, a single acknowledgement that were it not for the prevarications, the short-sightedness, often the downright dishonesty of those left in charge, the situation would never have reached its present level of crisis. At one point that morning, I found myself at the Shanghai Club, meeting with three eminent members of the "elite." And faced anew with their hollow pomposity, their continued denial of their own culpability in the whole sorry affair, I felt an exhilaration at the prospect of ridding my life of such people once and for all. Indeed, at such moments, I felt an utter certainty that I had come to the right decision; that the assumption shared by virtually everyone here—that it was somehow my sole responsibility to resolve the crisis—was not only unfounded, but worthy of the highest contempt. I pictured the astonishment that would soon appear on these same faces at the news of my departure—the outrage and panic that would rapidly follow—and I will admit such thoughts brought me much satisfaction.

Then, as I continued my lunch, I found myself thinking of my last meeting with Jennifer that sunny afternoon at her school: of the two of us, in the prefects' room, sitting awkwardly in our armchairs, the sun playing on the oak panelling, the grass leading down to the lake visible in the windows behind her. She had listened in silence as I had explained, to the best of my ability, the necessity of my going away, the overwhelming importance of the task awaiting me in Shanghai. I had paused at several points, expecting her to ask questions, or at least to make some comment. But each time, she had given a serious nod, and waited for me to continue. In the end, when I realised I had started to repeat myself, I had come to a halt and said to her:

"So, Jenny. What do you have to say?"

I do not know what I had expected. But after gazing at me for another moment with a look devoid of any anger, she had replied:

"Uncle Christopher, I realise I'm not very good at anything. But that's because I'm rather young still. Once I'm older, and it might not be so long now, I'll be able to help you. I'll be able to help you, I promise you I will. So while you're away, would you please remember? Remember that I'm here, in England, and that I'll help you when you come back?"

It was not quite what I had expected, and though often since arriving here I have thought over these words of hers, I am still not sure what she meant to convey to me that day. Was she implying that, for all I had just been saying to her, I was unlikely to succeed in my mission in Shanghai? That I would have to return to England and continue my work for yet many more years? Just as likely, these were simply the words of a confused child, trying hard not to display her upset, and it is pointless to subject them to any sort of scrutiny. For all that, I found myself yet again pondering our last meeting as I sat over my lunch that afternoon in the hotel conservatory.

It was while I was finishing my coffee that the concierge came to tell me I was wanted urgently on the telephone. I was directed to a booth on the landing just outside, and after a little confusion with the operator, heard a voice which was vaguely familiar to me.

"Mr. Banks? Mr. Banks? Mr. Banks, at last I have remembered."

I remained silent, fearing if I said anything at all I would jeopardise our plans. But then the voice said:

"Mr. Banks? Can you hear me? I have remembered something important. About the house we could not search."

I realised it was Inspector Kung; his voice, though croaky, sounded startlingly rejuvenated.

"Inspector, excuse me. You took me by surprise. Please, tell me what you've remembered."

"Mr. Banks. Sometimes, you know, when I indulge in a pipe, it helps me remember. Many things I have long forgotten drift before my eyes. So I thought very well, one last time, I shall go back to the pipe. And I remembered something the suspect told us. *The house we could not search. It is directly opposite the house of a man called Yeh Chen.*"

"Yeh Chen? Who is that?"

"I do not know. Many of the poorer people, they do not use street addresses. They talk of landmarks. The house we could not search. It is opposite Yeh Chen's house."

"Yeh Chen. Are you sure that was the name?"

"Yes, I'm sure. It came back very clearly."

"Is that a common name? How many people in Shanghai are likely to have that name?"

"Fortunately there is one further detail the suspect gave us. This Yeh Chen is a blind man. The house you seek is opposite that of Yeh Chen the blind man. Of course, he may have moved house, or passed away. But if you could discover where this man lived at the time of our investigation . . ."

"Of course, Inspector. Why, this is immensely useful."

"I am glad. I thought you would find it so."

"Inspector, I cannot thank you enough."

I had become aware of the time, and when I put down the phone, I did not return to my lunch, but went straight upstairs to my room to pack.

I recall a strange sense of unreality coming over me as I contemplated which items to take away. At one stage, I sat down on the bed and stared out at the sky visible through my window. It struck me as most curious how, only a day earlier, the piece of information I had just received would have constituted something utterly central to my life. But here I was, turning it over casually in my head, and already it felt like something consigned to a past era, something I need not remember if I did not wish to.

I must have completed my packing with time to spare, for when the knock came on my door at half past three precisely, I had been sitting in my chair waiting for a good while. I opened the door to a young Chinese man, perhaps not even twenty, dressed in a gown, his hat in his hand.

"I am your driver, sir," he announced softly. "If you have suitcase, I will carry."

AS THE YOUNG MAN steered the motor car away from the Cathay Hotel, I stared out at the busy crowds of Nanking Road in the afternoon sunshine, and felt I was watching them from a vast distance. I then settled myself in my seat, content to leave everything in the hands of my driver, who despite his youth appeared assured and competent. I was tempted to ask what his connection was with Sarah, but then remembered her caution about speaking any more than necessary. I thus remained silent, and soon found my thoughts turning to Macao and some photographs I had seen of the place many years ago in the British Museum.

Then after we had been travelling for perhaps ten minutes, I suddenly leant forward to the young man and said: "I say, excuse me. This is something of a long shot. But do you happen to know of anyone called Yeh Chen?"

The young man did not take his gaze from the traffic before him and I was about to repeat my question when he said:

"Yeh Chen. Blind actor?"

"Yes. Well, I know he's blind, though I didn't know he was an actor."

"Not famous actor. Yeh Chen. He was actor once, many years ago, when I was boy."

"Do you mean . . . you know him?"

"Not know him. But I know who he is. You interest in Yeh Chen, sir?"

"No, no. Not especially. Someone just happened to mention him to me. It really doesn't matter."

I did not say anything else to the young man for the remainder of our journey. We travelled down a baffling series of little alleys and I had quite lost any sense of where we were by the time he pulled up in a quiet back street.

The young man opened my door and gave me my suitcase.

"That shop," he said, pointing. "With phonograph."

Across the street was a small shop with a grimy window, within which indeed a phonograph was displayed. I could see too a sign in English reading: "Gramophone Records. Piano Rolls. Manuscripts." Glancing up and down the street, I saw that apart from two rickshawmen squatting beside their vehicles and exchanging banter, the young man and I were alone. I picked up the suitcase and was about to cross the street, when something made me say to him:

"I wonder, could you wait here a little?"

The young man looked puzzled. "Lady Medhurst say only to bring you here."

"Yes, yes. But *I'm* asking you now, you see. I'd like you to wait just a little longer, just in case I need your services further. Of course, I may not need you. But you know, just in case. Look here"—I reached into my jacket and took out some bills—"look, I'll make it worth your while."

The young man's face flushed with anger, and he spun away from the money as though I were proffering something quite repulsive. He sullenly got back into the car and slammed his door.

I saw I had made a miscalculation of some sort, but at that moment could not be bothered to worry about it. Besides, for all his anger, the young man had not started up the engine. I stuffed my money back into my jacket, picked up the suitcase again and crossed the street.

Inside, the shop was very cramped. The afternoon sun was streaming in, but somehow only a few dusty patches were lit by it. To one side was an upright piano with discoloured keys, and several gramophone records displayed without their sleeves along the music stand. I could see not only dust but cobwebs on the records. Elsewhere there were odd pieces of thick velvet—they appeared to be off-cuts from theatre curtains—nailed up on the walls, together with photographs of opera singers and dancers. I had perhaps expected Sarah to be standing there, but the only person present was a spindly European with a dark pointed beard sitting behind the counter.

"Good afternoon," he said in a Germanic accent, glancing up from a ledgerbook spread before him. Then looking me up and down carefully, he asked: "You are English?"

"Yes, I am. Good afternoon."

"We have some records from England. For example, we have a recording of Mimi Johnson singing 'I Only Have Eyes for You.' Would you appreciate?"

Something in the cautious way he had spoken suggested this was the first part of an agreed code. But though I searched my memory for some password or phrase Sarah might have told me, I could remember nothing. In the end, I said:

"I have no phonograph with me here in Shanghai. But I'm very fond of Mimi Johnson. In fact, I attended a recital of hers in London a few years ago."

"Really? Mimi Johnson, yes."

I got the distinct impression I had puzzled him with the wrong response. So I said: "Look here, my name is Banks. Christopher Banks."

"Banks. Mr. Banks." The man said my name neutrally, then said: "If you appreciate Mimi Johnson, 'I Only Have Eyes for You,' I shall play it for you. Please."

He ducked under the counter, and I took the opportunity to look out of the shop window back into the street. The two rick-shawmen were still laughing and talking, and I was reassured to see my young man still there in the car. Then just as I was wondering if there had not been some huge misunderstanding, the warm languid sound of a jazz orchestra filled the room. Mimi Johnson began to sing and I remembered how the song had been all the rage in London clubs a few years before.

After a while, I became aware of the spindly man indicating a spot on the rear wall hung with heavy dark drapes. I had not noticed before that there was a doorway there, but when I pushed, I indeed found myself stepping through into an inner room.

Sarah was sitting on a wooden trunk wearing a light coat and hat. A cigarette was burning in her holder and the cupboard-like room was already thick with her smoke. All around us were piles of gramophone records and sheet music stored in an assortment of cardboard boxes and tea-chests. There was no window, but I could see a back door, at that moment slightly ajar, which led outside.

"Well, here I am," I said. "I brought just the one suitcase as you insisted. But I see you've three yourself."

"This bag here's just for Ethelbert. My teddy bear. He's been with me since, well, for ever really. Silly, isn't it?"

"Silly? No, not at all."

"When Cecil and I first came here, I made the mistake of putting Ethelbert in with a whole lot of other things. Then when I opened the case, his arm had fallen off. I found it right in a corner, stuck inside a slipper. So this time, give or take a few shawls, he's got a whole bag all to himself. It is silly."

"No, no. I understand perfectly. Ethelbert, yes."

She carefully put down her cigarette holder and stood up. Then we were kissing—just like, I suppose, a couple on the cinema screen. It was almost exactly as I had always imagined it would be, except there was something oddly inelegant about our embrace, and I tried more than once to adjust my posture; but my right foot was hard against a heavy box and I could not quite negotiate the necessary turn without risking my balance. Then she had taken a step back, breathing deeply, all the time looking into my face.

"Is everything ready?" I asked her.

She did not at first reply, and I thought she was about to kiss me again. But in the end, she said simply:

"Everything's fine. We just have several more minutes to wait. Then we'll go out there"—she indicated the back door—"walk down to the jetty and a sampan will take us out to our steamer two miles down the river. After that it's Macao."

"And Cecil, does he have any idea at all?"

"I didn't see him all day. He set off for one of his little places straight after breakfast, and I expect he's still there."

"It's a great shame. Really, someone should tell him to pull himself together."

"Well, it's no longer up to us to do so."

"No, I suppose not." I let out a sudden laugh. "I suppose it's not up to us to do anything other than what we choose."

"That's right. Christopher, is something wrong?"

"No, no. I was just trying to . . . I just wished . . ."

I reached out to her, thinking to initiate another embrace, but she raised a hand, saying:

"Christopher, I think you should sit down. Don't worry, there'll be time to do everything, *everything,* later."

"Yes, yes. I'm sorry."

"Once we're in Macao, we can have a good think about our future. A good think about where would be good for us. And where would be good for Jennifer. We'll spread all our maps out over the bed, look out of our room on to the sea and argue about it all. Oh, I'm sure we *will* argue. I'm looking forward even to our arguments. Are you going to sit down? Look, sit here."

"I say . . . Look, if we have to wait a few minutes, let me just go and do something."

"Do something? What exactly?"

"Just . . . just something. Look really, I won't be gone long, just a few minutes. You see, I just have to ask someone something."

"Who? Christopher, I don't think we should talk to anyone at this point."

"That's not what I mean, exactly. I fully realise the need for caution and so on. No, no, don't worry. It's just that young man. The one who you sent, the one who drove me here. I just need to ask him something."

"But surely he's gone."

"No, he's not. He's still out there. Look, I'll be straight back."

I hurried out through the curtain back into the shop, where the spindly man with the beard looked up at me in surprise.

"You appreciated Mimi Johnson?" he asked.

"Yes, yes. Wonderful. I just have to pop out for a second."

"May I make it clear, sir, that I am Swiss. There is no impending hostility between your country and mine."

"Ah yes. Splendid. I'll be back in a moment."

I hurried across the road towards the car. The young man, who had seen me, rolled down his window and smiled politely; there seemed no trace of his earlier temper. Stooping down to him, I said quietly:

"Look here. This Yeh Chen. Do you have any idea where I might find him?"

"Yeh Chen? He lives very near here."

"Yeh Chen. I'm talking about the *blind* Yeh Chen."

"Yes. Just over there."

"His house is over there?"

"Yes, sir."

"Look here, you don't seem to understand. Are you saying Yeh Chen, the *blind* Yeh Chen, that his house is *just over there*?"

"Yes, sir. You may walk there, but if you wish, I take in car."

"Listen to me, this is very important. Do you know how long Yeh Chen has lived in his present house?"

The young man thought, then said: "He always live there, sir. When I was boy, he live there."

"Are you sure? Now look, this is most important. Are you sure this is the *blind* Yeh Chen, and that he's been living there for a long time?"

"I told you, sir. He there when I was small boy. My guess, he live there many, many years."

I straightened, took a deep breath and thought about the full implications of what I had just heard. Then I leant down again and said: "I think you should take me there. In the car, I mean. We have to approach this carefully. I'd like you to take me there, but to stop the car a little way away. Somewhere where we can see clearly *the house opposite* Yeh Chen's house. Do you understand?"

I got into the car and the young man started the engine. He turned the vehicle a full circle, then we took another narrow side-street. As we did so, many thoughts crowded into my mind at once. I wondered if I should tell the young man the significance of the journey we were making, and even considered asking if he was carrying a gun in the car—though in the end I decided such an enquiry might only panic him.

We turned a corner into an alley even narrower than the one before. Then we turned again and came to a halt. I thought for a second we had reached our destination, but then realised what had made us stop. In the alleyway before us was a crowd of young boys trying to control a bewildered water-buffalo. There was some sort of altercation going on between the boys, and as I watched, one of them gave the buffalo a clout on the nose with his stick. I felt a wave of alarm, remembering my mother's warnings throughout my childhood that these animals were as dangerous as any bull when riled. The creature did nothing, however, and the boys continued to argue. The young man sounded the horn several times to no avail, and finally, with a sigh, he began to reverse the vehicle back the way we had come.

We took another alley nearby, but this diversion appeared to confuse my driver, for after a few more turns, he stopped and reversed again, though this time there was no obstruction. At one point, we came out on to a broader rutted mud track with dilapidated wooden shacks all along one side.

"Please hurry," I said. "I have very little time."

Just then a huge crashing sound shook the ground we were travelling along. The young man continued to drive steadily, but looked nervously into the distance.

"Fighting," he said. "Fighting started again."

"It sounded awfully close," I said.

For the next few minutes, we steered around more narrow corners and little wooden houses, blasting the horn to scatter children and dogs. Then the car came to another abrupt halt, and I heard the young man let out an exasperated sound. Looking past him, I saw the way ahead was blocked by a barricade of sandbags and barbed wire.

"We must go all the way round," he said. "No other way."

"But look, we must be very close now."

"Very close, yes. But road blocked, so we must go all the way round. Be patient, sir. We get there soon."

But a distinct change had entered the young man's manner. His earlier assurance had faded, and now he struck me as ridiculously young to be driving a car, perhaps no more than fifteen or sixteen. For some time, we travelled through muddy, stinking streets, down more alleys where I thought we would at any moment plunge into the open gutters—but somehow the young man always managed to keep our wheels just clear of the edges. All the while, we could hear the sound of gunfire in the distance, and see people hurrying back to the safety of their houses and shelters. But there were still the children and dogs, seemingly belonging to no one, running everywhere before us, oblivious to any sense of danger. At one point, as we bumped our way across the yard of some small factory, I said:

"Now look, why don't you just stop and ask the way?"

"Be patient, sir."

"Be patient? But you've no more idea where we're going than I have."

"We get there soon, sir."

"What nonsense. Why do you persist in this charade? It's typical of you Chinese. You're lost, but you won't admit it. We've been driving now for . . . well, it seems like an eternity."

He said nothing, and brought us out on to a mud road that climbed steeply between large heaps of factory refuse. Then came another thunderous crash somewhere alarmingly near, and the young man dropped his speed to a crawl.

"Sir. I think we go back now."

"Go back? Go back where?"

"Fighting very near. Not safe here."

"What do you mean, the fighting's near?" Then an idea dawned on me. "Are we anywhere near Chapei?"

"Sir. We in Chapei. We in Chapei some time."

"What? You mean we've left the Settlement?"

"We in Chapei now."

"But . . . Good God! We're actually outside the Settlement? *In Chapei?* Look here, you're a fool, you know that? A fool! You told me the house was very near. Now we're lost. We're possibly dangerously close to the war zone. *And we've left the Settlement!* You're what I call a proper fool. Do you know why? I'll tell you. You pretend to know far more than you do. You're too proud to admit to your shortcomings. That's my definition of a fool exactly. A right fool! Do you hear me? A right and proper fool!"

He stopped the car. Then he opened his door and without glancing back, walked off.

It took me a moment to calm myself and assess the situation. We were most of the way up a hill, and the car was now in an isolated spot on a mud track surrounded by mounds of broken masonry, twisted wire and what looked like the mangled remains of old bicycle wheels. I could see the young man's figure marching up a foot-path over the rim of the hill.

I got out and ran after him. He must have heard me coming, but he neither quickened his pace nor looked back. I caught up and stopped him by grasping his shoulder.

"Look, I'm sorry," I said, panting a little. "I apologise. I shouldn't have lost my temper. I apologise, I really do. No excuse for it. But you see, you've no idea what all this means. Now please"—I indicated back to the car—"let's continue."

The young man would not look at me. "No more driving," he said.

"But look, I've said I'm sorry. Now please, be reasonable."

"No more driving. Too dangerous here. Fighting very near."

"But listen, it's very important I get to this house. Very important indeed. Now tell me truthfully, please. Are you lost or do you really know where the house is?"

"I know. I know house. But too dangerous now. Fighting very near."

As though to support his point, machine-gun fire suddenly echoed around us. It felt reasonably distant, but it was impossible to tell from which direction it was coming, and we both looked about us, feeling suddenly exposed on the hill.

"I'll tell you what," I said, and took from my pocket my note-book and pencil. "I can see you want no further part in all this, and I can understand your viewpoint. And I'm sorry again I was rude to you earlier. But I'd like you to do two more things for me before you go home. First, I'd like you please to write down here the address of Yeh Chen's house."

"No address, sir. There is no address."

"Very well, then draw a map. Write down directions. Whatever. Please do it for me. Then after that, I'd like you to drive me to the nearest police station. Of course, that's what I should have done from the start. I'll need trained, armed men. Please."

I gave him the notebook and pencil. Several pages were covered with notes from my enquiries earlier in the day. He turned the tiny pages until he came to a blank one. Then he said:

"No English. Cannot write English, sir."

"Then write in whatever you can. Draw a map. Whatever. Please hurry."

He appeared now to grasp the importance of what I was asking him to do. He thought carefully for a few seconds, then began to write rapidly. He filled one page, then another. After four or five pages he slotted the pencil back into the spine of the notebook and handed it to me. I glanced through what he had done, but could make no sense of the Chinese script. Nevertheless I said:

"Thank you. Thank you very much indeed. Now please. Take me to a police station. Then you can go home."

"Police station this way, sir." He took several further steps in the direction he had been walking. Then from the crest of the hill, he pointed down to the bottom of the slope where, perhaps two hundred yards away, a mass of grey buildings began.

"Police station there, sir."

"There? Which building?"

"There. With flag."

"I see, yes. You're sure that's a police station?"

"Sure, sir. Police station."

From where we were standing, it certainly looked like a police station. I could see, moreover, that there was little point in trying to drive to it; the car had been left on the other side of the hill, and the track we had just come up was not wide enough for the vehicle; I could see we might easily get lost again trying to find a way around the hill. I put the notebook back into my pocket, and thought about presenting him with some banknotes, before remembering how offended he had been earlier. I therefore said simply:

"Thank you. You've been of great help. I'll manage by myself from here."

The young man gave a quick nod of the head—he seemed still to be angry with me—then, turning, went off back down the slope in the direction of the car.

CHAPTER 18

THE POLICE STATION LOOKED to be abandoned. As I came down the slope, I could see broken windows and one of the entrance doors hanging off its hinges. But when I picked my way through the broken glass and went inside into the station's reception area, I was met by three Chinese men, two of whom pointed rifles at me, while the third brandished a garden spade. One of them—who was wearing a Chinese Army uniform—asked in halting English what I wanted. When I managed to convey who I was, and that I wished to speak with whomever was in charge, the men began to argue among themselves. Eventually the one holding the spade disappeared through into a back room, and the others kept their guns on me while we waited for his return. I took the opportunity to glance about me, and concluded it was unlikely there were any policemen left in the station. Although a few posters and notices remained up, the place looked to have been abandoned some time ago. Cables were dangling off one wall and the back section of the room had been gutted by fire.

After perhaps five minutes, the man with the spade came back. A few more exchanges followed in what I guessed was Shanghai dialect, before finally the soldier gestured that I should go with the man with the spade.

I followed the latter through into a back room, which turned out also to be guarded by armed men. But these stood aside for us, and soon I was going down some rickety stairs into the cellars of the police station.

My recollection is a little hazy now as to how we got down to the bunker. There were perhaps a few more rooms; I remember we walked along a kind of tunnel, stooping to avoid low beams; here too were sentries, and each time we encountered one of their looming black shapes, I was obliged to press myself right into the rough wall in order to squeeze past.

Eventually I was shown inside a windowless room that had been turned into some sort of makeshift military headquarters. It was lit by two bulbs dangling side by side from a central beam. The walls were of exposed brick, and in the wall to my right, there was gouged out a hole large enough for a man to climb through. There was a battered wireless set mounted in the opposite corner, while in the middle of the floor sat a big office desk—which I could see at a glance had been sawn in half, then crudely put back together again with rope and nails. Several upturned wooden boxes constituted the available seating, the only actual chair being occupied by an unconscious man who was tied up to it. He was in a Japanese marines' uniform, and one side of his face was a mass of bruising.

The only other people present were two Chinese Army officers, both on their feet, bent over some chart spread across the desk. They looked up as I entered, then one of them came forward and offered his hand.

"I am Lieutenant Chow. This is Captain Ma. We are both very honoured to have you visit us like this, Mr. Banks. Have you come to lend us your moral support?"

"Well, in actual fact, Lieutenant, I came here with a specific request. However, I would hope that once my task is completed, morale will be boosted no end. Yours and everyone else's. But I'll need a little assistance, and this is why I've come to you."

The lieutenant said something to the captain, who evidently did not understand English; then they both looked at me. Suddenly the unconscious Japanese in the chair vomited down the front of his uniform. We all turned to stare at him; then the lieutenant said:

"You say you need assistance, Mr. Banks. In what form exactly?"

"I have here some directions, directions to a particular house. It's imperative I reach this house without any further delay. The directions are written in Chinese, which I'm unable to read. But you see, even if I could read them, I'd need a guide, someone familiar with this locality."

"So you wish for a guide."

"Not only that, Lieutenant. I will need four or five good men, more if possible. They will need to be trained and experienced, since this will be a delicate task."

The lieutenant gave a little laugh; then making his features solemn once more, said: "Sir, we are at this moment very short of such men. This base is a crucial part of our defence force. And yet you saw for yourself how thinly it is guarded. In fact, the men you saw on the way in are either wounded, sick or inexperienced volunteers. Every man capable of sustained fighting we have pushed to the front."

"I appreciate, Lieutenant, that you're in a demanding situation. But you have to understand, I'm not talking about just some casual enquiry I wish to make. When I say it's imperative I reach this house . . . Well, Lieutenant, I'll tell you, there's no need to keep it a secret. You and Captain Ma here can be the first to know. The house I wish to find, which I know is very near us now, is none other than the one in which my parents are being held. That's right, Lieutenant! I'm talking about nothing less than the solving of this case after all these years. You see now why I felt my request, even at this busy moment for you, quite warranted."

The lieutenant's face remained fixed on mine. The captain asked him something in Mandarin, but the lieutenant did not reply. Then he said to me:

"We are waiting for some men to return from a mission. Seven went out. We do not know if they will all return. It was my intention that they be sent to another location immediately. But now . . . In this instance, I shall take personal responsibility. These men, however many of them may return, will accompany you on your mission."

I sighed impatiently. "I thank you, Lieutenant. But how long will we have to wait for these men? Isn't it possible for me to take a few of the men standing out there, just for several minutes? After all, the house is somewhere very near here. And you see, I have someone waiting . . ." I suddenly remembered Sarah, and a kind of panic seized me. I took another step forward and said: "In fact, Lieutenant, I wonder if I may use your telephone. I really should speak to her."

"I'm afraid there is no telephone here, Mr. Banks. That is a radio, connected only with our headquarters and our other bases."

"Well then, it's all the more imperative I clear this matter up without delay! You see, sir, there is a lady waiting, even as we speak! May I suggest I take three or four of the men out there guarding this base . . ."

"Mr. Banks, please calm yourself. We will do all we can to assist you. But as I have said already, the men outside are not fit for such a mission. They will only jeopardise it. I understand you have waited many years to solve this case. I would counsel you not to act hastily at this juncture."

There was good sense in the lieutenant's words. With a sigh, I sat down on one of the upturned tea-chests.

"The men should not be much longer now," said the lieutenant. "Mr. Banks, may I see these directions you have?"

I was reluctant to let go of my notebook even for a few seconds. But in the end I handed it to the officer, opened at the appropriate pages. He studied the directions for a while, then returned the notebook to me.

"Mr. Banks, I should tell you. This house. It will not be so easy to reach."

"But I happen to know, sir, it's very near here."

"It is near, that is true. Nevertheless, it will not be easy. Indeed, Mr. Banks, it may even be behind Japanese lines by now."

"Japanese lines? Well, I suppose I could always reason with the Japanese. I have no quarrel with them myself."

"Sir, if you will come with me. I will show you, while we wait for the men, our exact position."

For a moment, he spoke rapidly to the captain. He then walked towards a broom cupboard in the corner, flung open its door and stepped inside. It took me a moment to realise I was expected to follow, but then when I tried also to enter the cupboard, I almost walked into the heels of the lieutenant's boots—which were now directly in front of my face. I heard his voice say from the darkness above:

"If you will please follow me, Mr. Banks. There are forty-eight rungs. It is better you keep at least five rungs below me."

His feet disappeared. Stepping further into the cupboard, I reached out my hands and found some metal rungs on the brick before me. Far above in the darkness, I could see a little pond of sky. I guessed that we were at the bottom of a chimney, or an observation tower used by the police.

For the first few rungs, I found the going awkward; not only was I nervous of missing my grip in the dark, there was also the worry of the lieutenant slipping and falling down on to me. But eventually the patch of sky grew larger, and then I saw the lieutenant's figure clambering out above me. In another minute or so, I had joined him.

We were standing up on a high flat roof surrounded on all sides by miles of densely packed rooftops. Away in the distance, perhaps a half-mile to the east, I could see a column of dark smoke rising into the late-afternoon sky.

"It's odd," I said, looking around me. "How do people get about down there? There appear to be no streets."

"That is certainly how it looks from up here. But perhaps you will care to look through these."

He was holding out a pair of binoculars. I raised them to my eyes and spent some time adjusting them until I could see clearly, only to find I was gazing at a chimney stack a few yards in front of me. Eventually, though, I managed to focus on the column of smoke in the distance. The lieutenant's voice said somewhere close beside me:

"You are now looking at the warren, Mr. Banks. The factory workers live there. I am sure in all the time you were a child here, you never visited the warren."

"The warren? No, I don't think so."

"Almost certainly not. Foreigners rarely see such places unless they are missionaries. Or perhaps communists. I am Chinese, but I too, like many of my peers, was never permitted to go near such places. I knew almost nothing about the warren until '32, the last time we fought the Japanese. You would not believe human beings could live like that. It is like an ants' nest. Those houses, they were intended for the poorest people. Houses with tiny rooms, row after row, back to back. A warren. If you look carefully, you may see the lanes. Little alleys just wide enough to allow the people to get into their homes. At the back, the houses have no windows at all. The rear rooms are black holes, backing on to the houses behind. Forgive me, I am telling you this for a good reason, as you will see. The rooms were made small, because they were for the poor. There was a time when seven or eight people shared such a room. Then as the years went on, families were forced to make partitions, even within these small rooms, to share the rent with another family. And if they still couldn't pay the landlords, they would partition the room further. I remember seeing tiny black closets divided four times, each with a family in it. You do not believe this, Mr. Banks, that human beings can live like this?"

"It does seem unbelievable, but if you've seen these conditions yourself, Lieutenant . . ."

"When the fight against the Japanese is over, Mr. Banks, I will consider giving my services to the communists. You think that is a dangerous thing to say? There are many officers who would rather fight under the communists than under Chiang."

I moved the binoculars over the dense mass of shabby roofs. I could see now that many of them were broken through. I could decipher, moreover, the lanes the lieutenant had mentioned, narrow passageways threading here and there into the tenements.

"But this is no shanty town," the lieutenant's voice was continuing. "Even if the partitions erected by the tenants are flimsy, the essential structure, the warren itself, is brick. This proved crucial in '32 when the Japanese attacked, and it is proving so to us now."

"I can see that," I said. "A solid warren defended by soldiers. No easy prospect for the Japanese, even with their modern weapons."

"You are right. The Japanese weaponry, even their training, counts for almost nothing down there. Fighting is reduced to rifles, bayonets, knives, pistols, spades, meat cleavers. The Japanese line, in the past week, has actually been pushed back. You see that smoke, Mr. Banks? That point was held by the enemy only last week. But now we have pushed them back."

"Are there civilians still living down there?"

"There are indeed. You may not believe it, but even close to the front, some of the houses in the warren are still occupied. This makes it even harder for the Japanese. They cannot shell indiscriminately. They know the Western powers are watching and they fear ruthlessness will have a cost."

"How long can your troops hold out?"

"Who knows? Chiang Kai-shek may send us reinforcements. Or the Japanese might decide to give up and redeploy, concentrate instead on Nanking or Chunking. It is by no means certain we will not still be victorious. But the fighting recently has cost us dearly. If you will move your field glasses to the left, Mr. Banks. Now, do you see that road? Yes? That road is known locally as Pigs' Alley. It doesn't look an impressive road, but now it is very important to the outcome. As you see, that is the one road that runs along the edge of the warren. At the moment, our troops have sealed it off, and have managed to keep the Japanese out. If they are able to come down that road, the warren can be penetrated all along the side. There will be no point in our attempting to hold out. We will have been flanked. You asked for men to accompany you to the house where your parents are. The men who will accompany you would otherwise have been deployed defending the barricade at the top of Pigs' Alley. The last few days, the fighting there has become desperate. Meanwhile, of course, we are having also to hold our line across the warren."

"From up here, you wouldn't think there was so much going on down there."

"Indeed. But I can assure you, inside the warren, things are now very bad. I tell you this, Mr. Banks, since you are intending to go in there."

For a moment or two, I went on gazing through the glasses in silence. Then I said: "Lieutenant, that house, the house where my parents are being held. Will I be able to see it from up here?"

His hand touched my shoulder briefly, though I did not take my eyes from the binoculars.

"Do you see, Mr. Banks, the remains of that tower standing to the left? It looks like one of those Easter Island figures. Yes, yes, that's it. If you draw a line from that over to the remains of that large black building to the right, the old textile warehouse, that was, this morning, the line to which our men had beaten back the Japanese. The house where your parents are being held is roughly level with that tall chimney on your left. If you draw a line, very level with it across the warren, until you come to just a little left of where we are now standing. Yes, yes . . ."

"You mean near that roof, the one with the eaves pointing up into a kind of arch . . ."

"Yes, that's it. Of course, I cannot say with certainty. But according to those directions you showed me, that is roughly where the house is."

I stared through the field glasses at that particular roof. For some time I could not stop staring, even though I was conscious of keeping the lieutenant from his duties. After a while, it was the lieutenant who said:

"It must feel strange. To think you might be looking at the very house containing your parents."

"Yes. Yes, it does feel a little strange."

"Of course, it might not be that house. That was simply a guess on my part. But it will be somewhere very near it. That tall chimney I showed you, Mr. Banks. The locals refer to it as the East Furnace. The chimney you can see much closer to us, almost directly in line with the other one, belongs to the West Furnace. Before the fighting, the inhabitants used to burn their refuse at one or other of these places. I would advise you, sir, to use the furnaces as your landmarks once you are within the warren. Otherwise it is hard for a stranger to keep his bearings. Look again carefully at that far chimney, sir. Remember, the house you seek is only a little way away from it, in a direct line due south."

I finally lowered the binoculars. "Lieutenant, you've been most kind. I can't tell you how grateful I am to you. In fact, if it won't embarrass you, you will perhaps permit me to mention you by name during the ceremony that will take place at Jessfield Park to commemorate the freeing of my parents."

"Really, my help has not been so significant. Besides, Mr. Banks, you must not assume your task is accomplished. Standing up here, it does not look far away. But inside the warren there is a lot of fighting. Although you are not a combatant, it will still be difficult to move from house to house. And aside from the two furnaces, there are few clear landmarks surviving. Then you must bring your parents out safely. In other words, you still have a daunting task ahead of you. But now, Mr. Banks, I suggest we go back down. The men may well have returned by now and be awaiting my orders. And as for you, Mr. Banks, you must try and come back before nightfall. It is hellish enough moving about the warren in daylight. At night, it will be like drifting through one's worst nightmares. If you are overtaken by darkness, I would advise you to find some safe place and wait with the men until morning. Only yesterday, two of my men killed each other, they were so disorientated in the dark."

"I've taken to heart everything you've said, Lieutenant. Well then, let's be going back down."

DOWNSTAIRS, CAPTAIN MA was talking to a soldier in a badly torn uniform. The latter did not appear to be wounded, but seemed shocked and upset. The Japanese in the chair was now snoring, as though enjoying a peaceful nap, though I noticed he had vomited some more down the front of his clothes.

The lieutenant conferred quickly with the captain, then questioned the soldier in the torn uniform. Then he turned to me and said:

"It is bad news. The others have not returned. Two have certainly been killed. The remainder are trapped, although there is a good chance they will yet escape. The enemy has, if only temporarily, made an advance, and it may well be that the house your parents are in is now behind their lines."

"Regardless of that, Lieutenant, I still need to proceed, and without any further delay. Look here, if the men you promised me haven't returned, then perhaps, though I realise it's a lot to ask, perhaps you'd be good enough to escort me yourself. Honestly, sir, I can't think of a more suitable person to assist me at this point."

The lieutenant thought this over with a grave expression. "Very well, Mr. Banks," he said finally. "I shall do as you ask. But we must hurry. I should not really leave this post at all. To do so for any length of time could have the most awful consequences."

He issued rapid instructions to the captain, then opening a

drawer in the desk, began placing a number of items into his pockets and belt.

"It is better you do not carry a rifle, Mr. Banks. But do you have a pistol? No? Then take this. It is German and very reliable. You should keep it concealed and if we encounter the enemy, you must not hesitate to declare your neutrality immediately and clearly. Now, if you will follow me."

Taking a rifle that was leaning against the desk, he strode over to the hole gouged into the opposite wall and nimbly climbed through. I pushed the pistol into my belt, where it was more or less concealed by my jacket, then hurried after him.

CHAPTER 19

I T IS ONLY HINDSIGHT that makes the first part of that journey appear relatively easy. At the time, as I stumbled after the lieutenant's striding figure, it certainly did not feel that way. My feet quickly began to smart from the rubble-strewn ground, and I found terribly awkward the contortions required to negotiate the holes in each wall.

Of the latter, there seemed an unending number, all of them more or less similar to the one in the cellar command base. Some were smaller, some large enough for two men to squeeze through at the same time; but they had all been gouged out with rough edges, and required a little jump to climb through. Before long I found myself close to exhaustion; no sooner had I clambered through one such hole than I would spot the lieutenant ahead of me, smartly easing his way through the next wall.

Not all the walls were still standing; sometimes we would pick our way through the debris of what must have been three or four houses before encountering another wall. The roofs were almost all smashed, often absent altogether, so that we had plenty of daylight from the sky—though here and there, heavy shadows made it easy to lose one's step. More than once, until I grew more accustomed to the terrain, my foot slipped painfully between two jagged slabs or sank ankle-deep into fragmented rubble.

It was all too easy in such circumstances to forget we were passing through what only several weeks before had been the homes of hundreds of people. In fact, I often had the impression we were moving through not a slum district, but some vast, ruined mansion with endless rooms. Even so, every now and then it would occur to me that in among the wreckage beneath our feet lay cherished heirlooms, children's toys, simple but much-loved items of family life, and I would find myself suddenly overcome with renewed anger towards those who had allowed such a fate to befall so many innocent people. I thought again of those pompous men of the International Settlement, of all the prevarications they must have employed to evade their responsibilities down so many years, and at such moments I felt my fury mount with so much intensity I was on the verge of calling out to the lieutenant to halt, just so I could give vent to it.

The lieutenant did, though, pause at one point of his own accord, and as I caught up with him, said:

"Mr. Banks, please take a good look at this." He was indicating a little over to our left, towards a large boiler-like construction which, though covered in masonry dust, had remained more or less intact. "This is the West Furnace. If you look up there, you will see the nearer of the two tall chimneys we saw earlier from the roof. The East Furnace is similar in appearance to this, and it will be our next clear landmark. When we reach it, we shall know we are very close to the house."

I studied the furnace carefully. A chimney of some girth emerged from above its shoulders, and when I took a few steps closer and looked up, I could see the huge chimney going off way up into the sky. I was still staring up at it when I heard my companion say:

"Please, Mr. Banks. We must continue. It is important we complete our task before the sun sets."

It was several minutes after the West Furnace that the lieutenant's manner became noticeably more cautious. His tread became deliberate, and at each hole, he would first peer through, his rifle poised, listening intently, before climbing up. I also began to spot more and more stacks of sandbags, or coils of barbed wire, left within reach of the holes. When I first heard the machine-gun, I abruptly froze, believing we were under fire. But then I saw the lieutenant before me still walking, and with a deep breath, went on after him.

Eventually I came through a hole to find myself in a much larger space. In fact, in my exhausted condition, I thought I had entered the bombed remains of one of those grand ballrooms I had been taken to in the Settlement. I then realised we were standing in an area once occupied by several rooms; the partition walls had almost entirely vanished, so that the next good wall was all of twenty-five yards away. There I could see seven or eight soldiers lined up, their faces to the brick. I at first took them for prisoners, but then saw how each man was standing before a small hole through which he had inserted the barrel of his rifle. The lieutenant had already crossed the rubble and was talking to a man crouched behind a machine-gun mounted on a tripod. This machine-gun arrangement was positioned before the largest hole—the one through which we would have to climb to continue our journey. Coming closer, moreover, I saw the perimeters of the hole had been decked with barbed wire, allowing only enough space for the gun barrel to manoeuvre.

I supposed at first the lieutenant was asking the man to remove this obstacle out of our way, but then I saw how tense all those present had become. The man behind the machine-gun, all the time the lieutenant spoke to him, never took his gaze from the hole before him. The other soldiers too, all along the wall, remained still and poised, their attention utterly focused on whatever was on the other side.

Once the alarming implications of this scene had sunk in, I felt inclined to climb back through the previous hole. But then I saw the lieutenant returning towards me and remained where I was.

"We have some trouble," he said. "A few hours ago the Japanese managed to push forward a little way. We have now beaten them back again and the line has been re-established where it was this morning. However, it would seem several Japanese soldiers did not retreat with the others, and are now caught behind our line. They are completely cut off and thus very dangerous. My men believe they are at this moment on the other side of that wall."

"Lieutenant, you're not suggesting, are you, that we delay while this matter sorts itself out?"

"I am afraid we will have to wait, certainly."

"But for how long?"

"It is hard to predict. These soldiers are trapped, and they will be either captured or killed in the end. But meanwhile they have weapons and are very dangerous."

"You mean we could wait for hours? Days even?"

"That is possible. It would be very dangerous at this point for the two of us to continue."

"Lieutenant, I'm surprised at you. I was under the impression that you, an educated man, were fully aware of the urgency of our present undertaking. Surely there's some other route we could take to by-pass these soldiers."

"There are other routes. But it remains the case that however we proceed, we will be in considerable danger. Unfortunately, sir, I see no alternative but to wait. It is possible the situation will be resolved before long. Excuse me."

One of the soldiers by the wall had been signalling urgently, and now the lieutenant began to go across the rubble towards him. But just then the machine-gunner let loose a deafening burst of fire, and when he ceased there was an extended scream coming from beyond the wall. The scream began full-throated, then tapered off into a strange high-pitched whimper. It was an eerie sound and I became quite transfixed listening to it. It was only when the lieutenant came rushing back and pulled me down behind some fallen masonry that I realised there were bullets hitting the wall behind me. The men at the next wall were now firing too, and then the machine-gunner let off another burst. The authority of his weapon seemed to silence all the others, and thereafter, for what felt like an inordinate time, the only sound to be heard came from the wounded man beyond the wall. His high-pitched whimpers continued for several moments, then he began to shout something in Japanese over and over; every now and again the voice would rise to a frantic shriek, then die away again to a whimper. This disembodied voice echoed unnervingly around the ruins, but the Chinese soldiers in front of me remained utterly still, their concentration not wavering from what they could see through the wall. Suddenly the machine-gunner turned and vomited on the ground beside him, before immediately turning back to the wire-decked hole in front. From the way he did this, it was not easy to tell if his sickness had to do with nerves, the sounds of the dying man, or simply some stomach complaint.

Then eventually, though their postures hardly changed, the soldiers all perceptibly relaxed. I heard the lieutenant say beside me:

"So you see now, Mr. Banks, that it is no easy matter to proceed from here."

We had been crouching down on our knees, and I noticed my light flannel suit was now almost entirely covered in dust and grime. I took a few seconds to collect my thoughts before saying:

"I appreciate the risks. But we must nevertheless continue. Particularly with all this fighting going on, my parents shouldn't be left in that house a moment longer than necessary. May I suggest we take these men here with us? Then if these Japanese soldiers set upon us, we'd be much the stronger."

"As the commanding officer here, I cannot possibly sanction

such an idea, Mr. Banks. If these men leave their position, the head-quarters would become entirely vulnerable. Besides, I will be putting the men's lives at needless risk."

I gave a sigh of exasperation. "I must say, Lieutenant, it was pretty sloppy work on the part of your men to have allowed these Japanese in behind your line. If all your people had been doing their jobs properly, I'm sure such a thing would never have arisen."

"My men have fought with commendable bravery, Mr. Banks. It is hardly their fault that your mission is, for the time being, inconvenienced."

"What do you mean by that, Lieutenant? What are you implying?"

"Please calm yourself, Mr. Banks. I am merely pointing out it is not the fault of my men if . . ."

"Then whose fault is it, sir? I realise what you're implying! Oh yes! I know you've been thinking it for some time now. I was wondering when you'd finally come out with it."

"Sir, I have no idea what . . ."

"I know full well what you've been thinking all this time, Lieutenant! I could see it in your eyes. You believe this is all my fault, all this, all of it, all this terrible suffering, this destruction here, I could see it in your face when we were walking through it all just now. But that's because you know nothing, practically nothing, sir, concerning this matter. You may well know a thing or two about fighting, but let me tell you it's quite another thing to solve a complicated case of this kind. You obviously haven't the slightest idea what's involved. Such things take time, sir! A case like this one, it requires great delicacy. I suppose you imagine you can just rush at it with bayonets and rifles, do you? It's taken time, I accept that, but that's in the very nature of a case like this. But I don't know why I bother to say all this. What would you understand about it, a simple soldier?"

"Mr. Banks, there is no need for us to quarrel. I have only the most sincere good wishes for your success. I am simply telling you what is possible . . ."

"I'm getting less and less interested in your idea of what is and isn't possible, Lieutenant. If I may say so, you're hardly a good advertisement for the Chinese Army. Do I take it you're now going back on your word? That you're unwilling to accompany me beyond this point? I take it that's so. I'm to be left to carry out this difficult task by myself. Very well, I shall do so! I shall raid the house single-handed!"

"I think, sir, you should calm yourself before saying anything more . . ."

"And one other thing, sir! You can safely assume I will no longer be mentioning you by name at the Jessfield Park celebration. At least if I do, it will not be in a complimentary light . . ."

"Mr. Banks, please, listen to me. If you are determined to continue, despite the danger, then I cannot stop you. But you will undoubtedly be safer alone. With me, you certainly run the risk of being fired upon. You, on the other hand, are a white man in civilian clothes. As long as you are very careful, and announce yourself clearly before any encounter, it is possible you will come to no harm. Of course, I repeat my recommendation that you wait until the situation here is resolved. But then again, as someone myself with ageing parents, I can well understand your feelings of urgency."

I rose to my feet and brushed off as much dust as I could. "Well then, I shall be on my way," I said coldly.

"In that case, Mr. Banks, please take this with you." He was holding out a small torch. "My advice, as before, is to stop and wait if you do not reach your destination by dark. But I can see from your present attitude you might well be inclined to push on. In which case, you will certainly need the torch. The batteries are not new, so do not use it any more than you need to."

I dropped the torch into my jacket pocket, then thanked him somewhat grudgingly, already rather regretting my outburst. The dying man had now stopped trying to talk and was just screaming again. I had begun to walk towards the sound, when the lieutenant said:

"You can't go that way, Mr. Banks. You will have to move north for a while, then try to navigate yourself back on course later. Come this way, sir."

For a few minutes, he led me on a path perpendicular to the one we had been taking. In time we came to another wall with a hole gouged out of it.

"You should go this way for at least half a mile before turning east again. You may still meet soldiers, from either side. Remember what I told you. Keep your revolver hidden, and always announce your neutrality. If you encounter any of the inhabitants, ask them to direct you to the East Furnace. I wish you luck, sir, and I regret I cannot assist you further."

AFTER I HAD BEEN moving north for several minutes, I noticed the houses becoming less damaged. This did not, however, make my journey any the easier; the roofs being more intact meant I had to make do with a much murkier light—I had decided to save the torch till nightfall—and I would often have to feel my way along a wall for some distance before coming across an opening. There was, for some reason, far more broken glass in this vicinity, and also large areas submerged in stagnant water. I frequently heard the scuttling of large groups of rats, and once trod on a dead dog, but could not hear any sounds of fighting.

It was at around this stage of the journey that I found myself thinking again and again of Jennifer, sitting in the prefects' room on that sunny afternoon we had parted—and in particular, of her face as she had made that curious vow, uttered so earnestly, to "help me" when she was older. Once, as I groped my way forward, an absurd picture came into my head of the poor child struggling after me through this ghastly terrain, determined to make good her promise, and I suddenly felt a rush of emotion that all but brought tears to my eyes.

Then I came upon a hole in a wall through which I could see only pitch blackness, but from which came the most overwhelming stink of excrement. I knew that to keep on course I should climb through into that room, but I simply could not bear the idea and kept walking. This fastidiousness cost me dear, for I did not find another opening for some time, and thereafter, I had the impression of drifting further and further off my route.

By the time it grew completely dark and I began to use the torch, I was coming across many more signs of habitation. I would often stumble into a barely damaged chest of drawers or shrine, even whole rooms in which the furnishings were hardly disturbed, giving the impression the family had just gone out for the day. But then right next to such places I would discover more rooms utterly destroyed or flooded.

There were, too, more and more stray dogs—scrawny beasts I feared might attack me, but which invariably shrank away growling when I shone my beam at them. Once I came upon three dogs savagely tearing something apart, and drew my pistol, so convinced was I they would come for me; but even these animals meekly watched me pass, as though they had come to respect the carnage a man was capable of wreaking.

I was not so surprised, then, when I came across the first family. I found them in my torch beam, cowering back into a dark corner: several children, three women, an elderly man. Around them were the bundles and utensils of their existence. They stared at me in fear, brandishing makeshift weapons, which they lowered only slightly at my words of reassurance. I tried to enquire if I was anywhere near the East Furnace, but they returned only uncomprehending stares. I came across three or four more such families in the nearby houses—increasingly, I was able to use actual doorways rather than openings in walls—but found them no more responsive.

Then I entered a larger space, the far side of which was bathed in the reddish glow of a lantern. There were a lot of people standing about in the shadows—again, predominantly women and children with a few elderly men among them. I had begun to utter my usual words of reassurance, when I sensed something odd in the atmosphere, and stopping, reached instead for my revolver.

Faces turned to me in the lantern glow. But then almost immediately the gazes returned to the far corner where a dozen or so children had crowded around something down on the ground. Some of the children were poking with sticks at whatever it was, and then I noticed that many of the adults were holding at the ready sharpened spades, choppers and other improvised weapons. It was as though I had disturbed some dark ritual, and my first inclination was to walk on past. Perhaps it was because I heard a noise, or perhaps it was some sixth sense; but I then found myself, revolver still drawn, moving towards the circle of children. The latter seemed reluctant to reveal what they had, but gradually their shadows parted. I then saw in the dim red glow the figure of a Japanese soldier lying quite still on his side. His hands were tied behind his back; his feet too had been bound. His eyes were closed, and I could see a dark patch soaking its way through his uniform under the armpit further from the ground. His face and hair were covered in dust and speckled with blood. For all that, I recognised Akira with no difficulty.

THE CHILDREN HAD STARTED to gather round again, and one boy prodded Akira's body with a stick. I commanded them to get back, waving my revolver, and eventually the children retreated a little way, all watching carefully.

Akira's eyes remained closed while I looked him over. His uniform was torn away at the back, right down to his raw skin, suggesting he had been dragged along the ground. The wound near his armpit was probably caused by shrapnel. There was a swelling and cut on the back of his head. But he was so covered in grime, and the light was so poor, it was hard to ascertain how serious these injuries were. When I shone the torch on him, heavy shadows fell everywhere, making it even harder to see clearly.

Then, after I had been examining him for a few moments, he opened his eyes.

"Akira!" I said, bringing my face close. "It's me. Christopher!"

It occurred to me that with the light behind my head, I would appear to him no more than an intimidating silhouette. I thus called his name again, this time turning the torch beam on to my face. It is possible this action only served to make me look like some hideous apparition, for Akira grimaced, then spat contemptuously at me. He could not summon much force and the saliva dribbled down his cheek.

"Akira! It's me! How fortunate to find you like this. Now I can help you."

He looked at me, then said: "Let me die."

"You're not dying, old chap. You've lost some blood, and you've had something of a rough time of it lately. But we'll get you to some proper help and you'll be fine, you'll see."

"Pig. Pig."

"Pig?"

"You. Pig." Again he spat at me, and again the spittle dribbled out of his mouth without force.

"Akira. Clearly you still don't realise who I am."

"Let me die. Die like soldier."

"Akira, it's me. Christopher."

"I not know. You pig."

"Listen, let me get these ropes off you. Then you'll feel much better. Then you'll soon come to your senses."

I glanced over my shoulder, thinking to demand some tool with which to cut his bonds. I then saw that all the people in the room had gathered in a crowd just a little way behind me—many holding weapons of one sort or another—as though posing for a sinister group photograph. I was somewhat taken aback—I had for the moment forgotten about them—and felt for my revolver. But just at that moment, Akira said with a new energy:

"If you cut string, I kill you. You warn, okay, English?"

"What are you talking about? Look, you blockhead, it's me, your friend. I'm going to help you."

"You pig. Cut string, I kill you."

"Look, these people here will kill *you* just as quickly. In any case, your wounds will become infected soon. You have to let me help you."

Suddenly two of the Chinese women began to shout. One appeared to be addressing me, while the other was shouting to the back of the crowd. For a moment confusion reigned, then a boy of around ten emerged holding a sickle. As he came into the light, I could see a piece of fur—perhaps the remains of a rodent—dangling from the point of the blade. It struck me the boy was holding the sickle with such care so as not to let this offering drop, but then the woman who had shouted at me grabbed the sickle and whatever it was fell to the ground.

"Now look," I stood up and cried at the crowd. "You've made a mistake. This is a good man. My friend. *Friend.*"

The woman shouted again, indicating I should step aside.

"But he's not your enemy," I went on. "He's a friend. He's going to help me. *Help me to solve the case.*"

I raised the revolver and the woman stepped back. Meanwhile, everyone else was talking at once and a child began to cry. Then an old man was pushed to the front, a young girl holding his hand.

"I speak English," he said.

"Well, thank goodness for that," I said. "Kindly tell everyone present that this man here is my friend. That he's going to help me."

"Him. Japanese soldier. He kill Aunt Yun."

"I'm sure he didn't. Not him personally."

"He kill and steal."

"But not this man. This is Akira. Did anyone see him, this *particular* man, kill or steal? Go on, ask them."

Rather reluctantly, the old man turned and muttered something. This provoked more arguing, and another weapon, a sharpened spade, was handed round and grasped by one of the other women at the front.

"Well?" I asked the old man. "Aren't I right? No one saw Akira personally do any wrong."

The old man shook his head, perhaps to disagree, perhaps to indicate he had not understood. Behind me, Akira made a noise and I turned to him.

"Look, you see? It's just as well I came by. They've got you mixed up with some other fellow, and they want to kill you. For God's sake, do you still not know who I am? Akira! It's me, Christopher!"

I took my eyes off the crowd, and turning fully to him, shone the torch into my face again. Then when I clicked it off, I saw for the first time the beginnings of recognition on his face.

"Christopher," he said, almost experimentally. "Christopher."

"Yes, it's me. Really. It's been a long time. And not a moment too soon, it would seem."

"Christopher. My friend."

Rising, I looked through the crowd, then gestured to a young boy holding a kitchen knife to come closer. When I took the knife from him, the woman with the sickle moved threateningly towards me, but I raised the revolver and shouted to her to keep her distance. Then kneeling down again beside Akira, I went about cutting his bonds. I had imagined Akira had said "string" because of his limited English, but I now saw he was indeed tied with old twine that yielded easily under the blade.

"Tell them," I said to the old man, as Akira's hands came free, "tell them he's my friend. And that we're going to solve the case together. Tell them they've made a big mistake. Go on, tell them!"

As I turned my attention to Akira's feet, I could hear the old man muttering something and arguments starting again in the crowd. Then Akira sat up cautiously and looked at me.

"My friend Christopher," he said. "Yes, we friends."

I sensed the crowd moving in and sprang to my feet. Perhaps in my anxiety for my friend, I shouted in an unnecessarily strident tone: "Don't any of you come any nearer! I'll shoot, I really will!" Then turning to the old man, I cried: "Tell them to get back! Tell them to get back if they know what's good for them!"

I do not know what the old man translated. In any case, the effect on the crowd—whose belligerence, I now realised, I had much overestimated—was utter confusion. Half of them appeared to believe I wished them over the wall to our left, while the remainder assumed I had commanded them to sit down on the ground. They were all of them clearly alarmed by my demeanour, and in their anxiety to comply, were stumbling over one another and shouting in panic.

Akira, realising he had to seize his chance, made an attempt to climb to his feet. I hoisted him up by his arm, and for a moment we stood swaying together unsteadily. I was obliged to tuck the revolver back in my belt to free my other hand, and we then tried a step or two together. A putrid smell was coming from his wound, but pushing this out of my mind, I shouted over my shoulder, no longer caring how many of them understood:

"You'll see soon enough! You'll see you made a mistake!"

"Christopher," Akira murmured in my ear. "My friend. Christopher."

"Look here," I said to him quietly. "We have to get away from these people. That doorway in the corner over there. Do you think you can manage it?"

Akira, leaning heavily on my shoulder, looked into the dimness. "Okay. We go."

His legs appeared unhurt and he walked reasonably well. But then after six or seven steps together, he stumbled, and for a moment, in our efforts to keep from collapsing in a heap, we must have looked to the onlookers as though we were wrestling one another. But we managed to find a new arrangement, and recommenced our walk. Once, a small boy ran forward to hurl some mud at us, but was immediately hauled back. Then Akira and I were at the doorway—the door itself had disappeared—and staggered through into the next house.

$\mathcal{O}$NCE WE HAD COME through two further walls and there was still no sign of our being pursued, I felt for the first time a kind of exhilaration at being finally reunited with my old friend. I found myself laughing a few times as we staggered on together; then Akira too gave a laugh, and the years seemed to melt away between us.

"How long has it been, Akira? It's been such a long time."

He was moving painfully by my side, but he managed to say: "A long time, yes."

"You know, I went back. To the old house. I suppose yours is still next door."

"Yes. Next door."

"Oh, have you been back too? But of course, you've been here all the time. You wouldn't see it as anything so special."

"Yes," he said again, with some effort. "Long time. Next door."

I brought us to a halt and sat him on the remnants of a wall. Then carefully removing the ragged jacket of his uniform, I examined his wounds again, using the torch and my magnifying glass. I was still unable to ascertain a great deal; I had been afraid that the wound under his arm was gangrenous, but it now struck me the foul smell might be coming from something smeared on his clothes, perhaps from where he had been lying on the ground. On the other hand, I noted that he was alarmingly hot and utterly drenched in sweat.

Removing my jacket, I tore several strips off the lining to use as dressings. Then I did my best to clean the wound with my handkerchief. Though I tried to wipe the pus off as gently as possible, his sharp intakes of breath told me I was causing him pain.

"I'm sorry, Akira. I'll try to be less clumsy."

"Clumsy," he said, as though turning the word over. Then he gave a sudden laugh and said: "You help me. Thank you."

"Of course I'm helping you. And very soon, we'll get you proper medical help. Then you'll be fine in no time. But before we do that, you'll have to help *me*. There's a very urgent task for us first, and you'll understand better than anyone why it's so urgent. You see, Akira, I've located it at last. The house where my parents are being held. We're very near it at this moment. You know, old chap, for a time, I was thinking I'd have to go into that house alone. I'd have done it, but really, it would have been an awful risk. Goodness knows how many kidnappers are in there. I'd originally reckoned on getting a few Chinese soldiers to help, but that's proved impossible. I was even thinking of asking the Japanese to help me. But now, the two of us together, we'll do it, we'll manage the thing for sure."

I was all this time attempting to tie the improvised bandage around his torso and neck in such a way as to maintain some pressure on the wound. Akira watched me carefully, and when I stopped speaking, smiled and said:

"Yes. I help you. You help me. Good."

"But Akira, I have to confess to you. I've got myself rather lost. I was doing quite well till shortly before I came across you. But now, I really don't know which way to go. We have to look out for something called the East Furnace. A large thing with a chimney. I wonder, old chap, do you have any idea where we might find this furnace?"

Akira was continuing to look at me, his chest heaving. When I caught sight of him like that, I was suddenly reminded of those times when we had so often sat together at the top of the mound in our garden, recovering our breath. I was about to mention this to him when he said:

"I know. I know this place."

"You know how to get to the East Furnace? From here?"

He nodded. "I fight here, many weeks. Here, I know just like"—he suddenly grinned—"like my home village."

I smiled too, but the remark had puzzled me. "Which home village is this?" I asked.

"Home village. Where I born."

"You mean the Settlement?"

Akira was quiet for a moment, then said: "Okay. Yes. Settlement. International Settlement. My home village."

"Yes," I said. "I suppose it's my home village too."

We both began to laugh, and for a few moments we went on giggling and laughing together, perhaps a little uncontrollably. When we had calmed down somewhat, I said:

"I'll tell you an odd thing, Akira. I can say this to you. All these years I've lived in England, I've never really felt at home there. The International Settlement. That will always be my home."

"But International Settlement . . ." Akira shook his head. "Very fragile. Tomorrow, next day . . ." He waved a hand in the air.

"I know what you mean," I said. "And when we were children, it seemed so solid to us. But as you put it just now. It's our home village. The only one we have."

I began to put his uniform back on him, taking every care not to hurt him unnecessarily.

"Is that any better, Akira? I'm sorry I can't do more for you just now. We'll get you properly seen to very soon. But now, we've important work to do. You tell me where we go."

Our progress was slow. It was hard for me to keep the torch pointed before us, and we often stumbled in the dark, at great cost to Akira. Indeed, he more than once came close to losing consciousness on that lap of our journey, and his weight around my shoulders grew immense. Nor was I without my own injuries; most annoyingly, my right shoe had split apart, and my foot was badly gashed, causing a searing pain to rise with each step. Sometimes we were so exhausted we could go no more than a dozen steps without stopping again. But we resolved on these occasions not to sit down, and would stand swaying together, gasping for breath, re-adjusting our weights in an attempt to relieve one pain at the expense of another. The rancid smell from his wound grew worse, and the constant scuffling of the rats around us was unnerving, but we did not, at this stage, hear any sounds of fighting.

I did what I could to keep our spirits up, making light-hearted remarks whenever I had the breath. In truth, though, my feelings concerning this reunion were, during those moments, of a complex hue. There was no doubting my huge gratitude at fate's bringing us together just in time for our great undertaking. But at the same time, a part of me was saddened that our reunion—which I had thought about for so long—should be taking place in such grim circumstances. It was certainly a long way from the scenes I had always conjured up—of the two of us sitting in some comfortable hotel lounge, or perhaps on the veranda of Akira's house, overlooking a quiet garden, talking and reminiscing for hours on end.

Akira, meanwhile, for all his difficulties, maintained a clear sense of our direction. Frequently he would lead us along some route I feared would finish in a dead end, only for a doorway or opening to appear. From time to time, we came across more inhabitants, some no more than presences we sensed in the darkness; others, gathered around the glow of a lantern or a fire, would stare at Akira with such hostility I feared we would be set upon again. But for the most part we were allowed to pass unmolested, and I once even managed to persuade an old woman to give us drinking water in return for the last bank-notes in my pocket.

Then the terrain changed perceptibly. There were no more pockets of domesticity, and the only people we encountered were isolated individuals with abandoned looks in their eyes, muttering or weeping to themselves. Nor were there any more surviving doorways, but only the gouged-out holes of the sort the lieutenant and I had negotiated at the journey's start. Each of these presented us with much difficulty, Akira being unable to climb through—even with me assisting his every move—without inflicting dreadful agonies upon himself.

We had long since given up conversation, and were simply emitting grunts in time to our steps, when suddenly Akira brought us to a halt and raised his head. Then I too could hear a voice, someone shouting orders. It was difficult to say how near it was—perhaps two or three houses away.

"Japanese?" I asked in a whisper.

Akira went on listening, then shook his head.

"Kuomintang. Christopher, we now very close to . . . to . . ."

"The front?"

"Yes, front. We now very close to front. Christopher, this very dangerous."

"Is it absolutely necessary to go through this area to reach the house?"

"Necessary, yes."

There was a sudden burst of rifle fire, then from further away, the reply of a machine-gun. We instinctively tightened our grasp on one another, but then Akira freed himself and sat down.

"Christopher," he said quietly. "We rest now."

"But we have to reach the house."

"We rest now. Too dangerous to go in fighting zone in darkness. We be killed. Must wait morning."

I saw the sense in this, and in any case, we were now both too exhausted to go on much further. I also sat down and switched off the torch.

We sat in the dark for some time, the silence broken only by our breathing. Then suddenly the gunfire started again, and for perhaps a minute or two continued ferociously. It ended abruptly; then after another moment of quiet, a strange noise rose through the walls. It was a long, thin sound, like an animal's call in the wild, but ended in a full-throated cry. Next came shrieking and sobbing, and then the wounded man began to shout out actual phrases. He sounded remarkably like the dying Japanese soldier I had listened to earlier, and in my exhausted state, I assumed this must be the same man; I was on the point of remarking to Akira what a singularly unfortunate time this individual was having, when I realised he was shouting in Mandarin, not Japanese. The realisation that these were two different men rather chilled me. So identical were their pitiful whimpers, the way their screams gave way to desperate entreaties, then returned to screams, that the notion came to me this was what each of us would go through on our way to death—that these terrible noises were as universal as the crying of new-born babies.

After a time, I grew conscious of the fact that should the fighting spill into our room, we were sitting in a completely exposed position. I was about to suggest to Akira we move somewhere more hidden, but then noticed he had fallen asleep. I switched on the torch again and shone it about cautiously.

Even by recent standards, the destruction around us was severe. I could see grenade damage, bullet holes everywhere, smashed brick and timber. There was a dead water-buffalo lying on its side in the middle of the room no more than seven or eight yards from us; it was covered in dust and debris, a horn pointing up to the roof. I went on casting the beam about until I had established all the possible points from which combatants could enter our enclosure. Most importantly, I discovered, on the far side of the room, beyond the buffalo, a little brick alcove, which perhaps had once served as a stove or fireplace. This struck me as being the safest place for us to spend the night. Shaking Akira awake, I put his arm around my neck, and we both rose painfully to our feet.

When we reached the brick alcove, I pushed away some rubble and cleared an area of smooth wooden boards sufficient to allow us both to lie down. I spread out my jacket for Akira and carefully laid him down on his good side. Then I too lay down and waited for sleep.

But exhausted as I was, the continuing cries of the dying man, my fears of being caught in the fighting, and my thoughts of the crucial task before us all kept me from drifting off. Akira too, I could tell, remained awake, and when finally I heard him sitting up, I asked him:

"How is your wound?"

"My wound. No trouble, no trouble."

"Let me see it again . . ."

"No, no. No trouble. But thank you. You good friend."

Although we were only inches apart, we could not see each other at all. After a long pause, I heard him say:

"Christopher. You must learn to speak Japanese."

"Yes, I must."

"No, I mean now. You learn Japanese now."

"Well, quite honestly, old fellow, this is hardly the ideal time to . . ."

"No. You must learn. If Japanese soldier come in while I asleep, you must tell them. Tell them we are friend. You must tell them or they shoot in dark."

"Yes. I see your point."

"So you learn. In case I asleep. Or I dead."

"Now look here, I don't want any of that nonsense. You're going to be as fit as a fiddle in no time."

There was another pause, and I remembered from years ago how Akira would fail to follow me if I used colloquialisms. So I said, quite slowly:

"You're going to be perfectly well. Do you understand, Akira? I'll see to it. You're going to be well."

"Very kind," he said. "But precaution is best. You must learn to say. In Japanese. If Japanese soldier come. I teach word. You remember."

He began to say something in his own tongue, but it was much too extended and I stopped him.

"No, no, I'll never learn that. Something much shorter. Just to make clear we're not the enemy."

He thought a moment, then uttered a phrase only slightly shorter than the previous one. I made an attempt, but almost immediately he said:

"No, Christopher. Mistake."

After a few more attempts, I said: "Look, it's no good. Just give me one word. The word for 'friend.' I can't manage anything more tonight."

"*Tomodachi*," he said. "You say. *To-mo-da-chi*."

I repeated this word several times, I thought perfectly accurately, but then realised he was laughing in the darkness. I found myself laughing also, and then, much as we had done earlier, we both began to laugh uncontrollably. We went on laughing for perhaps as long as a full minute, after which I believe I fell asleep quite suddenly.

WHEN I AWOKE, the earliest dawn light was coming into the room. It was a pale, bluish light, as though just one layer of darkness had been removed. The dying man had now gone silent, and from somewhere came the singing of a bird. I could now see that the roof above us had largely vanished, so that from where I lay, my shoulder hard against the brickwork, there were stars visible in the dawn sky.

A movement caught my eye and I sat up in alarm. I then saw three or four rats moving around the dead water-buffalo, and for a few moments I sat gazing at them. Only then did I turn to look at Akira, dreading what I might find. He was lying beside me quite still, and his colour was very pale, but I saw with relief that he was breathing evenly. I found my magnifying glass and began gently to examine his wound, but succeeded only in waking him.

"It's just me," I whispered as he sat up slowly and glanced about him. He looked frightened and bewildered, but then he seemed to remember everything, and a look of numb toughness came into his eyes.

"You were dreaming?" I asked.

He nodded. "Yes. Dreaming."

"Of a better place than this, I should hope," I said with a laugh.

"Yes." He gave a sigh, then added: "I dream of when I am small boy."

We were silent for a moment. Then I said:

"It must have been a rude shock. To come from the world you were dreaming of into this one here."

He was staring at the buffalo's head protruding out of the rubble.

"Yes," he said eventually. "I dream of when I am young boy. My mother, my father. Young boy."

"You remember, Akira. All the games we used to play? On the mound, in our garden? You remember, Akira?"

"Yes. I remember."

"Those are good memories."

"Yes. Very good memories."

"Those were splendid days," I said. "We didn't know it then, of course, just how splendid they were. Children never do, I suppose."

"I have child," Akira said suddenly. "Boy. Five years old."

"Really? I'd like to meet him."

"I lose photo. Yesterday. Day before. When I wound. I lose photo. Of son."

"Now look, old chap, don't get despondent. You'll be seeing your son again in no time."

He continued to stare for some time at the buffalo. A rat made a sudden movement and a cloud of flies rose up, then settled again on the beast.

"My son. He in Japan."

"Oh, you sent him to Japan? That surprises me."

"My son. In Japan. If I die, you tell him, please."

"Tell him that you died? Sorry, can't do that. Because you're not going to die. Not yet anyway."

"You tell him. I die for country. Tell him, be good to mother. Protect. And build good world." He was now almost whispering, struggling to find his words in English, struggling not to weep. "Build good world," he said again, moving his hand through the air like a plasterer smoothing a wall. His gaze followed the hand as though in wonder. "Yes. Build good world."

"When we were boys," I said, "we lived in a good world. These children, these children we've been coming across, what a terrible thing for them to learn so early how ghastly things really are."

"My son," Akira said. "Five years old. In Japan. He know nothing, nothing. He think world is good place. Kind people. His toys. His mother, father."

"I suppose we were like that too. But it's not all downhill, I suppose." I was trying hard now to combat the dangerous despondency settling over my friend. "After all, when we were children, when things went wrong, there wasn't much we could do to help put it right. But now we're adults, now we can. That's the thing, you see? Look at us, Akira. After all this time, we can finally put things right. Remember, old chap, how we used to play those games? Over and over? How we used to pretend we were detectives searching for my father? Now we're grown, we can at last put things right."

Akira did not speak for a long time. Then he said: "When my boy. He discover world is not good. I wish . . ." He stopped, either in pain or because he could not find the English. He said something in Japanese, then went on: "I wish I with him. To help him. When he discover."

"Listen, you great ape," I said, "this is all far too morose. You'll see your son again, I'll see to that. And all this about how good the world looked when we were boys. Well, it's a lot of nonsense in a way. It's just that the adults led us on. One mustn't get too nostalgic for childhood."

"Nos-tal-gic," Akira said, as though it were a word he had been struggling to find. Then he said a word in Japanese, perhaps the Japanese for "nostalgic." "Nos-tal-gic. It is good to be nos-tal-gic. Very important."

"Really, old fellow?"

"Important. Very important. Nostalgic. When we nostalgic, we remember. A world better than this world we discover when we grow. We remember and wish good world come back again. So very important. Just now, I had dream. I was boy. Mother, Father, close to me. In our house."

He fell silent and continued to gaze across the rubble.

"Akira," I said, sensing that the longer this talk went on, the greater was some danger I did not wish fully to articulate. "We should move on. We have much to do."

As though in reply, there came a burst of machine-gun fire. It was further away than the night before, but we both started.

"Akira," I said. "Is it far now to the house? We must try and reach it before the fighting starts again in earnest. How far is it now?"

"Not far. But we go carefully. Chinese soldier very near."

OUR SLEEP, far from refreshing us, appeared to have made us even more depleted. When we stood up and Akira put his weight on me, the pain which went across my neck and shoulders obliged me to let out a moan. For some time, until our bodies grew accustomed again, walking together proved a torturous ordeal.

Our physical conditions aside, the terrain we traversed that morning was by far the most difficult yet. The damage was so extensive, we would frequently have to halt, unable to find a way through the debris. And while it was undeniably a help to see where we were setting down our feet, all the ghastliness that had been hidden by the darkness was now visible to us, taking a profound toll on our spirits. Amidst the wreckage, we could see blood—sometimes fresh, sometimes weeks old—on the ground, on the walls, splashed across broken furniture. Worse still—and our noses would warn us of their presence long before our eyes—we would come across, with disconcerting regularity, piles of human intestines in various stages of decay. Once when we stopped, I remarked to Akira about this, and he said simply:

"Bayonet. Soldier always put bayonet in stomach. If you put here"—he indicated his ribs—"bayonet not come out again. So soldier learn. Always stomach."

"At least the bodies are gone. At least they do that much."

We continued to hear occasional gunfire, and each time we did so, I had the feeling we had come a little closer to it. This concerned me, but Akira now seemed surer than ever of our route, and whenever I questioned his decisions, he shook his head impatiently.

By the time we came across the bodies of the two Chinese soldiers, the morning sun was coming down in strong shafts through the broken roofs. We did not pass close enough to examine them properly, but my guess was that they had not been dead for more than a few hours. One was face-down in the rubble; the other had died on his knees, his forehead resting on the brick wall, as though he had been overcome by melancholy.

At one point, my conviction that we were about to walk right into crossfire grew so strong that I stopped Akira, saying:

"Now look here. What's your game? Where are you leading us?"

He said nothing, but stood leaning against me, his head bowed, recovering his breath.

"Do you really know where we're going? Akira, answer me! Do you know where we're going?"

He raised his head wearily, then indicated over my shoulder.

I turned—I had to do so slowly, for he was still leaning on me—and saw through a broken section of a wall, no more than a dozen steps away, what was undoubtedly the East Furnace.

I said nothing, but led us over to it. Like its twin, the East Furnace had survived the assaults well. It was covered in dust, but looked virtually in working order. Letting go of Akira—he immediately sat down on some rubble—I went right up to the furnace. As on the last occasion, I could see the chimney above me pointing towards the clouds. I went back to where Akira was sitting and gently touched his good shoulder.

"Akira, I'm sorry about my tone just now. I want you to know I'm very grateful to you. I could never have found this by myself. Really, Akira, I'm so grateful."

"Okay." His breath was now a little easier. "You help me. I help you. Okay."

"But Akira, we must be very near the house now. Let me see. Along there"—I indicated—"the alley runs that way. We have to follow the alley."

Akira appeared reluctant to get to his feet, but I hoisted him up and we set off again. I began by following what was clearly the narrow alley the lieutenant had pointed out from the rooftop, but in almost no time we found our way completely barred by fallen debris. We climbed through a wall into a nearby house, then proceeded on what I imagined was a parallel course, picking our way through rubble-strewn rooms.

These houses we now found ourselves in were less damaged, and had clearly been more salubrious than those we had lately come through. There were chairs, dressing tables, even some mirrors and vases still intact amidst the wreckage. I was eager to keep going, but Akira's body began to sag badly, and we were obliged to stop again. We sat down on a fallen beam, and it was as we were recovering our breath that my gaze fell upon the hand-painted name-board lying there in the rubble before us.

It had split cleanly along the grain of the wood, but the two pieces were lying there side by side; I could see also part of the lattice-work by which it had once been fixed to the front entrance. It was not by any means the first time we had come across such a thing, but some instinct drew my attention to this particular item. I went over to it and, extricating the two pieces of wood from the masonry, brought them back to where we were sitting.

"Akira," I said, "can you read this?" I held the pieces together before him.

He gazed at the script for a while, then said: "My Chinese, not good. A name. Someone's name."

"Akira, listen carefully. Look at these characters. You must know something about them. Please, try and read them. It's very important."

He continued to regard the board, then shook his head.

"Akira, listen," I said. "Is it possible this says Yeh Chen? Could that be the name written here?"

"Yeh Chen . . ." Akira looked thoughtful. "Yeh Chen. Yes, possible. This character here . . . Yes, possible. This say Yeh Chen."

"It does? Are you sure?"

"Not sure. But . . . possible. Very possible. Yes"—he gave a nod—"Yeh Chen. I think so."

I put down the two pieces of the board and made my way carefully over the rubble towards the front of the house we were in. There was a broken gap where the doorway had once been, and looking through it, I could see into the narrow alley running outside. I looked across to the house directly facing me. The frontages to the adjoining properties were badly smashed, but the house I was looking at had survived strangely intact. There were hardly any obvious signs of damage: the shutters on the window, the crude sliding wooden lattice door, even the charm dangling above the doorway, had all remained unscathed. After what we had travelled through, it looked like an apparition from another more civilised world. I stood there staring at it for some time. Then I gestured to Akira.

"Look, come here," I said in a near-whisper. "This has to be the house. It can't be any other."

Akira did not move, but gave a deep sigh. "Christopher. You friend. I like very much."

"Keep your voice down. Akira, we've arrived. It's this house. I can feel it now in my bones."

"Christopher . . ." With an effort he rose to his feet and came slowly over the ground. When he was beside me, I pointed out the house. The morning sun shining down into the alley was causing bright streaks to fall across its front.

"There, Akira. There it is."

He sat down by my feet and gave another sigh. "Christopher. My friend. You must think very carefully. It is many years. Many, many years now . . ."

"Isn't it odd," I remarked, "how the fighting's hardly touched that house? The house with my parents inside."

Uttering these words, I suddenly felt almost overwhelmed. But I collected myself and said: "Now, Akira, we have to go in. We'll do it together, arm in arm. Just like that other time, going into Ling Tien's room. You remember, Akira?"

"Christopher. My dear friend. You must think very carefully. It is many, many years. My friend, please, you listen. Perhaps mother and father. It is now so many years . . ."

"We'll go in now together. Then as soon as we've done what we have to do, we'll get you to proper medical help, I promise. In fact, it's possible there'll be something, some first aid, in that house. At least some clean water, perhaps bandages. My mother will be able to look at your injury, perhaps put on a fresh dressing for you. Don't you worry, you'll be fine in no time."

"Christopher. You must think very carefully. So many years go by . . ."

He fell silent as the door across the alley slid open with a rattle. I had hardly started to fumble for the revolver when the small Chinese girl emerged.

She was perhaps six years old. Her face had a still expression, and was rather pretty. Her hair had been tied carefully into little bunches. Her simple jacket and wide trousers were slightly too large for her.

She looked about her, blinking in the sunlight, then looked our way. Spotting us easily—neither of us had moved—she came towards us with surprising fearlessness. She stopped in the alley just a few yards away, and said something in Mandarin, gesturing back to the house.

"Akira, what's she saying?"

"Not understand. Perhaps she invite us inside."

"But how can she be involved? Do you suppose she has something to do with the kidnappers? What's she saying?"

"I think she ask us to help her."

"We'll have to tell her to stand away," I said, drawing my revolver. "We have to anticipate resistance."

"Yes, she ask us to help. She say dog is injured. I think she say dog. My Chinese not good."

Then as we watched, from somewhere near where her carefully tied hair began, a thin line of blood ran down, over her forehead and down her cheek. The little girl appeared to notice nothing and spoke to us again, gesturing once more back to her house.

"Yes," Akira said. "She say dog. Dog is hurt."

"Her dog? *She's* hurt. Perhaps seriously."

I took a step towards her, intending to examine her wound. But she interpreted my movement as compliance, and turning, skipped back across the alley towards her door. She slid it open again, looked towards us appealingly, then disappeared inside.

I stood there for a moment hesitating. Then I reached a hand down to my friend.

"Akira, this is it," I said. "We must go in. Let's go in now together."

CHAPTER 21

J TRIED TO KEEP the revolver poised as we crossed the alley. But Akira's arm was around my neck, and I was having to support so much of his weight, that I imagine our gait as we staggered together into the house was far from authoritative. I was vaguely aware of an ornamental vase standing in the entrance way, and I believe the decoration I had seen dangling from the door frame gave a little chiming sound as we brushed past it. Then I heard the girl's voice speaking and looked about us.

Although the front of the house had remained virtually untouched, the whole of the back half of the room we were in lay in ruin. Thinking about it today, I would suppose a shell had come through the roof, bringing down the upper storey, and destroying the rear of the house, together with the property adjoining it behind. But at that moment I was looking first and foremost for my parents, and I am not sure what exactly I registered. My first giddy thought was that the kidnappers had fled. Then, when I saw the bodies, my terrible fear was that they were those of my mother and father—that the kidnappers had slaughtered them on account of our approach. I have to confess that my next emotion was one of great relief when I saw that the three corpses thrown about the room were all Chinese.

Near the back, over by a wall, was the body of a woman who might have been the young girl's mother. Possibly the blast had thrown her there and she was lying where she had landed. There was a shocked expression on her face. One arm had been torn off at the elbow, and she was now pointing the stump up to the sky, perhaps to indicate the direction from which the shell had come. A few yards away in the debris, an old lady was also gaping up at the hole in the ceiling. One side of her face was charred, but I could see no blood or any obvious mutilation. Finally, closest to where we were standing—he had been obscured at first by a fallen shelf—lay a boy slightly older than the little girl we had followed in. One of his legs had been blown off at the hip, from where surprisingly long entrails, like the decorative tails of a kite, had unfurled over the matting.

"Dog," Akira said beside me.

I stared at him, then followed his gaze. In the centre of the wreckage, not far from the dead boy, the little girl had knelt down beside an injured dog lying on its side and was gently caressing its fur. The dog's tail moved weakly in response. As we stood watching her, she glanced up and said something, her voice remaining quite calm and steady.

"What's she saying, Akira?"

"I think she say we help dog," said Akira. "Yes, she say we help dog." Then suddenly, he began to giggle helplessly.

The young girl spoke again, this time addressing only me, perhaps having dismissed Akira as a lunatic. Then she brought her face down close to the dog's and continued to pass her hand gently over its fur.

I took a step towards her, untangling myself from my friend's arm, and as I did so, Akira crashed over into some broken furniture. I looked back at him in alarm, but he had continued to giggle, and besides, the girl's pleading had gone on unbroken. Laying my revolver down on something, I went over to her and touched her shoulder.

"Look here . . . All of this"—I gestured at the carnage, of which she seemed completely oblivious—"it's awfully bad luck. But look, you've survived, and really, you'll see, you'll make a pretty decent show of it if you just . . . if you just keep up your courage . . ." I turned to Akira in irritation and shouted: "Akira! Stop that noise! For God's sake, there's nothing to laugh about! This poor girl . . ."

But the girl had now grasped my sleeve. She spoke again, carefully and slowly, looking into my eyes.

"Look, really," I said, "you're being awfully brave. I swear to you, whoever did all this, whoever did this ghastly thing, they won't escape justice. You may not know who I am, but as it happens, I'm . . . well, I'm just the person you want. I'll see to it they don't get away. Don't you worry, I'll . . . I'll . . ." I had been fumbling about in my jacket, but I now found my magnifying glass and showed it to her. "Look, you see?"

I kicked aside a bird-cage in my path and went over to the mother. Then, perhaps out of habit as much as anything else, I bent down and began to examine her through the glass. Her stump looked peculiarly clean; the bone protruding out of the flesh was a shiny white, almost as though someone had been polishing it.

My memory of these moments is no longer very clear. But I have a feeling it was at this point, just after I stared through the glass at the woman's stump, that I suddenly straightened and began to search for my parents. I can only say, by way of partial explanation for what ensued, that Akira was still giggling where he had fallen, and that the girl was continuing to make her pleas in the same even, persistent tones. In other words, the atmosphere had become fairly overwrought, and this might account to some extent for the manner in which I went about turning what was left of that little house upside down.

There was a tiny room at the back, completely destroyed by the shelling, and it was here I began my search, pulling up broken floorboards, smashing open with a table leg the doors of an upturned cupboard. I then returned to the main room and began to heave aside the piles of wreckage, smashing with my table leg at anything that failed readily to yield to my kicks and manoeuvres. Eventually, I became aware that Akira had stopped his giggling and was following me about, pulling at my shoulder and saying something in my ear. I ignored him and carried on with my search, not pausing even when I accidentally threw over one of the bodies. Akira continued to pull at my shoulder, and after a time, unable to comprehend why the very person I had counted on to assist me was instead bent on hindering me, I turned to him, shouting something like:

"Get off me! Get off! If you won't help, then just go away! Go off into your corner and giggle!"

"Soldiers!" he was hissing at me. "Soldiers coming!"

"Get off me! My mother, my father! Where are they? They're not here! Where are they? Where are they?"

"Soldiers! Christopher, stop, you must calm! You must calm or we killed! Christopher!"

He was shaking me, his face close to mine. I then realised that indeed there were voices coming from somewhere close by.

I allowed Akira to pull me to the back of the room. The little girl, I noticed, had now fallen silent, and was gently cradling the dog's head. The animal's tail was still making the occasional faint movement.

"Christopher," Akira said in an urgent whisper. "If soldier Chinese, I must hide." He pointed to the corner. "Chinese soldier must not find. But if Japanese, you must say word I teach."

"I can't say anything. Look, old fellow, if you're not willing to help me . . ."

"Christopher! Soldier coming!"

He tottered across the room and disappeared into a cupboard standing at an angle in the corner. The door was sufficiently damaged so that the whole of his shin and a boot were clearly visible through the panel. It was such a pathetic attempt to hide that I began to laugh, and was about to call out that I could still see him, when the soldiers appeared in the doorway.

The first soldier to come in fired his rifle at me, but the bullet hit the wall behind me. He then noticed my raised hands, and the fact that I was a foreign civilian, and shouted something to his comrades, who crowded in behind him. They were Japanese, and the next thing I remember, three or four of them began to argue about me, all the time covering me with their rifles. More soldiers came in and began to search the place. I heard Akira call out from his hiding place something in Japanese, then as soldiers crowded around his cupboard, I saw him emerge. I noticed he did not seem particularly pleased to see them, nor they him. Other men had gathered around the little girl, also arguing what to do. Then an officer entered, the men all stood to attention, and a silence fell over the room.

The officer—a young captain—glanced about the room. His gaze fell on the child, then on me, then settled on Akira, now supported by two soldiers. A conversation ensued in Japanese, in which Akira himself took no part. A resigned expression, with elements of fear, had come into his eyes. He once tried to say something to the captain, but the latter immediately cut him off. There was another quick exchange, then the soldiers began to lead Akira away. The fear was now very evident in his face, but he did not resist.

"Akira!" I called after him. "Akira, where are they taking you? What's wrong?"

Akira glanced back and gave me a quick, affectionate smile. Then he was gone, out into the alley, crowded from my view by the soldiers accompanying him.

The young captain was looking at the child. Then he turned to me and said:

"You Englishman?"

"Yes."

"Pray, sir, what do you do here?"

"I was . . ." I looked around. "I was looking for my parents. My name is Banks, Christopher Banks. I'm a well-known detective. Perhaps you've . . ."

I did not quite know how to continue, and besides, I realised I had been sobbing for some time, and that this was making a poor impression on the captain. I wiped my face and continued: "I came here to find my parents. But they're not here any more. I'm too late."

The captain looked around once more at the debris, the corpses, the little girl with the dying dog. Then he said something to the soldier nearest him, never taking his eyes from me. Finally he said to me: "Pray, sir, you come with me."

He made a polite but firm gesture that I should precede him out into the alley. He had not holstered his pistol, but then nor was it aimed at me.

"This little girl," I said. "Will you take her somewhere safe?"

He gazed back at me in silence. Then he said: "Pray, sir. You leave now."

I WAS ON THE WHOLE looked after decently by the Japanese. They kept me in a little back room within their headquarters—a former fire station—where I was fed and a doctor treated me for several injuries I had barely noticed receiving. My foot was bandaged and I was even provided with a large boot to accommodate it. The soldiers in charge of me spoke no English, and appeared uncertain whether I was a prisoner or a guest, but I was too exhausted to care; I lay on the camp bed they had put up in my back room, and for several hours, drifted in and out of sleep. I was not locked in; in fact, the door to the adjoining office would not close properly, so that whenever I came back to consciousness, I could hear Japanese voices arguing, or else shouting down a telephone, presumably about me. I now suspect I was suffering from a mild fever for much of that period; whatever, as I went in and out of sleep, the events not only of the past few hours, but of the last several weeks, circled around my head. Then gradually, one by one, the cobwebs began to clear, so that by the time I was awoken, towards the late afternoon, by the arrival of Colonel Hasegawa, I found I had an entirely fresh view on all that had been troubling me about the case.

Colonel Hasegawa—a dapper man in his forties—introduced himself politely, saying: "I am glad to see you are feeling so much better, Mr. Banks. I trust these men here have looked after you well. I am pleased to tell you I have come with instructions to escort you to the British consulate. May I suggest we set off at once?"

"Actually, Colonel," I said, rising gingerly to my feet, "I would prefer it if you could take me somewhere else. You see, it's rather urgent. I'm not sure of the exact address, but it's not so far from Nanking Road. Perhaps you know it. It's a shop selling gramophone records."

"You are so eager to purchase gramophone records?"

I could not be bothered to explain, so just said: "It's important I get there as quickly as possible."

"Unfortunately, sir, I have instructions to deliver you to the British consulate. I fear we shall cause great inconvenience if I do otherwise."

I gave a sigh. "I suppose you're right, Colonel. In any case, now I think about it, I fancy I shall be too late."

The colonel looked at his wristwatch. "Yes, I fear you might. But if I may suggest. If we set off straight away, then you will be enjoying your music again with minimum delay."

We travelled in an open military vehicle driven by the colonel's batman. It was a fine afternoon and the sun was beating down on the ruins of Chapei. We moved slowly, for though much of the debris had been cleared out of our path—there were huge piles of it on the roadside—the road was pitted with craters. Occasionally we would pass down a street with almost no sign of damage; but then we would turn the corner and the houses would be little more than piles of rubble, and every surviving telegraph pole would be standing at an odd angle between tangled cables. Once, as we moved through such an area, I found I could see a fair distance across the flattened ruins, and caught sight of the chimneys from the two furnaces.

"England is a splendid country," Colonel Hasegawa was saying. "Calm, dignified. Beautiful green fields. I still dream of it. And your literature. Dickens, Thackeray. Wuthering Heights. I am especially fond of your Dickens."

"Colonel, excuse me for bringing this up. But when your men found me yesterday, I was with someone. A Japanese soldier. Do you happen to know what became of him?"

"That soldier. I am not certain what became of him."

"I do wonder where I might find him again."

"You wish to find him again?" The colonel's face became serious. "Mr. Banks, I would advise you not to concern yourself any more with that soldier."

"Colonel, has he in your eyes committed some offence?"

"Offence?" He looked at the passing ruins with a gentle smile. "Almost certainly that soldier gave information to the enemy. It is likely that is how he negotiated his release from captivity. I understand you yourself said in your statement you found him near the Kuomintang lines. That is most suggestive of cowardice and betrayal."

I was about to protest, but realised it was in neither Akira's nor my interests to fall out with the colonel. After I had been silent for a time, he said:

"It is wise not to become too sentimental."

His accent, which was otherwise impressive, faltered on this last word, so that it came out as "sen-chee-men-tol." It rather grated on me and I turned away without responding. But a moment later he asked in a sympathetic tone:

"This soldier. You had met him somewhere previously?"

"I thought I had. I thought he was a friend of mine from my childhood. But now, I'm not so certain. I'm beginning to see now, many things aren't as I supposed."

The colonel nodded. "Our childhood seems so far away now. All this"—he gestured out of the vehicle—"so much suffering. One of our Japanese poets, a court lady many years ago, wrote of how sad this was. She wrote of how our childhood becomes like a foreign land once we have grown."

"Well, Colonel, it's hardly a foreign land to me. In many ways, it's where I've continued to live all my life. It's only now I've started to make my journey from it."

We passed through Japanese checkpoints into Hongkew, the northern district of the Settlement. In this region too there were signs of war damage, as well as those of anxious military preparation. I saw many piles of sandbags, and trucks filled with soldiers. As we approached the canal, the colonel said:

"Like yourself, Mr. Banks, I am very fond of music. In particular, Beethoven, Mendelssohn, Brahms. Chopin also. The third sonata is marvellous."

"A cultured man like you, Colonel," I remarked, "must regret all this. I mean all this carnage caused by your country's invasion of China."

I feared he would become angry, but he smiled calmly and said:

"It is regrettable, I agree. But if Japan is to become a great nation, like yours, Mr. Banks, it is necessary. Just as it once was for England."

We were silent for a few moments. Then he asked:

"I am sure, yesterday, in Chapei, you saw unpleasant things?"

"Yes. I certainly did."

Suddenly he let out a strange laugh, which made me start. "Mr. Banks," he said, "do you realise, do you have any idea, of the unpleasantness yet to come?"

"If you continue to invade China, I am sure . . ."

"Excuse me, sir"—he was now quite animated—"I am not talking merely of China. *The entire globe,* Mr. Banks, the entire globe will before long be engaged in war. What you just saw in Chapei, it is but a small speck of dust compared to what the world must soon witness!" He said this in a triumphant tone, but then he shook his head sadly. "It will be terrible," he said quietly. "Terrible. You have no idea, sir."

I DO NOT REMEMBER CLEARLY those first hours following my return. But I would suppose my arrival in the grounds of the British consulate, conveyed by a Japanese military vehicle, and looking more or less like a tramp, did little for the morale of an anxious community. I remember vaguely the officials rushing out to meet us, and then, as I was taken into the building, the look on the face of the consul-general as he came hurrying down the stairs. I do not know what his first words to me were, but I do recall my saying to him, perhaps even before any greeting had passed my lips:

"Mr. George, I must ask you to let me see your man MacDonald without delay."

"MacDonald? *John* MacDonald? But why do you wish to talk to *him*, old fellow? Look, what you need is to rest up. We'll have a doctor look you over . . ."

"I accept I'm looking a little the worse for wear. Don't worry, I'll go and freshen up a bit. But please, have MacDonald ready for me. It's very important."

I WAS SHOWN to a guest room in the consulate building, where I managed a shave and a hot bath despite a whole series of people knocking on my door. One of these was a dour Scottish surgeon who examined me for a good half-hour, convinced I was concealing some serious injury from him. Others came to ask after one or another aspect of my welfare, and I sent at least three of them back with an impatient query concerning MacDonald. I received only vague replies about his not yet having been located; and then, as the evening drew on, exhaustion—or perhaps something the surgeon had given me—sent me off into a deep sleep.

I did not awake until well into the following morning. I had breakfast brought to my room, and changed into some fresh clothes delivered from the Cathay while I had been asleep. I then felt a lot better, and decided I would go and seek out MacDonald then and there.

I thought I could remember the way to MacDonald's office from our last meeting, but the consulate building was rather deceptive and I was obliged to ask directions from a number of people I encountered. I was still a little lost, making my way down a flight of stairs, when I spotted the figure of Sir Cecil Medhurst standing on the landing below me.

The morning sun was streaming through the tall landing windows, lighting up a large area of grey stone around him. There was no one else on the landing, and Sir Cecil was stooping forward slightly, hands clasped behind his back, gazing down on to the consulate grounds below. I was tempted to retreat back up the stairs, but it was a quiet part of the building, and there was a chance my footsteps would make him look up at any moment. I thus continued my descent, and as I came up to him, he turned as though he had been aware all along of my approach.

"Hello, old fellow," he said. "Heard you were back. A bit of a panic when you went missing, I'll tell you. Feeling better?"

"Yes. I'm fine, thanks. Just this foot's a little awkward. Won't quite fit into my shoe."

The sun in his face made him look old and tired. He turned back to the window again and peered out; moving alongside him, I too looked out. Below us, three Sikh policemen were hurrying back and forth across the lawn, stacking sandbags into piles.

"You heard she's gone?" Sir Cecil asked.

"Yes."

"Of course, when you went missing at the same time, I jumped to conclusions. So did a few other people, I fancy. That's why I came along this morning. To offer you my apologies. But they told me you were sleeping. So I was just . . . well, just kicking my heels here."

"There's hardly any need for apologies, Sir Cecil."

"Oh yes there is. I fancy I went around saying a few things the other evening. You know. Jumping to conclusions. Of course, everyone knows now I was making a fool of myself. But all the same, thought I'd better come along and explain myself."

Down on the lawn, a Chinese coolie arrived with a wheelbarrow containing more sandbags. The Sikh policemen began unloading them.

"Did she leave a letter?" I asked, trying to sound nonchalant.

"No. But I did receive a cable this morning. She's in Macao, you know. Says she's safe and well. Says she's by herself, and that she'll be writing soon." Then he turned to me and grasped my elbow. "Banks, I know you'll miss her too. In some ways, you know, I'd have preferred it if she'd gone off with you. I know she . . . she thought jolly well of you."

"It must have come as a big shock," I remarked, for want of something to say.

Sir Cecil turned away and for a time went on gazing down at the policemen. Then he said: "Wasn't really, to tell you the truth. No shock at all." Then he went on: "I always told her she should go, told her she should go and find love, you know, true love. She deserves it, don't you think? That's where she's gone now. Off to find true love. Perhaps she'll find it too. Out there, on the South China Sea, who knows? Perhaps she'll meet a traveller, in a port, in a hotel, who knows? She's become a romantic, you see? I had to let her go." There were now tears welling in his eyes.

"What will you do now, sir?" I asked gently.

"What will I do? Who knows? Ought to go home, I expect. I suppose that's what I'll do. Go home. Just as soon as I've paid off a few debts here, that is."

I had been conscious of footsteps coming down the stairs behind us, but now they slowed to a halt and we both of us turned. I was rather dismayed to see Grayson, the official from the Municipal Council.

"Good morning, Mr. Banks. Good morning, Sir Cecil. Mr. Banks, we're all so pleased to see you back and safe."

"Thank you, Mr. Grayson." And when he continued simply to stand there on the bottom stair smiling foolishly, I added: "I trust all the arrangements for the Jessfield Park ceremony are progressing to your satisfaction."

"Oh yes, yes." He gave a vague laugh. "But just now, Mr. Banks, I came to find you because I heard you were wishing to speak with Mr. MacDonald."

"Yes, that's right. In fact, I was just on my way to find him."

"Ah. Well, he won't be in his usual office. If you'd follow me, sir, I'll take you to him now."

I gave Sir Cecil a gentle squeeze on the shoulder—he had turned back to the window to hide his tears—then followed Grayson with an eager step.

He led me through a deserted section of the building, and then we came to a corridor containing a row of offices. I could hear someone talking on the telephone, and a man who emerged from one of the doors nodded to Grayson. Grayson opened another door and waved for me to go in ahead of him.

I stepped into a small but well-appointed office dominated by a large desk. I stopped at the threshold because there was no one in the room, but Grayson nudged me further in and closed the door. He then walked around the desk, sat down, and gestured towards the empty seat.

"Mr. Grayson," I said, "I have no time for these foolish pranks."

"I'm sorry," Grayson said, "I know you wished to see MacDonald. But you see, MacDonald's domain is protocol. He discharges his duties very well, but his territory doesn't really extend much further."

I sighed with impatience, but before I could speak, Grayson went on:

"You see, old chap, when you said you wanted MacDonald, I assumed you wanted me. I'm the fellow you need to speak to."

I then noticed there was something different about Grayson. His ingratiating air had vanished, and he was watching me steadily over the desk. When he saw understanding dawn in my face, he gestured once more at the chair.

"Please make yourself comfortable, old chap. And I do apologise for having rather dogged you since your arrival here. But you see, I had to make sure you didn't do anything to cause a big stink with the other Powers. Now, let me see, I take it you want a meeting with the Yellow Snake."

"Yes, Mr. Grayson. I wonder if you can arrange such a thing."

"As it happens, we finally got word while you were away. All parties seem happy now to grant your request." Then leaning forward, he said to me: "So, Mr. Banks. Do you feel you're closing in?"

"Yes, Mr. Grayson. At last, I believe I am."

SO IT WAS that just after eleven o'clock last night, I found myself travelling by car through the elegant residential areas of the French Concession in the company of two officers from the Chinese secret police. We went down avenues lined with trees, past large houses, some entirely hidden behind high walls and hedges. Then we came through gates heavily guarded by men in gowns and hats, and halted in a gravelled courtyard. A dark house, four or five storeys high, stood before us.

Inside, the lights were low, and more guards lurked everywhere in the shadows. As I followed my escorts up the central staircase, I gained the impression the house had until recently belonged to a wealthy European, but had now, for some reason, fallen into the hands of the Chinese authorities; I could see crude notices and schedules pinned up on the walls right alongside exquisite works of Western and Chinese art.

To judge from its decor, the room I was shown into up on the second floor had until recently contained a billiard table. There was now a yawning space in the middle of the room, around which I paced while I waited. After twenty minutes or so, I heard the sound of more cars arriving down in the courtyard, but when I tried to see out of the windows, I found these gave on to the gardens to the side of the house, and I could see nothing at all of the front.

It was perhaps another half-hour before I was finally fetched. I was escorted up another flight of stairs, then along a corridor past more guards. Then my escorts stopped, and one of them pointed to a door several yards before us. I went the last lap alone, and entered what appeared to be a large study. There was thick carpet beneath my feet, and the walls were almost entirely lined with books. At the far end, where heavy drapes had been drawn across the bay windows, was a desk with a chair on either side of it. A reading lamp on the desk created a warm pool of light, but otherwise much of the room was in shadow. As I stood surveying my surroundings, a figure rose from behind the desk and, stepping carefully around it, gestured back to the chair he had vacated.

"Why don't you take this seat, Puffin?" Uncle Philip said to me. "You remember, don't you? You always loved to sit in my chair behind my desk."

CHAPTER 22

*H*AD I NOT BEEN EXPECTING to see him, it is perfectly possible I would have failed to recognise Uncle Philip. He had put on weight over the years, so that though he was not stout, his neck had thickened and his cheeks were sagging. His hair was wispy and white. But his eyes were calm and humorous in much the way I remembered.

I did not smile as I came towards him; nor did I go behind the desk to the chair he had offered. "I'll sit here," I said, stopping beside the other chair.

Uncle Philip shrugged. "Well, it's not my desk anyway. In fact, I've never set foot in this house before. Something to do with you, this place?"

"I've never been here before either. May I suggest we sit down?"

When we did so, we could see each other clearly for the first time in the light from the desk lamp, and we spent a moment carefully studying one another's features.

"You haven't changed so much, you know, Puffin," he said. "Easy to see the boy in you, even now."

"I'd appreciate you not calling me by that name."

"Sorry. Rather cheeky, I admit. So here we are, you managed to track me down. I kept refusing to meet you before. But in the end, I suppose I began to want to see you again. Owe you an explanation or two, I expect. But I wasn't sure, you see, how you regarded me. Friend or foe, that sort of thing. But then these days I'm not sure about most people on that score. Do you know, they told me to keep this with me just in case?" He produced a little silver pistol and held it up to the light. "Can you believe it? They thought you might wish to attack me."

"But I see you brought it along just the same."

"Oh, but I carry it everywhere. So many people wanting to do me mischief these days. I didn't really bring it on your account. One of those men standing out there. Perhaps he's been bribed to burst in here and stab me. Who can tell? That's the way it's been for me, I'm afraid. Ever since this Yellow Snake lark started."

"Yes. It would seem you're much given to treachery."

"That's a bit harsh, if you're implying what I think you're imply-ing. As far as the communists are concerned, very well, yes, I've turned traitor. Even there, it was never my intention, you know. Chiang's men got hold of me one day and threatened to torture me. I admit, I didn't fancy that much, didn't fancy it one bit. But in the end, they did a far cleverer thing. They *tricked* me into betraying one of my number. And then, you see, that was that. Because as you've seen, no one punishes turncoats more savagely than my old comrades. There was no other way for me to stay alive. I had to depend on the government to protect me from my comrades."

"According to my investigations," I said, "a lot of people have lost their lives through you. And not just those you betrayed. There was a time, a year ago, when you allowed the communists to believe the Yellow Snake was another man. Many of his family members, including three children, were killed in the first wave of reprisals."

"I don't consider myself admirable. I'm a coward, and I've known it a long time. But I can hardly be held to account for the

Reds' savagery. They've proved themselves every bit as vicious as Chiang Kai-shek ever was, and I've no respect left for them. But look here, I don't expect you came to talk about all this."

"No, I didn't."

"So, Puffin. I'm sorry. Christopher. So. What shall I tell you? Where shall we begin?"

"My parents. Where are they?"

"Your father I'm afraid is dead. Has been for many years. I'm sorry."

I said nothing and waited. Eventually he said:

"Tell me, Christopher. What do you believe happened to your father?"

"Is it any business of yours what I believe? I came here to hear it from you."

"Very well. But I was curious to know what you'd worked out for yourself. After all, you've made quite a name for yourself for such things."

This irritated me, but it occurred to me he would be forthcoming only on his own terms. So in the end, I said: "My conjecture has been that my father made a stand, a courageous stand, against his own employers concerning the profits from the opium trade of those years. In doing so, I supposed he set himself against enormous interests, and was thus removed."

Uncle Philip nodded. "I'd supposed you believed something like that. Your mother and I discussed carefully what to have you believe. And it was more or less what you've just said. So we were successful. The truth, I'm afraid, Puffin, was much more prosaic. Your father ran off one day with his mistress. He lived with her in Hong Kong for a year, a woman called Elizabeth Cornwallis. But Hong Kong is awfully stuffy and British, you know. They were a scandal, and in the end they had to rush off to Malacca or some such place. Then he got typhoid and died, in Singapore. That was two years after he left you. I'm sorry, old fellow, it's hard to hear all this, I know. But brace yourself. Because I've a lot more to tell you before the evening's out."

"You say my mother knew? At the time?"

"Yes. Not at first, mind you. Not for a good month or so. Your father covered his tracks rather well. Your mother only found out because he wrote to her. She and I were the only ones who ever knew the truth."

"But the detectives. How on earth did the detectives fail to discover what he'd done?"

"The detectives?" Uncle Philip let out a laugh. "Those underpaid, overworked flat-feet? They wouldn't have found an elephant gone missing in Nanking Road." Then when I remained silent, he said: "She would have told you eventually. But we wanted to protect you. That's why we had you believe what you did."

I had started to feel uncomfortable sitting so close to the desk lamp, but the upright chair did not allow me to sit back. Then after I had maintained my silence another few moments, Uncle Philip said:

"Let me be fair to your father. It was difficult for him. He always loved your mother, loved her intensely. I'm jolly sure he never stopped loving her right to the end. In some ways, Puffin, that was the trouble. He loved her too much, idealised her. And it was just too much for him, trying to come up to what he saw as her mark. He tried. Oh yes, he tried, and it nearly broke him. He might have just said: 'Look here, I can only do so much and that's it, I'm who I am.' But he adored her. Wanted desperately to make himself good enough for her, and when he found he didn't have it in him, well, he went off. With someone who didn't mind him as he was. It's my belief he just wanted *rest*. He'd tried so hard for so many years, he just wanted rest. Don't think so badly of him, Puffin. I don't believe he ever stopped loving you or your mother."

"And my mother? What has become of her?"

Uncle Philip leant forward on his elbows and tilted back his head slightly. "How much do you know already about her?" he asked.

The lightness he had earlier contrived to place in his voice had evaporated altogether. He now looked a haunted old man, consumed with self-hatred. He was gazing at me carefully despite his tilted head, and the yellow light from the desk lamp showed white whiskers growing out of his nostrils. From somewhere downstairs, I could hear a phonograph playing Chinese martial music.

"I'm not trying to annoy you," he said, when I did not answer. "I don't want to hear myself talking any more about it than I have to. Come on. How much have you found out?"

"I was until recently under the impression both my parents were being held captive in Chapei. So you see, I have not been so clever."

I waited for him to speak. He remained in his curious posture for a time, then sat back and said:

"You won't remember this. But shortly after your father went away, I came to your house to see your mother. And a certain man came also that day. A Chinese gentleman."

"You're referring to the warlord, Wang Ku."

"Ah. Then you haven't been so foolish."

"I found out his name. But thereafter, I suspect I've been too busy following a false trail."

He gave a sigh and cocked his ear. "Listen," he said. "Kuomintang anthems. They play them to tease me. Wherever they take me, it's like this. Happens too often to be a coincidence." Then when I said nothing, he rose to his feet and wandered into the shadows towards the heavy curtains.

"Your mother," he said eventually, "was devoted to our campaign. To stop the opium trade into China. Many European companies, including your father's, were making vast profits importing Indian opium into China and turning millions of Chinese into helpless addicts. In those days, I was one of those central to the campaign. For a long time, our strategy was rather naive. We thought we could shame these companies into giving up their opium profits. We wrote letters, presented them with evidence showing the damage opium was causing to the Chinese people. Yes, you may laugh, we were very naive. But you see, we thought we were dealing with fellow-Christians. Well, eventually we saw we were getting nowhere. We discovered that these people, they not only liked the profits very much, they actually *wanted* the Chinese to be useless. They liked them to be in chaos, drug-addicted, unable to govern themselves properly. That way, the country could be run virtually like a colony, but with none of the usual obligations. So we changed our tactics. We grew more sophisticated. In those days, just as they do still, the opium shipments came along the Yangtze. Boats had to bring them upriver through bandit country. Without adequate protection, the shipments wouldn't get much beyond the Yangtze gorges without being marauded. So all these companies, Morganbrook and Byatt, Jardine Matheson, all of them, they used to make deals with the local warlords through whose territories the shipments passed. These warlords were just glorified bandits really, but they had armies, they had the power to see the shipments through. So here was our new strategy. No longer did we plead with the trading companies. We pleaded with the warlords. Appealed to their racial pride. We pointed out it was in their hands to end the profitability of the opium trade, to reverse the one major obstacle to the Chinese taking command of their own fate, their own land. Of course, some were too keen on the payments they received. But we had some converts. Wang Ku was at that time one of the more powerful of these bandit lords. His territory covered several hundred square miles in the north of Hunan. A pretty brutal chap, but sufficiently feared and respected to make him valuable indeed to the trading companies. Now Wang Ku became very sympathetic to our cause. He often came to Shanghai, liked the high life here, and we were able to prevail on him during these visits. Puffin, are you well?"

"Yes, I'm fine. I'm listening."

"Perhaps you should go now, Puffin. You don't have to hear what I'm about to tell you."

"Tell me. I'm listening."

"Very well. My feeling is that you should hear it, if you can bear to. Because . . . well, because you must find her. There's still a chance you can find her."

"So my mother is alive?"

"I've no reason to suppose otherwise."

"Then tell me. Go on with what you're saying."

He came back to the desk and sat down once more in front of me. "That day Wang Ku came to your house," he said. "It's fitting you should remember that day. You're quite right to suspect it was important. It was the day your mother discovered that Wang Ku's motives were far from pure. Put simply, he planned to seize the opium shipments himself. Of course, he'd made complicated arrangements, so that it went through three or four other parties, very Chinese that, but in the end, yes, that's what it amounted to. Most of us already knew this, but your mother didn't. We'd kept her in the dark, perhaps foolishly, because we sensed she'd not accept it. The rest of us, naturally we had qualms, but we decided to work with Wang nevertheless. Yes, he'd sell the opium to the same people the trading companies did. But the important thing was to stop the imports. To make the trade unprofitable. Unfortunately, that day Wang Ku came to your house he said something that for the first time made clear to your mother the reality of his relationship with us. My guess is she felt foolish. Perhaps she'd suspected it all along, but hadn't wished to look at it, and was as angry with herself and with me as she was with Wang. In any case, she quite lost her temper, actually struck him. Only lightly, you understand, but her hand did touch his cheek. And of course, she said everything she had to say to his face. I knew then some terrible price would have to be paid. I tried to sort the thing out then and there. I explained to him how your father had just left, that your mother was really upset, I tried to convey all this to him as he left. He smiled and said not to worry, but I worried, oh yes, I worried all right. I knew that what your mother had done couldn't be undone so easily. I'd have been relieved, I tell you, if all Wang had done in response was stop participating in our plan. But he wanted the opium, he'd already made plenty of arrangements. Besides, he'd been insulted by a foreign woman, and he wanted to put things right."

As I leant towards him into the glare of the lamp, an odd feeling came over me that behind my back the darkness had grown and grown, so that now a vast black space had opened up there. Uncle Philip had paused to wipe some sweat from his forehead with the heel of a hand. But now he looked at me intently and continued:

"I went to see Wang Ku later that day at the Metropole. I did what I could to try and stop the calamity I knew would come. But it was no use. What he told me that afternoon was that far from being angered by your mother, he'd found her spirit—that's what he called it, her 'spirit'—highly attractive. So much so that he wished to take her back with him as a concubine, back to Hunan. He proposed to 'tame' your mother, as he would a wild mare. Now you must understand, Puffin, the way things were then, in Shanghai, in China, if a man like Wang Ku decided on a course like that, there was little anyone could do to stop him. That's what you must understand. Nothing at all would have been achieved by asking the police or whoever to guard your mother. That might have slowed things down a little, but that's all. There was no one who could protect your mother from the intentions of a man like that. But you see, Puffin, my great fear was for you. I wasn't sure what he intended to do with you, and that's what I was really pleading for. In the end, we came to an agreement. I would arrange things so that your mother was alone, unguarded, if at that same time I could take you right away from the scene. That's all I wanted to do. I didn't want him to take you too. Your mother, that was an inevitability. But for you, there was something to plead for. And that's what I did."

There was a substantial pause. Then I said:

"After this convenient arrangement, do I take it Wang Ku continued to co-operate with your scheme?"

"Don't be cynical, Puffin."

"But did he?"

"As it happened, he did. Taking your mother satisfied him. He did as we wished him to do, and I dare say, his contribution was a factor in the companies' eventual decision to end the trade."

"So my mother was, you might say, sacrificed for a greater cause."

"Look, Puffin, it wasn't anything any of us had a choice about. You must understand that."

"Did you ever see my mother again? After she was abducted by this man?"

I saw him hesitate. But then he said:

"Yes. As a matter of fact, I did. Once, seven years later. I happened to be travelling through Hunan and accepted Wang's invitation to be his guest. And there, in his fortress, yes, I did see your mother one last time."

His voice was now almost a whisper. The phonograph downstairs was no longer playing, so that a stillness hung between us.

"And . . . and what had become of her?"

"She was in good health. She was, of course, one of several concubines. Under the circumstances, I'd say she'd adapted well to her new life."

"How had she been treated?"

Uncle Philip looked away. Then he said quietly: "When I saw her, she asked about you, naturally. I told her what news I had. She was pleased. You see, until I saw her that time, she'd been utterly cut off from the outside world. For seven years, she'd only heard what Wang chose to have her hear. What I mean is, she didn't know for certain that the financial arrangement was working. So when I saw her, that's what she wanted to know, and I was able to reassure her that it was. After seven years of torturous doubt, her mind was put at rest. I can't tell you how relieved she was. 'That's all I wanted to know,' she kept saying. 'That's all I wanted to know.' "

He was watching me now very carefully. After another moment, I gave him the question for which he was waiting.

"Uncle Philip, what financial arrangement?"

He looked down at the back of his hands and studied them for a time. "Had it not been for you, her love for you, Puffin, your mother, I know, would have taken her own life without a moment's hesitation before allowing that scoundrel to lay a finger on her. She would have found a way, and she would have done it. But there was you to consider. So in the end, when she saw the situation for what it was, she made an arrangement. You would be financially provided for in return for . . . for her compliance. I saw to much of it myself, arranged it through the company. There was a man there at Byatt's, didn't have a clue what it was all about. Thought he was securing safe passage for his opium. Ha ha! He was a fool, that man!" Uncle Philip shook his head and smiled. Then his face darkened again, as though he were now resigned to the course our conversation would take.

"My allowance," I said quietly. "My inheritance . . ."

"Your aunt in England. She was never wealthy. Your real benefactor, all these years, has been Wang Ku."

"So all this time, I've been living . . . I've been living off . . ." I could not go on and simply stopped.

Uncle Philip nodded. "Your schooling. Your place in London society. The fact that you made of yourself what you have. You owe it to Wang Ku. Or rather, to your mother's sacrifice."

He stood up again, and when he looked at me I saw something new in his face, something almost like hatred. But then he turned and moved away into the shadows, and I could see it no more.

"That time I last saw your mother," he said. "In that fortress.

She'd lost all concern for the opium campaign. She only lived for you, worried for you. By that time, the trade had been made illegal. But even that news meant nothing to her any more. Of course I was bitter about it, as were the others of us who'd given years to the campaign. We'd finally achieved our goal, we thought. Opium trade abolished. It only took a year or two to see what abolition really meant. The trade had simply changed hands, that was all. It was now run by Chiang's government. More addicts than ever, but now it was being peddled to pay for Chiang Kai-shek's army, to pay for his power. That's when I joined the Reds, Puffin. Your mother, I thought she'd be devastated to know what our campaign had amounted to, but she no longer cared. All she wanted was for you to be looked after. She only wanted news of you. Do you know, Puffin"—his voice suddenly took on a strange edge—"when I saw her that time, she seemed well enough. But while I was there, I asked others in the household, people who would know. I wanted to find out the truth, find out how she'd really been treated, because . . . because I knew that one day this moment, this meeting we're having now, was bound to come. And I found out. Oh yes, I found out. Everything."

"Are you deliberately trying to torment me?"

"It wasn't just . . . just a matter of surrendering to him in bed. He regularly whipped her in front of his dinner guests. Taming the white woman, he called it. And that wasn't all. Do you know . . .".

I had already covered my ears, but now shouted out: "Enough! Why torture me like this?"

"Why?" His voice was now angry. "Why? Because I want you to know the truth! All these years, you've thought of me as a despicable creature. Perhaps I am, but it's what this world does to you. I never meant to be like this. I meant to do good in this world. In my way, I once made courageous decisions. And look at me now. You despise me. You've despised me all these years, Puffin, the closest thing I ever had to a son, and you despise me still. But now do you see how the world really is? You see what made possible your comfortable life in England? How you were able to become a celebrated detective? A detective! What good is that to anyone? Stolen jewels, aristocrats murdered for their inheritance. Do you suppose that's all there is to contend with? Your mother, she wanted you to live in your enchanted world for ever. But it's impossible. In the end it has to shatter. It's a miracle it survived so long for you. Now, Puffin, here. I'll give you this chance. Here."

He had taken out his pistol again. He came from the shadows towards me, and when I looked up, he was looming above me, much as he had done in my childhood. He flung back his jacket and pressed the pistol into his waistcoat near his heart.

"Here," he said, bending down and whispering so I could smell his stale breath. "Here, boy. You can kill me. As you've always wanted to. That's why I've stayed alive so long. No one else should have that privilege. I've saved myself, you see, for you. Pull the trigger. Here, look. We'll make it appear as if I attacked you. I'll be holding the gun, I'll fall over you. When they come in, they'll see my body collapsed over you, it'll look like self-defence. See, here, I'm holding it. You pull the trigger, Puffin."

His waistcoat was pushing against my face, moving up and down with his heaving chest. I felt a revulsion, and tried to move away, but his free hand—the skin felt indescribably parched—had grasped my arm in an effort to draw me to him. It occurred to me he would pull the trigger himself if my hand so much as touched the pistol. I pulled back violently, unbalancing my chair, and staggered away from him.

For a second we both glanced guiltily towards the door to see if the commotion would bring in the guards. But nothing happened, and eventually Uncle Philip laughed, and picking up the chair, positioned it carefully in front of the desk. Then he sat on it himself, put the pistol down on the desk, and spent some time recovering his breath. I took a few more steps away from the desk, but there was nothing else in that cavernous room, and I simply came to a stop, my back still turned to him. Then I heard him say:

"All right. Very well." He took a few more gulps of air. "Then I'll tell you. I'll make to you my darkest confession."

But for the next minute, all I could hear behind me was his heaving breath. Then finally he said:

"Very well. I'll confess to you the truth. About why I allowed Wang Ku to kidnap your mother that day. What I said before, yes, it's true enough. I had to safeguard you. Yes, yes, everything I said earlier more or less stands. But if I'd really wanted to, if I'd really wanted to save your mother, I know I'd have found a way to do so. I'll tell you something now, Puffin. Something I wasn't able to confess even to myself for many years. I helped Wang take your mother because a part of me wanted her to become his slave. To be used like that, night after night. Because you see, I always lusted after her, right from the days when I came to be a lodger in your house. Oh yes, I desired her, and when your father went off like that, I believed it was my chance, that I was his natural successor. But . . . but your mother, she'd never looked at me like that, I realised it after your father went away. She respected me as someone decent . . . No, no, it was impossible. Not in a thousand years could I put myself forward to her, not in that sort of way. And I was angry. I was so angry. And when it all happened, with Wang Ku, it excited me. Do you hear me, Puffin? *It excited me!* After he took her away, in the darkest hours of the night, it excited me. All those years, I lived vicariously through Wang. It was almost as though I'd conquered her too. I gave myself pleasure, many many times, imagining for myself what was happening to her. Now, now, kill me! Why spare me? You've heard it! Here, shoot me like a rat!"

For a long time, I went on standing in the darkened part of the room, my back to him, listening to his breathing. Then I turned to him again and said, quite quietly:

"You said earlier you believed my mother was still alive. Is she still with Wang Ku?"

"Wang died four years ago. His army, in any case, was disbanded by Chiang. I don't know where she is now, Puffin. I honestly don't."

"Well. I shall find her. I shan't give up."

"It won't be easy, my boy. There's war raging through the country. It'll soon engulf the whole of it."

"Yes," I said. "I dare say it will soon engulf the whole world. But that's not my fault. In fact, it's no longer my concern. I mean to start again, and this time to find her. Is there anything else you can tell me to help with my search?"

"I'm afraid not, Puffin. I've told you everything."

"Then goodbye, Uncle Philip. I'm sorry I'm not able to oblige you."

"Don't worry. No shortage of people willing to oblige the Yellow Snake." He gave a quick laugh. Then he said in a weary voice: "Goodbye, Puffin. I hope you find her."

PART SEVEN

*L*ONDON,
14TH NOVEMBER 1958

$\mathcal{I}$T WAS MY FIRST LONG TRIP in many years, and for two days after our arrival in Hong Kong I remained quite fatigued. Air travel is impressively fast, but the conditions are cramped and disorientating. My hip pains returned with a vengeance and a headache lingered for much of my stay, which no doubt jaundiced my view of that colony. I know of those who have made the trip out there and returned full of praise. "A forward-looking place," they always say. "And astonishingly beautiful." Yet for much of that week, the skies were overcast, the streets oppressively crowded. I suppose I did appreciate here and there—in the Chinese signs outside the shops, or just in the sight of the Chinese going about their business in the markets—some vague echo of Shanghai. But then again, such echoes were more often than not discomforting. It was as though I had come upon, at one of those dullish supper parties I attend in Kensington or Bayswater, a distant cousin of a woman I once loved; whose gestures, facial expressions, little shrugs nudge the memory, but who remains, overall, an awkward, even grotesque parody of a much-cherished image.

I was in the end glad of Jennifer's company. When she had first hinted she should come with me, I had deliberately ignored her.

For even by that late stage—I am speaking of only five years ago—she was still tending to regard me as some sort of invalid, especially whenever the past, or else the Far East, re-emerged in my life. I suppose a part of me had long resented this oversolicitousness, and it was only when it occurred to me she genuinely wished to get away from things for a while—that she had her own worries, and that such a trip might do her good—that I agreed we should travel together.

It had been Jennifer's suggestion that we try and extend our journey to Shanghai, and I suppose this would not have been impossible. I could have spoken to a few old acquaintances, men who still have influence at the Foreign Office, and I am sure we could have gained entry into mainland China without undue difficulty. I know of others who have done just that. But then by all accounts, Shanghai today is a ghostly shadow of the city it once was. The communists have refrained from physically tearing the place down, so that much of what was once the International Settlement remains intact. The streets, though renamed, are perfectly recognisable, and it is said that anyone familiar with the Shanghai of old would know his way about there. But the foreigners, of course, have all been banished, and what were once lavish hotels and night-clubs are now the bureaucratic offices of Chairman Mao's government. In other words, the Shanghai of today is likely to prove no less painful a parody of the old city than did Hong Kong.

I have heard, incidentally, that much of the poverty—and also the opium addiction against which my mother once battled so hard—has receded significantly under the communists. How deeply these evils have been eradicated remains to be seen, but it would certainly appear that communism has been able to achieve in a handful of years what philanthropy and ardent campaigning could not in decades. I remember wondering to myself what my mother would have made of such a reflection that first night we spent in Hong Kong, as I paced around my room at the Excelsior Hotel, nursing my hip and trying in general to regain my equilibrium.

I did not go to Rosedale Manor until our third day. It had long been understood that I would make the trip alone, and Jennifer, though she watched my every move throughout the morning, saw me off after lunch with no undue fuss.

That afternoon the sun had actually broken through, and as I climbed the hill-slopes in my taxi, the well-manicured lawns on each side were being watered and mown by teams of gardeners stripped to their vests. Eventually the ground levelled off and the taxi pulled up in front of a large white house built in a British colonial style with long rows of shuttered windows and an additional wing sprawling from its side. It must once have been a splendid residence, overlooking as it did the water and much of the west side of the island. When I stood in the breeze and looked across the harbour, I could see right into the distance to where a cable-car was climbing a faraway hill. Turning to the house itself, however, I saw it had been allowed to grow shabby; the paint on the window ledges and door frames in particular had cracked and peeled.

Inside, in the hallway, there was a faint smell of boiled fish, but the place looked spotlessly clean. A Chinese nun led me down an echoing corridor to the office of Sister Belinda Heaney, a woman in her mid-forties with a serious, slightly dour expression. And it was there, in that cramped little office, that I was told of how the woman they knew as "Diana Roberts" had come to them through a liaison organisation working with foreigners stranded in communist China. All the Chinese authorities had known of her when handing her over was that she had been living in an institution for the mentally ill in Chunking since the end of the war.

"It's possible she'd spent most of the war there too," Sister Belinda said. "It hardly bears thinking about, Mr. Banks, what sort of place that was. A person, once incarcerated in such a place, could easily never be heard of again. It was only because she was a white woman she was singled out at all. The Chinese didn't know what to do with her. After all, they want all foreigners out of China. So eventually she was referred here, and she's been with us now for nearly two years. When she first came to us, she was very agitated. But within a month or two, all the usual benefits of Rosedale Manor, the peace, the order, the prayers, began to do their work. You wouldn't recognise her now as the poor creature who arrived here. She's so much calmer. You're a relative, did you say?"

"Yes, it's certainly possible," I said. "And since I was in Hong Kong, I thought it only right I paid a visit. It's the least I could do."

"Well, any news of kin, close friends, any link with England, we'd be very glad to hear about. Meanwhile, a visitor is always welcome."

"Does she have many?"

"She has visitors regularly. We run a scheme with the pupils of St. Joseph's College."

"I see. And does she get on well with the other residents?"

"Oh yes. And she's no trouble to us at all. If only we could say the same about some of the others!"

Sister Belinda led me down another corridor to a large sunny room—it had perhaps once been the dining room—where twenty or so females all dressed in beige smocks were sitting or shuffling about. French doors were open to the grounds outside, and the sunlight was falling through the windows across the parquet flooring. Had it not been for the large number of vases filled with fresh flowers, I might have mistaken the room for a children's nursery; there were bright watercolours pinned all over the walls, and at various points, little tables with draughts, playing cards, paper and crayons. Sister Belinda left me standing by the entrance while she went over to another nun sitting at an upright piano, and a number of the women stopped what they were doing to stare at me. Others appeared to become self-conscious and tried to hide themselves. Almost all were Westerners, though I could see one or two Eurasians. Then someone started to wail loudly somewhere in the building behind me, and curiously, this had the effect of putting the women at their ease. One wiry-headed lady nearby grinned at me and said:

"Don't you worry, love, it's only Martha. She's bloomin' well off again!"

I could hear Yorkshire in her accent and was wondering what tides of fate had brought her to this place, when Sister Belinda returned.

"Diana should be outside," she said. "If you'd follow me, Mr. Banks."

We went out through the French doors into well-tended grounds which climbed and dipped in all directions, reminding us we were near the crest of a hill. As I followed Sister Belinda past flower beds abloom with geraniums and tulips, I glimpsed panoramic views over the neatly cut hedges. Here and there, old ladies in beige smocks were sitting in the sunshine, knitting, chatting together or muttering harmlessly to themselves. At one point, Sister Belinda paused to look about her, then led me down a sloping lawn through a white gate into a little walled garden.

The only figure to be seen here was an elderly lady sitting in the sun on the far side of the thinning grass, playing cards at a wrought-iron table. She was absorbed in her game and did not look up as we approached. Sister Belinda touched her shoulder gently and said:

"Diana. Here's a gentleman come to visit you. He's from England."

My mother smiled up at us both, then returned to her playing cards.

"Diana doesn't always understand what's said to her," Sister Belinda said. "If you need her to do something, you just have to keep repeating it over and over."

"I wonder if I may speak with her alone."

Sister Belinda was not keen on this idea and for a moment seemed to be trying to think of a reason why this was not possible. But in the end, she said: "If you'd prefer it, Mr. Banks, I'm sure that's all right. I shall be in the dayroom."

Once Sister Belinda had gone, I looked carefully at my mother as she dealt out her cards. She was much smaller than I had expected and her shoulders had a severe hunch. Her hair was silver and had been tied tightly in a bun. Occasionally, as I continued to watch her, she would glance up and smile, but I could see a trace of fear that had not been there in Sister Belinda's presence. Her face was not so greatly lined, but there were two thick folds beneath her eyes that were so deep they looked almost like incisions. Her neck, perhaps owing to some injury or condition, had receded deep into her body so that when she gazed from side to side at her cards, she was obliged also to move her shoulders. There was a droplet clinging to the tip of her nose, and I had taken out my handkerchief to remove it before realising that by doing so I might unduly alarm her. Finally I said quietly:

"I'm sorry I couldn't give you any sort of warning. I realise this might be something of a shock for you." I stopped, since it was clear she was not listening. Then I said: "Mother, it's me. Christopher."

She looked up, smiled much as before, then turned back to her cards. I had assumed she was playing solitaire, but as I watched, saw she was following some odd system of her own. At one point the breeze lifted a few cards off the table, but she appeared not to care. When I collected the cards from the grass and brought them back to her, she smiled, saying:

"Thank you so much. But there's no need to do that, you know. Myself, I like to leave it until many more cards have accumulated on the lawn. Only then do I go to gather them, all in one go, you see. After all, they can't fly away off the hill altogether, can they?"

For the next few moments I continued to watch her. Then my mother began to sing. She sang quietly to herself, almost under her breath, as her hands went on picking up and placing down the cards. The voice was faint—I could not make out the song she was singing—but it was effortlessly melodious. And as I went on watching and listening, a fragment of memory came back to me: of a windy summer's day in our garden, my mother on the swing, laughing and singing at the top of her voice, and me jumping up and down before her, telling her to stop.

I reached forward and gently touched her hand. Instantly she pulled it away and stared at me furiously.

"Keep your hands to yourself, sir!" she said in a shocked whisper. "Keep them *right* to yourself!"

"I'm sorry." I moved back a little to reassure her. She returned to her cards and when she next glanced up, she gave a smile as though nothing had happened.

"Mother," I said slowly, "it's me. I've come from England. I'm really very sorry it's taken so long. I realise I've let you down badly. Very badly. I tried my utmost, but you see, in the end, it proved beyond me. I realise this is hopelessly late."

I must have started to cry, because my mother looked up and stared at me. Then she said:

"Do you have toothache, my man? If so, you'd better talk to Sister Agnes."

"No, I'm fine. But I wonder if you've understood what I'm saying? It's me. Christopher."

She nodded and said: "No use delaying it, my man. Sister Agnes will fill in your form."

Then an idea came to me. "Mother," I said, "it's Puffin. *Puffin.*"

"Puffin." She suddenly became very still. "Puffin."

For a long time my mother said nothing, but the expression on her face had now changed entirely. She was looking up again, but her eyes were focused on something over my shoulder, and a gentle smile was creasing her face.

"Puffin," she repeated quietly to herself, and for a moment seemed lost in happiness. Then she shook her head and said: "That boy. He's such a worry to me."

"Excuse me," I said. "Excuse me. Supposing this boy of yours, this Puffin. Supposing you discovered he'd tried his best, tried with everything he had to find you, even if in the end he couldn't. If you knew that, do you suppose . . . do you suppose you'd be able to forgive him?"

My mother continued to gaze past my shoulder, but now a puzzled look came into her face.

"Forgive Puffin? Did you say forgive Puffin? Whatever for?" Then she beamed again happily. "That boy. They say he's doing well. But you can never be sure with that one. Oh, he's such a worry to me. You've no idea."

"IT MIGHT SEEM FOOLISH TO YOU," I said to Jennifer when we were discussing the trip again last month, "but it was only when she said that, it was only then I realised. What I mean is, I realised she'd never ceased to love me, not through any of it. All she'd ever wanted was for me to have a good life. And all the rest of it, all my trying to find her, trying to save the world from ruin, that wouldn't have made any difference either way. Her feelings for me, they were always just *there*, they didn't depend on anything. I suppose that might not seem so very surprising. But it took me all that time to realise it."

"Do you really suppose," Jennifer asked, "she had no inkling at all who you were?"

"I'm sure she didn't. But she meant what she said, and she knew what she was saying. She said there was nothing to forgive, and she was genuinely puzzled at the suggestion there might be. If you'd seen her face, when I first said that name, you'd have no doubt about it either. She'd never ceased to love me, not for a single moment."

"Uncle Christopher, why do you suppose you never told the nuns who you really were?"

"I'm not sure. It seems odd, I know, but in the end I just didn't. Besides, I saw no reason to take her away from there. She did seem, somehow, contented. Not happy exactly. But as though the pain had passed. She'd have been no better off in a home in England. I suppose it was much like this question of where she should lie. After she died, I thought about having her reburied here. But there again, when I thought it over, I decided against it. She'd lived all her life in the East. I think she'd prefer to rest out there."

It was a frosty October morning, and Jennifer and I were walking down a winding lane in Gloucestershire. I had stayed the night at an inn not far from the boarding house where she is currently living, and I had called on her shortly after breakfast. Perhaps I did not conceal well enough my sadness on seeing the shabbiness of her latest lodgings, for she had quickly insisted, despite the chill, on showing me the view from a nearby churchyard over the Windrush valley. As we came further down the lane, I could see at the bottom the gates of a farm; but before we reached them, she led me off the path through a gap in the hedge.

"Uncle Christopher, come and look."

We picked our way through a thick patch of nettles until we were standing by some railings. I could then see the fields sweeping down the valley side.

"It's a wonderful view," I said.

"From the churchyard, you can see even further. Don't you ever think of moving out here too? London's much too crowded now."

"It's not like it used to be, that's true."

We stood there for a moment, side by side, gazing down at the view.

"I'm sorry," I said to her, "I've not been up here much recently. I suppose it's been a good few months now. Can't think what I've been up to."

"Oh, you shouldn't worry so much about me."

"But I do worry. Of course, I worry."

"It's all behind me now," she said, "all of that last year. I won't try anything foolish like that ever again. I've already promised you that. It was just an especially bad time, that's all. Besides, I never really meant to do it. I made sure that window was left open."

"But you're still a young woman, Jenny. With so much ahead of you. It depresses me that you should even have contemplated such a thing."

"A young woman? Thirty-one, no children, no marriage. I suppose there is time still. But I'll have to find the will, you know, to go through all of that again. I'm so tired now, I sometimes think I'll gladly settle for a quiet life on my own. I could work in a shop somewhere, go to the cinema once a week and not do anyone any harm. Nothing wrong with a life like that."

"But you won't settle for that. Doesn't sound like the Jennifer I know."

She gave a small laugh. "But you've no idea what it's like. A woman of my age, trying to find romance in a place like this. Landladies and lodgers whispering about you every time you step outside your room. What am I actually supposed to do? Advertise? Now that *would* set them all talking, not that I care at all about them."

"But you're a very attractive woman, Jenny. What I mean is, when people look at you, they can see your spirit, your kindness, your gentleness. I'm sure something will happen for you."

"You think people see my spirit? Uncle Christopher, that's only because you look at me and still see the little girl you once knew."

I turned and looked carefully at her. "Oh, but it's still there," I said. "I can see it. It's still there, underneath, waiting. The world hasn't changed you as much as you think, my dear. It just gave you something of a shock, that's all. And by the way, there *are* a few decent men in this world, I'll have you know. You just have to stop doing your utmost to avoid them."

"All right, Uncle Christopher. I'll try and do better next time. If there is a next time."

For a moment we went on gazing at the view, a light wind blowing across our faces. Eventually I said:

"I should have done more for you, Jenny. I'm sorry."

"But what could *you* have done? If I take it into my silly head to . . ."

"No, I meant . . . I meant earlier on. When you were growing up. I should have been there with you more. But I was too busy, trying to solve the world's problems. I should have done a lot more for you than I did. I'm sorry. There. Always meant to say it."

"How can you apologise, Uncle Christopher? Where would I be now without you? I was an orphan, with no one. You mustn't ever apologise. I owe you everything."

I reached forward and touched the wet cobweb suspended across the railings. It broke and dangled from my fingers.

"Oh, I hate that feeling!" she exclaimed. "Can't bear it!"

"I've always rather liked it. When I was a boy, I used to take off my gloves just to do it."

"Oh, how could you?" She laughed loudly, and I could see suddenly the Jennifer of old. "And what about you, Uncle Christopher? How about *you* getting married? Don't you ever think about it?"

"Definitely too late for that."

"Oh, I don't know. You manage well enough living on your own. But it doesn't suit you much either. Not really. It makes you morose. You should think about it. You're always mentioning your lady-friends. Won't one of them have you?"

"They'll have me for lunch. But not for much more, I fear." Then I added: "There was someone once. Back then. But that went the way of everything else." I gave a quick laugh. "My great vocation got in the way of quite a lot, all in all."

I must have turned away from her. I felt her touch my shoulder, and when I looked around, she was peering gently into my face.

"You shouldn't always talk so bitterly about your career, Uncle Christopher. I've always so admired you for what you tried to do."

"Tried is right. It all amounted to very little in the end. Anyway, that's all behind me now. My major ambition in life these days is to keep this rheumatism at bay."

Jennifer suddenly smiled and slipped her arm through mine. "I know what we'll do," she said. "I have a plan. I've decided. I'll find a fine decent man whom I'll marry, and I'll have three, no, four children. And we'll live somewhere near here, where we can always come and look over this valley. And you can leave your stuffy little flat in London and come and live with us. Since your lady-friends won't have you, you can accept the post of uncle to all my future children."

I smiled back at her. "That sounds a fine plan. Though I don't know if your husband would so appreciate having me around his house the whole time."

"Oh, then we'll rig up an old shed or something for you."

"Now, that does sound tempting. Keep your end of the bargain and I'll think about it."

"If that's a promise, then you'd better watch out. Because I'll make sure it happens. Then you'll *have* to come and live in your shed."

OVER THIS LAST MONTH, as I have drifted through these grey days in London, wandering about Kensington Gardens in the company of autumn tourists and office workers out for their lunch breaks, occasionally running into an old acquaintance and perhaps going off with him for lunch or tea, I have often found myself thinking again of my conversation with Jennifer that morning. There is no denying it has cheered me. There is every reason to believe that she has now come through the dark tunnel of her life and emerged at the other end. What awaits her there remains to be seen, but she is not by nature someone who easily accepts defeat. Indeed, it is more than possible she will go on to fulfil the programme she outlined to me—only half-jokingly—as we looked out over the valley that morning. And if in a few years' time things have indeed gone according to her wishes, then it is not out of the question I will take up her suggestion to go and live with her in the country. Of course, I would not much fancy her shed, but I could always take a cottage not far away. I am grateful for Jennifer. We understand each other's concerns instinctively, and it is exchanges like the one that frosty morning which have proved such a source of consolation for me over the years.

But then again, life in the countryside might prove too quiet, and I have become rather attached to London of late. Besides, from time to time, I am still approached by persons who remember my name from before the war and wish my advice on some matter. Only last week, in fact, when I went to dinner with the Osbournes, I was introduced to a lady who immediately seized my hand, exclaiming: "You mean you're *the* Christopher Banks? The detective?"

It turned out she had spent much of her life in Singapore, where she had been "a very great friend" of Sarah's. "She used to talk of you all the time," she told me. "I really do feel I know you already."

The Osbournes had invited several other people, but once we sat down to eat, I found myself placed beside this same lady, and inevitably our conversation drifted back to Sarah.

"You were a good friend of hers, were you not?" she asked at one point. "She always talked so admiringly of you."

"We were good friends, certainly. Of course, we rather lost touch once she went out to the East."

"She often talked of you. She had so many stories about the famous detective, kept us quite amused when we grew tired of playing bridge. She always spoke most highly of you."

"I'm moved to think she remembered me so well. As I say, we rather lost touch, though I did receive a letter from her once, around two years after the war. I wasn't aware until then how she'd spent the war. She made light of the internment, but I'm sure it was no joke."

"Oh, I'm sure it was no joke at all. My husband and I, we could so easily have suffered the same fate. We managed to get ourselves to Australia just in time. But Sarah and M. de Villefort, they always trusted so much to fate. They were the sort of couple who went out in the evening with no plan, quite happy to see who they bumped into. A charming attitude most of the time, but not when the Japanese are on your doorstep. Did you know him also?"

"I never had the pleasure of meeting the count. I understand he returned to Europe after Sarah's death, but our paths have never crossed."

"Oh, I thought from the way she talked of you, you were good friends with them both."

"No. You see, I really only knew Sarah during an earlier part of her life. I beg your pardon, there's perhaps no way for you to answer this. But did they strike you as a happy couple, Sarah and this French chap?"

"A happy couple?" My companion thought for a moment. "Of course, one can never know for sure, but quite honestly, it would be hard to believe otherwise. They did seem utterly devoted to one another. They never had much money, so that meant they could never be quite as carefree as they might have wished. But the count always seemed so, well, so *romantic*. You laugh, Mr. Banks, but that's just the word for it. He was so devastated by her death. It was the internment that did it, you know. Like so many others, she never fully recovered her health. I do miss her. Such a charming companion."

Since this encounter last week, I have brought out and read again several times Sarah's letter—the only one I ever received since our parting in Shanghai all those years ago. It is dated 18th May 1947, and has been written from a hill station in Malaya. Perhaps it was my hope that after my conversation with her friend, I would discover in those rather formal, almost blandly pleasant lines, some hitherto hidden dimension. But in fact the letter continues to yield up little more than the bare bones of her life since her departure from Shanghai. She talks of Macao, Hong Kong, Singapore as being "delightful," "colourful," "fascinating." Her French companion is mentioned several times, but always in passing as though I already knew all there was to know about him. There is a breezy mention of the internment under the Japanese, and she pronounces her health problems "a bit of a bore." She asks after me in a polite way and calls her own life in liberated Singapore "a pretty decent thing to be getting on with." It is the sort of letter one might write, in a foreign land, on an impulse one afternoon to a vaguely remembered friend. Only once, towards the end, does its tone imply the intimacy we once shared.

"I don't mind telling you, dearest Christopher," she writes, "that at the time, I *was* disappointed, to say the least, at the way things transpired between us. But don't worry, I have long ceased to be cross with you. How could I remain cross when Fate in the end chose to smile so kindly on me? Besides, it is now my belief that for you, it was the correct decision not to come with me that day. You always felt you had a mission to complete, and I dare say you would never have been able to give your heart to anyone or anything until you had done so. I can only hope that by now your tasks are behind you, and that you too have been able to find the sort of happiness and companionship which I have come lately almost to take for granted."

There is something about these sections of her letter—and those last lines in particular—that never quite ring true. Some subtle note that runs throughout the letter—indeed, her very act of writing to me at that moment—feels at odds with her report of days filled with "happiness and companionship." Was her life with her French count really what she set off to find that day she stepped out on to the jetty in Shanghai? I somehow doubt it. My feeling is that she is thinking of herself as much as of me when she talks of a sense of mission, and the futility of attempting to evade it. Perhaps there are those who are able to go about their lives unfettered by such concerns. But for those like us, our fate is to face the world as orphans, chasing through long years the shadows of vanished parents. There is nothing for it but to try and see through our missions to the end, as best we can, for until we do so, we will be permitted no calm.

I do not wish to appear smug; but drifting through my days here in London, I believe I can indeed own up to a certain contentment. I enjoy my walks in the parks, I visit the galleries; and increasingly of late, I have come to take a foolish pride in sifting through old newspaper reports of my cases in the Reading Room at the British Museum. This city, in other words, has come to be my home, and I should not mind if I had to live out the rest of my days here. Nevertheless, there are those times when a sort of emptiness fills my hours, and I shall continue to give Jennifer's invitation serious thought.